# Orion
## *in the*
# Sunshine

*A Novel*

Jenny Poelman

ISBN: 978-1-966343-57-8  (hard cover)
        978-1-966343-58-5  (soft cover)

Edited by: Erika Nein

Published by WARREN Publishing
Charlotte, NC
www.warrenpublishing.net
Printed in the United States

*For my parents and my huge and wonderful family ...*
*and for all families who live with absence as a presence*

## PRAISE FOR *THE ALPHABET WOODS*

"The Alphabet Woods *is a testament to the triumph
of the human spirit. A beautiful story of unimaginable
adversity, betrayal, and loss as seen through the eyes
of a small boy and a kind-hearted woman who is dealing
with her own internal suffering. Jenny's raw emotion
and creative storytelling nestled amongst beautiful trees,
will leave an ineffaceable mark on your soul. It is a
juxtaposition of despair and hope.*

—RENÉE BENEVILLE

"*I was captivated by the characters and various mysteries
in* The Alphabet Woods *and am anxiously awaiting their
next adventures! Can't wait for a new page-turner.*"

—BETTY GRAY

"The Alphabet Woods *is a beautiful,
emotional story that shows that a little compassion,
time, and commitment can change lives. I think we
all know and need a bit of Key North in our lives.*"

—BROOKE SUMMERS/VO PERSONALITY

"The Alphabet Woods *will not only entertain you,
it will draw you into Key's life and the lives of those around
her. You will find yourself wishing you could sit down
with her, have some iced tea, and get to know her better.*"

—PATTI CLARK

# Prologue

## METEOR

*September 1998*

yo insisted on driving to Virginia in the van. Riggs stared out the window, oblivious to the trees swishing by and Pearl Jam blaring from the boom box positioned on the floor behind him. It was bad enough that every time he and Ayo Jones went anywhere together, he became the shotgun-riding copilot to a no-holds-barred jerk, but the van added a creepy element that Riggs especially despised. At least in the Camry they didn't look like stalkers, even though Ayo's whistling and hooting at any reasonably attractive female still commenced.

If women were enticed to join them, Riggs would be relegated to the Camry's back seat with whomever Ayo deemed less attractive, referred to as the "dingo." It was part of his game, creating code words and private jokes, always derogatory and always at the expense of someone else. "You Australian, sweetie?" Ayo would ask innocently, touching her shoulder or the small of her back or tugging on a lock of hair, that knowing smirk playing around his mouth as his defiant eyes met Riggs's embarrassed ones.

The confused target would inevitably say no (usually pulling away), and Riggs knew that was his cue to invite her into the back with him while, up front, Ayo made the moves on his decreed winner in the looks department. It didn't matter who ended up in the back with Riggs, though, because he was unavailable. The love of his life, to his everlasting dismay, had moved before their junior year in high school to outer space (well, Albuquerque) and was now attending college there.

He reached up and lightly grasped the nickel-sized medallion hanging from a sturdy gold rope chain around his neck, a gift from his girlfriend for his eighteenth birthday. In two years, he'd never taken it off.

"Clutching your pearls again, Eleanor?" Ayo's mocking voice cut through the music, accompanied by the supercilious sneer he reserved for the nickname Riggs despised. "Where have *y'all* been these days? I called and talked to your *mama*, and she said she didn't know where her baby boy was." He pushed his lower lip out in a wet, exaggerated pout.

"Around." Repulsed, Riggs gritted his teeth and lowered his hand.

He'd been seventeen to Ayo's twenty-three when he walked unseeingly into the stickiest kind of web. If his girlfriend hadn't left such a void when she moved, Riggs would never have been sucked into Ayo's sham camaraderie that, like quicksand, had dragged him into a constricting brand of friendship that played on his self-doubts, squelched his confidence, and allowed for none of his other buddies to be included. Ayo was the predator who'd expertly isolated Riggs from the safety of the herd.

Riggs's mother had recently handed him the pages of an article she'd torn out of a women's magazine. "Riggs, honey," she said tentatively in her soft Alabama drawl, "will you read this? I feel it exactly describes Ayo and who you are to him. Ask yourself whether he's *truly* your friend."

Because he loved his mama and she so rarely interfered in his business, Riggs read the article titled "Is There a Narcissist in Your Life?" It assigned a new label to Ayo's personality, but it was preaching to the choir because Riggs had already arrived at the full-color realization that Ayo was a manipulative, self-aggrandizing, counterfeit human devoid of empathy, who showed no signs that he would ever change—in other words, a natural-born narcissist. Riggs's parents would have been overjoyed to know that he and his high school best buddy had been ghosting Ayo for a month.

Yesterday, though, Ayo had dangled the one carrot Riggs could not resist, a prize worth the torture of this van ride: tickets to Sunshine Fest Richmond, featuring Riggs's favorite band of all time, the Foo Fighters, whom he'd never seen perform live. Even so, he'd agreed to go only because Ayo also invited Riggs's best friend, who was right there in the back seat. *Just this one last trip, then I never want to see Ayo's face again.*

It was the fight with his own father thirty minutes earlier, though, that had Riggs's emotions in turmoil, had him simultaneously boiling mad and feeling terribly guilty; in fact, his scolding conscience made him even angrier. He'd told his father (admittedly on very short notice) that he wouldn't be playing at their band's gig that evening. "It's the *Foo Fighters*, Daddy! Ayo got tickets last-minute!"

"Ayo! That snake in the grass? You *know* he's trouble!" His father's voice rose. "Your word is your life, son. You made a promise."

"Oh, for once, play without me!"

A promise to give up nearly every Friday and Saturday night for eternity? When he also worked with his father all day? No twenty-year-old adult male, still living with his parents or not, should have to schedule his life twenty-four seven according to his father's wishes! Why *shouldn't* he do something for himself?

Their escalating yelling match had brought his mama indoors from the garden and his younger brother down the stairs to gape in dismay as the two men they loved most threw foreign, accusatory words at each other. Words that, once uttered, would never be taken back, no apologies ever offered or accepted.

Because that day, Riggs inexplicably vanished.

Through the months, then the years, that followed, as the missing person flyers faded and disintegrated, his brokenhearted family incessantly arranged the splintered pieces as best they could, daily shoring themselves up to face a world without Riggs. When the younger son was sixteen, they migrated a few miles down the road to their newly constructed home on the outskirts of Troy, North Carolina, where most of the photographs of their beloved older son and brother were never put back up. The anguish and confusion contained in the frames were too heavy for them to lift, too burdensome for any nail to hold—and, in any case, they didn't need pictures to remind them of Riggs. He was never, ever gone from their thoughts.

# Chapter 1

## HONKER

*Mid–September 2018*

"*Relax*. There's plenty of time. Wain will be fine. He knows you'll be there." Key North exhaled in five calming puffs as she lifted her foot from the brake, allowing her olive-green Jeep to creep forward a few more yards in the dusty wake of a massive yellow tractor towing an extra-wide mowing apparatus along two lane Pike Road outside of Troy, North Carolina. There was nothing she could do except wait for an opportunity to pass.

She glanced in the rearview mirror. Wain's dog, Faro, appeared to be quite relaxed, enjoying his favorite road-unwinding view from the far back of the Jeep, the familiar shock of fur sticking straight up between his ears. Key smiled. Anymore, dogs without crazy hair looked almost bald.

*But I've never been late.* Wain had instructions to stay with his second-grade teacher if Key wasn't there when he dashed out of Troy Elementary, but would he remember? Though school had been in session for three weeks, she still sensed the little boy's endearing relief when he spotted her and a wagging, anticipatory Faro waiting near the frog-shaped green-painted school spirit boulder (#BULLFROGSTRONG!) with a phone-staring population of impossibly youthful parents and a few assorted caregivers, all of whom, like Key (for now), lived close enough to walk their young charges home from school.

Wain would race toward her, CartWheels backpack bouncing, and hug Key briefly as she relieved him of his lunch box, then he'd throw his arms around Faro, instantly transforming into the version of Wain that only Faro could elicit, as if the leash were a magical cord allowing that unique canine strength to inject extra confidence and joy directly to the little boy's still-healing heart.

A jarring honk broke the silence, startling both Key and Faro, who jumped to his feet, whining. Through the dog nose–smudged rear window, she watched the driver of the SUV behind her, a young(ish) brunette woman in gold-rimmed aviator sunglasses mouthing unseemly words and gesturing as though a nest of African killer bees had materialized inside her car.

Key rolled her eyes. Miss Aviator Glasses had to have come from Mistic Meadows Horse Barn, located at Pike Road's dead end, because there were only three properties along this stretch, and Key had just been at the other two, one of which was her own.

Like an obscene Morse code, another sharp toot followed by two progressively longer ones reverberated through the tranquil countryside, as if the blasts would somehow magically levitate both Key's Jeep and the tractor, allowing the Most Important Driver to zoom beneath them and sally forth to her Most Important Life.

"Goodness, settle down, lady! We'll all get there." *So rude. Probably not a local.* In Key's experience, most native North Carolinian drivers were polite nearly to a fault; nonemergency honking was not considered civil, much less (in this case) respectful of the tractor driver who simply needed to access a few miles of public roadway.

Once, in her previous life, Key had listened in bemusement while one of her late husband's friends loudly criticized the speed at which his elderly neighbor turned corners. His indignation had been so ridiculous that Key laughed, which offended the man *and* Jeff.

*Jeff.* Funny how he popped into her mind only when something made her uncomfortable or stressed. She took a deep breath, letting the thoughts flow through her, diverting them to her mental garbage can. *Empty trash. Open a new file.*

She raised her eyebrows. *New file, indeed.* As of this afternoon, she had a virtual drawerful of newly discovered files! Her day had started with an unexpected phone call from her neighbor Gayle Morgan, asking if Key could stay for a few hours with her elderly mother-in-law, Granny Jewel, while Gayle took her toddler to the doctor. "I think Dibs has got an ear infection; these things always start happenin' once school starts."

Hiding her surprise, Key instantly said yes, then rearranged her afternoon. Though she had known the Morgans for nearly the full five months since she'd moved into (and now temporarily out of) Pike House, they were a fiercely insular family, and Gayle had never made such a request before.

On the way to Granny Jewel's, she had stopped by Pike House, but neither her remodeling contractor, Dawson Plummer III (known as DP), nor his two-man work crew was there. She'd watered her plants, jotted a couple construction questions in her ever-present notebook, then motored the short distance south to Wildflower Lane, where the Morgan family lived in a double-wide mobile home a few hundred yards from Granny Jewel's tidy ranch house.

That afternoon Granny Jewel had freely explained her medical issues (debilitating osteoporosis and a few other age- and smoking-related issues), but it was the old woman's other topic of conversation that saturated Key's current thoughts: a shocking and terribly sad story starring characters whom Key knew, people whose lives she never would have imagined involved such ongoing, tragic turmoil. It wasn't small-town gossip. It was public knowledge. *How did I not know?*

The tractor finally made an extra-wide, sloth-speed turn onto a side road. Relieved, Key pressed on the gas, but not fast enough for Miss Aviator Glasses, who swerved around her and rocketed past in a blur of silvery indignation. On the passenger side of the Mercedes SUV, Key could just make out a large, ornate purple *M*.

She glanced at her watch. Fifteen minutes before the school day ended, just enough time to get back to her temporary rental house at 914 Veronica View and hoof it six blocks to Troy Elementary.

Five minutes later, Key set out at a very brisk pace, promising herself that later, after Wain was in bed, she'd take a deep dive online into the heartbreaking details of Granny Jewel's story.

# Chapter 2

## THE GOOD AND TOUGH JARS

Key patted her perspiring forehead with the unused paper napkin from Wain's lunch box. Autumn might have arrived in other states, but September in North Carolina was simply an extension of summer. "How'd school go today, honey? What goes in the good jar?" Every day, Wain added two events to their imaginary "good things" and "tough things" jars, and Key carefully recorded them in her day planner to share with Wain's father during his now-regular video calls from Dubai.

"We talked about pets, and I told about Faro. And guess what my teacher brought to school? A fuzzy brown-and-white rat thing! It runs on a wheel, and it's like, so, *so* cute. I think it's called a 'germ.'"

"Maybe a 'gerbil'?" Key hid a smile, hoping the germs at Troy Elementary weren't quite that large or furry. Twenty-some children and a gerbil. *Teachers are outliers.*

"Yeah! A gerbil. It's a she. We're gonna vote tomorrow about the name."

"What's your vote?"

"Sheba. We can take it treats if our parents say it's okay. Can I?"

*Parent.* Key was touched at how naturally he'd said it. "Of course! Let's look up what gerbils like to eat. What goes in the tough jar?"

"I saw Ell crying at recess," Wain replied instantly. Ell was Granny Jewel's nine-year-old granddaughter, Gayle and Lonny Morgan's child, and Wain's first and still best North Carolina friend.

Key's eyes widened. Gregarious, tough, empathetic Ell? *Crying?* She glanced at Wain. He was watching Faro, his mouth tucked in at one corner, a sure sign he was worried. *Go slow,* she cautioned herself. Wain would shut down if Key reacted too intensely to his words.

The Wain striding beside her today had navigated an astounding distance from the shell-shocked seven-year-old she'd brought from Florida in May to live with her, but he still bore the scars of the hellish, brutal years he'd endured with his now-jailed mother, Lyric, and her (almost) good-for-nothing boyfriend, Gary Callahan. There, Wain had been an unwanted bother and a target for their cruelty, and except for the hours he spent with an exceptionally caring housekeeper named Mrs. Titus, he'd lived for three years with no sense of safety, no trust, no freedom to simply be a child. His resilience was incredible, but Key still walked on eggshells when it came to their conversations. She'd learned to keep her tone unforced—not *flat*, exactly, but level. Calm.

"Ell was crying?" she asked almost nonchalantly. "Do you know why?"

Wain shook his head. "She was sitting on a swing, and she was crying. I was playing soccer with Greggo, and I saw her."

To Key's undying relief, Wain had already made several new friends. Greggo was the name most often mentioned.

"Oh, I'm so sorry. Poor Ell!" Key put her arm around Wain's shoulders as they stopped at a crosswalk. "Did you get a chance to talk to her?"

"Nuh-uh." He added seriously, "Second grade isn't allowed to talk to *fourth grade* at recess."

"Ah. Was there anyone else with Ell?"

"Yeah. Some other kids. I waved, but she didn't wave back."

"Move over, buddy." Key nudged Wain and Faro off the sidewalk as a frazzled woman hurried by, grasping a leash connected to the pink harness of a rat-sized lunging, yapping dog determined to annihilate them with its quarter-inch-long teeth. Faro, who was very selective in his choice of dogs to sniff, simply stared at it disdainfully, as though he were embarrassed to admit he shared DNA with such a creature.

The yapping faded. "Thanks for telling me about Ell, Wain."

"Uh-huh."

*He's told me all he knows.* Key sensibly dropped the topic but hoped that, somehow, she could uncover what lay behind it. Ell was the eternal optimist, everyone's cheerleader, as tough and outspoken as her grandmother. Key had never seen her cry.

"Do I have Cissy today?" Wain asked, jumping over a buckled triangular section of cracked sidewalk and the knobby tree root that had caused it.

"Yes." Key had interviewed four tutoring applicants before hiring Cissy Bellamy, a Troy High School senior who planned to study child psychology at the University of North Carolina. She'd instantly connected with Wain as she leafed through the three-ring binder he proudly showed her.

"So you're gonna use this totally awesome tree branch alphabet book to help with your reading?" Cissy had asked. "Okay, little guy, sounds good!"

They met from 4:30 to 5:30 p.m. Monday through Thursday, usually at the picnic table in the backyard, Faro flopped at Wain's feet. Already they'd made tremendous progress.

"I thought I don't have Cissy on Fridays."

"Today is Wednesday. Oh!" Key tugged her phone from her jeans pocket and pointed to a text. "Look at this!"

Wain didn't even flinch as he eagerly took the phone and began to read, a miracle that only Key truly understood. "It says, 'We ... S-A-V-E-D ...' I don't know what that is. And then '1, 4, U,' and a upside-down little *i*."

"That's an exclamation mark, because this is exciting! And this word is *saved*. Now try again."

"'We saved one for you.'" He frowned. "Saved what?"

"Remember Evie, the girl with pink hair at the store where we bought SunBolt? She sent this. What's going to be revealed in October?" Key asked, her eyes sparkling.

"The new CartWheel car?" Wain's face lit up. "They saved one for me?"

"Yes!" Key exclaimed. "*And* you get VIP access to the reveal party! We'll go to Porterville the night before—I'll book a hotel with a pool. How does that sound?"

"Yay!" Wain dropped the leash and did a little dance, causing Faro to emit a rare bark. "What's the car name?"

"They'll tell you at the reveal."

Wain picked up the leash, suddenly full of righteous indignation. "You know what, Key? Cissy *loves* my cars, but Mrs. Goos doesn't."

Key laughed. They'd had this conversation several times. "Wain, I promise, your teacher has nothing against CartWheels!"

The evening of Wain's first day of school, Key had received an email from his teacher, Mrs. Goos (Key couldn't imagine the jokes she'd endured over the years), whom she'd already pegged as a kind and caring woman who brooked no-nonsense, especially from her gaggle of second-grade goslings. Thankfully, Wain had no fear of her, which was a strong indicator, Key thought, of Mrs. Goos's good heart. Though Key had at least five years on the woman, she'd felt as though she were Wain's age as she read:

> Mrs. North:
>
> Wain is a wonderful addition to our classroom and has already made friends. He is bright and engaging and, as you and I have discussed, between his remedial class here and his home tutoring, he should soon reach grade-level skills. However, his Black Diamond car caused a minor uproar in the classroom today. Please have him leave his CartWheels collection at home, where they will not be a distraction nor temptation to others. I trust both you and he will understand.
>
> Thank you.
>
> Marcia Goos

Wain had reluctantly come to terms with the empty secret compartment in his backpack, but it still rankled, and every Friday afternoon, he slid his cars back into their designated mesh pockets.

"She's been a second-grade teacher for a long time," Key continued, "and she knows all about CartWheels. She doesn't want anything to happen to your cars at school."

"Like what? 'Cause I always take care of them."

"Yes, you certainly do." Recalling Mrs. Goos's use of the word *temptation*, Key thought for a moment. She didn't want to imply that Wain couldn't trust his schoolmates. "Just think how awful it would be if any of your CartWheels got lost or broken! After all the time you waited and wished for Black Diamond!"

"Yeah. Then my *real* dad gave it to me!" The rarest, most coveted CartWheel, Wain's unequivocal favorite, was a gift from his formerly absentee father, whose employment had recently taken him overseas. Through video calls, Guy was now working determinedly to connect with his son, and Black Diamond was a significant building block in their relationship. "What's my snack today?"

Key had long since gotten used to their whiplash conversations. "Grapes and oatmeal cookies. Milk or juice box?"

"Juice box!" Wain did another little skip. "Can we run?"

Faro was beginning to pull harder on the leash. No doubt he was thirsty, Key thought guiltily. "Run like the wind. I'll catch up."

# Chapter 3

## CISSY

"Hey, Miss Key!" Cissy entered the kitchen, removing her bike helmet and pushing her sunglasses to the top of her head. Tall, graceful, and athletic, she was half Cherokee, she'd told Key proudly, and the youngest of the three stunning Bellamy sisters, all of whom had been a sensation on the Troy High Lady Bullfrogs track and basketball teams. Today, with her straight black hair styled into two long braids wrapped at the ends in beaded leather laces, Key thought Cissy looked exactly like a young Rita Coolidge.

After hooking her backpack onto a barstool, Cissy selected a cookie from the plate on the island and walked to the sliding glass door. She waved at Wain, who was throwing a ball for Faro. "Aww, he's all ready for me!" On the picnic table in the backyard were the Alphabet Woods three-ring binder and a precise line of tiny cars. "We're barely using the tree book anymore, but he likes to have it there." When Cissy smiled, her high cheekbones crinkled the corners of wide light-brown eyes.

"What's on the docket today?" Key dropped a pod into the coffee machine. Her French press came into service when she had time, but lately she was using it less and less.

Cissy fished a colorful box out of her backpack. "Sidewalk-chalk fence art. I'm gonna have Wain draw his cars, then write the names underneath." Somehow, despite (or maybe because of) her youth, Cissy intuitively understood that Wain was especially receptive to any type of game that incorporated his own interests, so CartWheels and dogs and kid-friendly adventures factored strongly into her lesson plans.

"Oh, genius, Cissy! A gigantic wooden canvas! Don't hose it off before I get a picture for Wain's dad!"

"Okay." Cissy picked up her backpack. "So … yesterday I noticed something about that old lady next door."

"Mrs. Montgomery? Do you know her?" Key sat down at the table and opened her laptop.

"No, ma'am. But I think she talks to her flowers. She was saying, 'Thank you, honey. You are a full-on star,' or 'Thank you, beautiful, for blooming where you were planted'—and no one was in the yard with her. I think it was her flowers she was talking to."

"Sounds very sweet." Key grinned and pointed to her own eyes. "When you're writing on the fence, Cissy, please have Wain draw a big red A-R-R-O-W pointing to a peephole at my eye height."

Cissy laughed aloud and went out to join Wain.

# Chapter 4
## MULLING

Key rested her head on the back of the sofa and closed her eyes. Her card-ideas notebook remained unopened on her lap; she simply couldn't muster up one creative thought. *The thing I never could have predicted about caring for and living with a child,* she mused, *is how much mental space that little human will occupy.* She'd begun calling it "Wain brain."

Key had considered giving up her contract with CORE Cards but ultimately decided that she needed this slice of her very own life, and thanks to her interesting afternoon, she'd accomplished one card design during Wain's tutoring session. Granny Jewel, in her deep drawl, had asked Key to transfer a load of clothes from the washer to the dryer. "Always wash my unmentionables on Wednesdays." (Apparently, she was fine with Key seeing and handling what she couldn't mention.)

Key had immediately envisioned the front of the card: a grass skirt hanging from two clothespins, drips of water falling onto the ground below. And inside: "If you wash your grass skirt, are you doing *lawn*dry?"

Setting aside the notebook, she opened her day planner and hurriedly jotted down her usual daily recap. More power to the people who recorded everything on their phones, but oh, how she loved the authenticity and three-dimensional comfort of paper and pen. Just as she was finishing, her phone pinged.

Hey Key! Can you talk?

Yes!

She picked up on the first ring. "Mack! How was your fishing trip?" Key had known Guy's coworker, Maxwell Simons, for only a few months, but he had already become a trusted confidant. Though she refused to allow herself to think further than that, she willingly admitted to herself that over the past week, she'd missed his calls.

"Hi, Key! It was excellent. But six days is a long time to be out in the wild. It's great to be home."

After they'd chatted for several minutes, Key said, "Mack, this afternoon I heard a very intriguing story from Granny Jewel—a mystery, actually—involving people I know. I haven't done any research on it yet, but if you have time to mull it over with me ..."

"Do tell," Mack said wryly. "I can't resist a good mull."

Key laughed and stood as Faro appeared and wandered toward the back door. "I'm going to sit outside while we talk. It's beautiful tonight."

"Storming in Houston. Not complaining. We need the rain."

"It's probably coming our way." *Check the weather. Wain might need a ride to school. Hello again, Wain brain.* It was still so new to her.

Outside the back door, Key plopped down onto the nearest of four white Adirondack chairs, but the bevy of flying insects that immediately attacked the motion-sensor light sent her hustling to the one farthest away. Nose to the ground, Faro ambled around the yard, reacquainting himself with every inch of shrubbery.

She turned up her phone's speaker volume. "The story is about my contractor, DP, who's one of those salt-of-the-earth guys, in his early thirties. When DP was twelve, his older brother disappeared from a concert and has never been seen again. Vanished without a trace."

Mack made a dismayed exclamation. "Whoa. I wasn't expecting something so ... serious."

"Yes. Heartbreaking. I'm vague on details because Granny Jewel is, well, Granny Jewel, and she said that back then she was going through her third divorce, which she described as 'real macrimonious.'"

Mack laughed out loud. "Perfection. I may have to hijack that word."

"She's the queen of malapropisms. Anyway, the missing boy's name is Riggs Plummer, and, like DP does now, he worked for his father Dawson's construction company and played in Dawson's band, Orion. It seems Riggs was a budding guitar genius."

"He disappeared after one of the concerts they played?"

"No. Riggs was attending a concert in Virginia. Granny Jewel says the band they went to hear was real popular and the name was ridiculous."

"That narrows it down. Let's see, who were my kids into back then? Savage Garden? Third Eye Blind? Marcy Playground?"

Key laughed. "I'm impressed! What I can't believe, though, is that in all the months DP's worked at my house, he's mentioned his brother but never told me that he's missing!"

"Grief is tough to discuss," Mack said thoughtfully. "For a long time, it was hard for me to say my wife had died. I didn't want to make others uncomfortable."

"Yes." Key and Mack were on similar paths in the sense that they'd each lost their spouses, but that was where the similarities ended. While Mack genuinely grieved the loss of a loving partner and the mother of his children, Jeff's death had created far more complicated emotions for Key.

"What do people think happened to Riggs?" Mack asked.

Key waved a moth away from her face. "No one knows! Riggs left his group to go to the restroom and just … disappeared, no trace of him ever found. The Plummers have been searching for twenty years."

"Oh man. My heart goes out to them," Mack said sympathetically. "It's incredibly stressful to live without answers. Families with missing loved ones are sentenced to a hellish purgatory through no fault of their own."

"A hellish purgatory. That's a perfect description." Maybe, Key thought, Mack had dealt with similar situations in his line of work—about which she knew next to nothing.

"Did Riggs go to the concert with anyone?" Mack asked.

"Yes. Granny Jewel's son, Lonny, who was Riggs's best friend, and a guy named Arlo." Key opened the door for Faro and watched affectionately as he made a beeline back to Wain's room.

"Obviously both Arlo and Lonny must have passed the smell test if they're not suspects," Mack mused. "Have you met either of them?"

"Arlo is long gone, but I've met Lonny. He's a nice, polite guy, quiet—at least around me—and as far as I can tell, a good husband and dad. After his release from serving two years in jail in Florida for theft, the family moved back here. Actually, you met his daughter, Ell."

"'Swimming was a broken straw.' That Ell?"

"Didn't suck," Key retorted, making him laugh.

"Lonny's not the type to off his friend?" Mack asked.

"And here I was, admiring your eloquence!" Key exclaimed, amused but slightly shocked. "According to Granny Jewel, Lonny was devastated and has remained close with Riggs's family."

"I save my eloquence for victims .... Not blaming Lonny at all, but it wouldn't be the first time someone did something horrible in their twenties and then became an upstanding citizen for the rest of their lives. What's Lonny's last name?"

"Morgan. And Granny Jewel's is ... um, I have absolutely no idea."

"So she's like Cher. Or Beyoncé. Just goes by the first name."

"About as far from Cher and Beyoncé as you can get," Key replied, laughing. "Listening to her talk about Riggs, I felt like she was repeating an urban legend, not a story that involves people I know." Key picked up her phone. "What do you think, Mack? Should I bring it up to DP?"

"Hmm." There was a short silence. "I'm scratching my ear."

"And that means ...?"

"My wife used to say it meant I didn't have an immediate answer. DP's reticence may be masking too much pain for everyday conversations."

"Yes. I'll let him bring it up."

"Or look for an opening. Maybe he'd appreciate the opportunity to talk about his brother. You're a great listener, Key, and people trust you."

His compliment warmed her to the core. "In the good news category, DP and his wife Molly are expecting a baby in January; it's a little boy, so I hope he brings a new era of joy to that family."

"Grandkids do that."

Key smiled. "So do the sons of first cousins once removed."

"Guy never mentions Wain without bringing up his gratitude to you." Mack yawned mid-sentence. "I'm sorry, Key, it's been a long day, and it's even later for you. Talk tomorrow?"

"Yes, of course! Are you sure you're up to coming here next month for more fishing?"

"You obviously haven't met many fly fishermen! There is no such thing as too much. And my granddaughter Lainey would never forgive me if I didn't keep that promise."

They rang off. Key stood and walked to the fence, studying the smudgy chalk drawings she'd photographed earlier. Anyone unfamiliar with Wain's story would simply see four primitively drawn cars, each with their names written in a confident childish scrawl. But knowing the hurdles Wain had overcome, Key would have happily taken a chain saw to that section of fence and hung it in her living room like the priceless piece of art it was.

Above her, on an infinite navy canvas, myriad stars added pinpoints of light, and suddenly an overwhelming sadness for the fractured, stoic Plummer family flooded though Key. What story would Riggs tell if he could? What dots needed to be connected?

"Where are you, Riggs?" she said aloud to Orion, who was right where he should be, marching with bow drawn in his autumn arc across the night sky.

She said a heartfelt prayer for DP and his parents; for Ell, who was obviously struggling; for the beautiful, budding relationship between Wain and Guy; and for her weary, kind friend Mack, who she knew full well had not been fly-fishing in a remote wilderness for the past six days. And of course, he knew she knew.

# Chapter 5

## GOLDEN EARRING

"What goes in Friday's good jar?" Key asked cheerfully. They were in the Jeep, one stitch in the hemline of cars inching forward on the half-moon drive outside Troy Elementary.

Wain waved a small blue envelope. "This is Greggo's mom's phone number, so we can play sometime."

"How fun! I can't wait to meet Greggo and his mom and dad."

"I think he just has a mom." Wain stared out the window.

Key instantly sensed the downshift in his demeanor. Wain never asked about his own mother anymore; he knew, in his seven-year-old way, that Lyric was as treacherous as she was disengaged, a woman whose greed had landed her in jail. And now, due to a murderous plot Key had uncovered, Lyric was not allowed to communicate with her son. Not that she'd ever expressed any interest in doing so. *But Wain's heartache continues.* It must feel so confusing and unfair to him because … well, it was confusing and unfair, and Key was getting used to navigating the unexpected moments that brought those emotions to the surface. She decided to forgo the "tough jar" question. If this didn't qualify, what did?

They pulled into the driveway. "I'll text Greggo's mom. Maybe he'd like to come over after school sometime, or on a Saturday. Does he like CartWheels too?"

"Yeah." Wain slowly unbuckled his seat belt.

"After we carry these groceries in, let's take your bike out to Pike House. You can ride as long as you want." Key would appreciate a catch-up with DP, if he was there, but more importantly, Wain needed a comforting dose of the only place he had ever been allowed to call home.

Wain immediately brightened. "DP and Miguel and Benito are gonna be so happy to see me and Faro!"

"DP says he misses talking to you." It suddenly occurred to Key that DP's brother's disappearance could explain the sweet, caring connection he shared with Wain, who'd experienced an equally life-altering loss.

"Can Ell come ride with me?" Wain asked, wolfing down a banana as Key unpacked bags. He'd already collected his cars from his bedroom and slid them into his backpack.

"Not today, but let's see if she can join us on a hike to Dogleg Pond tomorrow. We'll pack a picnic. How does that sound?"

"Yay!" Wain tossed a treat to Faro, who expertly snapped it out of the air. "Can we go fishing at the pond?"

"I own zero fishing equipment, so unfortunately, that idea is out. But let's do some exploring!" Key patted him on the back. "Bring your bike around front."

As they turned off Pike Road and drove past the now-familiar queue of loblolly pines lining the driveway, Key took a deep breath, absorbing the tranquility this tiny slice of the world provided. Her porch swing was off the chains, sitting disconsolately like a tilted, legless bench on the lawn alongside two other chairs, but Pike House itself, even amid the renovation clutter, was as congenial as the day she'd discovered it. *Yes. We're home.*

She had unloaded the bike and filled Faro's water bowl when DP emerged from the front door holding a large Styrofoam cup. A wide grin spread across his face as he returned Wain's excited wave. "Well, howdy, strangers!"

"Hi, DP!" Key replied. "Wain's going to do some bike riding, and I'll soak in the happiness of being out here."

"Watch this wheelie!" Wain yelled excitedly, yanking on the handlebars, then pedaling furiously to the path behind the house.

"What's next? Two inches off the ground?" DP asked Key, grinning.

"He's ready for professional gigs," Key answered, glad to see DP's humor was still intact, then she immediately became annoyed at herself. There was no need to view him differently simply by virtue of what she now knew about his brother.

DP leaned against the gate. "It's good to see y'all. Even with all the construction noise, the place seems quiet." They strolled to the porch, and DP held the door open. "I apologize for the mess. It's all gonna be worth it, though. We're still on target for a December finish date." With his boot he swept at a few remnant blocks of wood, making an arc in the thick dust. "Got the wall down. Plumbing's almost done. Next week okay to meet with the electrician?"

"Of course! Oh, it's looking great!" It was a short tour, but Key found it very exciting. Light now flooded a newly spacious living area, and it was slightly disorienting but wonderful to see the oak trees outside the kitchen window from where she was standing in the living room. In her mind, she'd already moved back in and put milk in the fridge, added throw pillows to the sofa, and was enjoying a cup of coffee by a gently crackling fire while Wain and Faro played in the weedless front yard.

"Polish up these old pine floors and this place'll look brand-new while still showing off that antique twist you love. How y'all doing in the rental?"

"All good," Key replied. "The house is beautiful, but like any short-term rental, it's impersonal. It perfectly fits our need for a place right now, but ..."

DP nodded understandingly. "Nothing like your own bit of earth. Your own bed at night." They returned to the front lawn, and he sank with a grateful sigh into one of the displaced porch chairs, extending his long legs and stacking the heel of his right boot onto the toe of his left.

Key retrieved her water bottle, a container of cookies, and a denim shirt from the Jeep, then dragged the white rocker several feet closer to DP. She arranged the shirt on the back of the chair and brushed sawdust off her shorts. "I'm going to hang out here and let Wain ride."

"Mind if I stay? Molly's gone to visit her parents this weekend, doin' some shopping for the baby. I'm gonna practice my archery and watch college ball and drink cold beer and eat nachos all weekend."

"I'd love the company." Key held out the cookies. "Add these to your menu."

"Thanks, Miss Key." DP removed his cap and scrubbed at his longish light-brown hair, then locked his hands behind his head and closed his eyes. "Been a long week."

When they'd first met, Key had noticed the letters *R-I-P* tattooed inside a star on DP's inner forearm. She'd never asked about it, though, and now she wondered if they were his brother's initials. What a sad irony that would be. Now, too, for the first time, she was able to accurately interpret the layers of exhaustion on the face of the young man across from her. It wasn't only the sun or long hours of physical labor causing those creases at the corners of his eyes. Her heart went out to him.

She rose and took a stroll around the yard, plucking the most obvious weeds. She'd hired Ell's older brother Cavender to mow, but the gardens all needed a good tidying up. It was astonishing how fast plants and trees grew in this temperate state. From behind the house, she heard Wain calling happily to Faro. It sounded like they'd stopped by the tire swing.

Tossing the weeds over the fence, she rested her elbows between two pickets and watched as a small flock of never-still grackles perched here and there in the branches of a maple tree, shrieking at one another in their squeaky-gate bird voices. Suddenly they all swooped away as one, iridescent jet-black feathers reflecting the sun like rainbows in oil slicks. *Bird mental telepathy.* It never ceased to amaze her. Yes, this was exactly what they'd needed. She returned to the rocker, tugged on a tuft of crabgrass, then another.

DP's next words surprised Key. "How's Wain's daddy these days?"

She glanced at him. He'd put his hat over his eyes. "Guy's doing well. His travel schedule is nonstop, but he's working hard on being more engaged. He and Wain talk via regular video calls. They're looking forward to being together at Christmas. Well, we all are!"

"That'll be real nice. Feel sorry for the guy, not knowing his son like that. I haven't even met my baby boy, and I can't imagine being away from him for even a day."

"When's Molly's due date?"

"Mid-January. If I can, I'm gonna take a couple weeks off after our boy's born. I should be working on your garage and breezeway by then."

"No matter what's going on here, DP, of course you should take the time off!" Key replied fervently. "Even if the house isn't done, my landlords won't be back until early February."

"Y'all can move in soon as it passes inspection. I think we've uncovered everything, even the unforeseen unforeseens on this project." DP straightened himself in the chair, pulled his cap back on, and selected a cookie. "I know the house y'all are renting. Don't know the people that bought it though."

"Vern and Deirdre Olson. I didn't meet Vern; he'd already driven their RV out West, towing their car."

"Where are they from?"

Key shrugged. "I don't know. Deirdre told me that they moved to Troy on a whim. Well, actually, she said it was her husband's choice to move here."

"Bertie Montgomery, your neighbor to the south, is one of my mama's oldest friends. She seemed old even when I was a kid. Sweet lady. Always had the full-size candy bars at Halloween."

"I need to introduce myself. How are your parents, DP?"

"Doin' all right. Mama's settin' up a nursery at her place." He smiled. "Baby Riggs Dawson Plummer will be playing varsity football before he needs new clothes."

"Oh, I love the name!" Key scooted forward, the rockers on her chair bumping clumsily on the grass. *Goodbye, indecision. Hello, gut instinct.* "DP, the other day Granny Jewel told me about your brother. I'm … I'm just so very sorry for the sorrow your family has endured."

He nodded, his eyes showing his appreciation, but his brows were drawn together in a surprised frown. "Thank you, Miss Key. I figured you knew and just wasn't talking about it. It's not the kind of thing that's a secret, you know?"

"I had no idea. I'm truly so sorry."

"Twenty years this month." DP exhaled a deep, weary sigh that conveyed more to Key than any words. "I'm real happy Molly's willing to name our baby after my brother. In fact, it was her idea. Riggs was also my mama's maiden name."

"Did Molly know your brother?"

"Oh no, she was a bitty girl when he disappeared. I'm eight years younger than Riggs, and she's six years younger than me. Of course, she *heard* about it, growing up. Who hasn't."

"Me. Since I moved here, it's been all about getting Wain settled, this house renovation, becoming acquainted with the area …."

"New boy, new dog, new house—you've for sure taken on a lot, especially for—" He stopped and took a quick drink, then crunched a piece of ice.

"My advanced age of fifty-seven?" Key asked teasingly, and DP laughed.

"You're an inspiration, that's what you are."

"Nice backtrack!" Key laughed, then said seriously, "DP, it has to be exhausting, dealing with such a devastating … unknown."

He nodded slowly. "The anniversary, if you want to call it that, is always real hard on all of us, but especially on Mama, which makes it extra hard on my daddy. He hides it better, puts his feelings into his songs." DP rubbed the diamond-and-gold stud in his right ear, something Key had seen him do many times. She had always found that earring incongruous in a man so practical.

DP caught her look. "This earring is my lifetime reminder of my brother. Ever since he was fourteen, he had a stud in his right ear with a tiny diamond star in the center. I thought it was ultracool, you know?" DP leaned forward. "See the star?"

"Oh … yes!" She'd never looked that closely.

"The summer I was twelve, I convinced Riggs to pierce my ear, using the matching earring to his. He froze my earlobe with an ice cube and held the needle in a flame, then dipped it in rubbing alcohol and poked it through while I sat on the seat of our John Deere lawn tractor. Our parents was watching *NYPD Blue*, oblivious to the fact that their garage was an operating theater. Real safe, sterile environment, hospital-grade grass clippings and gas cans and oily rags and whatnot."

"And all those hammers and awls in case he needed them to finish the job." They laughed. "But *yikes*, DP." Key cringed at the thought of both the homegrown operation *and* what shenanigans might materialize a few years down the road with Wain. By then, though, she fully expected Guy to be present. *Thank goodness.* "How'd your parents react?"

"Well, Mama was a little worried about tetanus, scrubbed my ear with more rubbing alcohol, and Daddy said a pierced ear ain't the hill he intended to die on, and besides, the earring would have to come out when I started playing football. But at the time I thought I was the studliest thing going." He gave her a rueful grin. "Girls went crazy over Riggs playing his guitar, his long hair, earring, and all, so I was pretty sure it would make me as cool as him."

"Did it?"

He smiled sadly. "I never got to find out. It wasn't but two months later that Riggs disappeared. I didn't play football that year, no time for anything except living the loneliest existence while my parents searched for my brother. I started playing football a couple years later. The earring had stayed in, and the hole was healed." He rubbed his neck. "*That* hole was healed, anyway. Something I've always been grateful for, because now this earring and that memory mean more to me than just about anything I did with him."

"Riggs sounds like a brother who was a friend too."

"I *idolized* him. He was a natural musician, mesmerizing on the stage. His voice was … incredible. Old for his years. Things always came so easy to Riggs."

"Wain's dad is a lot like that," Key commented thoughtfully. "But the easiness is all on the surface."

"Yeah? Same with Riggs, now I think about it."

The sun had gone behind the clouds again. Key slipped on the denim shirt. "Granny Jewel told me how close her son Lonny was to your brother."

"Him and Riggs was best friends till Ayo came along." DP's voice took on an unfamiliar, bitter tone.

"Who?" Key asked. Granny Jewel hadn't mentioned this person.

"Ayo Jones." DP's eyes darkened. "Worst kind of human. Psycho. He tore up that friendship. Caused a lot of chaos in our family over the years with his manipulation of my brother."

"Ohhh. Granny Jewel called him 'Arlo.'"

"It was Ayo." DP gave a disgusted snort. "He left town real quick after Riggs disappeared. We think he knows something. I've looked for him online, but I think Ayo was a nickname, and with a last name like Jones, forget it. I don't even know where to start."

"And not a hint of where Riggs might be, in all these years?"

"Zero." DP compressed his lips. "We know Riggs *likely* ain't alive, but we don't know that for absolute sure. It locks us into a sorrowful place we can't escape, if that makes sense."

*Exactly Mack's description of the hellish purgatory.* "Yes, of course it makes sense. It's a terrible limbo."

DP tapped the earring again. "Twenty-five was a real hard birthday for me, because by then, I'd lived longer without Riggs than I did with him. Now I'm thirty-two, and Riggs would have turned forty, but in my mind he's still twenty, and in some twisted way I've become his older brother. You know?"

"Yes. I don't know how else you *could* see it," Key replied sympathetically. At least Wain had answers, as unsatisfying and hurtful as they were. "What exactly happened? If you don't mind talking about it."

"I don't mind. Talking about him makes him real." DP rubbed his star tattoo. "Riggs Inman Plummer."

So she'd been right. What heartbreakingly prophetic initials.

"It's rare I meet anyone these days who don't know the story," DP continued, "and then, a course, you also meet the people who *think* they know the story. Tellin' us Riggs left the concert, hitchhiked to New Mexico to see his girlfriend, Carly, and got murdered on the way."

"That's what they say?" Key had so many questions.

"Oh yeah. Mama and Daddy and I—when I got old enough to see things for what they were—we never bought into that. Riggs would *never* have left us or abandoned Carly. Hard to believe Ayo wasn't involved, but the cops ain't got one thing to go on. No body, no evidence, no crime. Want to hear something crazy, Miss Key?"

"What?"

He hesitated. "Uh, lately I've thought I heard my brother calling to me."

Goose bumps prickled the back of Key's neck. "Seriously?"

"Yeah. It's never happened before …. But we can talk another time." DP gestured toward the gate as Wain skidded his bike to a stop and tugged off his helmet, then retrieved his water bottle and flung himself onto the grass next to them, panting dramatically.

"What kinda motocross y'all got back there, bud?" DP asked.

"I made a zigzag track! Wanna see?"

"Only if I get the grand tour by the designer himself." They stood and started for the rear of the house. "So y'all are coming back tomorrow?"

Key stayed silent, giving Wain a chance to answer. He'd been ignored or told to shut up or commanded to leave the room so often by his mother and Callahan that he was still unsure of himself in conversations, so she was gratified to hear him say, "Uh-huh, we're hiking to Dog Pond. Ell's coming too."

"Dogleg Pond." DP ruffled Wain's hair. "Before the horse farm went in, that area was real popular for partying teenagers."

"Did you fish?" Wain asked. "I want to, but Key says we have to get a *fishing pole* first." He said it as though he'd never heard anything so preposterous.

DP laughed. "Miss Key ain't wrong, Wain. You want a fishing expert, ask Jukey King. He's an encyclopedia of the outdoors around here. You know, there was always a pair of swans on that pond. My pawpaw told me, you see a swan, it's a sign of good times and happiness ahead!"

They stopped as Wain proudly pointed to a very faint bike-tire indentation in the grass. "See my track? Jukey has one at his house. His boys made it."

"Real nice, son," DP replied agreeably. He turned to Key. "I better head out. Thanks for asking after my brother. I've got more stories, if you want to hear them?"

"Oh yes, DP. I absolutely do."

# Chapter 6

## JAIL BABY

Saturday morning was chilly enough that Key dug sweatshirts out of a plastic bin, and after packing a lunch, she and Wain headed out with an ecstatic Faro.

Ell was waiting outside her family's mobile home with her backpack in one hand and an ornately carved walking stick in the other, her dark-brown ponytail cascading out the back of a grubby pink baseball cap. She burst into the Jeep, tossing her items onto the seat, hugging Faro and Wain.

"Miss Key, Mama has eggs for you when we get back."

"Perfect timing! I'm almost out." Key headed back up Wildflower Lane. "Ell, it's wonderful to see you! Are you ready to hike?"

"Uh-huh! I made PB and J on a hot dog bun. And Mama said take fruit, so I have two packs of Skittles." Ell turned to Wain. "Look! My walking stick has animal faces carved on it. A fox and a rabbit. Granny Jewel's husband made it. I don't know which one. One died but Granny Jewel says the others ran off because she was a … a siren. Like a mermaid with shells to cover, um, you know." Ell brushed her hand surreptitiously across her chest.

"Granny Jewel was a mermaid?" Wain asked in awe.

"Not a real mermaid. A fem fatal."

Key gave up and laughed out loud. "It's pronounced *femme fatale,* Ell." Mack would love this one.

"Are you sure?"

"Pretty sure, darlin'." Before they could delve any further into the topic, they were back at Pike House.

"Want to see my motocross track?" Wain asked as they all shrugged into their backpacks.

*Five ... four ... three ... two ... one.*

"Miss Key, will you hold my walking stick?"

She took it from Ell. "Let's just put it in the Jeep. The trail isn't hilly." She suddenly couldn't wait to get into the woods.

Overnight, the cooler weather had brought about a subtle change; soon the woods would be fully ablaze with autumn color, but today they were still in a cool canopy of green, their path shielded most of the way from the sun. Wain and Ell scampered ahead, but Key took her time, absorbing the whole of her surroundings. Though she and Wain walked to and from school almost every day, the endless urban dissonance distracted them from nature itself. Here, though, the trees and grass and sky *were* the story, enhanced by a cathedral-like stillness interrupted only by singing birds and rustling leaves.

Except for Wain's skinned knee and one stop to remove several burrs from an unhappy Faro's muzzle, they made good time. Key consulted her fitness app: one and a half miles.

Dogleg Pond, a charming little body of water with a jetty poking out from the southwest, rippled and shone like hammered silver, its shoreline extended by five feet of crackle-patterned mud caused by a dryer-than-usual summer. Lining the far shore was a tidal wave of deciduous trees waiting patiently to show off their individual autumn finery.

While Faro swam and Wain and Ell waded and explored, Key searched for the perfect photographs: a tiny toad on Wain's muddy palm; a magnificent swallowtail butterfly clinging with impossibly fragile legs to a beech leaf; Ell standing with her back to Key, the sun creating a halo on her hair.

After lunch, while the children sprawled on the grass, loudly chewing Skittles and pointing out cloud shapes, Key began collecting scattered picnic debris. Near Ell's backpack was a small card featuring a cowgirl in a pink hat, twirling a lasso. *EVERYONE'S INVITED*, it said in a ropy cursive font.

"Ell, is this yours?" Key asked, holding it out.

"*Give me that!*" Ell sprang to her feet and rushed at Key, snatching the card and furiously wadding it up, then sank onto the grass and burst into tears, burying her face in her palms.

Instantly, Wain was beside her, his hand on her back, then Faro joined them, and all three huddled together like penguins against a blizzard. Blindsided, Key pulled off her sunglasses and slowly sat down. She had seen only the front of the invitation. What could possibly have provoked that kind of reaction?

"What happened?" Wain asked curiously.

"This. I got this at school." Ell hurled the crumpled card onto the ground, then wrapped her arms around her shins, hiding her face in her knees, rocking back and forth.

Wain picked it up and patted it smooth, then tried to read the loopy letters on the front but gave up and handed it to Key.

"Ell, may I read this?" she asked gently.

"I don't care."

Which of course, Key knew, meant just the opposite. "'Everyone's invited,'" she read out loud, then opened the card. "'Ex—'" She pressed a hand over her mouth. "*Ell.* What in the … Who is this *from*?" She couldn't bear to envision Ell's excitement, then absolute devastation caused by the hideous words inside.

"What? What does it say?" Wain asked.

"It says, 'Except you, jail baby, ha ha,'" Ell said dully, lifting her head and staring at the water.

"What does *that* mean?" Wain asked. "What's 'jail baby'?"

"I guess it means my dad was in jail," Ell answered bluntly.

"Who's it from?" Key asked again, almost vibrating with anger.

Ell gave a great, heaving sigh. "Tally Mayweather."

The way Ell said it, no doubt Tally was the It Girl of Troy Elementary's fourth grade. Key held up the card. "Ell, have you showed this to your parents? To your teacher? To anyone?"

"No!" Ell shouted, panicked. She again grabbed the card, then tore it to shreds, hurling tiny pieces of paper into the air. "My teacher loves Tally! And my mama and especially my daddy would feel terrible, and Granny Jewel would say something that would only make it worse! Please don't tell them, Miss Key. *Please!*"

"*I'm* not gonna tell," Wain said resolutely.

*What a terrible burden for a nine-year-old.* Key thought fast. "Okay. I won't, Ell, *if* you'll tell me about Tally."

Ell's words dropped like hailstones, stinging and cold. "She's having a birthday party at the horse barn, and she invited all the girls in our class, except me."

"You mean Mistic Meadows Horse Barn? The one right down *our* road?" Key asked, pointing south.

"Yeah." Ell stared at the ground. "They text about me on their phones. And Tally says my name is *L* for 'loser' because of my clothes and my hair and my dad being in jail, and when they walk by my desk, they do, like, a loser sign on their forehead with their hand." Almost involuntarily, she made the gesture.

Key couldn't count the times Ell had mentioned wanting to ride a horse; this would have been the party of her dreams. But even more unbearable, Ell would be reminded of the devastating "jail baby" rejection every time she saw the large road sign for Mistic Meadows near her house. What herculean effort today had it taken to hide *this*? *Is there anyone more capable of nuclear psychological warfare than mean girls?*

"Ell, I can't imagine our lives if we hadn't met you!" Key plucked a sliver of paper out of Faro's coat, ran her hands deeper into his fur (no ticks, thankfully), then scraped the pieces of the torn card into a tiny pile.

"Why don't they like me, Miss Key?"

"Ell, it *isn't* about you. Tally's cruel behavior is caused by an ugly emptiness inside *her.*"

"*I'm* your friend, Ell," Wain said encouragingly. "We're kinda the same, except my mom's still in jail. So I'm like a jail baby too."

The understanding way he said it, as though their shared parental woes were something to bond over (and no doubt they were), staggered Key. *How,* she thought, *out of all the places I could be, did I end up here, in this complicated conversation with two children who've already experienced more pain than I knew at twice their age?* It was beyond anything she could have ever imagined. "Wain, Ell, that term 'jail baby' is something I've never heard before, but it is extremely unkind and unfair. You have every right to tell Tally to knock it off, in fact—"

"Look! *Look!*" Wain grabbed Faro's collar and pointed toward the pond.

"Ohhh!" Ell exclaimed, as a pair of swans glided from behind the jetty to the open water, graceful necks bent, beaks starkly obsidian against impossibly white feathers. Once across, they floated in the shallows near the reeds, their elegant bodies creating undulating silvery reflections, paying no attention to their rapt viewers just a dozen yards away.

"DP *said* there were swans!" Wain whispered. "His pawpaw told him! It means a good thing's gonna happen!"

After she snapped several pictures, Key said, "We're going to make a good thing happen. Each of you collect four big rocks and set them in a ring around that pile of paper and twigs." Mystified, they easily obeyed; there were rocks everywhere.

From her backpack, Key produced the waterproof container of strike-anywhere matches she carried in case she needed to cook a campfire stew or send smoke signals or incinerate unspeakably malicious words. Handing one match to each child, she then struck hers on a rock. "Light yours from mine," she instructed, "and we'll torch Tally's mean words."

Wain immediately tossed his match onto the pile of paper, but Ell used hers to light individual pieces until the flame got too close to her fingertips.

"Paper has no chance against fire," Key pointed out, "and Tally Mayweather's weak, ugly words are no match for the fire in you, Ell.

I believe the swans swam over to say, 'There are better days ahead.' It's going to get better."

"Yeah," Ell replied with zero conviction, slumping against a tree, her fists crammed into her sweatshirt pockets, violet-blue eyes rimmed with red.

While Key prospected helplessly for instant, healing sentiments that simply didn't exist, Wain squatted beside the rock ring, poking at the ashes with a stick, sending the last smoky wisps drifting skyward. In the background, the almost-otherworldly swans floated, still as ice sculptures.

Ell's next words set in motion the ripples that would change lives.

"I wish I was a pirate," she said.

# Chapter 7

## DINNER WITH THE MORGANS

"e too!" Wain exclaimed. "I wanna be a pirate with you."

"Why a pirate, Ell?" Key asked, though she suspected she already knew.

Ell had regained at least some equilibrium. "Pirates have, like, buried treasure and stuff. If I found a box of buried treasure, we wouldn't be poor."

"You're not poor!" Wain retorted. "You sell eggs! 'Member? Key gives you money for the eggs?"

Ell finally laughed. "Not like *five dollars,* Wain. I mean like a whole box of coins and jewels. I'd give it to my daddy and mama, and I'd buy my own phone. And pirates get to go on adventures and sail away."

"I get it, Ell," Key said. In the past, hadn't she herself dreamed of sailing away to a new life? And hadn't that dream come true? Because here she was, not exactly sailing, but journeying with a host of new companions on an adventurous, intensely fulfilling path crammed with treasure, which, after all, was in the eye of the beholder.

It was after three. The swans drifted like feathery ballerinas back toward the jetty, as though they'd very much enjoyed their roles in this literal version of *Swan Lake,* but it was time to go home. Key had the children fill plastic sandwich bags with water and pour it inside the fire ring, then, with the sole of her shoe, she ground every last bit of ash into the mud, wishing that doing so would also forever obliterate the words *jail baby* in everyone's minds. She needed to shape this awful memory into a triumph. But *how*?

Someday, Key hoped, Ell would realize that having loving parents, siblings, and grandparents amounted to riches beyond which many children, including the little boy beside her, could ever dream. But now wasn't the time to point that out—nor was it at all helpful to wonder out loud, *Why does a fourth grader need a cell phone?* Instead, she put an arm around each child and turned them toward the pond. "Look around you. When you're outdoors, you're rich in a way that all the pirate gold in the world can't buy. This has been a pretty good adventure, hasn't it?" Wain nodded, and at least Ell didn't disagree.

The walk back on weary legs felt farther than their morning trek, but no one complained, and Ell cheered up as she and Wain played "shadow lava," jumping from one sunlit patch to another. It didn't change what Monday would bring, though, Key thought with a pang, wondering again how much Ell was hiding as she chased Wain down the path.

At the Morgans', Gayle emerged from the front door with Dibsy in tow, and after a quick recap (with no mention of the card), Wain and Ell scampered off to Granny Jewel's house a few hundred yards up the driveway to return her walking stick.

Key hunkered down next to Dibsy. "Hey there, baby! How's your ear?"

"Antibiotics are a miracle—wouldn't even know she's been sick," Gayle replied. "Thank you for inviting Ell. She's been out of sorts lately."

"Anytime! She's such a special kid." Key tamped down a wave of guilt. What was more important: a promise kept to a nine-year-old or Gayle's right to know why her daughter was struggling?

"Miss Key, would you and Wain like to have dinner with us? Lonny's grilling burgers, and we're setting up on Granny Jewel's veranda. Lon's older brother Larry and his wife Petra are up there now."

"We'd love to!"

Gayle bent to adjust a twisted strap on Dibsy's purple overalls. "Could Dibs hang with you for a few? I got a wagonload of food to run over to GJ's."

"Of course!" As Key strolled around, listening to toddler gibberish and leaning slightly to encase a tiny, trusting hand in hers, up at Granny Jewel's Ell and Wain were pulling Faro in Gayle's wagon, laughing and shouting. *How could anyone not like Ell?*

*Fourth grade.* How easily it all came flooding back: Key's crush *du jour* (not that the recipient had any idea), arguments with friends, slumber-party shenanigans, wishes and dreams, and nine-year-old frustrations, all recorded in Key's green fake-fur diary in a childish cursive she could see to this day. And not one of those thoughts was ever shared with her parents.

But this … this bullying? Was it right to keep Ell's secret?

Well, Key's other side argued, had she ever discussed her own shame for remaining a bystander while a girl named Jasmine was relentlessly mocked by the two popular girls Key most wanted for friends? Did she ever voice her relief (not only for Jasmine, but, shockingly, selfishly, for herself) when that poor girl moved away midyear and the problem of Key's own cowardice moved with her? No, she had not shared any of that with her parents. She'd navigated those rocky shoals alone and, to this day, chagrined.

*Maybe,* she mused, *helping Ell is a way I can make up for my own lack of courage so many decades ago.*

She sighed. It was complicated, but yes, she would keep her word to Ell, who had shown insight beyond her years when she argued that Lonny would blame himself.

Dibsy waddled over in her impossibly tiny pink Crocs and offered Key a dense egg-shaped magnolia cone covered in red seeds. "Ah *dah!*" she said cheerfully, displaying five fresh teeth.

"'Ah dah' back at you, baby. I'm going to do my best to help your sister," Key replied, giving her a squishy hug.

***

Granny Jewel, resplendent in a maroon bell-sleeved top and black-and-white-checked knit pants, welcomed Key with a hug and made the introductions. Larry, a stocky, balding dark-haired man with friendly gray-blue eyes, a broad smile, and a good bit of surplus hanging over his belt, looked so unlike lanky, blond Lonny that Key wondered if they might be half brothers. Considering Granny Jewel's macrimonious track record, it was a good possibility. Petra was short and equally sturdy, with a stylish bleached-blond pixie cut and a no-nonsense demeanor, her phone connected to her hand like an oxygen source. Though very friendly, they exuded far less of the energetic *zing* Key had come to associate with Ell and her family.

Dinner was a feast: bacon-topped cheeseburgers, three homemade salads, buttery corn on the cob, and a variety of chips and pickles. Wain and Ell, starving after all the fresh air, perched on cushions next to the glass-topped coffee table, gobbling their food, and Faro watched wistfully until, finally, Lonny took the biggest burger from the stack and handed it to him, bun and all. "Here, bud. Can't resist those soulful eyes."

When Key helped herself to seconds of Gayle's peppery potato salad, Petra said knowingly, "Duke's."

"Amen," Granny Jewel said, nodding. North Carolinians, Key had long-ago learned, were extremely loyal to their Duke's Mayonnaise.

She took a tiny sip of her sugary tea, far too sweet for her Midwestern palate, but she'd finish the entire glass before she'd be ungracious. This family was one of the nicest (and most entertaining) she'd ever met.

At one point, Key heard the word "restitution" during a brief but serious conversation held in low tones between Lonny and Larry. Suddenly, Ell's comment about being poor took on new context. Most likely, Lonny's wages were being garnished—something to do with his incarceration, no doubt.

"Y'all can watch TV inside if you want," Granny Jewel told Wain and Ell, who were now sprawled like exhausted puppies on the floor, with just enough strength remaining to inhale their chocolate cupcakes. "Got all the *Beverly Hillbillies* and *Gilligan's Island* on DVD."

"I'll set it up, Mama, and put some coffee on." Larry disappeared into the house with the children, who, Key suspected, would probably be asleep before the *SS Minnow* reached the island or the Hillbillies exited their ancient truck.

Lonny pulled a cigarette out of a box lying on the table next to him, tapped it on the arm of his chair, and tucked it between his lips.

"Ashtray, darlin'." Granny Jewel slid a used paper plate toward him. "Thought you was quittin'."

"Down to three a day," Lonny replied. "One after each meal." He took a long, blissful draw.

Gayle spoke up. "I'm done. Not one smoke in four weeks, and the money we save is goin' toward a car for me if Ell don't need braces."

"Hard thing, quittin'," Granny Jewel said sympathetically. "Proud of you, honey." She changed the subject. "I told Key the other day about Riggs. She didn't have no idea."

Lonny's eyes widened. "Y'all seriously didn't know?"

Key shook her head. "My heart goes out to the Plummers."

"Mine too, especially Riggs's mama," Petra said, finally tucking her phone snugly into the pocket of her tennis skirt and lighting her own cigarette. "How they manage is … well, I guess they just *got* to pick up and go on, 'cause they got no choice in the matter." With a sympathetic but philosophical shrug and an expert sideways lip move, she blew smoke out over the railing, saying to Key, "Our Liza's nineteen, and Tyla's twenty-one; both in college. If either one of them was taken, I'd hunt that outlaw to the ends of the earth. And heaven help him if *this* mama frickin' wildcat ever caught him." She raised her hands, clawlike, and scrabbled bright-red nails at the invisible kidnapper's face, the smoke from the cigarette adding a comically sinister element.

"Coffee in five," Larry announced, leaning against the doorframe, arms crossed and resting on his stomach. "Preach it, sister," he said equally to his wife, sliding right back into the conversation. "But why *him*? Could be a *her*. Y'all women ain't all saints."

Petra shot him a sassy look. "Fine. Him *or* her! I got no trouble tearin' it up with any man *or* woman hurts my baby. Show. Me. The. Way." She clapped her hands forcefully between the words, ash flying everywhere.

"Yessir, Sergeant!" Larry saluted, then said to Key with a proud little nod, "She ain't joking."

*Scratch that thought about Petra's lack of zing*, Key told herself. Wain's mother, Lyric, might benefit from a heart-to-heart with the mama frickin' wildcat.

"Riggs gone missin' is the worst thing that's ever happened in my life," Lonny said, instantly capturing everyone's attention. His blue eyes, so like Ell's, met Key's. "But my problems ain't nothin' compared to the Plummers'."

Key glanced at Gayle. Surely Lonny's incarceration and the ensuing difficulties were higher on her scale of tough times? But Gayle was nodding in agreement while rocking Dibsy, who had fallen asleep sucking her thumb. "That's right, Lon. At least our sentence ended."

Lonny kept his eyes on the tip of his cigarette. "DP had to shoulder a burden he never asked for, didn't deserve. The Plummers got a life sentence, courtesy of a man I wisht me and Riggs never laid eyes on."

"Arlo done wrong to the whole community, JMO." Granny Jewel took a cup from the tray Larry was holding, then looked bewildered as her sons burst out laughing. "Ell taught me that! Don't that mean *just my opinion*?" When they nodded, she scolded, "So you got no call to laugh!"

Larry continued his rounds. "Touché, Mama. But it's *Ayo*. And he was a natural-born SOB who wouldn't have been yanking my brother and his best friend around if I'd been here, you can bet your bottom dollar on that." He handed Key a mug, adding, "When all that went down, I was stationed overseas in the US Army."

"But without the army, wouldn't have been no *us*, Lar." Petra, too, turned to Key. "Me and Larry got married in Ansbach, Germany, when we were both in the service."

It was cooling off. Granny Jewel tugged a homemade lap quilt out of a bulging wheelchair pocket and offered it to Gayle, who snugged it around Dibsy.

"What exactly happened the day Riggs disappeared?" Key asked. She was dying to hear the story.

"How much time you got?" Lonny asked, stubbing his cigarette butt on the paper plate.

"As long as Granny Jewel's DVD collection lasts," Key answered, and they all laughed.

"Might take that long," Lonny replied.

# Chapter 8

## LONNY'S STORY

"From kindergarten on," Lonny began, "me and Riggs was tight. Loved bein' outside, playing sports, campin' by Dogleg, hangin' out with our group of friends. We did a lot of stupid crap but never got into no deep trouble, you know? Just crazy in that teenage way. By the time we was fourteen or so, though, Riggs didn't have a lot of freedom, because most Fridays and Saturdays he played with Orion, his daddy's band. He was a *real* good singer and guitar player, coulda been someone like Derek Trucks if he'd got the chance."

"Long as it's not M&M," Granny Jewel grumbled, screwing her face into a scornful sneer. "M&M is always gonna be chocolate candy to me and can't nobody convince me it's music. And I say, pull up them pants. No one gives a flying rat's patoot about layin' eyes on your unmentionables."

"Eminem is a *rapper*, Mama, a person, not a kind of music!" Larry retorted, exasperated but joining in the laughter. "Now, listen, you *gotta* let Lon talk or we are gonna be watching the *sun* come up."

Granny Jewel lifted her chin. "G'wan, then."

Lonny tipped his chair back, his handsome, thin face now in the shadows, his voice far more subdued. "Everything changed the summer before our senior year in high school, when me and Riggs started our own little business, L&R Painting. We was *hustlers*, advertised our services on those tear-off strips all over town. Our first job was repaintin' a shed, and the day we started, here comes this guy pushin' through the shrubbery, said he lived in the basement apartment next door. Tells us his name is Ayo Jones." He took a sip of coffee, grimaced, and poured the rest over the porch railing.

"You're supposed to drink it while it's hot," Larry pointed out.

"Thanks, big bro," Lonny replied humorously. "I'm real grateful you're helpin' me navigate the pitfalls of life, because I'm only forty."

"How old was Ayo when you met him?" Petra asked.

"Some older than us," Lonny replied. "Maybe five or six years."

"It's real strange he was hanging out with y'all young boys. He didn't have a job or nothin'?" Petra persisted. Mama wildcat was showing her claws.

"Yeah, he worked at a cleaning business, the kind that mucks out after disasters—you know, fires, floods, tornadoes, that kind of thing."

"What was your first impression of Ayo?" Key asked, wishing she had her notebook and pen.

Lonny shrugged. "We thought he was okay. Coupla country boys like us, yeah, we was impressed by Ayo's things, like Ray-Ban sunglasses, nice watch, expensive shoes, CD collection, all that. He drove a new white Camry."

"Where'd he get the bucks?" Larry asked. "Type of job he had don't pay for no Camry."

"He said he got a settlement from an injury where he used to work. Anyway, right from the get-go Ayo zeroed in on Riggs. Maybe it was that musician angle. He thought Riggs could 'attract chicks.'" Lonny sketched air quotes. "And it was true, Riggs had that kinda looks and personality. Girls thought he was cute as heck, and he come alive on that stage."

"Gettin' chilly." Granny Jewel tugged a shapeless black sweater from the same wheelchair pocket. Immediately, Petra jumped up and helped her into it.

Key stood. She simply had to get her notebook. "Excuse me." Inside the house, she was unsurprised to see that the children were sound asleep, Wain on the sofa with Faro curled up at his feet and Ell looking especially vulnerable in a battered recliner, both of them covered with colorful crocheted throws. On the TV, his drawling sentences punctuated by canned laughter, perennially phlegmatic Jed Clampett was in the process of unraveling Jethro's latest comic tangle. A rush of nostalgia blended with protective affection swept over Key. Why couldn't life always be this uncomplicated and safe? She foraged for the remote on Ell's chair and hit mute, then snapped off the overhead light, leaving the television to set a flickering glow.

"Do you mind if I take notes?" she asked when she returned, holding up her notebook. "I'd like to research Riggs's disappearance. Maybe I can find a new string to tug." *Maybe Guy and Mack can help is more like it.*

"Have at it," Lonny replied skeptically. "Fresh eyes can't hurt, but in twenty years, nothin' has ever changed." He picked up the pack of cigarettes, caught a look from Gayle, and set it back down with a sigh. Granny Jewel dug once again into her wheelchair pocket, this time producing an unwrapped peppermint that she dusted off and handed to her son.

*Once a mother, always a mother. Well, most of the time.* Key shook her head slightly, thinking of Lyric.

"Huge reward, too, right, Lon?" Petra asked. She tapped on her phone and read aloud, "'Two hundred thousand dollars for any information leading to finding Riggs Plummer.'" To Key she said, "But any online research just regurgitates the same old, same old."

Key nodded. "I found that out." She had seen the reward poster featuring two pictures: one a close-up of a boyishly handsome, smiling young Riggs (Key noted the earring) and the other of him playing guitar on a stage. Riggs favored their fair-haired mother, Olive, and DP was darker like Dawson, but the familial resemblance was there. "How long was it before you realized … you know, something was off about Ayo?" she asked Lonny.

"Not long, for me at least." Lonny crunched his mint. "That was a man loved to brag about *everything*. Whatever you did, he done it better. Whatever you saw, he seen it clearer. Wherever you traveled, he done more miles in a shorter time in a better rig while picking up the most beautiful hitchhiker. Whatever you bought, he had a better version, and not only that, he'd mock yours, do his best to make you feel small."

"A one upper." Petra nodded. "Got a ex-friend like that. I run when I see her coming."

Lonny grimaced. "It got to me real quick, but Riggs ... I don't know, maybe his bs meter had a higher tolerance level than mine. Maybe he felt sorry for Ayo. The guy had a rough childhood. *Supposedly.*"

"Rough how?" Larry asked, looking dubious.

Lonny shrugged. "He told us he was adopted and then when he was, like, nine, his adoptive parents had their own kid and changed their minds about him. Put him into the foster system."

"I did not know that!" Granny Jewel exclaimed amid dismayed gasps sparking around the porch.

*How close had Wain come to the same fate?* Key asked herself. What if she'd declined Guy's request to take him? She couldn't bear thinking about it.

"For real, Lon? Ayo told you that?" Gayle asked, clutching Dibsy a little tighter.

Lonny nodded. "Said he was looking for his birth mother. I think, you know, Riggs felt bad for the guy because the Plummers were such a tight family and all." He shook his head. "I'm sorry if that did happen to Ayo as a kid, but bear in mind, the guy was a liar. Made stuff up *all the time.* Played on sympathy however he could get it."

"Hard to believe a person would make up something like that!" Petra exclaimed.

Lonny laced his hands behind his head and stared at the porch ceiling. "Anyways, I stopped hangin' out with Ayo early on, but Riggs got sucked into that vortex, and it come between him and me, ruined our friendship. Exactly what Ayo wanted." He narrowed his eyes and looked directly at Key. "Why did the nicest, most talented guy—my best friend—have to be lost and that ... *cockroach* get to go on and live life?"

No one answered; the only sounds were the click of Petra's lighter, the snap of the American flag on the pole in the yard, and the cicadas singing their sandpaper songs.

Quiet Lonny was unexpectedly forthright, even eloquent, in such a homespun way. Key considered his words. "Do you think Ayo had something to do with Riggs going missing?"

"Question of the century, Miss Key," Lonny answered, as Granny Jewel nodded vigorously. "I can't see how, because I was there. Riggs was there. Foo Fighters was on stage. Riggs headed to the john, and then"—his face showed twenty years' worth of consternation—"I never saw him again."

"Fool Fighters!" Granny Jewel waved languidly at Key. "I knew it was something about fools."

Before Larry could correct his mother, Key hurriedly asked Lonny, "You came straight back to Troy from the concert?"

"Yes, ma'am. I drove Ayo's van back. Our friend Shasta Harrison snagged a ride because she had to be at work in Troy at the doughnut shop at five the next morning. She sat up front with me, and Ayo slept in the back." He hit the palm of one hand with the back of the other, emphasizing each sentence. "We stopped for gas once. Got here. Got out. Ayo drove away." He shook his head. "It was that simple."

Key glanced at her notes. "Van? I thought Ayo drove a Camry."

"That day he drove this beater white work van because we thought, if the concert went real late, we might want to sleep somewhere overnight. When all that happened with Riggs, though, we came on back."

"It was past three a.m. when Arlo dropped you off," Granny Jewel scolded as Petra draped a small quilt across her front and down her lap like a giant bib, tucking it here and there between her body and the wheelchair. "Y'all were exhausted. Had no business being on that road!"

"Not gonna argue, Mama," Lonny replied. "Never said we wasn't dyed-in-the-wool idiots back then."

"It must have been extremely hard to drive away from the concert without Riggs," Key said sympathetically.

"Yes, ma'am. We waited a couple hours, to see if he'd show up. I was close to panicking, but Ayo kept insisting he had left, gone to see his girlfriend Carly."

"It ain't that far-fetched to think Riggs took off on his own, maybe hitchhiked?" Larry said.

"That's the easy answer, ain't it?" Lonny's voice rose a notch. "Allows the law to wash their hands of it!" He crossed his arms. "Miss Key, Riggs told Ayo and me that maybe he'd leave after the concert and catch a bus to Albuquerque to visit his girlfriend. He even brought his saved-up money. See, he was *real* pissed at his daddy, 'cause they had an Orion gig that night and of course Dawson expected him to play. They fought about it." Lonny shrugged. "But in my opinion, all his talk of leavin' was just blowin' off steam."

"Weird," Key mused. "Why leave before the Foo Fighters finished?"

Petra gestured toward Granny Jewel, whose chin was on her chest. "She's fixing to fall asleep right there. Y'all keep talking. I'm gonna help her into bed."

"I'll help you, Petra," Gayle said.

Lonny jumped up and kissed his mother, then carefully extracted Dibsy from Gayle's arms. "Oooh. Warm baby. Better than a campfire."

"Please don't think ill of her sons, Key," Larry said. "Mama won't let us help her like she will Gayle and Petra. Pitches a full-dee fit if we try."

"Might see her unmentionables. 'G'wan! Git! Leave a grown woman to her privacy!'" Lonny added, tipping his chin and sounding uncannily like his mother.

"I don't think ill of anyone in your family," Key replied once they'd all stopped laughing.

"You'd never know we're family by our names, though," Larry said as the brothers exchanged a look, identical wry smiles playing across their faces." My daddy was Clarence Oakes, Lonny's was Bud Morgan, and then there was two others. It can get real confusing, real quick."

Out came Granny Jewel's voice again from Lonny's direction. "'Some men just cain't handle a siren!'"

They were still going back and forth when Petra returned. "What y'all laughing at?" she asked, shrugging into a denim jacket. "Oh. Never mind." To Key she said, "We all love GJ, but talk about a crazy childhood! They never had to wonder if their mama loved them, though. And she's real happy to have Lonny and Gayle back here. So are we."

Lonny's face grew serious. "I owe Mama everything. When I was incarcerated, she sent money every month. Bought us that mobile home too."

"Heart of gold," Larry agreed.

"Now y'all are going to have to quiet down some," Gayle said from the doorway. "We got four sleeping, and I want to keep it that way!"

"Where were we?" Lonny asked. "We've kinda derailed the train here."

# Chapter 9

## LONNY'S STORY CONTINUES

Petra peeled the paper off a cupcake, removed the bottom half with an expert twist, and positioned it on top of the icing.

Between nibbles she said, "Lonny, you was talkin' about Riggs maybe going to see his girlfriend."

"Carly Prescott. She moved after our tenth-grade year, and it about broke his heart. If Riggs woulda had a cell phone, he'd a been on it 24-7 with her."

"Cell phones was a luxury back then—cost near a thousand bucks," Larry said.

"Ayo had a Motorola. Of course." Lonny made a face. "But after Riggs disappeared, he never answered it."

Key frowned. "Ayo sounds truly awful, but I'm still confused as to why everyone suspects him."

Lonny nodded. "Understandable. I'll tee it up for you, Miss Key. A couple months before he went missing, Riggs had finally woke up to how psycho Ayo was, and he'd started hangin' out with me again. We got real good at ghosting the guy, but the one place he knew for a fact Riggs would be was wherever Orion was playing. Riggs would see him in the audience, glaring at him."

"Eww! That is so creepy!" Petra shuddered. "Scooch over by Lon, Lar." She raised her phone and snapped a quick photo, the flash sending a miniature lightning bolt across the dimly lit space. "Cute, y'all!" She tapped a few words to assure her daughters that their father, uncle, and baby cousin were still alive and well since the photo she'd sent an hour before.

"Mamarazzi, at it again," Larry joked.

"Let's go inside," Gayle suggested, gently lifting Dibsy. "We can move Ell and Wain to the spare bedroom."

"Don't have to tell me twice." Petra jumped up and grabbed her wooden chair. "My hiney feels like I been setting on gravel! And it's only sixty-seven frickin' degrees out here! I'm like to freezing!"

Key had long since gotten used to the "it's all relative" thermometer used in the American South, but it still amused her. Sixty-seven in her home state of Illinois was sunbathing weather.

In the living room, Faro regarded her with soulful eyes that seemed to say, *Take me home.*

"Soon," Key told him, rubbing his ears. "I want to hear the whole story."

Lonny picked up where he'd left off. "So we was ghosting Ayo, but then he scored three tickets for the Foo Fighters. Held 'em out like a carrot to Riggs." He shook his head. "The man was a master manipulator. He knew Riggs wouldn't go if I didn't, so he invited me, too, and a course I said I would. Got there around noon. Foo Fighters played in the early afternoon."

"Were you all together the whole time?" Key asked

"More or less. My memory's hazy due to a good dose of Mary Jane and alcohol. We was hanging out with friends, enjoying the music. Then Riggs went to the restroom and ..." He shrugged twice in quick succession, his lips tightly compressed. "*What happened?* Ayo told me he thought Riggs had left, decided to go see Carly, which sounded crazy, but it coulda happened because, like I said, Riggs had been talking about doing that on the ride up."

After three days, Lonny explained, when Riggs had not arrived at Carly's home, a frantic Dawson drove the route, stopping at every bus depot between Richmond and Albuquerque, desperately inquiring if anyone, anywhere, had seen his son. No one had.

"You okay, bro?" Larry asked suddenly, placing his hand on Lonny's knee.

"Yeah .... Sorry." Lonny gave an embarrassed little laugh and bent his head, using the hem of his T-shirt to dab at the corners of his eyes. "It sounds all kinds of crazy, but since we moved back here, at times I feel like Riggs is calling to me."

Key stifled a gasp. *DP had said the exact same thing.* "I'm sorry, Lonny," she said. "If this is too much, we don't have to talk about it."

"I'll talk all night if my words will allow you to—How did you put it? 'Tug a string.' Long past time for the Plummers to find peace." His eyes met Key's. "Know something funny? I watched Riggs walk away while the Foo Fighters played 'February Stars'—a song about missing someone. How crazy is that, when the star of Orion goes missing?"

# Chapter 10

## ICKY DILEMMA

Sunday was a comparatively low-key day after Saturday's exhausting string of activities. Wain had a late-morning video call with Guy, who seemed more upbeat. His work had been very fulfilling lately, he told Key, which she thought likely had nothing to do with gas or oil, even though ostensibly a company called Citron Oil was his employer.

They took Faro to the park, where Wain played with a group of children while Key chatted with their parents. They asked if she was his grandmother (an assumption she heard nearly every day) and seemed slightly nonplussed that Wain lived with her. She could tell they drew a distinct line between their role as parents and hers as Wain's caretaker. That conversation simply cemented an idea that had been simmering in Key's head ever since their Saturday hike: a plan to provide both Wain and Ell with a distinctly personal activity, one that might lessen the sting of a disengaged, uncaring mother and fourth-grade spitefulness.

A brief but deeply satisfying phone call to a woman Key had never met led to a second call, this time to Gayle, who put her on speaker so Lonny could listen, and Key heard in their voices excitement and relief on Ell's behalf.

Dinner was pepperoni pizza eaten on the sofa while watching a popular cartoon movie Wain had been begging to see called *The Ickies*, about a community of unattractive greenish elf-like creatures whose dialogue and actions, as far as Key could tell, revolved mostly around kid-grade ribald humor and random bodily noises. (When she'd called them "elves," Wain had corrected her nicely but firmly. "Um, Key, they're not elves. They're *Ickies!*" To which she had replied with an extra-wide grin, "You got *that* right, mister.") Key didn't mind working on her laptop while Wain devoured his pizza and giggled at the antics, but after enduring what seemed like the hundredth Icky belch, she did find herself irritated at the movie's creators. Surely they could do better.

Ickies aside, though, most of her still-fresh life with Wain rolled along as easily as if they were the only runners on a flat, open road. As far as Key could tell, Wain's primary need was a loving, safe space in which to traverse the joys and trials of childhood. She would be there as a boundary if he tried to gallop off into the mud and weeds, but she trusted him—he was smart, savvy, and engaging, and in his seven-year-old way, he understood and appreciated her part in rescuing him from Lyric and Callahan. Or maybe it was because every time Wain talked with Guy, his father said, "Make sure you mind Key, buddy." Whatever the reason, Wain was simply a great kid, and she already loved him more than she'd ever loved anyone.

The conundrum was how to recognize the boundary lines. For instance, this seemingly plotless cartoon—Key could almost feel her brain cells shriveling. Were they in the mud and weeds here? Was this the best use of Wain's time? Did that matter? Did he not deserve to choose some things for himself, banal as she may find them? After all, *The Beverly Hillbillies* wasn't exactly Montessori.

She thought back to DP's story. His parents hadn't known that their calm reaction to their twelve-year-old son's newly pierced ear would add precious elements of parental grace and patience to DP's most priceless memory of Riggs. But it had. *You just never know what the ripples of parenthood will deliver.*

But *The Ickies*? Key honestly couldn't fathom how this buffoon-laden cartoon would lead to meaningful conversation or beautiful memories. At least she and Wain had spent most of the weekend outdoors. The thought of Dogleg Pond brought her right back to Ell. *Talk about pitfalls and bumps in the road.*

After Wain went to bed, Key chatted with Mack.

"Jail baby," he commented somberly. "That is oddly, specifically targeted and spectacularly unkind. Kids live in the moment, which makes friction like this especially painful."

"Ell is a natural-born leader, but she's comparing herself to the other girls and coming up short in her own eyes. And since she doesn't want to tell her parents, even that support is unavailable. But I have an idea." Key explained her plan.

She could hear the smile in his reply. "It's great. Hopefully your idea'll give Ell and Wain some coping skills that will last the rest of their lives."

Before Key could tell him about her evening with the Morgans, Mack had to take another call, then he texted that he'd be gone for a few days.

Key still had no idea what either Guy or Mack actually *did*, but she hoped that, somehow, Mack might be able to track Riggs's movements from twenty years ago or (more likely) find Ayo. And because Mack had been very clear when they first met that there should be no reference via phone, texts, or email to the hidden side of his and Guy's employment, she'd wait to talk in person when he came to North Carolina.

★★★

Monday was chilly and sputtering rain, promising a downpour later that evening. Key drove Wain to school, waving her thanks to the cheerful greeters in bright rain gear who, Wain observed before exiting the Jeep, looked like walking crayons. "Some are like those big crayons that babies use. And some are the really old ones, and some are the regular ones." Key laughed to herself as she headed out of town. Was she extra-large, really old, or regular? Wain's penchant for noticing details and expressing them in amusing and colorful terms was one of her favorite parts of their conversations.

She gassed up the Jeep, then headed for Pike Road, where she continued to the end and entered an open gate leading to a gravel parking lot. After backing in, she left the windshield wipers on and sat for a moment, taking in the view.

*This is someone's dream come true, created for the dreams of others to come true.* It was the first time she'd ever been to Mistic Meadows Horse Barn, and she was immediately entranced. Directly across from her was a long two-story barn, to her left an office-tack shed combo. Both structures were light gray with corrugated red metal eaves supported by log posts and set off by white-framed windows. In the fenced pasture, several horses stood patiently under the dripping branches of a majestic live oak. The entire area telegraphed, *Serious fun to be had here.*

The only other vehicle in sight was a late-model pickup sitting outside the barn, tailgate down. In the bed of the truck, lying with its chin on its paws atop a bale of hay, a damp black-and-white border collie kept ice-blue eyes fixed intensely on the Jeep.

Zipping up her windbreaker, she hopped out, waved to the collie, and made her way to the office. The courtyard smelled and sounded wonderful—horses and hay and real life. The perfect venue to discuss an adventure.

# Chapter 11

## HORSE SENSE

ey swiped her suede ankle boots on a black rubber mat (what had she been thinking, wearing these to a horse barn on a rainy day?) then knocked lightly on the door.

"Come in!" called a raspy, muffled voice. Whoever it was sounded a bit harried; Key turned the knob, hoping she wasn't interrupting the myriad morning chores that inevitably came along with caring for a stable full of horses.

Before she could shut the door, a hard, wet swish hit her legs, and the border collie shook vigorously, then plunked itself onto the floor and began nonchalantly grooming its coat.

"Nice stealth move, collie." Key patted its head, then brushed droplets off her jeans and took a look around.

Behind an imposing wooden desk were two tall bookshelves featuring an entire set of equine encyclopedias, several horse figurines, a perpetual calendar frozen on August 27, a thirsty potted philodendron, an almost-empty jar of jelly beans (someone either didn't like the green ones or was saving the best for last), and an overflowing box marked *Lost and Found*. On the desk next to the keyboard, a cell phone with a cracked screen lay atop two folders.

Photos of horses and their people populated every inch of available wall space. *If I had to guess, these people are perpetually in a hurry.*

There was a commotion through the open door to her right—Key could see that it led into the tack shed—and then the same voice said, "Aha! Found it!" Thirty seconds later a stout woman staggered backward into the office carrying a box that she immediately dropped from waist height. It would be a miracle if everything inside hadn't broken.

"Blank trophies," the woman announced, dusting her hands together. "Donations for a fundraiser. They're tougher than they sound." She had a headful of gray curls, sparkling but steely greenish-yellow eyes, and a heavily freckled face. "I see you've met our hardworking farmhand, Emmaline." With a hand as worn and scuffed as her calf-hugging leather boots, she clasped Key's in a solid, two-pump shake. "I'm Jessie Mistic. I don't work in the office, that's my co-owner Regina's purview, but something came up this morning, so she asked me to meet with you."

"Key North. Nice to meet you! So your last name is actually Mistic? I thought it was a play on words."

"You can't believe how many people have told me I've misspelled my own last name," Jessie replied with a touch of asperity. "As *if!*" She seized a glove and vigorously brushed hay sprinkles from one of the two leather chairs positioned in front of the desk, then abruptly disappeared into the tack room. A toilet flushed; moments later Jessie emerged with two chipped mugs, one of which she offered to Key. "Coffee? We're out of creamer. Well, not exactly *out*. But it's curdled. Didn't think you'd want that. Dumped it down the commode."

"Oh, um, thank you! I drink it black, anyway." Key sat down and took a tentative sip, hoping she'd successfully hidden the grimace that followed. Clearly none of the dozens of blue ribbons on display had been awarded for best (or even palatable) coffee, but on the bright side, a cup of this nearly chewable inky caffeine would easily fuel a few hours of horse-related chores.

Jessie eased into the chair behind the desk and checked the labels on two creased folders. "We understand you'd like to enroll ... ah,

Wain Banfield and Ell Morgan … in our Saddle Happy program?" She glanced at the clock on the wall and made a face. "I have about twenty minutes. Tell me about the kiddos."

"I'll make it short," Key replied, hoping she'd done the right thing. Jessie's rough-around-the-edges personality wasn't necessarily off-putting; she'd define her as someone whose full and physically grueling life wasted neither words nor motions. "Wain lives with me because his mother is incarcerated in Florida and his father works overseas. He is seven and a half and in second grade. His father is my cousin's son."

"Child lives with foster grandmother. Mother incarcerated," Jessie murmured each drawn-out word as she wrote. "How's he doing with the change?"

"Much better than I could ever have expected," Key replied. "He was removed from a very unhappy, abusive home this past May."

Jessie suddenly softened, leaning her chin on her fist. "So trauma is not very far in his rearview mirror. And you're his guardian angel."

Key smiled. "Long story." If Jessie wanted more information, she'd supply it, but obviously time was of the essence.

"The biographies of our Saddle Happy kids are always much longer than their short lives deserve," Jessie reflected. "That's the best part of what we do—the children are allowed to put it all on the back burner for an hour or two." She opened the second folder. "Now, how about Ell Morgan?"

"She's nine, in fourth grade. She lives with both her parents, but her father Lonny was recently in prison in Florida, and since they moved back here, Ell has been struggling at school." Even with the ceiling fan, the small office was getting warm. Key pulled off her windbreaker.

Jessie lifted the folders. "Because both children have parents who are or were incarcerated, they meet our criteria. Can you bring them out here to meet their horses? Maybe later this week?"

"They're in? Just like that?" Key asked, bewildered. "I thought you needed proof."

Jessie batted a hand. "Eh. Not necessary. I know where to find you if we discover you've falsified the children's Saddle Happy credentials, which, by the way, is punishable by five years in prison, which means that Wain and Ell would qualify for the program in any case." She tucked a curl behind her ear and grinned as Key laughed.

"Oh, thank you, Jessie! I was expecting the process to be much more ... I don't know, *formal*."

"Formal? Wherever did you get that idea? Was it the wet dog, the clutter, the cold coffee, or the curdled creamer? Now, tell me more about the children—it helps us match them to the right horse. I've already got one in mind for Wain, but Ell ... hmm." Jessie pursed her lips and tapped her pen on the desk. "You mentioned she's struggling at school. Do you mind sharing some details?"

Without naming names or party details, Key briefly described Ell's school situation.

Jessie slapped her hands on the desk with startling fierceness, causing her pen to fly onto the floor beside a startled Emmaline. "*Jail baby?* You are *kidding* me. How are such young children able to inflict such cruelty?" She sighed slightly, shaking her head. "Has anything changed, though? I remember very clearly the mean kids during my elementary grade years. I was the target until I fought back."

Key picked up the pen and laid it on the desk. It wasn't hard to imagine the woman across from her fighting back. "Ell is quite alone in this." She explained Ell's reluctance to add to Lonny's deep regrets. "I'm far from an expert on children, Jessie, but I believe Ell will thrive here, with her love of horses and a focus on something other than problems at school."

"We'll certainly do all we can." Jessie handed Key two packets. "Paperwork to fill out, waivers to complete, yadda. Your biggest expense will be riding boots. All other equipment is covered by the scholarship funds. Let's plan on one-hour lessons at six-thirty on Wednesdays. This week will be an introductory meeting, a safety talk, and a tour. We are *always* dead serious about ensuring a positive and safe experience with our horses!"

"You cannot know how wonderful ... Well, yes, you do," Key concluded as Jessie nodded, smiling. *Of course she knows.*

"By any chance, Key, are you going back to Troy?"

"Yes. Is there something I can do for you?"

"This box of trophies needs to be dropped off at SouthPaws, a consignment store on Marshall Road."

"I know SouthPaws! I love Jukey and Mary!"

"We do too." Jessie carried the box to the Jeep. "Thank you, Key! I am so pleased we finally met our new neighbors!"

"See you Wednesday! Bye, Emmaline." She could feel the children's joy already.

# Chapter 12

## ELEANOR

To Key's disappointment, a sign in the window at SouthPaws read, *Sorry We Missed You!*

*Of course.* SouthPaws was closed on Mondays. She nosed around a little, puzzled momentarily over the words *FUN RAZOR* written clumsily in black marker on two boxes stacked to the left of the door and was still chuckling when her phone rang. Hurrying to the Jeep, she retrieved it from the cupholder, almost dropping it when she saw who was calling. "Jukey! Are you psychic? I'm at your place right now!"

"Hey, Key North! Yes! I'm psychic! Move forward and to your right, look up and wave, and I'll use my crystal ball to tell you which hand you're using." As usual, Jukey's easygoing voice belied his quick wit. He was one of the sharpest people Key had ever met.

"It wouldn't take much to convince me that you're psychic." As she waved at a gray orb attached like a single protruding eyeball to a crossbeam in the eaves, Key explained why she was there.

"You're waving your left hand, and all signs point to good fortune coming your way," Jukey joked. "That'll be ten dollars, slide it under the door. Seriously, you can put Jessie's box by the other donations. They'll be picked up today."

"What's the fundraiser for?" Key asked.

"Some worthy cause, I'm sure," Jukey replied. "I admit I don't always pay attention. So you finally met your horsey neighbors!"

Key laughed. "Yes! Well, I met Jessie."

"Jessie *Mistic*." His amused tone told Key that Jukey no doubt knew exactly what kind of conversation she'd had that morning. "She's tough as Yogi Berra's catcher's mitt, but if *you're* on her good side, you've got a friend for life. And maybe you're the psychic, Key North, because Mary planned to call you today. I'll put her on the phone."

Mary, as it turned out, was going to be babysitting her niece's son Reynold for the next two days. "He begged me to ask Wain to come play tomorrow after school. You all could have dinner with us." Reynold attended a different school, and the boys had not seen each other since the summer.

Key made a snap decision: She'd give Cissy and Wain tomorrow off. "We'd love that, Mary! Wain will be so excited."

Returning to Veronica View, Key made a quick sack lunch, then backtracked to Pike Road, this time accompanied by Faro and wearing sensible waterproof shoes.

By the time she arrived at Pike House, the misty rain had stopped, and ever-expanding patches of autumn blue were fast overtaking the few leftover clouds that proved no match for the still-strong Carolina sun. The air felt cleansed, fresh; in response, she could feel her entire body relaxing. Retrieving a canvas chair from the shed, Key tromped through the damp grass down to the outdoor patio DP and his crew had built that summer. *Add to to-do list: Find six Adirondack chairs.*

She set up her chair facing the trellis, noting happily the new tendrils of star jasmine clinging to the latticework of wire she'd placed around the posts. This view was almost as satisfying as the oak trees and the woods. Scooting down until her head rested on the back of her chair, Key closed her eyes and laced her fingers together across her stomach. A few minutes of pure alone time were exactly what she needed. *It's how I always feel out here.*

Faro suddenly abandoned the scolding squirrel he'd chased up a tree and raced past her.

"Hey there, good boy!" Key heard a familiar voice say, then "Morning, Miss Key! Am I interrupting?" DP, carrying a soft-sided cooler and a plastic gallon jug, materialized in front of her.

She shaded her eyes with her hand. "Hey, DP! Not at all! There's an extra lawn chair in the shed."

"Got one right here." From behind the fireplace, DP retrieved a five-gallon plastic bucket, turned it upside down and plopped down with his back against a trellis post. "Most versatile patio furniture ever."

"And here I was going to buy Adirondack chairs."

"These buckets are four dollars each at the hardware store, double as a firewood holder, stack up nice and tidy too. I'm all about saving you money. You're welcome."

Laughing, Key asked, "Where are Miguel and Benito?"

"They're helping my daddy today. He's up against a deadline on some finish work."

"And how was your bachelor nacho fest?"

"Delicious the first time, pretty dang good the next meal, threw them out after a few bites the third time." DP removed a sandwich from his cooler and unwrapped it. "Molly had a real nice time with her parents, but she's always ready to come home after a couple days. She's twenty-six years old, married, baby on the way, but they've never gotten past the helicopter stage. Doubt they ever will." He took a giant bite.

"Helicopter?" There was an entire parenting language Key didn't speak.

"Hovering. Nice people, just *real* protective. In their eyes she's still, like, eight years old. Luckily Molly has a younger brother and sister, so it's not all on her." DP waved his sandwich at Key. "Mmmm. Country ham and Duke's mayo on good old white bread. Best combo ever. Also, not nachos."

"You guys and your Duke's," Key commented, smiling.

For a few minutes, they discussed the renovation, then DP crumpled his empty potato chip bag and tossed it into his cooler. "Uh, Miss Key, do you want to talk some more about my brother?"

"Oh, yes!" Key quickly stood. "DP, do you mind if I take notes? Please don't think I'm crazy, but I want to do some research, see if I can chase down any kind of information."

"Be my guest." He didn't sound the least bit surprised.

Key hustled up to the Jeep and retrieved her notebook. "Thank you," she said when she returned.

DP inclined his head. "You can't believe the people who've tried to help. Amateur detectives, online sleuths, journalists, even a few psychics .... Finally, Daddy put his foot down and said no more interviews unless it's official. It's too much for Mama—and all of us— to get our hopes up and then be let down. Mama, especially, is a real private person. She hates the ... the ... Is *notoriety* the right word?"

"Yes. Oh, DP, how draining that must be."

"All we want is answers." DP took a deep breath. "And Daddy ain't ..." He hesitated. "Well, he ain't keen on discussing Riggs with, uh, outsiders. *I* don't see you that way, Miss Key; I'm *real* happy to talk with you, but he wouldn't be. I mean no offense."

"None taken," Key assured him, struck by the fact that all through life, children had ways of protecting their parents. She consulted her notes. "The other night, I ate dinner at the Morgans' and heard Lonny's side of the story. I have a glimmer of how Ayo acted, but how did his relationship with Riggs play out at your house? I mean, you were ... what? Nine years old when your brother started hanging out with Ayo?"

"Yes, ma'am." DP stretched his legs straight, stacked one heel on top of the other toe, and rubbed his earring.

"At that age, did you sense anything was off about the guy, or is it mostly what your parents have told you?"

DP raised his eyebrows. "Good question. It's hard to separate the two. Since you and I talked on Friday, I've tried to pull up more memories of Ayo, but it ain't much. Riggs knew better than to bring him over to our place. The guy made Mama real uncomfortable."

"Ugh! Why?" Olive was a gracious, reserved, and elegant Southern woman. Key couldn't imagine anyone acting indecently around her.

"Oh, not anything like he was coming on to her, nothing like that!" DP replied hastily. "If that had been the case, Daddy would have buried him somewhere in a concrete coffin. Naw, it was how Ayo treated Riggs. Like, he'd talk down to him, make fun of him, that kind of thing."

"Lonny said the same thing, that Ayo dictated that friendship."

"Lonny had Ayo pegged almost from the git-go but Riggs ..." DP shrugged. "Riggs was too nice a guy. Ayo twined himself into Riggs's life like a ... a ..."

"Leech?"

DP lifted a forefinger. "Leech is good. Bloodsucking poisonous vampire snake is better. Ayo knew better than to knock on our door. But he showed up at Orion concerts and other places."

"Other places? Like where?"

"Once in a while, if Mama and Daddy were busy, Riggs took me to my baseball games." DP smiled to himself. "That's a real good memory, having my brother watch me play. We'd go for ice cream afterward at King Tastee, and I always got this sundae called the Nut Cup. Riggs would have me spitting out my ice cream because him and his friends called it 'the jockstrap,' and you can imagine me at eleven, twelve ...." He crossed his arms and leaned back, laughing, and Key joined him. "Didn't matter where we were, my brother attracted people, bees to honey. Even at that age he had a fan club from his Orion gigs." DP paused, pressing one of the squishy orange earplugs draped on a cord around his neck. "We'd be eating our ice cream, talking to people, having a good time and then ... there was Ayo, like some kind of dark force. I think back on it now, and I see that Ayo was real jealous, couldn't stand Riggs getting attention that didn't include him. Even worse, it was like he was jealous of *me*."

"*Why?*" Like an ever-mutating virus, Ayo had contaminated even DP's few precious memories of his brother. Key was heartily sick of him.

DP shrugged. "No idea. It's all real vague after so long. But ... I do vividly recollect one time ...." He reached into his back pocket, pulled out his phone and began searching. "Miss Key, I've never told anyone this. Not Molly, not my parents. Wouldn't do a bit of good."

"Okay ...?"

"It was spring 1998, and it was just me and Riggs at my baseball game. I hit a double that scored two runs, and we won. Not sure who was prouder, him or me." He smiled wistfully. "Anyway, afterward we was sitting at a picnic table outside King Tastee and here comes Ayo. First thing he said to Riggs was 'Thought I'd find you here with baby bro sucking on his jockstrap, *Eleanor*.' Like, real snarky."

"Gross." Wain's favorite word of late was a perfect fit.

"Yeah. I can still see his eyes. Ugly. Jealous. Later, I asked my brother why Ayo called him 'Eleanor.'" DP shook his head. "Riggs said it was a play on words, from a Beatles song called 'Eleanor Rigby.'"

There was obviously more to the story. Key waited.

"This next part's hard to tell." DP's words emerged jerkily, as though they'd lain corroding in the dark recesses of his memory and he was still reluctant to drag them into the light. "For years I forgot about that conversation until one day in college. I was in the cafeteria real early, eating a banana muffin and thinking about Riggs, and out of the blue, 'Eleanor Rigby' starts playing over the sound system. I ... well, I had never truly *listened* to it. I couldn't believe what I was hearing. I went back to my dorm and looked up the lyrics online. Right then and there, I knew. *I knew.* Cried like a baby."

Key frowned. "I know the song, of course, but not all the words."

The bucket tipped and rolled off the pavers as DP stood and handed her his phone. "Not sure why that song of all things made me break down when so much else didn't." He hunkered down and petted Faro while she read.

Key pressed a hand over her mouth. "*Oh, no.*" It was cunning, cruel—Tally Mayweather's "jail baby" in much more sophisticated form. Handing his phone back, she said, "DP, this is ... insidious!"

He retrieved the bucket and wearily sat down. "Yeah. Another coded way to remind Riggs that he was nothing."

"Do you think Riggs knew?"

DP shrugged. "Can't say how Riggs took it. But yeah, I think he knew. Mama says Ayo used words against Riggs like a stiletto instead of a sledgehammer. This is just another one of those ways. How you gonna get anything else from the lyrics of that depressing song, Miss Key." It wasn't a question.

*These Southerners and their heartbreakingly poetic rhetoric.* "Yes. It's demeaning in such a subtle way. You're right; it does reveal a lot about Ayo. He obviously had his private, devious ways of twisting the knife. Lonny alluded to that too." How did people become this way? What created such ugliness?

Lifting his head, DP said quietly, "And you know, Miss Key, it was almost a prophecy. We got zero proof, but me and Daddy and Mama can't help but think Ayo was involved in my brother's disappearance and most likely his, uh ... death." DP picked up his container of water, dangling it from one finger like a jug of moonshine, and took a long swig. "And wherever he is, I guarantee Ayo Jones is creating misery one way or another. Those leopards don't change their spots."

A little cautiously, Key countered, "Based on what Lonny said, it's hard to see how Ayo could have been involved."

DP nodded. "I know. But if not Ayo, then who?"

"By any chance, do you have any pictures of Ayo?" Key asked.

DP scoffed. "No. Would have used them as target practice or burned them if I did. I remember the guy had dark hair and brown eyes. He was shorter than Riggs, a muscular kind of guy. You might ask Lonny."

Key doubted that, given all the upheaval in his life, Lonny owned any kind of Ayo mementos either, but she made a note to ask him. "Okay. Now tell me a memory about Riggs that *doesn't* involve Ayo."

For the next twenty minutes she listened as DP recounted memories of fishing at Dogleg Pond, vacations (his favorites were Yellowstone Park and Washington, DC), and trips to Alabama to visit relatives on his mother's side of the family.

"Thanks for sharing, DP." The stories, happy as they were, simply underscored the loss. Key wanted to weep.

There was a long pause while DP stared at his hands. "The memories after Riggs went missing are colored all wrong because … well, because it was all wrong. You remember the song 'Snake in the Grass,' from our concert last summer? That snake in the grass was Ayo. Daddy wrote it *before* Riggs went missing, and now we sing it every gig, just in case Ayo is somewhere he can hear it. Daddy says it's his way of telling him, 'I see you for what you are. You ain't won.'"

Key gaped at him. "You're kidding!" DP had no idea how well she remembered that song. She would never forget it as long as she lived. The title had provided the answer to her own mystery involving two very toxic people. *So strange how this is all playing out.*

"Miss Key, I don't want you to think I'm unhappy. Riggs would kick my butt if I lived that way, and I *am* truly happy. How could I not be, with Molly, and my new baby coming? But *I want to find my brother.*" He pressed the inner corners of his eyes with his forefingers, then quickly stood. "I gotta get back to work, but … it feels real good to talk. Makes Riggs come alive. Appreciate it."

# Chapter 13

## BULLY FOR ELL

"Guess what I accidentally did!" Wain burst out as he approached Key, who was waiting at Bullfrog Rock. The light rain had made his hair curlier, he had a splotch of blue paint above his left eyebrow, and his dinosaur-skeleton T-shirt hung crookedly, tucked into one side of his shorts. He had never looked cuter.

"What?" Key asked, trading Faro's leash for his lunch bag.

Wain cupped his hands around his mouth and said in a stage whisper, "I forgot to take my CartWheels out of my backpack."

"Oooh. Yikes," she replied, matching his tone and briefly looking around in an exaggerated, wide-eyed way. "How'd that go over with Mrs. Goos?"

"She doesn't know. I kept them secret. I really, *really* wanted to show Greggo, but I didn't."

"Smart boy." She gave him a quick hug.

"Does that go in the good jar or the tough jar?" Wain asked. "Because *nothing* else happened today."

Key laughed. "How about both? You forgot to do something, but you managed it like a pro. But what about painting? I bet that was fun?"

Mystified, Wain asked, "How'd you know we painted?"

"Because I'm psychic!" Key told him, tapping the top of her head. "Or it could be the tiny dab of blue paint right here." She touched his eyebrow.

"Ohhh." Grinning, he rubbed it off with the hem of his shirt. "Can I take Faro onto the grass?"

"Of course. I'll wait here for Ell." Key had asked Gayle if Ell could come over after school to help weed a small, overgrown flower bed during Wain's tutoring session. The garden wasn't Key's responsibility—the Olsons employed a lawn service—but she hoped the conversation would flow more freely if she and Ell were engaged in some type of minor chore.

In the next wave of noisy children, Key spotted Ell, eyes on the ground, clutching her backpack to her chest like a shield. *Walking alone doesn't necessarily mean anything*, Key thought with a sinking heart, *but her posture does.* And why was she being teased about her clothes? Key was no expert on elementary school fashion, but except for her high-top Converse sneakers, Ell was dressed no differently from any other little girl hustling past.

Key's welcoming smile turned to outraged disbelief as a dark-haired, round-faced girl in the front passenger side of a silver SUV stuck her head out of the open window and yelled, "Bye, jail baby! See ya! Don't wanna be ya!" then rolled the window back up, laughing shrilly. Key saw Ell step slightly sideways and flinch, but she didn't raise her eyes.

Whirling around, Key watched as the Mercedes made a right turn onto the main road and sped away, the ornate purple *M* on the side advertising its rude contents like a neon billboard. *Well, well, well. If that isn't the most fitting pair I've ever seen. But what kind of mother allows her child to do that? The honker kind, that's who.*

Wain, who was proudly showing Faro to a group of children, had thankfully missed the whole debacle, but Key was seeing-red furious. This wasn't the time or the place to address what she'd just witnessed, but something had to be done. "Hi, Ell!" she said brightly.

"Hi." Ell seemed happy to see them but was understandably subdued on the walk home. She and Wain were in the backyard with Faro when Cissy arrived.

"Before you get started, Cissy," Key said, "Would you mind giving me some advice?"

"Sure," Cissy replied immediately, leaning on the kitchen island, holding her ever-present water bottle. "What's up?"

Key hoped Cissy never lost that confidence, that way of simply facing whatever challenges presented themselves and addressing them head-on to the best of her teenaged ability. Pointing outside at Ell, she briefly explained.

"Oof. I *hate* mean girl drama." Cissy crossed to where Key was standing and watched Ell trying unsuccessfully to turn a cartwheel. "She's starting on the wrong foot …. Love her high-tops though. Can I ask, is there any one kid that's teasing Ell, or is everyone ganging up on her?"

Key hesitated, then decided to go for it. "The instigator is a girl in her class named Tally Mayweather."

"Ohhhh … Mayweather." The way Cissy said the name, it obviously meant something.

"Do you know them?" Key put a pod in the coffee maker and a mug under the spout.

"Ever seen that kids' boutique downtown? Mayweather's?" It took a moment for Key to decipher a cursive *M* from Cissy's swooping air sketch. "Big purple *M* on the window."

"I haven't," Key replied, "but I know exactly what the *M* looks like because I'm positive I've seen it on a car. So they own a boutique?"

"Yeah. Bougie kids' clothing. I've shopped for my baby niece there."

"Bougie?"

"You know, like high-end."

"Oh! Got it." Flintstones to Jetsons, that's what her life had become—not that Cissy would understand that reference. Key found it fascinating, this generational strata stacked like layers of rock on an exposed mountainside, each adding its version of slang, fashion, and attitude to its predecessors. She took a sip of coffee, grateful for the uncomplicated, deliciously bitter warmth. "So, Cissy, did anything like that ever happen to you?"

"Not really. I found my place early in sports. And my older sisters watched out for me."

*An older sibling!* Why hadn't she thought of that? "Do you know Cavender Morgan?" Key asked impulsively.

"Yeah …?" Cissy rolled her eyes like a starstruck fan. "Everyone knows Cav. He's so cute and funny!" She paused. "Wait … Morgan …?"

Key nodded. "Ell's his little sister."

"Are they close? Does he know what's going on?"

"Ell adores Cav. I doubt she's mentioned it to him though."

"She should tell him." Cissy slapped the countertop with both palms. "Tell her to tell him!"

"What if Ell doesn't *want* to tell Cav?" Key asked sensibly, raising her eyebrows.

"Oh, she'll tell him," Cissy assured her with all the confidence of a trusting younger sibling. "He *needs* to know."

"All right, I'll encourage her to tell her brother. But Cissy, please don't mention this."

"I promise I won't. Will you let me know, though, Miss Key? Because I'm supposed to write a paper for my child psychology class. I'd use … What do you call them? Aliases. Not that I see Ell as a guinea pig," she added hastily, and Key laughed.

"I don't think you do. And I think the words you want are *pseudonym* and *case study*. I'll keep you posted." She leaned against the counter, smiling. "You know, you're already well on the way to being an excellent child psychologist."

Cissy beamed. "Thanks, Miss Key."

As Cissy was gathering up her backpack, the door slid open. With the addition of two children and a dog, the kitchen was suddenly very full.

"Ready, Ell?" Key picked up two pairs of garden gloves. "We've got about an hour before the rain starts. Cissy, leave a little early if you need to."

Outside, Key and Ell got to work, an empty bucket between them. "Thanks, honey, for helping me! I want to hear how school went today."

"I kinda figured. Will I still get paid?"

Key laughed. "Of course! I heard Tally yell at you when you were walking to Bullfrog Rock."

"You *did*?" Ell sounded dismayed.

"Yep." Key sat back on her heels. "She's a piece of work."

"What does that mean?"

"It means ... Well, in a nutshell, it means Tally thinks her unkind behavior is somehow okay and it doesn't matter who she hurts. I suspect she's been raised to think she can say or do anything she wants."

"She talks about her party in front of me—like how much fun they're gonna have. She's having a slumber party after that, and they're gonna swim in her pool."

"Ell, if you could say anything to Tally, what would it be?"

"Stop calling me 'jail baby,'" Ell replied promptly. "Like if I walk up to her and ask what they're doing, she says, like, 'None of your business. Byyyeee, jail baby.'"

"Who told her your dad has been in jail?" Key asked. It was something that had been bothering her.

Ell shrugged. "Everyone knows." One by one, she dropped three weeds into the bucket. "It's not *my* fault."

"Absolutely not." Key kept her voice neutral as she loosened the dirt around a bunch of nasty broadleaf thistles. "Do you *want* to be friends with Tally? Be in that group of girls?"

Ell hesitated, which Key interpreted as a wistful *yes*. "I mean, I try to talk to her and be friends with her and Brandy and Renata." She hadn't put on the gloves, and as she rubbed her hands together, pills of mud dribbled onto the grass. Her bleak resignation, her acceptance that she somehow wasn't worthy of being included, broke Key's heart.

Key took a deep breath. "Ell, I want to be honest with you. I told Cissy what you're going through, and she suggested you talk to Cav about it."

"What could *he* do?" Ell sat back on her heels, sounding more intrigued than betrayed, Key was relieved to see.

"He may surprise you with how well he understands." Key patted Ell's thin shoulder. "It's completely up to you. Also, I'd encourage you to talk to your school counselor and tell him or her what's going on. Tally needs to be told that what she's doing is *not* okay." Key tossed a handful of dead leaves into the bucket.

"No! Everyone would know I tattled. I might tell Cav though," Ell added grudgingly.

"Wonderful. For what it's worth, here's my advice for today: You're a very strong girl. Use your strength to ignore Tally Mayweather."

"I can't ignore her! When we line up, she's right next to me! Mayweather, Morgan!"

That was an unfortunate coincidence. "So you try to talk to her?"

"I'm not gonna be *rude*."

*I'm about to impart such lonely advice.* Key picked two daisies. "Hold out your hand, palm up."

"Why?" Ell asked, but she did as Key asked.

Key placed the flowers onto Ell's muddy palm. "Now, tell me you've brought me flowers."

Ell rolled her eyes and said in a perfect monotone, "Miss Key, I brought you flowers."

"Well, I don't *want* your flowers!" Key knocked Ell's hand sideways, catapulting the daisies to the ground, then she snatched them back up, tore them to pieces, and hurled the petals and stems and leaves onto the grass.

"Hey!" Ell gave a little gasp, sounding shocked and hurt.

"It's to illustrate a point, Ell," Key said, giving her a reassuring hug. "A picture of what Tally is doing to you. You're naturally friendly, and that's a wonderful thing. But Tally twists your friendliness and throws it back in your face. *She deliberately hurts you.*"

"Poor flowers." Ell scraped together some of the daisy petals and let them flutter from her fingertips.

"Exactly. Ell, your feelings are those flowers. When you talk to Tally or try to be friends with her, it's like you're holding out your hand and saying, 'Here's all my power.' And she slaps your hand away and stomps on your power. It takes away *her* power when you don't speak first *or* respond to unkind words." Key picked two more daisies, reached for Ell's hand, and placed them inside, then wrapped the little girl's fingers around the stems. "That's *your* power. You *hang on* to your power, Ell Morgan. Do you think you can do that?"

Ell opened her hand and stared at the flowers. "I'll try."

"And one more thing, Ell. Look for others who might be lonely, someone who appreciates you. Someone who's a real friend."

"She *took* my friends." Tears filled Ell's eyes. "They were my friends first." She swallowed hard and put the flowers on the grass, then went back to weeding.

"They were," Key replied gently. "And they're not sticking up for you. I know that's what hurts the most. But BOLO, Ell!"

"BOLO?"

"It stands for 'Be on the lookout.' Believe me, there are kids in the fourth grade at Troy Elementary who need a friend like you. And talk to Cav!"

"I'll try."

"I know you will!" Key gave her another hug and dug into her pocket. "Last thing: Hold out your hand again. BOLO for the money you earned." She folded Ell's fingers around a twenty-dollar bill and finally saw her smile.

# Chapter 14

## STORMY OUTCOMES

At two in the morning the predicted thunderstorm finally unleashed with uncommon fury directly above Troy. At first, Key was only sleepily aware of angry winds battering quarter-sized raindrops against the windows, but when a bolt of lightning lit up the entire street, followed almost simultaneously by a vociferous crack of thunder, she snapped fully awake, switched on the bedside lamp, and checked her phone for any type of warning (no tornado looming, thankfully), then threw back her covers and hurried to check on Wain and Faro. Wain remained deeply asleep, one arm draped over his CartWheels backpack, but Faro was gone.

She discovered him in the main bathroom, curled into a ball against the tub, as far under the pedestal sink as he could squeeze himself. His anxious, apologetic brown eyes met hers, as though he felt guilty for abandoning his guard duties.

"Smart boy," she told him softly, gently kneading the topknot on his head. "This is probably the safest room in the house."

A quick walk-through revealed no issues, but as she padded back to bed, the hallway night-light flickered twice, then surrendered, and immediately the entire house was enveloped in an inscrutable black unrest. No glowing red or green dots from power buttons, no hum of refrigerator or air-conditioning, no whispery snick from the ceiling fan, the only sounds a lonesome, determined ticking from the kitchen wall clock and the wail of a faraway siren. Key cautiously felt her way back to the primary bedroom, confirmed that her phone was on the nightstand, then fell back asleep as the grumbling thunder faded. For the rest of the night, she chased oblique dreams, which, except for a lingering foggy uneasiness, she could not remember when she was awakened by the restored electricity switching on the bedside lamp.

*No wonder my dreams make me uneasy,* she told herself as she slid aside the ivory damask drapes and surveyed the leaves and branches littering the soggy yard and the street beyond, *considering the heavy conversations I've had lately! Missing people. Sad families. Bullies.* It would be a welcome relief to have dinner with Mary and Jukey tonight.

She let Faro out, then did a quick room-to-room survey. No windows broken, no leaks in the walls or ceiling, no water seeping under the doors. Well, the downstairs was intact, anyway; she couldn't check the second story because the door to the enclosed stairwell was secured with a large steel padlock attached to a substantial hasp.

"It's safer this way," Deirdre Olson had explained when she showed Key the house. "Kids like to explore, and our entire life is up there in boxes."

After resetting the flashing clocks, Key sat down at the table with her coffee (was it wrong to be most relieved that the coffee maker worked?) and, as usual, checked her tablet for emails. Mrs. Goos often sent reminders. ("Chilly today, please have your child bring a jacket;" or "Please sign and return paperwork in your child's backpack.") Key had heard some of the young parents at Bullfrog Rock disparaging what they considered the teacher's micromanagement, but as a novice caretaker of a second grader, she found it very helpful.

However, there were no new emails on her tablet because there was no internet connection. Up until now the Wi-Fi had worked perfectly. *Probably just needs a reset.* Toting her coffee, Key unsuccessfully searched every closet, cupboard, and shelf and concluded that the router and modem had to be somewhere upstairs. Of course, her phone still worked, but it wasn't ideal for bigger email files or Wain's video calls with Guy. She'd contact Deirdre later. With the time difference between North Carolina and Arizona, it was much too early to do it now.

"I never heard the storm! This is like a tree boneyard!" Wain exclaimed as they walked to school. He dragged a large branch off the sidewalk, then stacked another one on top of it. "Hey, Key, 'member when the Ickies threw all their meat bones in that pile outside their cave? And it stunk?"

*Please. Not the Ickies.* Key wrinkled her nose. "Mmmm ... maybe I was making popcorn. But old bones *would* stink." She changed the subject. "Wain, you slept right through the thunder and lightning, but Faro got very anxious. When I checked on you, he was hiding in the bathroom."

"I used to hide from Cal," Wain declared stoutly, as though Faro needed defending. It came out of nowhere, this rarest of rare statements; Wain almost never mentioned his life in Florida, especially Callahan.

"I know you did, buddy. Do you ever think about those days?"

"Sometimes. Cal was like Picky Icky. Like, mean and stuff."

*Oh, seriously? The Ickies, of all things, are the gateway to talking about Wain's previous life?* Key wanted to laugh out loud at the irony. "Tell me about Picky."

"He yelled a lot and kicked chairs and threw things. He punched a hole in the wall!"

"Sounds scary," she said sympathetically.

"Yeah, but at the end he had to turn nice 'cause the other Ickies made him be nice. Nice like my *real* dad." Wain was so proud of Guy.

"Your real dad is *very* nice," Key agreed, stunned that, from somewhere in all that ickiness, Wain had mined a priceless nugget of truth. "You should tell your dad about the movie next time you talk! He'd love that story." She was especially struck by the fact that Wain had erased the mean Icky Callahan by transforming him into the freshly minted kind and nice Icky, Guy. Somehow it all seemed so weirdly fitting. She grudgingly gave the movie's creators a tiny bit of credit.

At Bullfrog Rock, as Key watched Wain dash off to join his friends, her phone rang. She checked the number. *Seriously?* What was it, six-something a.m. out West? "Hi, Deirdre!"

"Hello!" Deirdre sounded as cheerful as ever. "Key, Vern is wondering if your internet is out?"

"Yes! How did you know?" Key asked.

"The doorbell camera. Vern got a notification."

"Oh, of course. Yes, the electricity went out last night. It's back on, but I couldn't find the modem to reset it, and I can't check upstairs."

"That's why I'm calling. The modem *is* up there," Deirdre replied. "I'm so sorry about this. We—I mean, *I* didn't even think about it. Vern's got the only key. He'll come fix it."

Key stopped in her tracks. "From *Arizona*?" she asked incredulously. "Deirdre, that's a *lot* of bother! If you want to send the padlock key, I can wait. I know how to reset a modem, and I can manage without it until then."

"Well, crazily enough, Vern's been saying he needs to get out there anyway. He needs some paperwork and wants to check on our horse." She lowered her voice. "Frankly, I think he's bored already with RV life. I've made friends, but ... well, anyway."

"Did you say, 'check on your horse'?" Key asked.

"Oh, didn't I tell you about our horse?" She gave a little laugh. "My husband, a man who knew nothing about horses, bought one on a whim when we moved to Troy. We board him at Mistic Meadows."

"On my road! Small world!"

"Vern is looking at flights now."

*What a week.* It seemed all Key had to do these days was stand still and life itself would simply swirl in like high tide and flood her schedule.

Later that morning, she took her laptop to Chix on Broadway and splurged a blissful ninety minutes sitting in an easy chair, savoring a latte and working on a card featuring a tipped-over red bucket (thank you, DP) spilling the words *relax, refresh, restore, reflect* onto a sandy beach. Inside, she wrote *Here's hoping your vacation checks every item on your bucket list!* She added four more to the file, emailed them, and shut her laptop. Good. Another month's work done.

*You need to take your own card advice.* Key suddenly felt tugged in so many directions. But why? Did she really need to be involved in other peoples' problems? She pondered for a few minutes. Ell's issue had fallen into her lap at Dogleg Pond, so that one she could not ignore. She would be a source of support as long as needed.

But Riggs? *Seriously, Key,* she admonished herself, *is it your job to solve Riggs's disappearance? More to the point, why do you think you can?* She resolved to share what little information she had with Mack when he and Lainey came to North Carolina, then she would let it go.

# Chapter 15

## CATCH-UP

fter stopping to pick up flowers and a bottle of cabernet, Key and Wain headed to SouthPaws, where Wain and Reynold visited Petey, the Kings' colorful, charismatic bird, then followed Jukey to a storage room where he retrieved an oversized bin, loaded it on a hand truck, and carted it to the enclosed patio.

"You're looking at a collection years in the making," he proclaimed loudly to an astonished Key over a clattering rainbow of cascading plastic bricks and the boys' excited squeals. "We add to it every time we come across loose bricks in our junking forays. Our retirement plan consists solely of having our offspring build us a mother-in-law apartment out of these."

"You could build an entire retirement *community* with that many!" Key laughingly exclaimed.

Jukey grinned. "Feel free to retire next door. I can't guarantee the color of your walls, but you can rearrange your floor plan anytime. I'll be back after I close up the store. Have fun, boys!"

Key and Mary settled in the living room with wine and an artistically arranged platter of cheeses and raw vegetables surrounded by a selection of crackers.

"When will you see Mack next?" Mary asked after they'd caught up on several other topics.

"In a couple weeks. He's bringing his eight-year-old granddaughter, and the four of us are going fly-fishing. He's rented a cabin in the western part of the state. You know, Mary, sometimes I think, *What am I doing, going off for a weekend with a man I've met in person one time, to fly-fish, which I've never done!* It's so far out of my comfort zone that it doesn't even register."

"It sounds adventurous," Mary countered. "And you don't have to have the entire relationship mapped out right this minute."

"True. Mack's become a good friend; that much is established. I'm fine if it stops right there. But I live in fear of getting myself into an awkward situation. I never thought I'd be saying this, but what if I don't like him as much as he likes me? Or vice versa? Well, I'm just glad we live a thousand miles apart. I can survive anything for two days." She took a bite of cheese, mostly to make herself stop talking. It wasn't like her to blather on like this.

"Maybe, instead of trying to categorize it, just call it a fishing expedition that may or may not involve a trout," Mary replied teasingly, causing Key to almost choke. "And having two little kids with you kind of quashes the whole romantic element, anyway, doesn't it? Bottom line: what's your gut telling you?"

"No red flags. Mack's a great listener, insightful, and genuinely caring." Key smoothed a tiny wrinkle on the linen sofa pillow resting against her thigh. *Except for the fact that he disappears for days at a time with no true explanation. Nothing red-flaggy about* that. "Guy would never have put him in touch with me if he didn't trust Mack implicitly, which is important because I also want to have them, ah—" She caught herself. *Watch it, Key.* As much as Mary knew about Key's recent circumstances involving Wain and his father, she had no idea that Guy and Mack did anything other than work for an oil company. It had to stay that way.

"You want to have them …?" Mary prompted curiously.

Key deflected. "Mary, do you know anything about Riggs Plummer?"

Mary sat up straighter. "Oh, Key, if I could solve any mystery on God's green earth, it would be that one! Not a day goes by that I don't think of the Plummers and say a prayer for them."

Through the window, Key watched Jukey walk briskly down the glass-enclosed breezeway that connected their store to the house. He stopped briefly to chat with the boys, who were now building an extremely tall and skinny brick tower, then poured himself a beer and joined the women, tilting a frosty glass in Key's direction. "Ahhh. This is more like it. Cheers. Glad to have you here, Key North."

"Thank you! Cheers."

Mary patted Jukey's knee. "Honey, Key was asking what we knew about Riggs."

"It's Troy's biggest mystery." Jukey shook his head, his expression suddenly serious. "Riggs was just an all-around great kid. I got to know him when Badger and I did some guiding for the Plummers back in the day."

"Guiding?" Key asked.

"Birds. With my dogs." Jukey set down his glass and held up an imaginary shotgun.

"Oh, right!" Key had met the Kings' ancient dog Badger only once before he'd died, but she was very familiar with Jukey's shotgun, which had been instrumental in prodding Gary Callahan to reveal Lyric's diabolical plot.

"That poor family," Mary said sadly.

*How exhausting it must be,* Key thought, *for the Plummers to have their lives defined by an indelible, mysterious tragedy and the incessant accompanying sympathy.* No wonder Dawson and DP found such solace in music. It was probably an escape as much as a passion. Key wondered what kind of reprieves Olive sought. "Did your boys know Riggs?"

"Yes," Mary replied, pointing at an artful assortment of framed pictures on the wall across from the sofa. "Kurtis, our oldest, played baseball with him for a couple years. Our other two are younger, but of course they knew of him."

Jukey picked up a cracker. "We had several conversations when Dawson and DP were building this house. Can't imagine losing one of our boys, much less not having answers."

"DP told me that this month has been especially difficult because it's the twentieth anniversary of Riggs's disappearance."

"Twenty years already?" Mary exclaimed. She picked up her phone and tapped it. "Key, I'm texting you the link to a missing persons podcast I follow. It's called *Inside Outlines,* and it's produced right down the road in Porterville."

"*Inside Outlines.* What does that mean?"

"The way the host, Wolverine, explains it, families of missing persons are sentenced to live inside the outline of their missing loved one. He tells the story from their point of view."

It sounded very intriguing. "Does he cover only North Carolina cases?"

"Oh no, they're from all over the country. He's very popular, has—" Mary consulted her phone again. "My goodness … over four million subscribers! I didn't realize it was quite *that* popular. I can't remember the host's real name offhand."

"Gabriel Mink," Jukey replied, laughing at Mary's shocked expression. "Can't help but hear now and then, honey. One of those things that sticks in my crossword puzzle–clue mind. Mink … Wolverine."

"Why am I still surprised at the random facts you carry in that brain?" Mary lightly punched his shoulder. "Anyway, Key, several years ago, for his very first podcast, Wolverine featured Riggs."

"Oh, wow! Seriously?" *So much for my vow to drop it.* Key rustled in her purse for her notebook and pen. "Did Wolverine interview the Plummers?" she asked.

Jukey and Mary exchanged a look, then he said slowly, "No, the Plummers didn't participate."

"Wolverine said he invited them, but they declined." Mary's expressive face showed her consternation. "Of course, we respect Dawson and Olive's decision but … we don't quite understand it."

"Maybe it's as simple as self-preservation." Key crunched a bite-size dill pickle, remembering DP's words about Dawson's refusal to do interviews.

"Well, we don't walk in their shoes," Mary mused. "I'm glad Wolverine went ahead with the podcast anyway."

"I wish it would have driven that deadbeat out of the woodwork," Jukey said. "Someone's gonna have to bird-dog him out of the underbrush. Or bait a trap." Hunting metaphors were in abundance tonight.

"You mean Ayo Jones," Key said. When they nodded, she added, "Did you ever meet him?"

"Not formally, but we saw him once at an Orion concert." Using a toothpick, Jukey made a tiny kebab with cherry tomatoes, cheese, and olives. "I remember he was kinda Italian looking. Full lips. Not a bad-looking guy, but off-putting in that way you pick up from some people. Wolf in sheep's clothing."

"Gut instinct, right there!" Mary exclaimed to Key.

"I wanted to punch him right in the gut instinct!" Jukey said. "He was trying to put the moves on our son Kurtis's girlfriend—she was maybe sixteen—and I was going to intervene when I saw Riggs pull him away."

Key made a face. "Gross." It seemed to be her go-to word where Ayo was concerned. "What do either of you think happened to Riggs?"

"We just can't fathom it," Mary replied. "The sheriff's office here has done zero"—she made an O shape with her fingers—"to look into it because, according to Dawson, they said Riggs was an adult who had every right to leave on his own."

"Well, honey, you can't blame the law around here. Riggs disappeared in Virginia," Jukey said solemnly, rubbing his neck.

Everyone, it seemed, knew the talking points. *Urban legend* indeed.

"Did the Richmond police investigate?" Key asked.

Jukey shook his head. "Dawson filed a report, but it went nowhere because there was not a whiff of foul play."

On the patio, Wain and Reynold cautiously added bricks one by one to the tower, which was now almost as tall as they were. It teetered precariously, then crashed, and the boys erupted in laughter. They'd be cleaning up with scoop shovels.

Jukey looked at his watch, then stood up. "I'll fire up the barbecue and make sure Wain and Rey aren't drowning in plastic."

Dinner was every bit as delicious as Key knew it would be. The boys declined the homemade peach chutney, but Key could have eaten the whole jar. "That kick at the end of every bite!" she told Mary, piling another forkful onto a small slab of pork chop. "Peach and red pepper go so well together!"

Mary pointed her ear of corn at Jukey. "I can't take the credit. That's Jukey's specialty."

"What don't you do, Jukey? This is fantastic!"

"Thank you, Key North." Jukey looked pleased. "I make it for friends and family. I've had people ask me to sell it, but that would steal time from my junking, and that's my bigger addiction. Happy to send a jar home with you."

"I'd love some!"

"Okay, boys, let's hear about your lives." Jukey had a way of finding common ground with everyone. First Reynold, then Wain, told him what they liked best about school. When Wain finished up with "… and my teacher's name is Mrs. Goos," Reynold broke into giggles.

"What?" Wain asked him. "What's funny?"

"Mrs. Goos." Reynold was still laughing.

"It doesn't have an 'e' on the end though," Wain said seriously. "It's G-O-O-S. So she's not like a bird goose, you know?"

*Wain just spelled a word like it was the most natural thing in the world.* Key played it cool, but she could hardly wait to tell Guy.

# Chapter 16

## BERTIE

"Hello there!" Bertie Montgomery called from her front lawn, waving a handful of leafy twigs as Key and Faro passed her house after walking Wain to school. "I hope Deirdre's house survived the thunder boomer the other evening! That was a gully washer!"

"It sure was!" Key replied, smiling. "Fortunately, our internet connection was the only casualty. It's nice to finally meet in person, Mrs. Montgomery! I'm Key North."

"Bertie." Using her teeth to tug off a glove, she clasped Key's hand, regarding her with intelligent denim-blue eyes magnified by thick lenses. "Well, internet issues are one problem I'll never have. The world has jetted forward without me." She pushed her glasses up and tossed the twigs into a rusty wagon filled with storm detritus. Despite her short, rotund build and advanced age, the woman was spry and energetic, with a headful of white curls accented by a woolen headband. She wore a long-sleeved black T-shirt under a button-front housedress that had to be at least as old as the wagon, and her swollen feet puffed like mushrooms out of soaking wet leather moccasins. All were perfectly in sync with a smile-lined, compassionate face bearing testimony to a lifetime of looking on the bright side.

"It looks like your world is pretty busy without help from the internet," Key said with a smile, adding impulsively, "Would you like some help cleaning up your yard? Then maybe join me for a cup of coffee?"

"Oh ..." Bertie seemed caught off guard. "Well, that would be wonderful, honey! I haven't been inside that house in years. It used to belong to my very dear friends Gerald and Georgia. I had coffee with them every morning."

With both of them working and the occasional stick thrown for Faro, the yard cleanup took only twenty minutes. Panting slightly, Bertie pulled off her headband and brushed leaf fragments out of her hair. "Thank you, Key! I'll just change my wet shoes and be over in a tick."

"No need to knock!"

★★★

"Cinnamon rolls I made yesterday," Bertie announced ten minutes later, placing a tray on the kitchen island. She had applied bright-red lipstick and dark-brown brows with a shaky hand, and Key found the wavy effect slightly disconcerting but touching. "I'm taking some to bridge club today at the senior center." She pointed to a foil-wrapped packet the size of a dinner platter. "An extra roll for your boy."

"Oh, thank you! He can share it with his tutor."

"The Bellamy girl that comes at four-thirty on the bike? She's a pretty thing."

"Cissy. She's wonderful!"

"Nice family." Bertie removed the cover from a small glass bowl. "Here's homemade maple icing," she said, adding hopefully, "and the rolls are even better with a pat of butter." She peered into the living room, then exclaimed in dismay, "Oh! There's none of Georgia's zippy personality left! All her lovely flocked wallpaper, the gold light fixtures, the shag carpet! Gone! Like a story has been erased! Ach! It's very dull in here now!"

"Probably because the Olsons are renting this space," Key said mildly. The decor *was* very bland, but she wasn't going to mourn an old shag carpet.

"Well, you can't keep fashion or Father Time from marching on, can you?" Bertie mused, slathering butter and icing onto her roll. "Saying fare-thee-well to people who knew you way back when is the worst part of growing old, but I'm very thankful for the many wonderful memories." She unselfconsciously licked both sides of the knife, then clattered it into the sink. "Unfortunately, after Gerald passed, the house sat empty for years while their three kids duked it out over inheritance issues." She clucked her tongue disapprovingly, started to say more, then changed the subject. "Your landlords, on the other hand, kept to themselves. I'd chat with Deirdre now and then—she's friendly enough—but I think she was intimidated by *him*."

"By her husband?" Key handed Bertie a mug and the sugar bowl. "I've never met him." She decided not to mention Vern's upcoming visit.

"Vern is ... Well, honey, I'm an astute judge of character, and I don't trust him. He's rude and standoffish, almost a recluse." Lifting her chin, Bertie put a stubby forefinger under her nostrils, saying in an atrocious British accent, *"A bit of a snob. And that beard! Ugh! I've never liked beards on a man."* She shuddered. "I could never be Amish."

Key laughed out loud. She couldn't quite get a fix on Bertie's accent, which, while decidedly *not* British, contained a nasal twang that Key would have pegged as upper Midwest. If that was the case, though, Bertie had lived in the South a good long time to have incorporated such a drawl.

"Oh, the truth is, I barely know him," Bertie admitted. "I give him a little wave and keep my head down, and he never bothers me. But he's a cold fish."

Key led the way into the living room and flipped a switch on the gas fireplace.

"Oh, my, how nice that it's working again!" Bertie exclaimed. "Georgia would be delighted. Gerald had many fine traits, but he wasn't the handiest of men."

"How long have you lived in Troy?" Key asked.

"Half a century, honey. I moved here in the early sixties after I married Jimmy Dean Montgomery."

"How did you meet Jimmy?"

"Ah-ah!" Bertie wagged a finger. "*Jimmy Dean*. Both names—like the sausage. He was in the army, stationed at Fort McCoy, Wisconsin, near my home. We met at a dance on base." She shook her head, smiling. "Oh my, could that boy shag dance! We got married three months later, he moved me into that very house next door, and within a year he'd died in combat in Vietnam."

Key gasped. "Oh, Bertie, that's tragic. I'm so sorry."

"Thank you. I once counted the actual days we'd been in one another's company. One hundred thirty-seven. I was a widow by age twenty-four, mourning a man and a future that—let's face it—I barely knew, living in a town I'd never heard of, in a state I knew nothing about, and yet ... here I am," Bertie finished, waving her hand.

"Did you marry again?" Key asked.

"No, honey. Never married again; never had children. My own, anyway." Bertie stabbed a last buttery bite with her fork and used it as a tiny mop to swipe bits of icing off her plate. "But over the course of twenty-two years I had twenty-six of the loveliest daughters you could ever hope to meet. And I planted a rose bush for each of them."

"Twenty-six daughters!" Key waited for Bertie to elaborate.

But the old woman bided her time. Picking up one of Wain's books from the coffee table, she riffled the pages and said pensively, "Your boy is younger than my charges were, but I imagine you understand a bit of what I experienced, taking in a child not your own."

"Well, maybe one twenty-sixth of what you experienced!" Key briefly explained the circumstances.

Bertie nodded. "When you bought Elvin Grimes's house, then hired my very dear friends the Plummers to help you remodel ... Well, you know. I heard some of your story." She picked up her lipstick-stained coffee cup and gave Key a bemused smile.

"DP told me you and his mother were friends. He also told me you gave out the big candy bars when they'd go trick-or-treating."

Bertie laughed. "Trust DP to remember that! Such a wonderful family." She took a slurpy sip. "And so much loss. I assume you know about their older son, Riggs."

Key nodded. "My heart goes out to them."

"And all these years later, not one iota more information than they had that first day. Tch. Watching what they've gone through and not being able to help ..." Bertie shrugged sadly. The common thread in every conversation about Riggs was bewilderment. *How does a person simply disappear?*

Key let Faro out and refreshed their coffees. "I'm very curious. How did you come to have twenty-six daughters? Were you a foster parent?"

"Not in a formal sense, but yes. A very particular kind of short-term foster mother to a very specific kind of foster daughter." Bertie raised her wavy eyebrows, further puckering an already-lined forehead, and nodded knowingly, as though Key should understand the code.

"What do you mean?"

Bertie took a careful sip before replying. "In the late 1960s, I was doing medical transcription for the hospital, and one day my boss pulled me aside. He knew someone who was looking for a woman, preferably single, who might consider renting a room for a few months to a teenage girl who was ... well, back then we called it 'in the family way.' Adelaide was my first girl. She'd be well over sixty now, but in here"—Bertie tapped her head—"she's still seventeen."

"Ohhh." A vision of Bertie planting rose bushes for twenty-six confused young girls who'd found acceptance and solace in the little ranch house next door flashed as clearly through Key's mind as if she'd witnessed it. "So all of them were—"

"Pregnant. All in their teens, all from out of state, and do you know, Key, to this day I don't know the surnames of most of them. They'd stay with me for a few months; I'd take them to Porterville during the last week before their due date and drop them off with Rose—a lovely woman, an ex-nun. Is that the term? Ex-nun? That sounds so ... stark. Like ex-military. Maybe that's not too far off."

"Maybe *former* nun?" Key suggested, smiling.

"*Former* nun. Yes, much better. Rose was a conduit; she had connections with adoption agencies and attorneys. She and I had a tremendous mutual respect, a partnership rather than a friendship. She knew my house was a private, safe haven and that I knew how to keep my mouth shut, because in every case, the pregnancies were to stay a secret. Prominent families who couldn't withstand the scandal, religious issues, racial issues, illicit affairs with teachers or bosses or married men .... Oh, it ran the whole gamut. So hush-hush. They came to me under the guise of summer camp, or helping an old relative for a few months, or a semester of school out of state .... I housed two girls whose own *fathers* had no idea they were expecting! Such an immense burden placed on those young shoulders! You hope that they've felt free to tell at some point, but you never know."

What a stunning turn this conversation had taken. "Did the girls return to your house once the babies were born?"

"Never. The babies went to the new parents immediately, and their little birth mamas returned home. Oh, I'm making it sound so clinical, but it was quite the opposite, Key! I loved my girls! And by and large, they loved me back."

"Do you stay in touch with any of them?"

"A couple three," Bertie replied, confirming to Key her Wisconsin *bona fides*. "It was up to them to contact me, and most did not. But some friendships *are* seasonal, aren't they? A time for every purpose under heaven." She shrugged, but not in resignation; more, Key thought, in acceptance.

"Did you ever meet the girls' parents?"

Bertie shook her head. "Not once! Oh, I'd get a vague thank-you note now and then with no return address, but for the most part, I suspect the parents wanted to forget I ever existed. Too painful." Her kind blue eyes met Key's. "I simply loved their girls, then let them go."

"It must have been difficult, knowing what they faced."

"Yes, it was." Bertie gazed at the back of her age-speckled hands for a moment, then placed them, folded, into her lap. "I always stressed that they were giving a precious, selfless gift to another family. Let me tell you, Key, I heard it all." She gave a gentle little laugh. "Here I was, this childless woman they didn't know from Adam's off ox, trying to help them visualize a future that neither of us quite understood."

"They were fortunate to have you while they were going through the hardest experience of their lives," Key said sympathetically.

"Oh, honey, I'd like to think so. It was a two-way street. They kept me young."

"When did you stop hosting the girls?" Key heard her phone vibrating on the kitchen table. It could wait.

"My last, Natalie, came in 1988." Bertie smoothed her dress over her knees. "I started the garden after she left. And while I presume my neighbors think I'm crazy, I talk to my flowers, say a prayer for them and their little buds." Her face lit up. "I encourage them all to bloom where they are planted, as they say!"

"That's a beautiful story." Key was in awe of the selflessness of the woman sitting across from her.

"Do you have time now to see them?" Bertie asked hopefully after a moment. "My roses?"

"I'd love to! It would be like meeting your girls."

"What a lovely thing to say." Bertie stood and stretched. "Oh, I'm going to feel all that yard work in these arms! Thank you again, honey, for helping me, and for the coffee."

Key switched off the fireplace and collected the dishes. "Thank you. I wouldn't have missed this conversation for the world." In the kitchen, she saw she had a voicemail from Deirdre Olson but left her phone where it was.

They took a shortcut through the hedge dividing their front yards, and as she stepped through a door-like gate in Bertie's privacy fence, Key let out a gasp. Around the entire perimeter of the yard, rose bushes created a vibrant hedge, their dark green leaves and final, graceful blooms of the season outlined by a scalloped concrete border. "It's gorgeous, Bertie! It smells heavenly back here!"

"Thank you, Key. The storm tore them up some, but they'll heal." Given what she'd just heard, Key thought the words held extra significance. "And they all have names," Bertie added proudly. In front of each rosebush sat a small granite rectangle a little larger than a postcard. "I made wooden markers, but they deteriorated, so I had a monument company engrave these. It probably looks like a cemetery, but I love it!"

"Just the opposite! It's a garden of life!" As they strolled, Key read aloud so many of the names of her own high school era. "'Diane. Frieda. Aletha. Tina. Jody. Audrey.'" They stopped by an especially beautiful bush that still held a few blooms. "'Voile.' What an unusual name! Do you remember them all?"

Bertie pinched off a torn leaf, then gently cupped a bruised peachy rose in her gnarled hand and leaned down to speak directly to it. "My lovely, sweet girl! You will heal!" To Key she said, "Some memories have remained more vivid than others, but oh yes, honey. I remember them all."

# Chapter 17

## VERN, BACKLIT

*very life is a story*, Key mused as she showered and readied herself for the day. Abiding under the veneer of what others were allowed to see were the myriad complexities comprising every individual, molded by influences and paths both chosen and unchosen. Who would ever have guessed that Dawson and DP, playing an exuberant Orion concert, had been missing a beloved family member for two decades? Or that Guy and Mack, under the guise of staid oil company employees, were involved in a business so mysterious that they couldn't discuss it? By simply chatting with family-man Lonny, no one would know he'd spent two years in prison. Or that Granny Jewel'd had four husbands. (Well, maybe that one wasn't so hard to believe.) And now she'd learned that Bertie, a sweet old lady with whom Key had simply exchanged waves now and then, was a Vietnam War widow whose story, and that of her girls, deepened and expanded with each adoption into opaque layers of subterranean, ongoing mysteries, beautifully represented by a backyard populated with colorful roses. Key found the old woman's unquestioning acceptance of the circumstances especially touching. *It takes a special kind of person to be willing to love and let go that many times.*

Reaching for her makeup bag, Key smiled, recalling Bertie's wavy eyebrows and her dismissive description of Vern Olson. "Oops!" she said aloud. Deirdre's message! She'd forgotten all about it. Retrieving her phone, she accessed her voicemail and put it on speaker.

"Hello," said a bored male voice. "This is Vern Olson. I'll be there around ten tomorrow morning. Please plan to be there."

All the way from Arizona to reboot a modem! Key still couldn't believe it. The whole situation was bizarre. There was a short silence, then Vern's voice continued, more muted, as though he'd moved away from the phone. His tone had changed, condescension dripping frigid as cave water from sentences not meant for her. She turned up the volume.

"You should have reminded me to move the modem, Dee! No! Don't give me that stupid doe-eyed look. You are such a f—" There was a fumbling noise, and the message abruptly ended.

*Well, well, well.* Key raised her eyebrows and compressed her lips. She had just been provided as perfect a vision of Vern Olson as if he were standing fully exposed in a backlit window. (And that was as far as she'd allow *that* mental image to percolate.) *Forewarned is forearmed.* She immediately dialed Mary and relayed what she'd just heard. "Want to come over for coffee while he's here? I'd prefer to have someone with me. He was just awful to his wife!"

Mary, as usual, instantly understood. "Jukey and I call them 'demoralizers.' We can spot them a mile off, usually by that how-stupid-can-you-be look they give people. Demoralizing others is their love language …. And the love is all for themselves. It oozes from their pores."

"It was oozing from his *voice*, that's for sure." The concept wasn't unfamiliar. Many times over the course of her marriage, Key had been the recipient of Jeff's lofty condescension, but this was different …. Uglier.

"While I'm there, we can listen to the *Inside Outlines* podcast about Riggs," Mary suggested. "You provide coffee, Key, and I'll bring a new pie I'm testing out."

"Oh, sure, make *me* do all the work," Key joked.

★★★

"Why can't Faro go?" Wain asked, pouring a scoop of dog food into the dog bowl. Cissy had just pedaled away with her half of Bertie's cinnamon roll tucked into her backpack, and it was nearly time to introduce Ell and Wain to Saddle Happy. Key could hardly wait.

"Faro needs to stay home tonight," she replied, filling a plate with lasagna, seven green beans (Wain was a reluctant vegetable-eater), and a buttered slice of bread. "Run and wash your hands. And every bean needs to disappear!" Wain's schedule lately had been unusually hectic. After tonight, Key vowed, she'd slow the pace.

Thirty minutes later, as they passed Pike House, Wain exclaimed, "Hey! You missed our turn! Are we going to Ell's?"

"You'll see," Key said mysteriously as they continued down Pike Road and through Mistic Meadows's open gate.

"There's Ell!" As soon as they parked, Wain dashed to join the Morgans. Key returned Gayle's enthusiastic wave and picked up a manila folder. Neither Jessie nor Regina was in sight, but there were lights on in the barn. As long as they didn't serve coffee (with or without cream), this was going to be a memory to savor.

# Chapter 18

## BOBCAT AND COCO

"Hello all!" Jessie emerged from the barn with Emmaline at her heels. "Gina will be out in a few minutes with some friends who want to meet ..." Slowly and dramatically she pulled a wadded piece of paper from her front jeans pocket. "Oh, yes! Which ones in this good-looking group are Wain and Ell?" She was far more relaxed than she had been on Monday.

"Me! I'm Ell! And he's Wain!" Almost vibrating with excitement, Ell propelled Wain forward by his backpack strap. "Are we gonna pet some horses?"

"We're gonna pet horses?" Excitedly, Wain turned to Key. "Did we bring some carrots? Or apples? That's what the Ickies fed their horses!"

Apparently, there was to be no escaping a lifetime of lessons from the Ickies. Key pulled a plastic bag from her jacket pocket. "As a matter of fact, I did! But let's wait until we talk to the ladies here."

"Let's get acquainted," Jessie replied warmly, shaking hands all around. "From what I understand, this is a neighborhood confab!" When she got to Cav, she studied him for a moment, as though, Key thought in amusement, Ell's brother were being assessed by the same standards Jessie might employ in choosing a horse. "Like horses? Looking for an after-school job?"

Cav shuffled his feet, glancing at his parents before he answered. "Uh, maybe, ma'am. I do some lawn mowin' and yard maintenance, but that's mostly seasonal. I don't know nothing about horses though."

Jessie snorted. "That's fixable! *A*, you've got muscles and *B*, you're not glued to your phone. Based on those two qualities alone, I think you'd be a fit. Let's talk, Mom and Dad included!" She clapped him on the shoulder.

From inside the barn came the unmistakable, beautifully musical *clop-clop-clop* of horseshoes ringing on concrete, and a tall, angular woman in a straw cowboy hat emerged leading two haltered, unsaddled horses that stepped gracefully from the wide doorway. Key had her eyes fixed on the mesmerized faces of Ell and Wain as the woman wound the horses' ropes loosely around a log railing.

"Hello! I'm Regina, but everyone calls me Gina." Like Jessie, the woman wore jeans, boots, and a T-shirt featuring a SADDLE HAPPY logo. "And before you two, Wain and Ell, meet these two"—she patted the horses' necks as the children's mouths dropped even farther open— "let's have a very important talk." She collected paperwork as the group settled onto the benches under the eaves. "Welcome to Mistic Meadows! Wain and Ell, you've both been selected to participate in our Saddle Happy program, where friendships are created between children and horses. Every Wednesday evening you will learn about, care for, and of course ride your horses. And because you both live so close, Jessie and I hope you'll visit your horses more often. We'll discuss that."

Wain still looked slightly mystified, but Ell let out an overjoyed squeal. "What? *Really?* Which one is mine?"

"Yours is the white mare with the gray mane and tail," Regina replied as everyone laughed. "Her name is Coco, and she is twelve years old. Coco wants to be friends with the other horses, but she's new here, and they haven't quite accepted her yet. Jessie and I think she needs a friend like you, Ell."

Ell's serious blue eyes met Regina's. "I kinda know what that's like."

Regina nodded understandingly, caressing Coco's neck. "Lots of kids do. And lots of horses do too. I just have a feeling you and Coco are going to hit it off."

Ell beamed. "I'm gonna take the best care of her!"

"And Wain," Regina continued, "This brown horse with the white blaze on his face is Bobcat. He's fifteen and has lived at Mistic Meadows for several years. We match him with the kids who will be best friends with him. Guess who we think that might be?"

"Me!" Wain pointed to his chest. "I can do that! I take care of my dog every day! Will Bobcat eat carrots? I know you're s'posed to hold your hand flat when you feed carrots to a horse. I saw it in a Ickies movie." Beside him, Ell was practically launching herself off the bench.

"Horses love carrots!" Regina replied. "Also apples, cantaloupe, and watermelon. On special occasions we even give them a piece of hard candy or a sugar cube!"

"Oh yeah, my teacher's gerbil likes all that stuff too." Wain's outspoken confidence surprised Key. Apparently Faro, the Ickies, and Sheba the gerbil had prepared him well for the equine phase of his life.

As Regina continued with a hands-on lesson, the children stroked the horses' velvety noses and fed them apples and carrots, with even Dibsy completely absorbed in patting Coco's neck and playing with her mane. *How do horses do it?* Key wondered, as she took several pictures. *They erase every bad feeling and replace it with a joy that only a horse can bring.*

She could still feel the magic of riding her neighbors' mare, learning to move with the gait, appreciating the acquiescent power of the huge animal carrying her. Maybe down the road, she, too, would ride again. For now, though, it was enough that Wain and Ell had a new focus, one she hoped would obliterate the words *jail baby* like rain on chalk.

# Chapter 19

## DEMORALIZER

"And the last thing on Wain's Saddle Happy list is a pair of sturdy riding boots, which we'll buy at the big farm store in Porterville." Key and Mary were enjoying coffee and a warm fire on the coolest autumn morning so far.

"If it allows growth and affirmation, only good can come from it." Sitting to Key's right in the Olson's sage-green easy chair, wearing a yellow V-neck sweater, Mary reminded Key of the cheery sunflowers her parents had grown along their split rail fence in Illinois.

Key glanced at her watch. "Mary, how long is the podcast about Riggs? My landlord is supposed to show up any minute."

Mary consulted her phone. "'Inside the Outline of Riggs Plummer,' forty-seven minutes long. Four years already since it was released." Her phone pinged. "And here's a text from a caterer asking for thirty-six mini apple pies by the middle of next week. Mercy. These short-notice requests." She typed a reply, then jumped up, slapping her forehead. "Pie! I left my three-berry crumble in the back seat of my car!"

Key laughed and stood, too, accompanying her to the front door. "It sounds delicious!" She'd briefly wondered when Mary had arrived carrying nothing but her handbag, but she didn't want to ask.

"Blueberry, boysenberry, gooseberry. I've never made it before. There's enough to share, and from what you told me, your landlord could use some sweetening up." As Mary reached for the knob, the doorbell rang.

When Mary opened the door, the man on the steps looked completely confounded. "Uh, you're not our—"

"No, I'm her friend, Mary. This is Key." Mary turned and pointed, then said politely, "Excuse me." She stepped past him onto the front steps.

"Hello! You must be Vern," Key said, momentarily stunned. No doubt she had the same look on her face as he had when he saw Mary. Manicured, fashionable Deirdre was married to this? Unkempt beard-mustache combo flowing from wildly shaggy shoulder-length hair of the same pewter gray. Green corduroy jacket, rumpled shirt with buttons straining. Baggy khakis. Leather loafers with thick soles that added inches to his height. If the man's intended look was fashion-challenged middle-ager, he'd handily win the prize. With an already strained smile, she extended her hand, which was instantly enveloped in his sweaty one. "I'm Key North."

Vern pushed toward her, continuing to grip much too tightly. Repulsed, she backed two steps into the house, and he followed, his full lower lip curving in the right direction but conveying no warmth whatsoever. "So you're my renter," he commented dismissively, as though Key were a stray he'd allowed to live under the porch.

*A crocodile smile full of dental implants. Hurry up, Mary.* Attempting again to free her hand from his, Key met his eyes, barely visible behind bizarre rectangular blue lenses in wire-framed hipster glasses. "Yes. I appreciate the—"

"Would have been nice if you'd told your friend I was coming. I had to park my rental on the street." With a final crushing squeeze, Vern dropped her hand and returned to the doorway to retrieve a brown leather briefcase. Though there was plenty of room for them both, Key was pressed against the small entryway table as he passed, brushing his body against hers. "So you crashed the internet. Good excuse to get the key, eh? Some people will do anything to get a chance to snoop around."

"Um, I'm sure it was the storm. I didn't—"

"*Kidding.*" With a short laugh, Vern unlocked the padlock and gave it a yank. "I'll get the equipment taken care of. Then I gotta sort through files up there." He paused, one foot on the first step, and added offhandedly, "By the way, your grandson and his cute little tutor are quite the fence *arteests.*"

Stunned by his almost farcical loutishness and the implications of the last sentence, Key didn't reply, and to her great relief, Mary reappeared, saying ruefully, "Sorry, Key. Jukey called, looking for the stapler. He finally found it in the safe. The *safe!*" Mary shook her head. "I've seen him leave hundred-dollar bills on the counter when he gets distracted, but at least our *stapler* won't get stolen." She held up a covered pie pan. "Mr. Olson, would you like a slice of pie?"

Key turned. Vern hadn't moved. *Why was he still standing there?*

"As long as it's not apple." From under the grungy mustache, Vern's upper lip curled. "Cinnamon and I aren't friends."

"Triple-berry crumble. No cinnamon."

"I'll try it," he replied grudgingly, as though he were doing Mary a favor. "Got any coffee? No decaf crap."

"Yes," Key replied, coolly enough to cause Mary to look questioningly at her.

Vern grunted. "Cream and sugar." He clomped heavily upstairs, each aged wooden step protesting with its own distinctive squeak.

# Chapter 20

## PODCAST, INTERRUPTED

"I've never seen him before. I'd for sure remember those glasses and that *hair*," Mary whispered as they made their way into the kitchen. "You look upset! What *happened* while I was outside?"

"Tell you in a minute." Key scrubbed her hands (her right one was still smarting from that painful squeeze), snapped a pod into the coffee maker, then opened the back door and took a gulp of fresh air. "Do your business, buddy," she said loudly but casually to Faro, who'd been dozing in a sunbeam. Taking a few steps onto the grass, Key quickly scanned the rear of the house. *Where is it?* That man *wanted* her to know he had a camera trained on the backyard. Wherever it was, she couldn't immediately see it.

Back inside, before she could explain anything to Mary, the stairs again creaked, and Vern reappeared with a toolbox, a drill, and two black plastic boxes with dangling cords, all of which he dumped in a tangled heap onto the table.

Faro gave the man a quick sniff, found him uninteresting and padded out of the kitchen, proudly carrying a ridiculous featherless rubber chicken Wain had chosen for him on their latest trip to the hardware store. Yet another scene so far from her previous staid and predictable life that Key wondered if she'd entered a wormhole.

"The pie's especially good heated," Mary told Vern.

"And your coffee's on the counter, sugar and cream beside it," Key added, determined to be civil. Vern Olson was obviously a disgusting, self-indulgent boor who reveled in making others uncomfortable, but she would not give him the satisfaction of knowing he'd thrown her off-balance.

"Stick around," Vern said peevishly, fixing his coffee as Mary and Key headed for the living room. "'Cause I'm gonna need to give you instructions." His accompanying guttural chuckle made the words sound almost obscene.

Key suppressed a shudder. She could hardly wait for the man to finish his tasks and leave. She just hoped he'd choose to eat upstairs.

"Whoo-ee!" Mary said under her breath as they sat down. "I'm glad you called me, Key."

Vern appeared in the doorway. "Think I'll join you in *my* living room," he announced, crossing in front of them to sit in the easy chair next to the fireplace. He poked suspiciously at his pie with his fork. "What kind of berries are these?"

Mary told him.

"It's delicious, Mary!" The gooseberries, which Key had never had before, were tart, juicy, and blended perfectly with the other fruit in a creamy filling, creating a sublime combination of sweet and sour, and the buttery crumble topping melted on her tongue.

Vern shoveled a forkful into his mouth, then slurped his coffee. "Crust could use some salt." Key gaped at him. The man's manners were unbelievable.

"Really?" Mary tried a bite. "Maybe. I took a few liberties with the ingredients." She added jokingly, "I may have to sell this pie under the table, like moonshine. Certain types of gooseberries are illegal in North Carolina."

"Illegal?" Key asked. "Why?"

"It's an odd little piece of history. Jukey knows more about it, but from what I understand, certain species of gooseberries can be host plants to a disease, and way back in the early—"

"Hold on. *Hold on.*" Vern burst out, waving his fork. His nails were bitten to the quick, Key noticed, and he wasn't wearing a wedding ring. "It's called white pine blister rust. To protect the pine trees, the US government outlawed currants and gooseberries in the early 1900s. They're not illegal everywhere anymore, but a few states still don't allow them to be grown." He sat back, rubbing his significant midsection. "I was an arborist back in the day."

"And yes, North Carolina is one of those states that prohibits gooseberries," Mary added, graciously overlooking the interruption. "These berries came to us frozen, from a farmer in Kentucky."

Key was floored. "I had no idea."

"Learn something new every day," Vern said, superciliously, as though Key had flunked the pop quiz. He scraped his fork across his plate. "Think I'll have seconds. Not every day I get illegal pie." It was probably as close to a compliment as he'd get.

"Help yourself." Mary set her phone on the end table. "Okay, Key, no Bluetooth speaker since your Wi-Fi's not working, but we should be able to hear just fine."

Over the fading introductory music, a friendly deep voice filled the room. "Welcome to the premier episode of *Inside Outlines*. I'm your host, Wolverine. Today our story covers the mysterious disappearance of a talented, popular young man from the small town of Troy, North Carolina, who vanished from an outdoor concert on September 5, 1998. Join me as we go inside the outlines of Riggs Plummer."

Vern, who had propelled himself to his feet, suddenly stumbled sideways, almost as though he'd been shoved. His fork slid off the plate and bounced onto the off-white area rug, creating an arc of purple splatter stains. Mary paused the podcast and both women rose to help.

Vern waved them back. "Got it, got it!" He snatched up his napkin and swiped at the rug, his ample rear end facing them. Key bit her lip and kept her eyes on her notes, a bubble of laughter threatening to explode if she so much as glanced at Mary.

While Wolverine explained that the Plummers had declined to be interviewed, Vern took an inordinate amount of time stomping from the kitchen to the living room, finally collapsing into his chair with a fresh piece of pie and an overly dramatic huffing sigh. Pointing his fork toward Mary's phone, he asked, "So what's all *this* about? Local yokel goes missing? Guarantee it was a drug overdose or some redneck feud between him and Lonny."

Key shot him a curious glance. Wolverine hadn't mentioned Lonny. *How does Vern Olson know that Riggs and Lonny were friends? Well, he did live in Troy …. And it wasn't a secret.*

Vern's insolent eyes briefly met Key's, then he pressed his lips tightly together and began brushing invisible crumbs off the arm of his chair. He said nothing more, but even after he'd finished eating, he made no move to fix the modem. Key got the distinct impression he was more interested than he was letting on.

Wolverine recounted how he'd interviewed two now-retired law enforcement officers from Richmond. Weeks after the concert, they'd finally conceded that something may have happened to Riggs, but rounding up witnesses from among tens of thousands of long-gone concert attendees had proven impossible. "Long story short," he said soberly, "it was another dead end. And his best friend, Lonny Morgan, who attended the concert with him, is unfortunately incarcerated in Florida. I wasn't allowed to interview him."

Vern snorted. "Hippies and druggies and felons make bad witnesses. Who'd a *thunk*!"

Wolverine had, however, found the girl who'd begged a ride home.

"Ayo told us he thought Riggs had gone out West to see his girlfriend," Shasta Harrison nervously told the podcast host. "It made sense, 'cause Riggs was crazy in love with that girl. But he never made it to New Mexico, and now I don't know what to think. Ayo Jones was at the concert too. He might know something, but that man's been gone from Troy forever."

Wolverine asked her to describe Ayo. "Well, he wasn't *bad lookin'*, but good gosh, he was way too old for me, and besides, he had a real high opinion of himself. Thought he was God's gift to women." She described the concert, then finished in a rush. "And then Riggs was just *poof*! Gone! And poor Lonny was *super* rattled about it the whole ride home."

"It's very important to note—Ayo Jones is not presumed guilty," Wolverine said hastily. "If any of my listeners could point me in his direction, please contact me via my website or on social media. And if you're listening, Ayo Jones, it would be my pleasure to interview you."

Key jotted Wolverine's contact information next to the few facts she'd found significant, but in truth, her chats with Lonny and DP had provided more information.

"It's hot as Hades in here." Vern stood, his armpits drenched in perspiration, and flicked off the gas flame. Jamming his phone into his jeans pocket, he grabbed his coffee cup and plate and lurched out.

"What in the ..." Key mouthed to an equally bewildered Mary, who had again stopped the podcast. They heard the dishes clatter into the sink. Returning with the equipment, Vern dumped it all onto the coffee table, rolled up his sleeves, and tugged a sideboard away from the wall, revealing an outlet and a cable connection. "I gotta get this done. Listen somewhere else or put up with the noise."

# Chapter 21

## UNWINDING

"He's the most off-putting person I've ever met, Key, and that's saying something!" The women were standing by Mary's car, having given up on the podcast. "And that gravestone tattoo ..." Mary grimaced.

"Gravestone tattoo? Ugh. I didn't see it—I tried not to look at him."

"Right forearm. Will you be all right here? I'm sorry to abandon you!"

"I'm leaving shortly," Key assured her. "I'm meeting with DP and the electrician at Pike House, then sorting through boxes in the shed."

Mary looked doubtful. "You're leaving the demoralizer in there alone?"

Key shrugged. "It's his house. I've got nothing he'd want. Unless it's your leftover pie." She gave Mary a hug. "I'm not sure what we accomplished today, but it was ..."

"One for the books." Mary finished for her, chuckling. "Jukey is going to be so sorry he missed this. Let's do this again soon! Minus Vern!"

After Vern explained how to reboot the modem (using far too many words for such a simple process), he went upstairs and didn't come back down. Key browned pork chops and added them to the crockpot with potatoes, onions, and carrots, then made herself a sandwich. Taking Faro, her notebook, and her computer, she left the house. She had no plans to return until she picked up Wain. By then, surely, Vern would be gone.

★★★

Wain spent the six-block drive from school reliving the evening before, asking when he could visit Bobcat again, and planning the various horseback adventures he and Ell were bound to have. "Bobcat goes in the good jar, but I can't think of anything for the tough jar because I'm too happy! Hey! Whose blue car is that?"

*Blue car?* Sure enough, there was Vern's high-end rental, sitting possessively in the driveway where she normally parked her Jeep. Key rolled her eyes. Apparently, the tough jar was all hers today. "It belongs to the man who owns this house." She pulled alongside the curb. *What is he still doing here? How hard is it to find a few documents?*

"Oh. I thought it was somebody, like, interesting." Wain clambered out of the Jeep. "I'm starving! I'm gonna get a snack!"

The delectable smells that greeted her had Key's exhausted, grubby, late-afternoon self thanking her energetic morning self for providing dinner. As she put away groceries, she could hear Vern's heavy tread above them, then the creak of the stairs, then to Key's dismay, he appeared around the corner holding a white banker's box and announced, "Too hot up there. Gonna sort this in the living room."

Wain stopped digging through his snack bin and stared openly at Vern.

"Wain, this is Mr. Olson, who owns this house."

"Hi." Wain's frank, unwavering gaze seemed to unnerve Vern, who self-consciously smoothed his unruly hair down over his ears.

"You the one drew all over my fence?" Vern asked. "You and the girl?" To Key's great surprise, he sounded almost friendly. At least less peevish.

"Um, yeah." Wain still hadn't taken his eyes off Vern.

"Mm." Vern pulled a bottle of water from the box and took a swig. "Windy out there. Been outside most of the afternoon. Had to check on my horse."

"Wait. You have a *horse*?" Wain asked excitedly. "So do I!"

*Of course.* Key had forgotten about the horse. "Deirdre said you board your horse at Mistic Meadows?" she asked Vern.

"Uh-huh." Vern kept smoothing his hair.

"That's right by our *real* house!" Wain burst out.

"I know." Vern poured a little water into one hand, rubbed his palms together and again smoothed his hair. It didn't do much good.

"My horse Bobcat lives there. What's your horse's name?"

"Zee."

"Zee? Like, um ..." Wain expertly sketched a *Z* in the air. "Like that?" Even in these odd circumstances, Key felt a glow of pride. There would come a day when she took Wain's fearless knowledge of the alphabet for granted, but today was not it.

"Pretty much, yeah." Vern picked up the box.

"Did you get to ride your horse today?" Wain tore open his bag of Cheddy Chipsters and followed Vern into the living room, crunching enthusiastically, Faro at his heels hoping for a dropped chip. From where she stood at the refrigerator, Key could still hear the conversation.

"Yep." The box thumped onto the coffee table; a chair cushion sighed.

"Where did you go?" *Crunch, crunch.*

"The woods."

Key surreptitiously snapped a photo of the two of them. Considering that Vern was a stranger, Wain was uncharacteristically very chatty. It had to be the horse.

Wain droned on. "Me and Key go exploring in the woods. We look for, like, letters and birds and nature things. I'm gonna ask if we can ride horses in there!" There was no answer. "Does Zee live in that big barn? The one with the bench in front? Bobcat does. And my friend Ell, she got a horse named Coco, but it's not like cocoa that you drink! It's mostly white, and it's a girl, and mine is a boy; he's brown with white on his face. Gina, that's the lady who showed me Bobcat, she says they love cucumbers and cantaloupe, just like Sheba, she's a gerbil, and next time we go, we get to—"

"Listen, little bro, it's been nice chatting all things equine, but I've got work to do." Vern's voice had risen a couple notches. "You and Fido here need to blow this pop stand."

"Wain!" Key called, a broad smile pasted across her face. Oh, how she loved that kid. Though it was shamefully ungraceful, she couldn't help hoping that Wain was inflicting upon Vern exactly the level of irritation she and Mary had experienced that morning. "Please take Faro out for a bit before Cissy gets here. Did you fill his water?"

"Oops!"

The leftover pie Mary had set on the counter, Key suddenly realized, was gone—aluminum pan and all.

Vern was back upstairs by the time Cissy arrived, and Key asked her to do the tutoring session outside. A few minutes later Vern reappeared with papers stuffed haphazardly into the outside pocket of his bag. *The pie is probably taking up all the room in the main section of that briefcase*, Key thought cynically. He locked the padlock, checked it twice, flapped a hand in Key's direction and departed.

Her phone pinged as she parked the Jeep on the drive.

Internet restored? Are we still on for 7 p.m.?

Guy! She'd completely forgotten their scheduled call. She mentally moved Wain's bedtime to a half-hour later. How Guy could be so chipper at 4 a.m. Dubai time was beyond her, but it spoke volumes as to his determination to consistently connect with his son.

Absolutely! Wain has so much to tell you!

★★★

Key busied herself around the house, half listening as Wain first read several pages of his library book to his father, then described everything that had transpired since their last call: swans, horses, playing with Reynold, school, and storms.

Guy waited while Key tucked Wain in. "Sheesh, Key, your schedule sounds worse than mine." Below him, the lights of Dubai twinkled to the horizon.

"It's been an *especially* crazy week," Key told him. "Nearly every day Wain adds something new to the list of things he wants to show you at Christmas. And Guy, his knack for noticing details is remarkable. Maybe it comes from studying his CartWheels like he does." She explained Wain's comparison of the teachers' raincoats to crayons, the tree branches to bones, and the insights he'd gathered from the awful Icky movie, which, with all that had happened, Wain had forgotten to tell his father about.

"He said that? That I'm the good Icky dad? That sounds, um, complimentary?"

"He recognizes a good Icky dad when he sees one." They laughed, then there was a silence.

"It's very humbling. I have a lot to make up for."

Key was determined to end the call on a positive note. "Guy, even though you're so far away, Wain gains a lot of strength and confidence knowing that you're in his life again. You're his hero. Black Diamond is his most treasured possession. You know, listening to parents converse while I wait at the school, I realize no one has all the answers. Wain's situation is different but certainly not unheard of, and honestly, it's better than that of many children. Wain simply … accepts his situation and soldiers on. I learn from him every day."

"Out of the nightmare into the dream. Thanks to you. I can't wait to hang out with him." Guy sounded wistful. "I need to wrap this up. Take care, Key, and thanks again. Love you both."

# Chapter 22
## GREGGO

"I'll call you back in twenty minutes," Key said to the "Mack" readout on her Jeep's dashboard. "We're on the way to pick up Wain's friend Greggo and his bike, then going out to Pike House so they can ride on the motocross trail. Anticipation level: nuclear."

"Motocross trail? How did I miss that when I visited?"

"I made it!" Wain called excitedly, leaning forward as far as his seatbelt would allow. "*And* we're gonna roast hot dogs and marshmallows *and* show Greggo my horse, Bobcat!"

"Hopefully we can see Bobcat," Key added hastily. "We'll stop by."

"Trails? Horses? How many years have I been asleep?" Mack exclaimed teasingly. "You live the life, Wain! Talk in a few, Key."

Greggo's home was one-half of a duplex. As Key parked behind a green Subaru, a husky red-haired, freckled boy in gray gym shorts and an orange Tennessee Volunteers hoodie hurtled outside, then stopped to hold open the fingerprint-covered glass door for a similarly dressed, barefoot woman pushing a well-used bike.

Key grinned and opened the rear of the Jeep. No mistaking that relationship; except for the daisy tattoo traveling up the side of her calf and a cascade of wavy curls versus her son's crew cut, Greggo's mother was his double in thirty-something female form. From the house came the sounds of another child wailing and a frenzied yapping that brought Faro to the Jeep window.

"Hi," the woman said distractedly, then called out to the boy, "Your helmet and backpack, G-man!"

"Come. With. Me. Wain." With his arms held stiffly at his sides, Greggo executed an exaggerated, robotic U-turn, making Wain giggle.

"Hi! I'm Key North, Wain's guardian." *Guardian*. It sounded so … *institutional*, more of a sterile assignment than a relationship. She needed to come up with a better term when casually introducing herself in relation to Wain.

"Raven Barbie. Nice to meet you. Wain, you're a legend in this house; no other boy Greggo knows has Black Diamond." The most incongruously named woman Key had ever met wheeled the bike over the gravel to the Jeep, saying, "Ow! Ow!" every step. "Sorry to make this fast, but …" she tilted her head toward the door. "It's a zoo in there. My husband just left, we're in the process of moving to a real house with a real yard, and as you can see, I'm absolutely rocking the single-mom life." She pulled an elastic band off her wrist and expertly twisted her hair into a bun, then helped Key load the bike.

Raven seemed very cavalier about being abandoned by her husband, Key thought sympathetically, remembering the conversation she'd had with Wain. *Probably putting on a brave face*. "I'm sorry. Single motherhood must be a huge adjustment. How old is your baby?"

"Single …?" Raven looked at her quizzically, then let out a hearty laugh. "Tate's almost two. But I mean, my husband left for a few *days*. He's a long-haul trucker. Unless you know something I don't!"

"Oh! Wow, we got that *completely* wrong." Key joined her laughter.

"And this is how rumors get started. Gimme hugs." Raven gave Greggo a quick embrace as Wain watched, his face unreadable. "Thanks very much for having him."

"Our pleasure. We'll be back by four, and I guarantee he'll be grubby. We're making s'mores."

"We call them dirt-glue sandwiches," Raven replied. "Be your best self, G-man."

★★★

At Pike House, after the boys had raced off on their bikes and she'd done a quick check on the remodel, Key fetched the wagon from the shed, loaded it with chairs and lunch supplies, and made her way with a happy sigh to the patio, anticipating a long chat with Mack. Though they needed the rain, it was impossible to complain about another stellar autumn day.

Down by the woods, Wain had picked up a stick and was jabbing at whatever Faro was sniffing, while Greggo pointed toward the path. As she put in her earbuds, Key heard a couple distinct *ewwws*. The grass was too tall to see what they'd found, and Key couldn't venture that far without her cell service fading. *Hopefully not a snake.* Probably a bug. North Carolina had more crazy bugs than she'd ever known existed.

She began collecting fallen branches, breaking them into smaller pieces, stacking them neatly beside the fireplace. To create the kind of red coals perfect for roasting hot dogs and marshmallows, the fire needed to burn for a while. Once it was lit, she dragged her chair closer to the fire and dialed Mack.

He answered on the fourth ring. "Sorry. I left my phone on the charger in my office." Key suddenly wished he was there with her, conversing in person, sharing the sunshine, the splash of red from her potted geraniums, and the exuberant voices of Wain and Greggo mingling with the scolding crows who'd taken exception to the motocross invasion.

While Mack agreed that Vern sounded "cartoonishly obnoxious," he saw nothing wrong with the camera Key hadn't been able to locate. "We've become a nation of cameras. Some are very sophisticated and well hidden. Just don't do or say anything that you don't want the man to know."

"*Say?* He can hear us too?"

"Depends on the setup, but I'd bet on it. My guess is it's in the motion-sensor light."

"Hmm." Key thought a moment. "I sat out there and talked to you about Riggs the day I stayed with Granny Jewel, but other than that, snooze fest. Dogs and tutoring sessions. Maybe he hears something now and then from the adorable and slightly eccentric neighbor lady next door who talks to her flowers." She explained how Bertie's rose garden had come to be.

"*Wow*. What an amazing story. You do seem to attract the unusual characters."

"Moths to a flame," Key deadpanned, and Mack laughed.

"Moth here," he said enigmatically.

Still smiling after they hung up, Key put the boys to work gathering more wood, then allowed them to add twigs to the flames. "It'll be a perfect hot-dog fire in no time," she told them. *Once a Girl Scout, always a Girl Scout.*

# Chapter 23

## DREAMS AND RECOLLECTIONS

A half-hour later, the coals were ready, and as Key helped Wain and Greggo skewer their hot dogs on roasting sticks, she heard a lawn mower start up in her front yard. Cav must have come to cut the grass.

"Hold your hot dogs above the coals and rotate them slowly," she instructed the boys, adding in a tone firm enough to make Wain look questioningly at her, "But do *not* mess with the fire! I'll be right back."

To her surprise, it wasn't Cav but Lonny in her front yard. He cut the engine and removed a pair of earplugs.

"Hi, Lonny! I never heard you arrive!"

"Hey, Miss Key! I rode Cav's bike. He's helping out at Mistic today. They got a big ole birthday party goin' on."

*Tally Mayweather's party!* Key's heart sank. "Where's Ell? Would she like to come over to roast hot dogs with Wain and his friend?"

"Gayle took the girls to Porterville today. Ell is near beside herself—they're gonna get her riding boots."

Key breathed a sigh of relief. "A girls' day out! How fun! How about you, Lonny? Do you have time to roast a hot dog?"

"I'd take you up on that. Skipped breakfast this morning." They started down the path. "Your place is looking real good, Miss Key."

"All thanks to DP." Key checked the patio. The boys were right where she'd left them, still carefully rotating their sizzling hot dogs.

"I stopped by to see DP yesterday." Lonny kicked a rock out of the path with the side of his boot. "His mama's havin' a rough time. It just never goes away."

"A friend of mine calls it a 'hellish purgatory.'"

"Not exactly clear on what purgatory constitutes, but I been in prison."

Key nodded. "Apt comparison."

Back at the patio, she introduced Lonny to Greggo, then asked, "Would you boys like to eat on the big rock?" After she'd delivered their plates, she took a seat across from Lonny.

"I had a dream about Riggs a coupla days ago," Lonny said, slowly turning his roasting stick. "You know how some dreams disappear the minute you open your eyes? Well, this one wan't like that. It was real vivid."

"What was it about?"

"Riggs was his twenty-year-old self, standin' by Dogleg Pond, leanin' against a tree trunk lookin' straight at me. It was misty out, and his shoes was muddy. He was holding one hand up by his neck, and the other one was making an *L* on his forehead, like how people say 'loser.'"

"But that's what—" Key caught herself mid-gasp. She couldn't tell Lonny that his own daughter was being taunted with that exact same gesture. "*Wow.* What do you think your dream means?"

Lonny leaned over to stroke Faro, who had chosen to keep his nose as close as possible to the hot dogs. "Gayle says dreams are about the dreamer. She says it's about me, not Riggs. Like he's tellin' me somethin' I need to learn. Like move forward, you know? Get out of the mud, stop beating myself up, go back to bein' more confident, like I was at age twenty. Gayle says maybe I miss who I was when Riggs and me was friends. Which I most definitely do."

"I've heard the same thing about dreams," Key replied. "That who or what we see in our dreams are a representation of some part of our subconscious, illuminating hidden aspects of our thoughts and actions."

"Yeah. Even if it's about me, it was *real* good to see him, then he just … faded away." Lonny gave a little laugh that ended in a sigh. "Kinda crazy, you know? That your asleep mind is saying, *Wake up to what you're doin' when you're awake.*"

"That's a perfect way to put it." Key said, squeezing mustard onto a bun. Lonny was obviously still struggling to find his place as a husband and father; his older brother, after all, had procured him a job, and his mother was providing their housing. And most likely his wages were being garnished. The whole picture underscored the reasoning behind Ell's reluctance to add to his burden. Unsure how to express encouragement without sounding too familiar (or much worse, condescending), Key decided on a question. "What would you choose to do if you could start over, Lonny?"

Lonny took his time answering. "I don't dislike what I'm doin' now, working at the block plant. I mean, it's good steady work, and I get to be outdoors. But if I could start over? Like, *way* over, back to when I was twenty? Probly go out West, find work on a ranch or somethin'. I love the space and them huge mountains out there. I love winters and hiking and archery hunting. Good thing, too, 'cause as a felon I can't own a gun. Had to sell mine."

Family issues, guilt, the struggle to rebuild, loss of privileges formerly taken for granted …. All consequences of one terrible decision. *What a price to pay*, Key thought.

"That's not to say I regret the life and family I have!" Lonny added quickly. "That ain't it at all. It's just, sometimes …" He shifted uncomfortably in his chair and adjusted the plate on his lap. "I'm not sayin' this real well. Makes me sound ungrateful for the blessings in my life."

Key smiled. "You don't sound ungrateful at all. I think it's human nature to wish we knew at twenty what we know at forty. But speaking from experience, I'm going to step out on a limb here and say, give yourself grace."

"You sound like Gayle. And my brother."

"You have a great support system, Lonny. I love that about your family. You know, I think Wain's father would relate to what you're saying." Key briefly recounted Guy's struggles with his own poor choices where Wain was concerned. "Maybe that's what Riggs was telling you in that dream. Don't let guilt and regret from your worst choice be a ball and chain that stops you from making the best of the rest of your life. For you and those around you." She took a bite of coleslaw, hoping she didn't sound like some trite meme.

"Maybe so. Thanks, Miss Key." Lonny gave her a rueful smile and stood, tossing his plate and napkin into the fire. Pulling a wrinkled cigarette from his shirt pocket, he rolled it straight on his jeans. "Mind if I smoke?"

"Not at all." She passed him the lighter she'd set on the woodpile.

Lonny remained standing, leaning against a trellis post, one ankle crossed over the other. Watching the boys on the rock, he commented wistfully, "Reminds me of me and Riggs."

Key met his eyes. "Lonny, some mysterious sequence of events aligned so faultlessly that Riggs literally vanished into thin air."

"Yep."

Key dug into her purse for her notebook. "I've been looking at it from as many angles as I can, making a timeline from what I've learned, listing absolutely everything that might be pertinent."

Lonny raised his eyebrows. "When you said you was gonna tug at strings, you wasn't just sayin' that."

"They're very tenuous strings," Key answered wryly. "Nothing ventured, nothing gained though, right? I did a little research on that concert. It was called Sunshine—" She checked her notes.

"Sunshine Fest Richmond."

"Right. And it was held outdoors at a farm west of Richmond. Not at a stadium or anything."

"In a huge field." Lonny took another pull on his cigarette.

"By any chance, do you remember where you parked in relation to where you entered?" Key asked.

Lonny rolled his eyes and exhaled smoke accompanied by a derisive snort. "Easy one. Ayo *of course* had to be in the VIP lot. He hung the tag from the mirror, bragged about it all the way up."

"So you didn't have far to walk, to the entrance."

"We was real close. Like, you could almost see the stage from there."

Key held out the notebook. "Would you be willing to draw me a diagram? Include where you best remember Ayo parked. And which way Riggs walked to the restroom."

"Gotta think a minute. Been a couple decades." As Lonny sat back down, his phone pinged. "Miss Key, check this out." He showed her a photo of a beaming Ell in a brand-new pair of black riding boots, one arm around Dibsy, adorable in a pink cowboy hat.

"Oh, I'm so happy for Ell!"

"Me too. She's such a sweetheart. Cav gave her some of his mowing money to help buy the boots. We're real proud of him too." He tossed his cigarette butt into the fire.

"Cav did that? You have the sweetest kids, Lonny!"

"They got the sweetest mama in the world." Lonny took the notebook from Key and quickly drew a map. "It ain't to scale, but this here's a parking lot, then a fence, and the entrance gate." He drew a curve. "Stage was here. And these little *x*'s, that's our group. Riggs walked toward a bank of portable toilets that was on the way to the entrance." He drew an arrow.

Key studied it. "Were you allowed to go out and come back in?"

"Yeah. I myself didn't try, but we got them numbered plastic wristbands when we gone in that allowed it. Nothin' was as locked down as it is now."

"It's sad how security is such a necessity nowadays." Key scribbled a shorthand version of his answer. "Okay, this is the question that I believe is central to the entire mystery: At any time, *especially* when Riggs said he was going to the restroom, was Ayo ever out of your sight?"

Lonny leaned forward, forearms on his thighs, years of frustration evident in his voice. "You're askin' the wrong guy. I *always* ignored and avoided Ayo. But for *sure* I remember Riggs saying to me, 'I'm going to the john.' If I could have a piece of my life to live over, it would change right there. I'd a gone with him. But I was like, yeah, okay, buddy. How could I know it was the last time I'd ever see Riggs?"

"And where was Ayo?"

Lonny shrugged. "Honestly, Miss Key, no idea."

"So—bottom line—Ayo *could have* followed Riggs when he went to the restroom. It's not out of the question."

Lonny gave a little shrug. "Well, in normal circumstances Ayo was on Riggs like white on rice. Acted like he owned him. But I doubt even Ayo would follow him to the *john*." Tipping his chair back, he tracked a jet overhead. "You know, bein' locked up gives you a good bit of time to think, so every day I'd work on remembering, look for that one extra thing I maybe forgot. If I could help the Plummers, at least I'd be doin' *some* good while I was in there. *Who was standin' next to me? How was Riggs acting? What kind of things was we talkin' about?* Just ... anything, you know? But Miss Key, *every dang time* it's the same .... Nothing. Nothing odd or out of place."

Key studied the map. "This is pure conjecture, but what if we went on the premise that Ayo *did* do something to Riggs during the concert?"

"You mean, like, murdered him," Lonny said flatly.

His words were so starkly, horribly matter of fact that Key flinched. "Well ... I guess I do."

"Thought that scene over a million times too." He sighed, then sat up straight. "Okay. Let's say he *did* follow Riggs, let's say he *did* murder Riggs. Where'd Riggs *go*? That parking area was a field of grass. No trees, no shrubs or whatnot. You're gonna hide a body ... where? In some rando's pickup bed? Under a car to be discovered soon as folks start leavin'? You see what I mean? No way, man."

"Where did Ayo himself say he was? When Riggs went to the restroom?"

"Around. Hangin' out."

Key sighed. It was all so vague. Twenty years (not to mention marijuana- and moonshine-fogged memories) certainly didn't allow for the clearest of pictures. "How much time went by before you noticed Riggs hadn't come back from the restroom?"

"Probably forty-five minutes."

Key's jaw dropped. "That long?"

"Yep. But Miss Key, they needed at least twice as many portable johns as they had. Everyone was talking about the wait. And I thought Riggs coulda gone to get food, whatever. Them lines was long too. So it wan't all *that* weird."

"Makes sense. So back to Ayo's assertion that Riggs had left ...."

"Ayo said he *assumed* Riggs had left. Which is the one concession I will give Ayo. Like I told you the other night, Riggs did say he might take off for Albuquerque 'cause he was so royally pissed off at his daddy after their fight. But why would Riggs leave right then and there? He *loved* that band. Why didn't he tell *me*? Makes *no* sense. You know?"

*Same song, hundredth verse.* They'd beaten this topic down to a nub. Key consulted her notes. "Let's switch gears. Do you remember the name of the company that Ayo worked for?"

"No, ma'am," Lonny replied. "There wasn't nothin' written on the van, I know that."

"Was the van clean?"

"Yes, ma'am. Real clean. Rakes and shovels and such on the walls inside. Nothin' in the back that coulda been a body rolled up in a tarp or nothin'. No big box the size of a coffin." Catching her surprised glance, he lifted his hands. "No joke. Dawson grilled me and Shasta about that."

Dawson had obviously left no stone unturned, except the eternally elusive one that would reveal the whereabouts of his son. "Last thing, Lonny—do you have any pictures of Ayo?"

He squinted over her head, thinking. "Mmm, doubtful. But my mama's got my old things stored in boxes, in her garage loft. Gayle's over there every day, and most afternoons she's lookin' for things to do. She might be willin' to dig through them."

"No pressure," Key assured him, feeling a sharp pang of sympathy for Gayle. "I'd love to see a picture of the guy."

"I'll talk to Gayle. Better get back to cuttin' grass. Thank you for lunch, Miss Key." Lonny turned down her offer of a s'more and waved to the boys, who were back on their bicycles.

Key was adding wood to the fire when Wain and Greggo skidded to a stop beside the patio and pulled off their helmets, cheeks flushed, eyes sparkling. "Can we make s'mores now? And can Faro have this last hot dog?"

"Yes to s'mores, no to the hot dog since I already gave him one." Key opened the cooler. "By the way! What were you guys looking at earlier? Down there on the path? The thing you poked with a stick."

Both boys giggled, then said simultaneously, "Horse poop."

# Chapter 24

## THE MISTIC STRING

Judging by the dozen or so cars they met on their way to Mistic Meadows (including a familiar SUV with a purple *M* on the side), it appeared that Tally Mayweather's birthday party had ended. *By crazy circumstance*, Key thought ruefully, *Cav got to attend the party, and his little sister didn't.*

Under the eaves by the Mistic Meadows office were torn wrappings, sagging crepe paper, and other colorful party remnants. Hoping her unscheduled visit with two very excited little boys wouldn't be a bother after what had surely been a full day for the horses and the staff, Key cracked the Jeep windows for an unhappy Faro and was digging in the cooler for a bag of carrots when Regina and Cavender emerged from the stable, both sporting straw cowboy hats and hot-pink bandanas.

"Well, howdy, Wain and crew!" Gina drawled theatrically.

"I hope it's okay that we stopped by to see Bobcat," Key said apologetically. "I tried to call, but there was no answer."

"It's no problem, Key! We simply haven't checked our phones all day. Here, cowboys." Regina pulled two crisp new bandanas from the bag she was carrying. Hot pink probably wouldn't have been their first color choice, Key thought with a smile as she helped the boys tie them around their necks, but with Cav as a model, it was.

"Y'all look bangin'." Cav gave each boy a light fist bump, which, Key could tell, instantly elevated their coolness factor in their own minds. And without a doubt, she thought, laughing inwardly, she'd hear the word *bangin'* from either Wain or Greggo before the day was done.

Gina turned to Cav. "You're off cleanup duty! Please take the boys to the small corral."

"Yay!" Wain did a fist pump, and Greggo executed another full-circle robot move.

"Come on, y'all," Cav sounded proud to be the guide.

"Thank you, Gina! Wain has talked about nothing but Bobcat for days." Key pointed to Faro, who was pressing his shiny black nose through three inches of open window. "Do you mind if I let Faro out? I'll keep him on the leash."

"Not at all. Let's go sit on the bench by the office. My legs are about to give out. *What* a day. Twenty-two fourth-grade girls. Endless laps around the arena."

"Sit. I'll tidy up." Key began throwing garbage into a wooden barrel lined with a black plastic bag. "Um, Gina, I have a question. You don't have to answer if you're breeching client confidentiality, but ..."

Gina laughed. "We're not a law firm. Ahhhh." Sinking gratefully onto the bench, she smacked her hands from thighs to boot tops, releasing small puffs of dust, then pulled off her hat, undid her ponytail and combed her hands through shoulder-length graying hair, which somehow made her look younger and older all at once. "What's your question?"

"I wondered if any of your clients ride their horses in the woods over by my place."

"Several of our regulars do. The trails in the pastures are more popular though. It's too soon for Wain and Ell to ride in the woods, if that's your question."

"Oh, no, not that, I ... uh ... There was fresh horse manure on the edge of my property, and I've never seen that before."

Regina grimaced. "Gosh darn it. Elvin Grimes, the old guy who previously owned your house, had that same complaint. He visited us one day and made it abundantly clear that he did not appreciate having to clean it up. Which of course we understood." She redid her ponytail and replaced the hat.

"It's not a complaint …."

"It's a confusing little slice of geography." Regina waved a hand toward the north. "Most of the forest is owned by the railroad, open to the public, but anyone wanting to get to Dogleg Pond must either hike through the woods or get permission to access the trail through your property or ours. Anyway, once Mr. Grimes posted *No Trespassing* signs, that seemed to end the problem."

"When did Mr. Grimes come to see you?"

"Hmm. Three or four years ago?" Gina answered after a moment. "We'd been open for a few years by then, so we were surprised that suddenly it was an issue."

Key made a mental note. "Off topic, but do you know Vern and Deirdre Olson?" she asked. "I'm temporarily renting their house. They board a horse here."

"Oh, McKenzie! Nickname Zee. That's him, the buckskin, right over there." Gina pointed to the east pasture where a lovely golden-tan gelding with a dark mane and tail grazed with two other horses.

"Beautiful horse!" Key wadded up a stained, cowgirl-themed paper tablecloth. *McKenzie. McKenzie.* Where had she heard that name recently?

"He is," Gina agreed. "Vern was here just the other day. He's not the most talented rider I've ever met, but for the past several years he's been a very loyal boarder." She chuckled. "Zee is such a patient horse."

"Vern stopped by the house the other day, and Wain immediately connected on the expert horseman level, what with having been around Bobcat for one hour of his life."

Gina laughed. "Love it. Vern of all people would know the boundaries, as much as he's ridden those trails. You know, Key, maybe you should put up the *No Trespassing* signs again."

Key flapped her hand. "I'm not worried about it." She changed the subject. "How's Cav working out?"

"Great kid. Hard worker. I'll tell you what, all those fourth-grade girls left today with crushes on the handsome young cowboy. They almost preferred him to the horses." Gina stood and struck a pose, placing her hand on a jutted-out hip, then said in a high, singsong voice, "Oh, Cav! Will you help me get on this horse? Cavender! Tie my bandana? Cav! Want some cake?"

Key laughed. "I can imagine. He is a cute kid."

"It's those dimples and the thousand-watt smile. He's very funny too—kept the waiting girls entertained while others rode. We don't often host such large parties, but the Mayweathers pulled out all the stops. Anything for their baby girl, you know? To tell the truth though, as much as I appreciate the income, I'm glad it's over. The drama! When we refused to let Ursula Mayweather bring balloons to the corral, it almost derailed the whole thing."

"Seriously?" Key unwound pink and white crepe paper from a post.

"Dead serious. Horses dislike unpredictable movement, which of course is the very definition of a helium balloon in the breeze. And what if one *popped*? It was the most ridiculous argument. We finally settled on allowing them to tie the balloons to the sign out on Pike Road, at the intersection."

Key hoped Ell had been well on her way to Porterville before the sign had been decorated. "Well, congratulations on pulling it off. That's a huge undertaking."

"Ursula Mayweather is ..." Regina stopped and clapped a hand over her mouth. "Oops. I'm getting dangerously close to breaching client confidentiality." They laughed.

*You're not telling me anything I don't already know,* Key thought, reaching for the broom and dustpan leaning against the doorframe, *except that Miss Aviator Glasses is named Ursula.*

Regina stood and said wearily, "I need to go help Jessie. Thank you, Key! I owe you a horseback ride!"

"I'd love that! Bye, Gina." Key checked her phone. A text from Mack.

"Oh no!" she exclaimed aloud as she read:

Hi Key, please call me when you get the chance. Lainey badly broke her arm today -both radius and ulna. =/ fell off a chair while getting candy from the top of the fridge. poor kid! she's going to be fine but this changes our fishing trip plans =/

She sent a quick text back, expressing her sympathy, telling him she'd call when they could talk without interruption. Then she headed for the corral in search of a cowboy and a robot wearing pink bandanas.

# Chapter 25
## MOTION SENSOR

"Come, Faro, I need your motion," Key whispered, tucking the covers around Wain's shoulders. After luxuriously scrubbing off smoke and dust and melted marshmallow, she was now in her comfiest sweats and slippers, wet hair pulled back in a ponytail, earbuds dangling on a cord around her neck. She tugged a fleece blanket from the foot of Wain's bed and draped it over her shoulders, then tiptoed out of the room. "You're always up for anything, aren't you?" she asked, giving Faro a long head scratch once they were in the kitchen waiting for her coffee to brew. She might stay awake a little longer, but tonight, that wasn't a bad thing. She needed to have her wits about her.

*Lights, camera, action.* "Do your business, buddy!" she called softly, once they'd stepped out the back door. Ignoring the moths that instantly fluttered like groupies around the motion-sensor light, she settled into the Adirondack chair closest to the steps and arranged the blanket on her legs, then ostentatiously wedged her earbuds into her ears, pulled her phone from her sweatshirt pocket, tapped it, and set it screen side down onto the arm of the chair. After a few seconds, refusing to acknowledge how foolish she felt, she lifted the tiny microphone on the cord, brought it close to her mouth, and began talking at a volume that, while loud, could still pass for normal.

"Hi, Sylvia!" (She didn't know anyone named Sylvia.) "Sorry I missed you earlier. Wain's asleep, and I finally have a minute. We spent the day out at Pike House." Picking up her cup, she opened the door to let Faro inside, then began slowly pacing in front of the motion-sensor light, making fake small talk for another minute.

"My *detective* case?" she said a little more loudly with a laugh. "Oh, you mean Riggs Plummer. Eh. The podcast was a waste of time. Way back, the Plummers hired a detective who suspects Riggs was hitchhiking to New Mexico to see his girlfriend and something bad happened along the way." She sat back down, cringing inside as she went on, "... Uh-huh, all that open land between Richmond and Albuquerque—he could be anywhere." After she'd elaborated a bit more on the futility of ever finding Riggs, she ended the call with a promise to get together soon.

Tightening the blanket around her shoulders, Key rested her head against the back of the chair, illogically feeling remorseful, as though her faked conversation had somehow betrayed DP and his family. Over the faint grinding of katydids, the occasional acorn plopped with the tiniest of rustles onto layers of crisp leaves while, above her, a nearly full moon joined the constellations in welcoming her to their chilly, star-studded nightlife. She smiled ruefully at Orion. *Hey there, fellow hunter. Sorry. Just in case, I wanted to throw him off the scent. Thanks to Wain, we may have finally tugged a string.*

She still needed to process what had happened earlier as they were leaving Mistic Meadows. It was too soon, though, to share her thoughts with anyone but the night sky and her notebook.

★★★

They'd dropped Greggo off with a grateful Raven, then picked up a pepperoni-pineapple pizza before finally heading home, where Key sent Wain straight to the shower and called Mack.

"I'm so sorry about all this, Key," he said as soon as he picked up.

"Oh, please don't apologize! How's Lainey?"

"It's painful, but she's going to be fine. She's the kind of kid who rolls with the punches. The sparkling turquoise cast helped." He filled Key in on the details. "I hope Wain isn't too disappointed."

"He won't be, because fortunately I never mentioned it to him. I figured I'd tell him a few days before you arrived, so we weren't living in 'Are we there yet' mode."

"Are you sure you haven't raised a whole passel of kids? Because that's a seasoned-parent move."

Key laughed. "I'm a quick learner. I made the mistake of telling him about the October CartWheels reveal. We made a countdown calendar the other day, which has alleviated the questions somewhat. Mack, what about your cabin reservations? Plane tickets?"

"I can rebook everything, but it'll have to be next spring. I'll look at some dates." Mack sighed. "It was my one free weekend in the next few months. I'm truly sorry, Key."

"Would you like to come alone?" Key asked, throwing caution to the wind. "You'd be welcome to stay at the rental with me. There's an extra bedroom," she added, hoping that didn't sound either too familiar or too off-putting.

Mack didn't seem to notice. "I would in a heartbeat, but Lainey's with me that weekend. Her parents are going on a trip. I can't back out now."

"No, definitely not! Spring works for me." There was a sliver of silence.

"But first chance I get, Key, I will come to North Carolina by myself. Fair warning—it will be short notice. I was really looking forward to spending time with you."

An unfamiliar warmth touched her cheeks. "Me too, Mack. You're welcome anytime. Tell Lainey I hope her arm heals fast!"

★★★

"Today was fun," Wain had said at dinner, and in those three simple words, Key detected his childish comparison of today's activities to the hundreds of darkly unfun days he'd endured with his mother and Callahan. *Today was fun because I am acquainted with the opposite. Today was fun because I wasn't walking on eggshells.* But she also heard, *I wish I could tell my mom about it, like Greggo got to tell his.*

She gave Wain an extra-warm hug from behind his chair, grateful that she didn't have to disappoint him with news of the canceled fishing trip. "It was so fun, buddy. I really like Greggo. Your dad is going to love hearing about it!"

But it wasn't those poignant words that had affected her most today and inspired her conversation with "Sylvia." No, that prize was awarded to a throwaway comment Wain made as they were about to leave Mistic Meadows. From the driver's seat in the Jeep, Key had pointed through the windshield to bright-yellow conductors attached to a wire running along the inside of the white board fence. "That wire with the yellow things is an electric fence," she'd told them. "Don't touch it. It'll zap you."

The boys slid forward to peer through the windshield. "Don't. Touch. Zap. Wire," Greggo echoed robotically.

"Unless you're a robot. Then it provides robot energy." Key turned to face the boys, whose mouths were open in wide O's. Laughing, she added, "Just kidding! Oh, and that's Vern's horse, Wain. The tan one."

Wain frowned. "Who's Vern?"

"The man who owns the house we're in. Zee's owner. You met him the other day."

"Oh yeah, the fat guy with the beard and that, like, *hair.*" Wain made wild waving motions around his head.

"Bangin'. Sounds. Like. Santa," Greggo intoned, and Key laughed again.

"Eww! He's not Santa!" Wain retorted, giggling and shoving Greggo with his shoulder. "He had blue glasses! And a gravestone tattoo! And a earring!"

Key turned. "Really? An earring?" Mary had mentioned the tattoo, which Key had seen when Vern was overexplaining the modem, but she'd missed the earring. So typical of Wain to notice.

"Yeah." Wain pushed himself a little farther between the two front seats, then brushed back his dark hair and pinched the helix of his ear.

"It's, like, way up under this curved part of your ear, you know? Eww! On a *old* guy! *Gross.*" He sounded so indignant.

Key pushed the ignition button. "It's not all that unusual for someone to have a piercing there, but I did not see that. You should be a detective, Wain. Nothing escapes your notice. Buckle up, buddy."

Wain clicked his seat belt. "And you know what else, Key?" he said nonchalantly. "It has, like, a star diamond in it. It's *just* like DP's!" He began giggling again at something Greggo said.

Key froze, goose bumps traveling down her spine, as finally, the memory that had been flickering in her subconscious fully lit up. *Zee. McKenzie. The lyrics to "Eleanor Rigby." Father McKenzie, who walks away from a grave.*

# Chapter 26

## AS NORMAL AS CAN BE

Sunday was rainy, and though he'd slept in until almost ten that morning and had jeep-shaped pancakes and a smoothie for brunch, Wain was uncharacteristically out of sorts. Key was positive he knew nothing about the canceled fishing trip, but it was almost as though he sensed that something he'd been anticipating had been snatched away.

She asked if he wanted to play a game (he didn't) or watch a movie (no), then tried to engage him by asking CartWheels questions and mentioning their upcoming trip to Porterville for the new car reveal, but even that elicited only flat, abbreviated replies.

"I'll be around if you want to do any of those things," Key told him kindly, after placing a hand on his forehead to see if he had a fever (he didn't). She switched on the gas fire and put soothing piano music on the Bluetooth speaker before she went about her chores, giving Wain an occasional affectionate rub on the back as she walked by the kitchen table where he'd spent the last hour sitting sideways on a chair, his head laying on his forearm, quietly studying a perfect line of CartWheels led by, as usual, Black Diamond. Maybe, Key mused as she tugged bed linens from the dryer, the cars' connection to his past helped Wain process the very real complications of his current seven-year-old life. *And he's probably exhausted.* It had been an extremely busy week.

Key suspected, too, that Wain's emotions had bubbled to the surface after observing Greggo with Raven. It was a terrible conundrum. She couldn't tell Wain just *how* dangerous his mother was, couldn't explain that in the safety deposit box at the bank was Lyric's letter signing away her parental rights after Key, with the help of Jukey and Mary, had uncovered her unthinkable plot to drown her own son for insurance money.

Guy knew only that Lyric had been complicit in Wain's abuse, nothing of the murder plot. Key was sticking to her plan to tell him at Christmas. It needed to be a face-to-face discussion.

During their latest call, after Wain went to bed, Guy had informed Key that Lyric pleaded guilty to the embezzlement charges and would remain incarcerated while awaiting sentencing. "She deserves what she gets. And more."

"I agree, Guy, but when I look at it through Wain's eyes, Lyric's sentence—whatever it is—won't alleviate his loss."

"You're right," Guy had said contritely. "It's hard for me to believe Wain misses her, but *of course* he does."

Barely aware of the rain lashing at the window, Key finished smoothing Wain's comforter over fresh sheets, then flopped onto his bed, leaning back on her elbows, studying the room. For Christmas, she'd order a set of custom canvas prints made from photos she'd taken. *Faro. Black Diamond. Guy. Bobcat. Bicycle. Tire swing.* "Oooh, and the fence chalk art!" she said aloud.

*Christmas.* She chuckled, remembering Greggo's observation about Vern. *Sounds. Like. Santa.* In the light of day, she was slightly embarrassed about the previous night's throw-Vern-off-the-scent conversation with her fake friend Sylvia. *An earring and a horse's name that matches one in a Beatles song.* Not exactly a smoking gun. Hardly even a smoking *coincidence.* At least no one had heard her.

After snuggling Wain's stuffed green dog next to the pillows, Key went to find her melancholic little boy, who was now slouched on the sofa next to Faro, tipping Black Diamond back and forth. He appeared a little less morose.

"Want to make cookies, buddy?" she asked casually. "We'll take some to Miss Bertie next door."

His eyes lit up. "Chocolate chip?" When she nodded, he said, "Yeah, okay. Hey Key, guess what. If you tip Black Diamond like this, you can see a jewel inside!"

"Seriously? Show me."

"Look in the window. You have to get your eye, like, really close. Like you're a giant, looking inside." He held the car close to her face and Key trained her "giant" eyeball on the window as Wain slowly tilted the car. A hologram of a diamond appeared, then disappeared. "Did you see that?"

"I did! Very cool! Is this the first time you've seen it?"

"Yeah, I noticed it today. I can't wait to show Ell and Greggo. And my dad." He slid Black Diamond into its mesh pocket, then zipped up the secret compartment.

Two hours later, they trooped through the rain to Bertie's front door.

"Can I give Miss Bertie the cookies?" Wain asked.

"Of course!" Key handed him the plate. With her foot, she lightly tapped the toe of Wain's rain boot. "Please take these off if she invites us in."

"Okay. She's gonna love these," Wain whispered, pressing the doorbell, then rocking eagerly back and forth on his heels.

It was worth every soggy step to see the delight on Bertie's face. "Oh my goodness, such welcome company on this gray day!"

"Hi Bertie! I would have called, but I realized I don't have your phone number."

"It's unlisted, but remind me to give it to you." Bertie pushed open the screen door. "Come in! Y'all have saved me from a nap that would have kept me up all night."

"We brought you these," Wain said shyly, handing her the plate.

"Oh my, don't these look delicious." The stream of animated chatter continued as she led them into her front room.

Fortunately, Bertie was ahead of them and still talking when Key bumped into Wain, who stopped short in the doorway and said, "Whoa. This is—" He stopped as Key touched his shoulder and looked back at her, eyes like saucers. When she put her finger to her lips, he nodded in understanding, and she patted his head, hearing in her mind the term her own very tidy and organized mother used to use. *Bunches and bundles*, she'd say cryptically, clicking her tongue on their way home from visiting people whose standards of acceptable clutter failed to meet hers.

Obviously, when Bertie wasn't outside or in her kitchen, the recliner Key had seen through the expansive bay window was her hangout. On the Formica table beside her chair, a landline telephone vied for space with myriad knitting supplies, several books, two bottles of lotion, the television remote, a chipped ceramic angel, a box of tissues, and a pile of wrappers beside a glass dish of hard candies. Under the table was a clear plastic bin holding more books, stacks of gardening magazines, and a heating pad, its cord dangling over the side.

Bertie thumped the plate of cookies on top of an ancient metal trunk in front of the couch, then gestured toward a card table across the room. "I checked out a new puzzle from the library, but these old eyes need a break! Let's have some coffee and maybe fresh apple juice? Troy Grocery has it in stock again. I used to pick apples and make it myself, but I gave that up years ago. Have you ever picked apples, Wain?" Wain shook his head. He hadn't stopped staring around the room.

"That sounds fun," Key said. "Is there an orchard near here?"

"A couple three. My favorite is Brunswick Acres. You'll enjoy all the activities." Bertie stated it positively, as though they'd already made plans to go. "Now you two stay put. I'll be right back." She indicated a weathered oak buffet with a bulky television on top. "Look in there, young Wain! I've got Tinkertoys, a tea-party set, a jar of marbles and … I can't recall what all. Oh, this makes my day!" She pulled the plastic wrap off the plate of cookies, scooped up two almost-empty coffee cups, and bustled out of the room.

"Should I look in there?" Wain whispered.

"Definitely!" Key set aside three crocheted throw pillows so old that they were back in fashion and sank like a stone into the decrepit sofa cushions, watching as Wain pulled out a jar of marbles and a bin of doll dishes, then an ancient, lidless cardboard box held together by yellowed, disintegrating tape.

"Whoa! Look at this!" He was almost squealing. Inside the box were at least a dozen miniature horses, plastic bales of hay, fencing, farm implements, and a roll of green felt decorated to look like a garden. "Horses! And a dog! Two dogs!"

It was wonderful to see his sunny equilibrium bouncing back. "Here, use the top of the trunk." Feeling as though she were playing a living room version of the square-sliding number games she'd had as a kid, Key moved the cookies to Bertie's Formica table and a precariously tipping pile of unopened mail to the puzzle table. She arranged the mail in two stacks. Judging by the envelopes, it looked like every charity known to man had Bertie Montgomery on their mailing list. The irony, Key thought wryly, that three thick envelopes were from the Save The Trees Foundation.

"Here we are!" Bertie handed Key a homely painted mug that said *MISS BERTIE'S the BEST* in a childish script, set a cup of apple juice on the trunk for Wain, and after retrieving her own coffee, helped herself to a cookie and settled with a happy sigh onto her recliner. "Oh, you've found my very favorite, Wain!"

# Chapter 27

## THE PINE PATCH STRING

"But nowadays I can't keep up—there are so many new folks." For the past half hour, Bertie had been regaling Key with what seemed like the full history of Troy, North Carolina. "This little pinpoint on the map is not the same small town it was in the sixties, when Jimmy Dean bought this house."

"Over fifty years of living in the same house. That's amazing!"

"This part is the original." Bertie gestured around the room. "The two bedrooms down the hall are much newer. I call that section the 'Pine Patch.'"

"Oh, did you add on?" Key sipped watery coffee and watched Wain add the finishing touches to a miniature Mistic Meadows. It had to be over eighty degrees in Bertie's house, and the sofa cushions were hypnotically soft. She'd have to be careful not to shut her eyes.

"No, honey, I had to have it rebuilt. One night during a storm, Mother Nature decided to topple the neighbor's enormous pine tree onto that end of the house."

"Oh, Bertie, how scary!"

"Fortunately, I was gone when it happened, on a tour of Maine with Georgia. Gerald called our hotel room to tell me about the hole in my roof, rainwater pouring in." She clucked her tongue. "He arranged for Mayweather's to cut up the tree that very day."

"Mayweather? Tree trimming?" Key asked, suddenly alert.

"They're a very prominent family in Troy. Jack-of-all-trades, really. Tree trimming was just one of their businesses."

"I've seen the Mayweather boutique downtown, but I've never been in there."

Bertie sniffed. "Oh, that's what's her name's hobby. Ursula. The one who married the younger Mayweather boy, Adam, who is probably twenty-five years older." Bertie chuckled. "You know what my friend Doris at the senior center calls her? The atrophy wife! Because Adam's gonna be a shriveled-up old man when that gal is still kicking up her stiletto heels! And then Yolanda Henson said, 'So she's a fool's gold digger?' And we about fell off our chairs!" Key burst out laughing, and Bertie was so amused at her own jokes that she began to cough. "She's not from around here," she gasped, wiping tears from her eyes when she could finally talk.

*I knew it.* Key could still hear Ursula's discordant honking behind her.

"The older Mayweathers were the salt of the earth, but ..." Bertie grimaced. "*Well.* If I can't say anything nice, I'll say nothing at all."

Though she would have loved to hear more, Key changed the subject. "How did the falling tree miss your roses?"

"Eh? Oh! That's my miracle." Bertie sketched an air-picture explanation. "The branches of another tree prevented it falling onto my roses. A few bushes were damaged but not killed. Oh, what a mess I came home to!" she declared, shaking her head. "I lived in a rental apartment for months while Plummer Construction rebuilt that part of the house. Riggs was on that crew. Nearly every day, I brought them cinnamon rolls and saved the gooiest middle one for my Riggs." She paused, sighed, then added, "After the roof and walls were repaired, there was a full week of residual cleanup. Mud. Tree bark. Sawdust. Leaves. I found pine needles in odd places for years after."

Key sat up straighter. "What year did this happen?"

"1996 …. No, 1997?" Bertie tapped her chin, then heaved herself out of her recliner and selected two framed pictures from a dusty bookshelf. Handing one to Key, she said, "Take the picture out of the frame, honey, and check the back. That was taken the day before the tree fell."

The photo showed a much-younger Bertie with another vibrant woman, both in rain jackets, arms around one another, standing in front of a lighthouse. Key removed the picture and read aloud, "'West Quoddy Head, 8/97.'" She replaced the picture and the backing. "That looks like a fun trip."

"It's all fun and games until a tree falls on your house, right?" Bertie quipped jovially. She held up the other picture. "Here are the Plummers, Christmas 1997. Less than a year before Riggs disappeared. Look at little DP! He's eleven!"

"Can I see?" Wain fetched the picture and sat down by Key, his lower extremities almost disappearing between the cushions. Together they studied the four formally dressed Plummers, parents seated and boys standing. They looked … so very happy. Successful. Confident. A family unaware of the seismic heartache to come. *Riggs,* Key telegraphed wistfully to the smiling young man next to Olive, *ask Lonny to walk to the john with you.*

"Which one's DP?" Wain asked.

"The younger one, honey," Bertie answered. After checking out an as yet earringless DP, Wain slid off the couch and went to get a cookie.

*Riggs's earring!* Key looked closer. Yes, there it was, a blurry little glint, visible under a mop of wavy blond hair framing a handsome young face with an irresistible slightly crooked grin. Easy to see how he'd charm the socks off female fans. "That's a beautiful picture."

"It makes me so happy and so sad all at the same time." Bertie picked up her knitting. Needles began to click. "Tch, tch. What Olive has gone through!" A pause. "She's never been the same."

"I don't see how it could be any other way," Key said soberly, again watching Wain. What if he disappeared? She couldn't think about it.

*Click, click.* "Such tremendous, ongoing loss," Bertie said, more to herself than to Key.

"Did you hire the cleanup crew, Bertie? The one that did the mucking out after your home repair was finished?"

"No, honey, that was all done through insurance."

"Do you recall the name of the business?"

Bertie shot her a curious look. "Who? The cleanup crew? Not offhand. They were hard workers, but I made sure to be there when they were cleaning. They were a rather … shady outfit."

"Bertie, is there *any* way you still have the paperwork? Like, receipts or bills or insurance information?"

Bertie thought for a moment. "I don't like to hang on to junk," she replied seriously, and Key had to look away to compose herself. "But I may have kept it for tax purposes or in case I sold the house. But that company is long gone. If you're looking for someone to clean your new place, I can provide recommendations."

"Thank you! I may need postconstruction cleanup." Key thought quickly, then decided to take a chance. "Bertie, may I tell you something in confidence?"

"Of course, honey." Bertie set her knitting in her lap, her eyes bright and interested.

"I'm trying to track down a guy who may have worked in 1997 for the company that did your cleanup. If I could get the name of that business, it might give me a place to start."

"Who's the fella?"

Key took a deep breath. "Ayo Jones."

"Riggs's so-called friend. What do you want with *him*?" Bertie asked, screwing up her face in distaste. The needles began clicking again, much more furiously. "He wasn't on the crew that cleaned up here. I would have recognized him. Oh, Dawson and Olive did *not* like that man."

"I'd like to find him," Key said again. "Employment records could help."

"You're a sleuth?" Bertie's expression had turned inscrutable.

"I'm not a sleuth." Key said. "I'm just looking for—"

"Because the Plummers have been very clear that they don't want to live in a state of upset. Do Olive and Dawson know you're doing this?"

"No," Key answered bluntly. "But DP does."

Bertie tipped her head, thoughtfully studying Key's face, then again pushed herself out of her chair. "Come with me, honey. I store my files in the Pine Patch. Let's take a look."

# Chapter 28

## A MEETING OR TWO AT JAVA U

From: wolverine@insideoutlines.com

To: k.e.y.n.@underlinemedia.net

RE: Riggs Plummer

Hi, Key. I'm very interested in talking with you. Do you have time to meet me in Porterville tomorrow morning, Monday? If so, please tell me when and where. If that doesn't work, I'll be out of town until next Thursday and will contact you once I'm back. My thanks for reaching out. Wolverine

till tremendously surprised at the almost-instantaneous reply she'd received to the impulsive email she'd sent using the Contact Me button on the *Inside Outlines* website, Key considered her options. *It's doable, and I need to go to Porterville anyway.* Before she answered Wolverine, though, she texted Cissy, who agreed to meet Wain at Bullfrog Rock if Key wasn't back in time.

*Yes,* Wolverine replied to her follow-up email, he would meet her at Java U at 10 a.m. He'd look on the patio for the woman in a blue jacket with a black dog on a red leash. *Sounds like a cold war spy novel*, he wrote at the end, to Key's amusement.

Key let Faro out and went to check on Wain. He'd gone to bed his normal upbeat self, telling Key he was excited to see his classmates and Sheba the gerbil the next morning. She was even more grateful than usual for the structure and social outlet his school provided.

***

On the drive to Porterville, Key replayed *Inside Outlines*: "The Disappearance of Riggs Plummer." Without Vern Olson's obnoxious, distracting interruptions, the story Wolverine told was far more cohesive.

She arrived at Java U fifteen minutes early, and after looping Faro's leash around a patio column, she entered through the back door and joined a queue that snaked around several tables. It was all so familiar: the cheery baristas in their collegiate-themed aprons; the caffeinated conversational buzz; the comfy, eclectic, always-occupied seating arrangement by the front window. No, Java U hadn't changed, but she was New Key, visiting a spot where Old Key, whom she barely recognized anymore, had spent countless hours designing cards or visiting with friends. *Do I* look *different?* Her life now was so fundamentally altered; how could her face—her entire *being*—not reflect that?

She was feeling quite fashionable in black skinny jeans, a royal-blue blazer, heeled black ankle boots, and pearl drop earrings. Plucking several decidedly unfashionable dog hairs from her sleeve, she grinned, recalling her earlier conversation with Wain. He had been eating breakfast at the kitchen island, watching Key transfer everything from her normal purse to a leather crossbody messenger bag roomy enough to include her laptop. She'd explained that she was going to Porterville for a meeting and to run errands, assuring him that Cissy would be at Bullfrog Rock if she wasn't.

Wain contemplated her while chewing a chunk of cantaloupe. "I like your earrings."

"Thank you, honey! I like them too. They're pearls."

"Why do you look so different today? I mean, like, pretty?" he'd asked, and she nearly choked on a bite of granola bar, then thanked him, explaining that she wanted to look nice for her meeting. As she waited to order her latte, she kept an eye on the front door. Based on the few pictures she'd found online, she was looking for a nice-looking man in his mid-forties.

"Oh my good *gosh*! Key North! Hello! I'd give you a hug, but my latte might spill!"

Key turned to see a woman balancing an oversize green-and-blue coffee cup on an orange saucer. Nina LaDane, former Sage Pointe neighbor. Buxom, flirty, gossipy, perfumy, almost-invisibly enhanced. She looked years younger than Key knew she was.

Key gave her a wide smile and a light arm squeeze. "Hi, Nina! How are you?" Her conversations with Nina had always stayed in safe, uncomplicated territory: fashion, shopping, the latest cosmetic procedures (about which Nina knew everything and Key knew nothing), Florida Gators football (ditto), or dogs.

"Doing well!" Nina beamed at her. "You look very chic, Key! Love the jacket. Are you back living in Porterville? The rural experiment with the little boy is over?"

"No, I'm still living in Troy with Wain. I love it." Key reminded herself to be on guard. Nina was close with Iris, Key's former friend who had adamantly disapproved of her move to Troy and (especially) her budding relationship with Wain. Iris had gone incommunicado after Key finally found the courage to stand up to her, and of course, Nina would have heard some version of this (one that made Key the villain, she was sure). Hence the term "rural experiment." Coming from Nina, though, the comment held none of Iris's acidity.

"Join us?" Nina pointed with her chin at a table where three women sat, watching. They smiled and waggled fingers at her, and Key waved back. She knew them by sight but couldn't remember their names.

"I'm sorry, Nina, I can't—I'm meeting someone."

"Oooh! A *someone*?" Nina raised her perfectly shaped eyebrows and glanced around. "Is the *someone* here?"

Patting her messenger bag, Key replied nicely but firmly, "A business meeting. I've also got my dog with me, so we're sitting out on the patio."

"Ooo, you got anothow pup-pup?" Nina exclaimed, lapsing into the peculiar lisping baby talk Key suddenly recalled from previous canine-related chitchat. "Well, Key, stop by our table with your *someone* if you have time!" She swished away, her texting fingers no doubt heating up as fast as her latte was cooling. Iris would be reading the latest before Wolverine darkened the coffee shop's door. Key could see it now: *Saw Key at Java U! With a man!!*

The patio, with its teak furniture, hanging planters, blue umbrellas, and ivy-covered walls, was cool but not uncomfortably so. Key selected a table near the door, wiped up a few wet spots on the chairs, and laid out her laptop and notebook. With one hand wrapped around her sophomore-sized to-go skinny latte, she listened to traffic and watched the leaves drift lazily down, as though they knew this first day of October would not tolerate their procrastination as permissive September had. As much as Key loved her new life, it was pleasant to be here again, absorbing the energy of the city. When Faro suddenly stood, she looked up.

"Is there a code word, ma'am, or am I allowed to sit?" A smiling man in jeans and a black hoodie sweatshirt bearing the *Inside Outlines* logo took the seat across from her and slid a small paper cup full of whipped cream across the table. "Pup'n'Fluff. For the pup, if he's— she's?—allowed."

"He. His name is Faro. Thank you!" Never would she tell this kind stranger that two minutes before, she'd discarded the exact same cup (empty) after Faro practically inhaled the one she'd purchased. She extended her hand. "I'm Key North. Thank you very much for meeting with me."

# Chapter 29

## GABRIEL

"Gabriel Mink." He telegraphed a sincere, confident kindness that instantly put her at ease. "A pleasure, Key. Thank *you* for meeting on such short notice, and for making the drive."

He was just over six feet tall, with a runner's fat-free body, dark-blond hair cut short enough that the gray at his temples was almost invisible, wide-set blue eyes, strong chin sporting a few days' stubble, high cheekbones, and an effortless smile. She'd describe him as very attractive rather than handsome—and in Key's mind, there was a difference.

"Have we met?" she asked. "I lived in Porterville for several years before I moved to Troy, and you seem familiar to me."

He smiled. "It's the voice. I was a radio DJ in various parts of the country until I moved to Porterville." That explained his lack of a Southern accent. "And now it's the voice of the podcast."

*No. It's more than that.* Key decided not to press it. "I once stood in line behind Tom Brokaw in a grocery store, and as soon as he said something to the clerk, I knew instantly who it was. I never would have noticed him otherwise. It was the voice."

"I'm no Tom Brokaw, but that's exactly what happens. It drives people crazy trying to figure it out." Gabriel pulled the lid off his cup and waved the steam away, then turned his chair sideways, stretched his legs out, stacked one foot on the other, and interlocked his hands behind his head. "I love Java U."

"It was one of my favorite haunts when I lived here."

"So what took you to Troy?" Gabriel asked. He had plenty of questions for her as she recounted Jeff's death, her impulsive purchase of Pike House, how Wain and Faro had come to join her, and their temporary move to Veronica View. *Of course* he'd want to vet her, she thought. He was the one publicly telling others' heartbreaking stories; he would be on the hook if a source turned out to be some kind of crackpot, fangirl wannabe detective attempting to piggyback on his podcast success.

Gabriel became even more attentive when she mentioned that DP was doing her remodel. "Very, very interesting. How'd you hear about my podcast?"

"A woman named Mary King. She and her husband own an antique store in Troy—and she is locally famous for her pies and baked goods. She's one of your biggest fans."

"Pies, you say?" Gabriel grinned. "Sounds like someone I need to meet. Please thank her for me. So, Key, may I ask—why the interest in this case? No offense, but your connection to the Plummers seems a bit ... tenuous. Are you an online sleuth?"

Key laughed. "No. But you're the second person to use the word 'sleuth' on me in two days."

Gabriel picked up his cup. "Online sleuths are both a blessing and a curse. We spend an inordinate amount of time confirming leads and information. We can't be too careful."

"I completely understand. Like I said in my email, I *might* have a tiny lead on where to find Ayo Jones, but I don't know what to do with it. I'm hoping you can help." Key smoothed the small stack of papers she'd set on the table.

Gabriel lifted his hand. "Before we get to that. Do you know Olive and Dawson?"

"I've only briefly met them, once at an Orion concert, and once at a party at my house. DP, as I said, is my contractor, so I know him best."

"I *really* wanted to interview the Plummers for my first podcast," Gabriel said wistfully. "But when I called Dawson, I got shot down almost before I formed a full sentence."

"Everyone grieves differently," Key said, thinking how difficult it must be for Gabriel to approach these families and ask them to examine unhealed wounds, then share their pain publicly. "There's a huge reward still being offered for information on Riggs, so the Plummers are obviously still hopeful."

"Yes. My podcast has donated. We have a charitable foundation that contributes to search efforts and reward funds. You'd think with all that money at stake, someone would have come forward by now. Unless they were guilty."

"My thoughts exactly," Key replied, still racking her brain. *Where* had she seen this man? Faro wandered toward Gabriel's chair, accepted a back scratch, then flopped down with a noisy sigh like a bored child. Around them, the patio was filling up, and at one table, three women were staring and surreptitiously snapping photos. If Gabriel was aware, he paid no attention.

"And by the way," Key continued, "I thought you covered Riggs's case very well. Talking to the Richmond police, interviewing the girl, getting Ayo's name out there …."

He smiled. "Thanks. It was adequate, but I had to leave a lot on the cutting-room floor, so to speak. Riggs's girlfriend, Carly, being one of them."

"I wondered!" Key exclaimed. "I noticed Carly was never mentioned."

Gabriel grimaced. "Yep. That's the main question I got after that podcast. *What about the girlfriend?* Bottom line, she told me Riggs never told her he was coming and, as we all know, never showed up."

"You talked to her?"

"Yes. She's a dermatologist, lives in Albuquerque. Happily married, young children. We had a pleasant conversation over the phone, but she asked me not to mention her, not even with an alias, because it's too disruptive. Her part in the story is minimal, it hasn't changed in twenty years, and she especially doesn't want to cause more pain to the Plummers. She also said she thinks about Riggs every day."

"Wow," Key said. "You've done so many podcasts since, and you still remember everything."

Gabriel held up his phone. "It's all in a cloud file. But every day I feel it *here*." He laid his fist on his heart. "This one is just ... extra heavy."

"I feel the same way. And so does Lonny Morgan, Riggs's best friend."

Gabriel's eyes widened. "You know Lonny?"

"Yes. His daughter is friends with Wain. Wonderful family."

"*Wow!* So he's out now! Man, I was so bummed when the prison turned down my interview request."

"I can tell you what he's told me." Key leafed through the papers she'd copied for Gabriel.

"What's your opinion, Key? Could Lonny have been involved somehow?"

She stared at him. Was he serious? "There's *no* way," she answered emphatically. "Lonny was a lifetime friend who loved Riggs like a brother. To this day, he regrets that he didn't, as he puts it, 'walk with Riggs to the john.'"

"But didn't he run away to Florida shortly after Riggs went missing?"

Key suppressed a prickle of protective irritation. "He did leave Troy, to get away, and the theft that put him in prison was years later."

"Online forums were full of suspicion about Lonny."

"Well, they're wrong," Key replied, completely exasperated. "Shasta, who you interviewed, can vouch for Lonny's whereabouts both at the concert *and* the drive home. And DP told me that his family absolutely believes Lonny and Shasta."

"Hey, look, Key, I've got no axe to grind with anyone," Gabriel said mildly, picking up his cup. "When I called Shasta to ask her opinion about the online speculation, she got angry—said she never would have consented to an interview if blaming Lonny was the outcome."

Slightly mollified, Key detailed every answer Lonny had provided while Gabriel took notes in the speedy *tick-tick-tick* thumb-typing way that she despaired of ever mastering. She slid a copy of the concert venue sketch toward him and traced a finger along the arrow Lonny had drawn. "Here's their group. Here's the portable toilets. Look how simple Riggs's route is."

"He wasn't hiking alone on a treacherous trail or meeting drug dealers in a back alley or living a life of skullduggery owing money to shadowy Mafia figures." Gabriel's face reflected the mystified look Key had come to associate with every conversation involving Riggs. "So what's your theory, Key? Unlucky hitchhiker?"

"Nope," Key said firmly. "I believe one person—Ayo Jones— knows what happened. I believe Ayo is the key to solving *all* of it. As you so aptly put it on your podcast, 'Why did Ayo get out of Dodge so fast?'"

"I said that? Get out of Dodge?" Gabriel rolled his eyes. "Classy, Wolverine," he said to himself.

"I liked it! It evokes the sense of someone sneaking away from Troy, which is what I believe Ayo did." Key handed Gabriel another paper. "I have *no* idea where Riggs is, but this potential lead to Ayo materialized smack-dab in the living room of the house I'm renting. It's my landlord."

"Your landlord," Gabriel repeated flatly, looking skeptical.

Key flushed. "Yes. To be honest, I'm terrified of wasting your time, Gabriel, but"—here she held up her thumb and forefinger, nearly touching—"I believe there is a tiny bit of evidence pointing to him."

"'Vern Olson,'" Gabriel read aloud, holding his phone horizontally over the paper and snapping a photo. "Okay, so ..." He gave a humorous little shrug. "You seem like a sane, logical person, Key. I mean, you must have *some* reason to suspect this guy."

Key sat forward, leaning her forearms on the table. "Yes. A few very strange tiny coincidences that I promise to share with you later, but maybe it would be best to see what, if anything, you can find on Vern Olson without my saying more." Her words sounded as foolish as she'd feared.

He sighed. "Can you elaborate just a little, at least?"

"Aside from my evidence, which is so thin that it's literally a wisp of circumstantial smoke, I have nothing more than what's on that paper: his wife Deirdre's phone number, the Troy address, and the fact that they are currently living in an RV somewhere in Arizona. They plan to return in February. Oh, and I have this photo." She handed him her phone. "Not my best work." She smiled despite the awkwardness.

Gabriel laughed out loud. "Well, the guy's got a lot of wild gray hair, and I can see part of a messy-looking beard. I can't see his face. The kid's back is in the way."

"That's Wain."

"Okay. Mind if I text it to myself?" After handing her phone back, he began asking questions, again typing her answers. "The Olson's address in Arizona?"

"No idea. I send all correspondence to a PO box in South Dakota. It's forwarded from there."

"Huh. Okay, Vern's or Deirdre's birth date? License plate of the car and/or RV? Deirdre's maiden name?"

"No idea. No idea. No idea. But I searched for Vern and Deirdre Olson online, and it's a blank page. Neither he nor his wife are on social media either, at least not with those names."

Gabriel perked up a little. "That is odd. There's almost always something out there. What name is associated with the purchase of the house?"

"I didn't think to look that up!" Key exclaimed. "At least you know I was telling the truth. I'm not a sleuth."

Gabriel laughed. "Not a problem, we'll do it. You said you had one other lead."

"Back in the late nineties, Ayo Jones worked for a disaster cleanup company, which may have been called 'Castle Phoenix.'"

*Tap-tap-tap.* "'Phoenix' as in the city, or 'phoenix' as in rising from the ashes?"

"Ashes, I'd guess. They were based out of Porterville at the time. The lady who lives next door to my rental used them in 1997."

Gabriel nodded. "You're thinking they may have employment records. Are they still in business?"

"My neighbor says no. She also says they were sketchy but did good work."

"Okay. Anything else?"

"This." Key handed Gabriel the timeline she'd made. "Here's what I have so far. If it's in green ink, it's a fact. If it's in red, it's a possible scenario."

"Impressive! How did you compile all this?"

"Mostly conversations with Lonny and DP. And the neighbor lady. But this is interesting, Gabriel." She touched the paper. "Look at the date your podcast on Riggs came out."

"I don't have to look. Tuesday, April 1, 2014. April Fool's Day."

"Now look at when Deirdre Olson told me they moved to Troy."

"June 2014." He raised his head. "You're saying there's a correlation between my podcast and their move to Troy? That's a bit of a stretch, isn't it?"

"Most likely. But it's a fact. I put it on there because, added to other strange coincidences, it may be significant."

"The coincidences you're not telling me about."

Key inclined her head. "*Yet*. And here's another thing." She pointed to green printing that said *TALK WITH MACK*. "Vern has a security camera in his backyard, and a couple weeks ago, when I first found out about Riggs, I talked to my … my good friend Mack about it on the phone while sitting in a chair near the house. Which means Vern heard that conversation and knew I knew about Riggs." She described the storm, the internet outage, the lock on the stairway door, and Vern's oddly timed appearance. "I offered to reboot the modem if they sent me the key, but I got the distinct impression he did *not* want me upstairs. Now why would that be? What's up there?" She didn't mention Vern's horse or the ride he'd taken that afternoon.

Gabriel rested his chin on his palm. "The living room, the upstairs, and the yard. Apparently, you don't go searching for intrigue, it comes to you. You've got me hooked simply because it's so … so …"

"Nutty?" The more she talked, the more preposterous it all sounded. Gabriel was very gracious, but she could sense his disappointment. Key scooped up Faro's paper cup and tossed it into the garbage can. "Swish," she said lightly, but inside she was cringing.

Gabriel leaned back in his chair and reviewed his notes. "The neighbor lady you mentioned, who hired Castle Phoenix. What's her name?"

"Bertie Montgomery. She's around eighty and still sharp as a tack." *Does Gabriel resemble someone famous? Did he sit next to me on a plane? Speak at one of Jeff's many conventions?* It was driving her crazy.

Gabriel whirled to face Key, his eyes wide, his face pale enough to showcase a faint sprinkle of freckles across his nose.

"What is it?" she asked curiously, glancing around the patio.

"Oh, uh, nothing." Swallowing hard, he sat back, then shut his eyes and ran his hand over his face, saying with a shaky chuckle, "Whew! I sometimes get names and faces mixed up. Hazards of living so many places."

Key hoped her face looked as neutral as her voice sounded. "The same thing happens to me."

*Is* that *how I know him? This cannot be.*

# Chapter 30
## CLOUDY CLARITY

"Key!" A familiar voice trilled from Java U's back doorway, making both her and Faro jump. Gabriel simply sat, staring at his phone, as though he hadn't recovered from whatever had shocked him.

"Yikes. Town crier," Key said softly, standing up and closing her laptop. It would never do for Nina LaDane to catch even a whiff of what they'd been discussing. Gabriel took another deep breath and stood too, tucking the papers Key had given him into the kangaroo pocket of his hoodie. He'd pasted on a polite smile by the time Nina sashayed over to their table, carrying yet another Pup'n'Fluff, this one with a tiny, frosted bone-shaped biscuit topper.

"Key, I just came out to say it was so nice to see you! And I thought maybe your pup-pup might like the Fluff Supremo, if that's all right with you?"

"That's very nice, thank you, Nina! His name is Faro." *Curiosity fed the dog*, Key thought humorously.

"Ooh, Farrell!" Nina hunkered down, making kissy noises. "My three itsy-bitsy Yorkie-barkies wouldn't add up to one of ooo, big bubba!"

"Nina, this is—" Key stopped, unsure how Gabriel preferred to be introduced.

"Oh, I *know!*" Nina quickly stood,  baby talk replaced by a simpering gush of words. "Wolverine, we saw you come out here, and we said, 'No way, *that* can't be who's meeting with our *friend* Key!' I came out to bring this to Key's adorable dog Farrell, and it turns out it *was* you!"

"In the flesh." Gabriel flashed a practiced but genuine smile.

Nina stepped closer. "There are a group of ladies from our neighborhood who meet at our clubhouse every Tuesday afternoon to have sangria and tapas and listen to true-crime podcasts! Yours is our favorite! We call ourselves the 'Sage Sleuths'! We've donated to your fundraisers, and we have an online club too! Oh, I wish I'd worn my sweatshirt! We'd be twins!" She fluffed her hair and tugged at her denim jacket, then smoothed her hands down her thighs.

"Thank you very much," Gabriel said sincerely. "So many families have depleted all their resources looking for missing loved ones."

"Sage Pointe has a podcast detective club?" Key asked Nina. That was one club she would have joined. "How long have you been meeting?"

"Oh, let me think." Nina placed a finger on her chin, frowning prettily. "At least four years now, because we've heard all your podcasts, Wolverine!"

"Thanks," Gabriel said again.

"We're very selective about who we invite to join!" Nina rattled on, now addressing Key. "Iris is in it, *of course!* Actually, Key, when we started meeting, I thought you'd be a perfect fit, but Iris said you weren't interested and not to bring it up because you told her you aren't a joiner—which is totally cool, not everyone is—then um ... well, Jeff passed, and ... you know ... and then you moved."

Key leaned down to pick up the third empty paper cup. It wasn't Nina's fault, but how *should* she react to discovering yet another way Iris had been manipulating her life and sidelining her friendships? *It doesn't matter now.* She tossed the cup into the garbage. How appropriate to this discovery.

Nina dug into her handbag for a small notebook. "May I get your autograph, Wolverine? Make it to *N-I-N-A* and the Sage Sleuths? Sounds like a rock band!" She giggled and held out her phone toward Key. "Do you mind?"

Gabriel obligingly posed and signed. "Nice to meet you, Nina. Please keep spreading the word, encourage everyone to share reviews, and if you have information, you can contact me through my website."

"Oooh! I will!" Nina wasn't inclined to go. "So how do *you* two know each other?"

Before Key could answer, Gabriel smiled and said easily, "Friends slash associates. Key and I go way back."

*Oh, the Sage Sleuths will have a heyday with that one.* Key eased her messenger-bag strap over her shoulder and unhooked Faro's leash. "Well, errands to run and miles to drive and a little schoolboy to pick up. Thanks for Faro's treat. It was good to see you, Nina!" She meant it. Ironically, this cloudy day had provided clearer views of the most unexpected vistas.

Gabriel pushed his chair under the table. "And I've got a plane to catch."

Nina waggled her fingers and reluctantly returned inside.

"I've got some merch in my truck for you and your friends." Gabriel appeared fully recovered as they headed to the parking lot. "Regardless of where your information takes us, Key, it was good to discuss Riggs again. His case is still number one on my 'Want to Solve' list. In fact, it's how I ended up in Porterville! I came to research his disappearance, and I unexpectedly fell in love with this area."

"North Carolina seems to have that effect." Key had met countless people with similar stories. Visitors became residents. "I sincerely hope my piece of the Riggs puzzle isn't a huge waste of time," she added, feeling anything but hopeful.

Gabriel touched her shoulder. "Hope's what it's all about, Key. You never know how things will connect."

"It's obviously close to your heart." She was bursting with questions she couldn't ask.

"Yes. Solving this case would be ... *tectonic*." At his truck, he filled a large bag, then shook her hand with both of his. "I enjoyed our Cold War spy meeting, Key North."

"Same here," she replied, her mind still racing, refusing to acknowledge what she thought she saw. "Thank you for everything, Gabriel Mink."

# Chapter 31

## THE HEART STRING

"I'll be right down the street for a few minutes, buddy." Key stashed the bag Gabriel had given her in the Jeep and cracked the windows. It was a cool day, she was parked in the shade, and Faro never minded dozing in the back.

At Imagine That, the tiny hobby store where they'd found Wain's latest CartWheel, SunBolt, Key was greeted by a friendly older woman who told her regretfully that they didn't carry fishing poles. She took a quick walk down the red-and-black-checkered aisle anyway, checked the CartWheels display (empty, with a sign that read *WATCH THIS SPACE*), and soon found herself with an armload of projects: an art kit, a model car, two games, and a box of beginner science experiments. Wain loved the precision of baking and cooking; maybe he'd enjoy making a mini volcano or a tornado in a jar. She also found a toddler's veterinarian set and couldn't resist buying it for Dibsy. At the clothing rack, she scored a rare CartWheels-logo T-shirt in Wain's size. Feeling as though she'd won the lottery, she set everything on the counter and went back for one last look.

A colorful box caught her eye. *Yo Ho PIRATES!! FIND BURIED TREASURE!!* Below the proclamation, a boy and a girl in pristine pirate garb ecstatically unearthed a chest of gold coins. "Are you kidding me?" she said aloud. Who was she to resist fate? Laughing, she added two more boxes to the stack.

The woman she'd spoken to earlier wedged herself behind the counter. "Looks like some lucky kids are going treasure hunting."

"Yes. My ... grandson, Wain, has a friend who wants to be a pirate. This is probably as close as she'll get. I hope."

"Metal detecting is addictive; you never know what you'll find! Just walking down our driveway, my husband found fourteen cents, a nice old metal button, and a bunch of handmade nails."

"They'll love it. Wain is also very excited for the CartWheels reveal party."

"Oh, did y'all get an invite?" the woman exclaimed. "With the QR code?"

"Yes. From Evie."

"I'm Evie's mom, Charlie. Well, honey, you've already hit buried treasure! That code gives you VIP access! CartWheel reveals are always such exciting days. Door prizes, a drawing for some special one-of-a-kind items, and best of all ... the new car! We will see you both on Saturday!"

Key's next stop was Porterville Farm Store, a sprawling two-story structure on the south edge of town. Riding boots in Wain's size were easy to find, and with the help of a friendly employee, she found two child-sized fishing poles and a prefilled tackle box with lures and bobbers and hooks and sinkers. She'd have to watch YouTube videos; when it came to fishing, she had no idea where to begin. Maybe Mack or Guy would do a tutorial video call.

*One more thing.* In the home-goods section, she added a coffee maker, an assortment of pods, and four horse-themed stoneware mugs to her cart.

While in line, she sent a text to Cissy, telling her she'd be back in time, and after wolfing down two delectable tacos from the farm store's crowded café, she gassed up the Jeep and headed back to Troy.

*What a day.* She muted the radio, thankful for the silence and the chance to reflect and plan. The next several days would be busy, but thankfully, she had pockets of free time.

Tuesday. She'd invited Ell to come home from school with Wain. Key missed her and was eager to hear if she'd spoken to Cav about Tally Mayweather.

Wednesday. Wain had his first Saddle Happy riding lesson that evening. It was all he'd been talking about—well, that and the CartWheels reveal party. She loved seeing him so excited.

Thursday. She had an early evening parent-teacher conference with Mrs. Goos, who'd instantly approved Guy's suggestion that he participate via video.

Friday. After school, they'd drop Faro off at the kennel, and Key and Wain would go to Porterville to stay at the hotel.

Saturday. CartWheels reveal party at Imagine That. It was sure to be a wonderful memory for Wain.

*What a week.* She sighed happily. Yes, she might be asleep on her feet by Wain's bedtime, but the whirlwind of activity generated by his presence also energized her, gave her purpose and fulfillment. Add to that Mack's potential visit, Guy's calls, her fascination with the mystery surrounding Riggs, and her home renovation, and she woke up every day with a sense of anticipation she hadn't had since childhood.

She turned up the radio. Humming to the Lumineers' "Cleopatra," she searched for a word to describe her life. *Restored.* That was it. Admittedly, seeing Nina LaDane at Java U had awoken a twinge of familiar hurt when Key learned how Iris had excluded her, but it had quickly faded. She would never choose that life again, so why should their actions affect her anymore? She laughed to herself, thinking of Gabriel's words. *Friends slash associates. We go way back.* The Sage Sleuths would be attempting to unravel that one over sangria and tapas for at least a month.

*Gabriel.* She was ten miles from Troy when she finally allowed her mind to address the current star in her meteor shower of thoughts. What was the peculiar word he had used? *Tectonic.* She frowned. *Stay focused, Key. Curious as you may be, those are not your tectonic plates to shift.*

She pulled into the driveway at Veronica View. Another Riggs string tugged from a completely unexpected direction; and this time it was tugging mightily at her very curious heart.

# Chapter 32

## GOLD STAR

Key stashed her purchases in the recesses of her bedroom closet, hurriedly changed into walking clothes, and arrived hot and out of breath at Bullfrog Rock just as the children spilled out, as colorful and bouncy as beads breaking free from a necklace. After such a hectic, impactful day, the simple task of meeting Wain was a soothing reminder of what mattered most.

Wain told her about a girl in his class who'd given him a gummy worm that looked exactly like a real worm, then burst out, "Hey, Key, aren't you gonna ask what's in the good jar today?"

"Oh … yes!" Lately, Key had let up on the good/tough jar conversations. Some days simply weren't that exciting *or* tough, and she never wanted Wain to dread the question or feel forced to answer. "What goes in the good jar?"

"Well …" he said dramatically as he stopped and pulled off his CartWheels backpack. "I got fifteen gold stars, and Mrs. Goos gave me the key to the treasure chest, and I got to choose a prize!"

"You did? Wain! Way to go, buddy!" Gold-star behavior was a strong theme in Mrs. Goos's classroom, and no pirate treasure chest provided more intoxicating loot than the boxful of trinkets available to the lucky students who'd earned the right to unlock it. "What prize did you choose?"

"You're gonna love it." Wain knelt and unzipped the backpack. "I picked this." He held up a sparkling gold plastic star pin about the size of a half dollar.

"Very cool!" Key said admiringly. "Look how glittery it is! Do you want me to help you pin it on your backpack?"

"No …. It's for *you*." He offered it up on grimy palm, his deep-blue eyes full of the gratification and joy that accompany the purest of gifts.

It was the last thing she'd expected to hear. "For *me*?" She could barely choke out the words.

"Uh-huh. You can wear it on your shirt, 'cause I know you like pretty stuff. 'Member? Your earrings?" He was glowing with pride.

The star morphed into a misty blob. "Wain, I *love* it. I'm going to put it right over my heart." She pinned the most valuable piece of jewelry she would ever own onto her shirt, then swept him into a bear hug. "Thank you, honey. This is the nicest gift I've ever gotten in my whole life."

"I thought you'd like it." Wain slipped his backpack on and took off running down the sidewalk with Faro, leaving Key swiping at her eyes.

A breeze picked up, providing a break in the cloud cover and sending down a ticker-tape shower of sugar maple leaves, as though the sun itself were sprinkling her world with heart-shaped portions of autumn glow. Even the sun was no match, though, for the warmth emanating from a glittery plastic star.

From her jacket pocket, her phone chimed. A blurry text from Gayle.

Ell is going to MM tmrw to c Coco, so she cant come over but I got ur eggs. Stop by anytime. BTW, found 3 boxes of Lons to look thru but didn't get 2 it 2day. fussy baby & cranky old lady lol

Key wiped her eyes and texted back that she'd be out the next day to pick up the eggs and hoped Gayle and Granny Jewel had time for a short visit. So much for an uncluttered Tuesday. She'd need an early start.

★★★

Tuesday morning, after she'd walked Wain to school, Key left Faro at the house and headed not for the coffee shop as she'd originally planned but for SouthPaws, where a smiling Jukey answered her knock, wearing a black canvas apron featuring a picture of a T-bone steak and the words *GRILLY MAN* in white stenciled letters. "Good morning, Key North! Come in!"

In the kitchen, the huge island was covered with a mini-pie assembly line: Granny Smith apples, a bowl of butter resting on ice, flour, rolling pins, spices, and a stack of miniature aluminum pie pans. Delectable aromas mingled like longtime best friends with the enticing scent of freshly brewed coffee. Key sighed. Even Java U couldn't compete.

Jukey picked up a paring knife. "I'm counting the minutes until I can start on my easier work, like tossing around hay bales."

Key laughed. "I saw all those bales stacked out front."

"We've got pumpkins and gourds coming. Gonna do an autumn display."

"Key! Hello!" Mary emerged from the hallway. She, too, was wearing an apron, a frilly pale-pink number splashed with red and yellow roses, and her hair was pulled off her face with a pink fabric headband.

"Hi! You look so pretty! I brought you something." Key handed her the gift bag she'd prepared.

"Oooh." Mary's brown eyes widened as she pulled out a sweatshirt, two hats, and a rolled-up T-shirt. "*Inside Outlines* merch! Did you order all this?"

"It's a gift from the man himself. A hat and hoodie for you, Mary, and a T-shirt and hat for you, Jukey."

"From *what* man?" Mary asked curiously.

"Wolverine. Well, Gabriel Mink. I met with him yesterday in Porterville."

Mary stared in disbelief. "Key! You can't waltz in here handing out swag and acting all nonchalant, then hit us on the head with this kind of information! How did all this come about?"

"Crazy story. Hand me a knife, and I'll help peel." Key settled onto the barstool next to Jukey, who'd already put on the hat. Laying the groundwork with DP's "Eleanor Rigby" story, Key recounted her every suspicion about Vern Olson: the fresh horse manure inside her property the day after he'd gone riding in the woods; Vern's horse's name; and most importantly, Wain's observation that Vern's earring exactly matched DP's. (Mary gasped out loud at this.)

"Wain's an observant little kid," Jukey commented.

"What *are* the lyrics to 'Eleanor Rigby'?" Mary picked up her phone and tapped a few times, pressing two floury fingers to her mouth in dismay as she read, then she handed the phone to Jukey and said to Key, eyes wide, "And the horse's name is *McKenzie*? That can't be a coincidence!"

"If you're right, Key North, it's like he's advertising a smug secret," Jukey said soberly.

"That's right, honey. Like a—a what do you call it? A token. His secret is like a token." Mary slapped a wad of dough onto the counter and began rolling it out with a vengeance.

Key nodded. "If—and it's a *big if*—he's our guy, I'd bet he has no idea that DP remembers that Ayo called Riggs 'Eleanor.' He thinks that knowledge is his, and his alone. And Mary, did you catch that Vern mentioned Lonny's name before it came up in the podcast? Something about a redneck feud."

"I remember the redneck feud part," Mary replied, "but I was so irritated with his interruptions that I missed the Lonny part." She tipped her head. "So if he knew of Lonny ..."

"Exactly!" Key said. "Of course, he's been living in Troy, so he could have known about Lonny, but ..."

"But he pretended he'd never heard of Riggs before that! Remember?" Mary exclaimed.

"Yes! Speaking of pretending, two can play that game." Key described her outdoor conversation with her fake friend Sylvia.

"You and your fake phone calls," Jukey said with a grin. "Well, it worked with Wain's mama, so maybe it'll work here too."

"I hope so! While we try to establish a connection between Vern and Ayo, I want him to think the Riggs story has faded back into the woodwork."

"Have you told DP about this Vern guy?" Jukey asked.

"No, because *nothing* is provable." Key sighed. "We could be barking up the completely wrong tree, which would be—"

"Catastrophic." Jukey broke in. "I agree, Key North. Wait until we know more. I say we because you've just hired us as your sidekicks." He tipped his hat. "See? Got the official gear. But—devil's advocate here— this Vern you've described doesn't fit at all with how I remember Ayo."

Mary gave a little shrug and began pressing circles in the pie dough with a fluted cutter.

"Twenty years is a long time, honey. People do gain weight. And who could see past that mess of hair all over his head and face?"

"So what's your plan, Key North?" Jukey asked.

"Let's wait to hear back from Gabriel," Key replied, relieved and very happy to have them so enthusiastically on board. "I gave him one other piece of information that may or may not pan out. There was a company called Castle Phoenix."

"Yeah, they did disaster cleanup some years ago." Jukey pushed a bowl of sliced apples across the island.

Key stopped peeling. "Do you know if Ayo Jones worked for them?"

"I don't know about Ayo, but I do know a guy who worked for them," Jukey replied.

Of course he did. Jukey knew everyone. *Small-town knowledge*, Key thought. *Two sides to that coin.* The same congenial network that might provide a quick answer was a loaded minefield if you didn't want your secrets discovered.

"Who's that, honey?" Mary asked.

"Cornel Johnston, out on Dermott Road."

"Oh, Corny!" Mary was already doing a search. She read a phone number to Jukey, who left the room and returned a few minutes later, just as the last of the pies were tucked into the Kings' massive oven.

"Bring Loretta and come by the store sometime! Thanks, Corny." Jukey referred to a few scribbles on a small notepad. "Castle Phoenix went out of business when Joe Castle, the owner, got sick, but Corny left before that; said he didn't care for the vibe there. Both Joe and his wife have passed away."

"But the million-dollar question, honey!" Mary exclaimed, filling coffee cups.

Jukey nodded. "Yes, Ayo Jones worked there for a few years. Then one day he didn't show up for work, and they never saw him again. Corny called Ayo a lying braggart and an arrogant fool. Among other colorful terms."

"Ayo wasn't winning any popularity contests, was he? When did he stop coming to work?" Key asked.

Jukey stirred cream into his cup. "Fall of '98. Corny remembers it well because Dawson Plummer visited them after he got back from searching for Riggs. It got heated because Joe couldn't—or wouldn't—give Dawson Ayo's information." He added somberly, "Corny said he'd never seen a man so tore up as Dawson was that day."

"Thanks, Jukey," Key said quietly, not sure exactly what they'd gained with this knowledge but adding the information to her notebook. After a short, solemn silence, she said, "Oh! I almost forgot. There's no school on Monday, so I'm taking Wain and Ell on a picnic to Dogleg Pond. Would you two like to join us?"

"Oh, that sounds fun!" Mary exclaimed. She consulted her phone. "Just one catering consultation at eight a.m. We could meet you at the pond around ten."

Jukey did a cast-and-reel motion. "The boys and I used to fish Dogleg almost every week. Some of our best times. Life lessons are honed through fishing."

"Funny you should say that," Key replied, smiling a little sheepishly. "I may have a bit of an ulterior motive. Wain is dying to try his hand at fishing. If you'll give him some pointers, I'll provide lunch."

"Deal!" Mary said instantly. "You can't do better than Jukey as a fishing guide!"

"Wonderful!" Key slid off her barstool. "Are you okay with a short hike? It's about a mile and a half."

Jukey slapped his hand on his thigh. "No need to walk," he said happily. "We've got a four-wheeler in that shed out there, just dying to take to the trails. We can cart you all and your gear, too, Key North."

There seemed to be no end to the Kings' abilities. "You just elevated lunch from smashed peanut butter and jelly to a semigourmet picnic basket!"

Mary clattered dishes into the sink. "Oh, I can't wait! It will be a treat to be back in those woods."

# Chapter 33

## CARE

Key returned to Veronica View to collect Faro, then headed to Granny Jewel's. Thanks to Jukey's friend Corny, they now knew that Ayo *had* worked for Castle Phoenix, but how, she wondered again, did that information shine light into the right crevices?

She was pleasantly surprised at her own determination to inch forward, gathering information. Old Key would never have offered to research a twenty-year-old mystery, or impulsively contacted a podcast host, or faked a phone call to throw an admittedly unlikely suspect off the scent. *It might all come to nothing, but why not keep trying?*

*On the flip side, Key,* warned that ever-present annoying inner voice, *you need to watch yourself. Running off your mouth about Vern could do more harm than good.*

"True," she answered aloud, reluctantly. Doubt flooded over her. *My gut instinct does not mean Vern Olson is Ayo Jones.* For every suspicion she harbored, there existed a logical explanation. Most terrifying of all, in her eagerness to help, she might cause more pain to the Plummers by implicating an innocent man. The thought made her blood run cold.

By the time Key turned onto Wildflower Lane, she'd lost all her optimism and was regretting that she'd ever insinuated herself into Riggs's story, sorry that she'd contacted Gabriel Mink or involved Lonny and Jukey and Mary. What had she been thinking? Why couldn't she just let sleeping dogs lie?

Dejected, she parked and let Faro out, lifting her hair off her already-damp neck. Today was one of those strangely warm, humid, breezeless October days that North Carolina invariably sandwiched between pockets of more autumn-like weather. As if in solidarity with her mood, Granny Jewel's American flag hung limply on its pole in the front yard, and the drooping, thirsty geraniums on the front porch looked as though they'd partied too hard the night before.

A welcome rush of cool air met her as Gayle answered the door, holding Dibsy, who made a dive for Key. "Good morning, Miss Key! Baby's happy to see you. Come in! Faro too."

"Hi!" Key set down her bags and took Dibsy, giving her a kiss on the cheek. She hadn't been friends with a toddler since Guy was little, but Dibsy had recently begun climbing onto her lap, playing with Key's jewelry, giving her hugs. It was humbling and heartwarming and one more reason she loved visiting the Morgans.

"GJ's in the bath," Gayle said. "After I get her settled, Miss Key, do you want to go through Lon's boxes with me?"

"Oh, I'd love to!" Key hunkered down with Dibsy. "I brought you something, baby."

"Miss Key, you didn't have to get her nothing!"

"I couldn't resist," Key said. "It's actually a selfish move on my part. Dibsy is helping me live out my childhood dreams by giving me an excuse to play with this toy."

Gayle laughed. "Well, if you put it that way, I'm sure Dibs is happy to help. Thank you, Miss Key, very much." They watched as Dibsy pulled the toy out of the bag, pushing away Faro's intrusive nose. He loved bags.

"It's a veterinary set, complete with a stuffed dog, cat, and bunny," Key said, struggling with the hard plastic shell encasing the toy. "I should have opened it before I came. This packaging is ridiculous."

"Dibs will love it! I'll get you some scissors."

"Maybe a chain saw," Key suggested, and Gayle laughed again.

Dibsy's vocabulary contained about five recognizable words, but her veterinary skills had been honed to perfection by a popular cartoon she watched as ardently as her grandmother watched her afternoon soap operas. By the time Granny Jewel thumped her walker into the living room, Key and Dibsy had set up the practice, healed the stuffed animals several times, and rescued the pink bunny from Faro, who'd kidnapped it twice.

"Good morning, Key!" Clutching her walker, Granny Jewel crossed the room step-by-deliberate-step, looking uncharacteristically vulnerable with her tangled wet hair and a white towel draped around her shoulders. "Thank you, honey," she said, once Gayle had finished combing out her hair. "That felt real nice. Now, y'all are gonna want to get them boxes."

"I'll just get your medication." Gayle disappeared into the kitchen, and Dibsy followed with the stethoscope around her neck, carrying the purple cat and a gigantic plastic syringe.

Key arranged the toys, then stood up, ignoring her protesting knees. "I can't sit on the floor for long periods like that anymore," she commented to Granny Jewel.

"Oh, honey, I'm lucky to get from bed to chair these days. I can't remember the last time I sat on the floor—voluntarily, that is. I ended up there the other day when I fell. I sat there for probably half an hour. Couldn't stand up or get to my phone. Lonny come up to bring my dinner and found me. Got me situated. I was lucky. Could have been much worse."

"Oh, Granny Jewel, how scary! I hope you're all right."

"Mostly frightened the living daylights out of me." Granny Jewel pushed up a saggy sleeve to reveal a nasty triangular bruise on her upper arm. "Courtesy of the corner of this coffee table. I'm real apprehensive to be up here alone if my body is gonna go all wacky. We're gonna get me one of those alert necklaces, but me and the kids got to figure out the next phase." She seemed unusually pensive today, and no wonder, Key thought sympathetically. It would be terrifying, knowing that a failing sense of balance or atrophying muscles could betray you at any moment. *The things we take for granted.*

Gayle caught the tail end of the conversation. "We're so relieved you're all right, GJ." She set a mug of coffee, a bottle of water, and two pills on the side table. "Now I'll get those boxes."

"How can I help?" Key asked.

"If you don't mind keeping an eye on Dibs? She can have a cheese cracker."

Key went in search of Dibsy, who was tugging a chair over to the kitchen sink. "Bath," she said clearly, holding up the stuffed cat. The syringe and stethoscope lay in an opened drawer atop a scrambled mess of plastic storage containers. Key slid the chair back into place, took the toys out of the drawer, and wrestled once again with packaging to extract a cracker. Gayle was the caretaker for demanding family members at both ends of the life spectrum and on various points in between; how did she make it look so effortless?

Granny Jewel put on her glasses and sat forward, watching eagerly as Gayle stacked two boxes near the front door then carried the third into the living room and wiped it off with a damp paper towel. "Gotta be eighteen years of dust. Can't say what's in there. Probably trophies and whatnot. Treasure your days with those little ones, girls. It all goes by in a blink of an eye." It was strange, Key thought, to be included in the same category as Gayle, a woman easily twenty years her junior.

With Granny Jewel reveling in telling story after story, they spent the next hour going through the history of young Lonny Morgan: a blue ribbon for artwork in fifth grade, the game ball after a winning home run, the awkward school pictures of the boy who would eventually morph into the handsome man Gayle had married. And Riggs. At every turn, they saw Riggs growing up right along with Lonny: in yearbook photos, sharing sports teams, swimming, camping, fishing, goofing around. None of the pictures had any explanation on the back, but Granny Jewel was surprisingly sure of herself as to the era. "Oh, that's seventh grade. I remember that shirt; we bought it in Destin when we went on vacation that summer." Or, "Lonny got that haircut right before the prom, so that's his junior year." Whatever drama her multiple marriages had created, she had not lost touch with her son.

"Oh … my goodness." Granny Jewel picked up one picture and pressed it against her heart, then held it up. Riggs and Lonny on the beach, backs to the camera, a football positioned between them, Riggs's arm slung easily around Lonny's shoulders. "The boys are thirteen here. I was between husbands"—she said this with no irony whatsoever—"and Riggs went with us to the Outer Banks. We crammed ourselves into some shabby hotel in Kill Devil Hills and had us the time of our lives!" Pointing to Riggs, she preached a brief disconsolate sermon, tears welling in her eyes. "*This* boy is the son the Plummers lost. *This* is the brother DP don't have no more. *This* is the friend Lonny can't never replace. Riggs Plummer ain't no urban tall tale. He was a *real person*, good-hearted and kind, who left a hole in all our hearts when he was lost. Lonny ain't never had a friend like that again."

The coffee table and the floor around it were now littered with mementos of Lonny's past, and Gayle was having trouble keeping her toddler out of the mess. While she retrieved a high chair, plopped Dibsy into it with a peanut butter and jelly sandwich, and turned on a children's show, Granny Jewel continued sorting through the pictures, carefully examining each one, pointing out those she knew. But no, the old woman told Key, handing the last photo back to her, none of those young men were Ayo.

Ayo Jones was as elusive in the past as he was in the present.

# Chapter 34

## GOLDEN BRACELET

After Gayle put a whimpering Dibsy down for a nap with the purple cat and a warm bottle, Key helped her assemble Granny Jewel's favorite sandwiches: pimiento cheese and spicy bread-and-butter pickle on store-bought white bread.

"I love the pickles!" Key said, reaching for one more triangle. Pimiento cheese was something she'd never eaten until she moved to North Carolina, and she loved it.

Gayle nodded. "It's Ell's favorite too. With the crusts off. My daddy woulda had my hide if I didn't eat the crust."

"Been eating pimpics since I was Dibsy's age," Granny Jewel said casually. "I used to make spicy pickles every summer, and now Petra's using my recipe. These are from her. This store-bought pimiento cheese ain't as good as my homemade, but it'll do."

"Pim ... What did you call them, GJ?" Gayle looked puzzled. "I've never heard that word before."

"Pimpics. Grew up calling them that. But I had to stop when Larry started calling 'em 'pimpwiches,' and of course that got passed on to Lonny like some kinda manly tradition. Even Riggs called 'em 'pimpwiches.'" Granny Jewel compressed her lips and fluffed her thin now-dry curls with her fingers, the embodiment of prim indignation.

"Then they'd *bust a gut*. You want to get my boys going, you ask about pimpwiches." She shook her head. "And now y'all are laughing fit to kill too. It's a desecration of a beautiful sandwich, is what it is."

"Oh, GJ, you made my stomach hurt." Gayle wiped her eyes. "I can't believe Lonny's never mentioned pimpwiches!"

Granny Jewel wagged a warning finger. "Don't get him started. Cav would latch on to that joke like a squirrel on a nut, and you'll regret it." She took another enthusiastic bite and talked while she chewed. "It's been real fun, though, seeing Lon as a boy. Brings back a boatload of memories. And look, we got over a dozen pictures of Riggs too."

"One to go. Not heavy, but it's rattly." Gayle set the third box on the coffee table, dusted it off, and pulled the flaps open. "It's a mishmash of trinkets and what all." She held up a jingly collar and read the ID tag. "Buster! Lonny's told us about him."

Granny Jewel gave a little snort. "Did he tell you that dang animal ate half my Christmas ornaments one year? Plus, he'd take off and chase cars way up there on Pike Road. It was a wonder he wan't kilt. No more dogs for us after that. Lonny had that collar hanging on his doorknob for years after Buster crossed to the rainbow pastures."

"Looks like Lon dumped his desk drawers in here," Gayle said. She began laying items in a tidy line on the coffee table. "Sunglasses …" (these she put on) "… playing cards, socks—What are those doing in a desk? Pocketknife, Swatch watch, fishing license, old mail …" She pushed the sunglasses to the top of her head and sorted through several letters, then held up a midsize manila envelope. "Feels like a card. The envelope's not sealed. Should I …?"

Granny Jewel leaned forward. "Should you open it? Glory, yes, honey! What can it hurt? Ancient history, whatever it is."

"It's two pictures, held together with a paper clip," Gayle said, moving closer to Granny Jewel's chair. "And there's a note attached to them." She began reading, then smacked a hand onto her mouth. "It's from Shasta! The girl from the concert!"

In the silence, Key heard the hum of the refrigerator, Faro's even breathing.

"What does it say, darlin'?" Granny Jewel asked urgently. "G'wan, read it to us."

> Lonny,
> Sunshine pics as promised! in the first one, you got your eyes closed, making that face! I still remember you saying jackass!!!! Haha!! but in the 2nd one, you look smoking hot as ever, haha!!! Riggs is missing in that one. he was probably still in line at the john!! Hope we hear from that boy soon. thx again for the ride & taking me to work. call me when you & riggs want to hang out!!
> xoxo shasta

The backs of the two pictures were blank. Gayle handed them to Granny Jewel as she and Key knelt on either side of her chair. "Is Ayo in these, GJ?"

"*Oh, my glory.*" Granny Jewel rested a hand on her heart. "Yessir. That's him right next to Riggs in the first one and next to Shasta in the second one. And there's Lon, a course." Her pearly pink fingernail moved slowly as she examined both pictures "Don't know these others."

Both photos were similar—typical group shots of exuberant young adults, surrounded by coolers and blankets and bags and chairs. Most held cups or cigarettes in their hands, and one of the boys was proudly displaying what looked like a joint.

Key zeroed in on Ayo Jones. *He's more country club than outdoor concert.* Obviously several years older than the rest of the group, he stood out in a pink polo shirt, crisp khaki shorts, and stylish leather deck shoes, while all around him were girls in bikini tops and cutoff shorts next to shirtless, barefoot guys. Shorter and more muscular than either Lonny or Riggs, Ayo had a headful of wavy jet-black hair, heavily lidded eyes, full lips, and distinct brows.

In the first picture Ayo held a red Solo cup, smiling insolently while making rabbit ears behind Riggs's head, and in the second, he stood between two girls at the edge of the group. Key could sense his arrogance and the girls' discomfort radiating from the picture.

"Notice anything?" Granny Jewel asked, then answered her own question. "Not a phone in sight! No one snapping selfish pickies or telling the world their business on Facebook and Ticker."

"I know exactly what you mean," Key countered, "but if Riggs had had a phone, the technology we have now could have helped track his location."

Gayle nodded. "Cav's gotta keep location services on. No phone allowed, otherwise."

"Fair points," Granny Jewel replied grudgingly. "Not sayin' there ain't pros and cons. But ain't it good to see young folk enjoying life, with no thought to broadcasting their every dang breath."

"Shasta and this other girl don't look like they're enjoying Ayo," Gayle observed. "She's real cute. Was her and Lonny ever …?"

"Not to my knowledge," Granny Jewel replied, patting Gayle's back. "Nothin' serious anyway. Lonny kept himself to himself when it come to girls. That's why we was so sure you was the right one when he told us about you."

"Wait a second!" Gayle exclaimed. "Look at this, y'all!" Plucking a gold plastic wristband from the box, she held it up. "It's what Lon's wearing in the picture! This is his Sunshine Fest admission band!"

"I can't believe he kept that," Granny Jewel took the band and held the two ends together. "Number 559467. Huh. Musta cut it off and dropped it in the drawer."

As Key photographed the note, both photos, and the wristband, she felt she was treading on solemn ground. On the coffee table were images and mementos of the very day Riggs Plummer vanished. By their deferential silence, she suspected Gayle and Granny Jewel felt the same.

# Chapter 35

## GREEN

He'd had another good day, Wain told Key at dinner, unsuccessfully twirling his fork around his spaghetti. He'd refused her offer to cut the noodles. "But at lunch Brady said I was bragging. But I wasn't." He sounded confused.

"What were you talking about when Brady said that?"

"I said I got to ride a horse tomorrow and I'm gonna get the new CartWheel."

"Both true." *Oh, the irony.* If only Brady understood the pain that had led to Wain's good fortune. "Let's flip it around, honey. If Brady told you those same things, would you think he was bragging?"

"No."

Key believed him. The deprivations Wain had experienced with Lyric and Callahan had molded him into a child who'd stood wistfully on life's sidelines, but to her knowledge, he'd never acted jealous of others' good fortune and, certainly—until lately—had nothing about which to be excited, much less brag. "What did you say when he accused you of bragging?"

"Nothing. I ate my chips." Wain managed to capture two noodles.

"Well, sometimes, other people can take our words the wrong way. It sounds like that's what happened here. Tell me about Brady."

"Um, he gets in trouble a lot. He took Greggo's Panthers hat at recess and wouldn't give it back."

"Oh, okay." Key waited, but no further descriptions were forthcoming. "Wain, you did nothing wrong by telling your friends what you'd be doing this week. It sounds like Brady is having a hard time." Key thought a moment. "It's complicated, but ... instead of telling you he wishes he could do those same things, he accused you of bragging. What do you think you should do if he does it again?"

Wain shrugged. "I'll, like, play with him, but I'm not gonna tell him anything."

Key bit her lip to stop a smile. "Did you already have that figured out?"

"Yeah. Hey, look, I got all these at one time!" Wain hurriedly shoved a forkful of noodles into his mouth before they could fall off.

*Conversation over.* "Awesome job, buddy. All the way around." Someday, all these mini conversations might homogenize into a complete life lesson.

After Wain was in bed, Key fixed a mug of salted caramel hot tea, switched on the fireplace, and dropped wearily onto the sofa. She texted Mack.

-Hi! How's Lainey? Do you have time to talk tomorrow afternoon? Want to talk now?

-If it works for you, tomorrow would be better.

She was probably way off base, Key thought, but she'd begun to wonder if Vern Olson had cameras or microphones *inside* the house. The man had *wanted* her to know he was watching the backyard, had taken pleasure in seeing her consternation when he'd mockingly mentioned the "fence arteests." Well, two could play that game. From now on, her conversations in and around Veronica View, unless she was talking to "Sylvia," would be so innocuous that her landlord, if indeed he was watching or listening, would conclude that she was the most stodgy, tedious renter ever.

Another ping. Call anytime! Lainey is doing great. Kids. =) Wish I was that resilient!

Key opened her pictures app and studied the photos she'd taken earlier. Even in a gaggle of attractive young people, Riggs stood out, effortlessly hip in a worn green Foo Fighters T-shirt, jeans, and Nike sneakers, with a red bandana tied Willie Nelson-style around shoulder-length blond hair. He *looked* like a star. In his left hand he held a pair of sunglasses, and with his right he clasped a medallion hanging from a gold chain around his neck. He was unsmiling, leaning away from Ayo's mocking rabbit-ears gesture.

Long-haired Lonny, impossibly young in a white tank top and denim shorts, stood on Riggs's right, a red cup in his left hand, his other arm around the shoulders of the barefoot girl Granny Jewel hadn't recognized. Lonny's eyes were squeezed shut, his mouth (at least according to Shasta's note) forming the word *jackass*.

Ayo was smirking. His Ray-Ban sunglasses were attached to the placket of his polo shirt, and he, too, held a red cup in his left hand—his right making the rabbit ears behind Riggs's head. Everyone whose wrists were visible was wearing a gold admission band, including Ayo, Riggs, and Lonny.

*Could that man possibly be Vern Olson?* Key zoomed in, pixelating the already slightly blurry picture, making it impossible to detect any fine details. She zoomed back out. Ayo was very fit, but over the course of twenty years, he could certainly have piled on a few dozen pounds. The height was about right. Vern had been taller than Key's own five foot seven by several inches, but his thick-soled shoes had added height. This man's black hair could have grown out curly and gray, same with the bushy, untrimmed beard. Vern's overgrown mustache covered his top lip, but his bottom lip had been quite full, as was Ayo's, and the curve of Vern's fake smile was similar. The teeth were different, but Vern absolutely had implants. It wasn't an impossible stretch to think they could be the same man.

Key swiped to the second photo, wishing she knew how much time had lapsed between the two. Lonny was now shirtless, holding a cigarette, and Ayo, who had a pair of binoculars around his neck, stood near the other end. His pristine pink shirt was now rumpled, his armpits soaked with perspiration, and he was possessively clutching an unsmiling Shasta's waist with his right arm while resting his left forearm on the shoulder of an annoyed-looking blond girl in a bikini top. His hand dangled much too close to her chest. Key hoped both girls had bolted as soon as the camera clicked.

*Wait a second.* Key frowned and leaned in for a closer look. *What am I seeing? Shadows?* Again, zooming in only made the picture blurrier. She rose and went to check on Wain. Sound asleep. Taking Faro, her phone, and tablet, she walked to the mailbox, out of view of the doorbell camera, and tapped Lonny's number. She was about to hang up when he answered. "Hey, Miss Key. Sorry. We're outside—kids are roasting marshmallows."

"That sounds fun!" Key said. "Lonny, do you have a minute?"

"Yes, ma'am. Gayle said y'all had a good time looking through my old boxes today. The kids was laughing at my hair in them pictures." He chuckled softly, then added, "I totally spaced that I had those. You know, Miss Key, it took me right back to that day. I can still feel how sick to my stomach I felt when we drove home without Riggs."

Key cleared her throat. "Lonny, in the first photo, did you notice how Riggs has his hand up by his neck? Just like your dream!"

"You serious?" Lonny said, then, "Ya'll watch the fire." A door squeaked open. "Whoo-ee. I see what you mean about my dream. That's crazy! You think my subconscious remembers that?"

"Maybe! Do you see anything strange when you compare the two pictures?"

There was a short silence. "Well, in the second one, Ayo is sweatin' like the pig he was, and Shasta looks real unhappy to be next to him, and so does the other girl. But nothin' is really standin' out."

"Look at Ayo's wrist in that second picture." Key was shivering, as much from the adrenaline coursing through her body as the chilly evening air.

"Miss Key, I just tried to enlarge this paper picture with my fingers like I would on a phone." They laughed, then Lonny said, "Wait a second. Ayo's wristband don't look like the ones ..."

Though she was positive of what she'd seen, Key rechecked the picture. "At first, I thought it was because his wrist is in the shadow of that poor girl's neck, but it's green, Lonny! Why did Ayo's wristband switch from gold to green?"

"*Dang. No idea.*" Lonny sounded completely bewildered.

"Would Shasta know?"

"She might. I can try to find out tomorrow." In the background, Key could hear Dibsy crying, then the door squeaked again. "I better get goin' now, though."

"Oh, of course, I'm sorry!"

"No problem. I'm gonna show Gayle once the kids are in bed. I'll call you tomorrow, Miss Key."

Key was barely back on the sofa when another text popped in.

Hi. Do you have time to talk?

Gabriel. As much as she wanted to hear his news, it would have to wait. She sent a quick reply.

Hi! Tomorrow morning would be better- after 8:30?

He sent a thumbs-up.

She took her cup to the kitchen and rinsed it out. What she needed more than answers right now was a bed and a pillow.

# Chapter 36

## THREE PHONE CALLS

Wednesday dawned clear and much cooler. Wain, looking sporty in a new Bullfrogs sweatshirt, practically danced to school, brimming with anticipation over his upcoming horseback ride.

Key walked back as fast as she could, past her rental house and on toward a nearby park, so deep in thought that when Faro barked sharply at a scarecrow decoration, she jumped sideways. *Halloween!* Instead of the annual Sage Pointe parties, this year she'd be helping Wain find a costume and possibly joining the trick or treat parade. Such thoughts, so inconceivable even six months ago, didn't even faze her anymore.

When her phone vibrated, she stopped to put in her earbuds. "Good morning, Gabriel!"

He dove right in. "So, Key, your guy Vern Olson has proved difficult to track down."

"Seriously?" She'd half expected him to tell her that Vern and Deirdre were a ten out of ten on the dull-suburban-couple scale.

"We found many Vern Olsons, or variations of that name, but none of them live in Troy, North Carolina. Same with the wife. No social media, at least under those names. No criminal records. Bottom line, with the vague information we have, and the fact that they're now in an RV somewhere out West, we hit a dead end. It's like chasing water droplets in a river."

Key hadn't expected this level of invisibility. "Who bought the house I'm renting on Veronica View?"

"That's another story. Who do you pay rent to?"

"DV Property Management. They do a draw on an account I set up at the local bank. The rent money is the only money in there."

"Smart."

"My late husband was a banker. You'd be amazed at the way people can be scammed." Key smiled at two young mothers pushing bundled-up toddlers in high-tech strollers.

Gabriel laughed. "After four years of podcasting? Bet I wouldn't. Records show the house was purchased and paid for in full by Zeetime Properties." He spelled it. "No mortgage, no personal names attached. Zeetime led us to another layer of the onion, a second LLC behind that one with the completely generic name of 'Practical Solutions.' It dead-ended there—at least what we can find with our limited resources."

"Wow. Who *are* these people?"

"Good question. They're odd, for sure, but nothing at all connects your landlord to Riggs Plummer."

*Mrs. Goos, gooseberry pie, wild-goose chase.* "Thank you, Gabriel. I do have an update on Castle Phoenix!" Key filled Gabriel in. "So Ayo Jones did work there. But it's out of business. Probably another dead end."

"All pieces of the puzzle," Gabriel replied congenially. "We'll bow out for now, Key, but please keep me in the loop. Riggs will always be number one on my 'Want to Solve' list."

*How many times has he said that?*

At Chix on Broadway a few hours later, Key settled with her drink at the counter facing the window and began updating her notes. Maybe it wasn't a wild-goose chase …. What she hadn't told Gabriel was that Zee, as in *Zeetime*, was a name with which she'd become very familiar. A text popped in.

Call me?

Lonny answered immediately. "Hey, Miss Key. I gotta eat and talk. One of the guys here at work knows Shasta and her husband. Her last name is McCord now, so I texted Gayle, she found her on Facebook and messaged her, and Shasta called me a few minutes ago."

"Wow!" *Oh, the joys of small towns and social media.* Lonny and Gayle had found Shasta in mere minutes, compared to Gabriel's expert but fruitless search for the Olsons. People who didn't care if they were found were easy to locate.

"She was real surprised to hear from me. I asked if she still had pictures from the concert, and she said all her old stuff was in her parents' storage unit, but when her parents split up, like, fifteen years ago, they stopped payin', and the unit got cleaned out and auctioned off."

"Oh no!" Key exclaimed, loudly enough that three women who'd settled in a nearby booth glanced over in concern. She lowered her voice. "Thankfully you saved your copies, Lonny!"

"Thank Mama, who can't throw nothin' away," Lonny replied around a mouthful of food. "It's a bummer, though, 'cause Shasta says she woulda had a bunch more." He sighed heavily. "Sometimes I think, what is the *deal*, man? You know? Seems like anything has to do with Riggs, it just ain't straightforward."

"So true. Did Shasta know anything about the wristbands?"

"That's a *big* ole yes. Get this, Miss Key. I asked her why Ayo would be wearin' that green band, and she said it's because he got the VIP parking pass. His endless bragging made her want to vomit—her words, not mine."

Key frowned. "But he was wearing a gold one in the first picture."

"Shasta says it's because when he went to get the binoculars out of the van, they made him switch wristband colors in order to access the VIP lot."

"*What?*" Key whispered, sitting straight up. "He went *out*? To get binoculars?" She felt as though she were shouting.

"Yep." Lonny sounded as smug as she'd ever heard him. "And you know what, Miss Key? Those wasn't his binoculars. They was

Riggs's. I know that for a fact. But at the concert, I never saw Riggs with them."

"But Ayo has them in the second picture." Key felt the hairs prickle on the back of her neck. Writing as fast as she could, she asked, "Did you ask Ayo back then why he had Riggs's binoculars?"

"No, ma'am. If it wasn't for this picture, I wouldn't remember him having them at all."

"Why didn't you get a green wristband, Lonny?"

"'Cause I never went out." Lonny crunched something. "According to Shasta, Ayo told her mine and Riggs's wristbands *should have been* green. If we had gone out, they would of switched the color before we could access that VIP lot."

"Shasta's got an amazing memory."

"Well, she says that on the way home, when I was out of the van pumping gas, Ayo asked her to cut his wristband off. She didn't think nothing of it, just cut it off with a teeny little pocketknife he had. That's how she remembers the band was green. And Ayo wasn't acting any stranger than usual, which to say he was a jerk—but what else is new."

"She didn't mention any of this in the podcast."

"Yeah, she never remembered it at all until I called her today! It didn't register no significance. She still don't see how Ayo coulda done somethin' to Riggs." Key could hear the shrug in his voice as he added, "Me neither, for that matter. Unfortunately."

"It's still huge news. We now know that Ayo left the concert!" She heard wrappings crinkle, a door squeak, voices, and engines.

"Real soon, I'm gonna stop by to see DP, show him the pictures y'all found of Riggs and the concert pictures too. See you tonight, Miss Key. We're gonna watch Ell ride. Feels like Christmas around our place."

When Key's phone rang yet again and it was Mack, she took her belongings and went outside, leaning on the front bumper of the Jeep in the Chix parking lot, enjoying an uncomplicated and upbeat conversation.

"I'm still planning to come to North Carolina," Mack said, before they hung up. "It would have to be during the week. Are there some dates that work for you?"

"Any time after this weekend should work." She took a deep breath and said carefully, "Honestly, Mack, I'd love to see you sooner rather than later. It would be good to ... catch up."

"I'll check flights."

As Key opened the Jeep door, the sun glinted off a penny at her feet. She picked it up and looked at the year. *1998*. Feeling strangely encouraged, she slid it into her pocket, and as she drove back to Veronica View contemplating how to move forward, she heard her father's voice: *An intersection is often mistaken for a dead end.* Lonny in his plain but lyrical way had expressed it even better: *Seems like anything has to do with Riggs, it just ain't straightforward.* She touched the penny. She would be searching for the turn.

# Chapter 37

## BROTHERLY LOVE

"Wain went to change," Cissy told Key. "He did awesome on his sight words today!" With her shiny black hair in a ponytail and the usual sunglasses perched on top of her head, she was the picture of radiant teenage energy.

"He's grown more confident by leaps and bounds, Cissy!" Using a folded tea towel as a potholder, Key slid a foil-covered glass casserole dish from the oven. "You're a big reason why he's doing so well!"

Cissy beamed. "Thanks, Miss Key. Mmmm, that smells so good."

"Oven-baked chicken thighs, rice, and roasted carrots. We're going to eat very fast because we have to be at the horse barn at six thirty, but you're welcome to join us."

"Oh, I wish! I have track. Um … did Cav tell you our plan?"

"What plan?" Key handed her two sugar-dusted molasses cookies.

Before Cissy could answer, Wain swaggered into the kitchen, his miniature Levis tucked inside his new red-and-tan riding boots, which, to Key's amusement, he'd been wearing constantly, even in his pajamas. "Look, Cissy!" He lifted a foot. "See? It's called a 'cowboy heel' 'cause my feet have to stay in the stirrups when I ride Bobcat."

"Dude! You're one handsome cowboy."

"My two favorite Bullfrogs! Stand together, you two. Sit, Faro." Feeling a bit like Mamarazzi Petra on Granny Jewel's porch, Key lifted her phone, snapped two quick pictures, and sent one to Guy with a quick explanation. Cissy's generation might take it for granted that in seconds this photo would materialize across the world, but Key (and most of her generation, she suspected) never would.

Cissy gave Wain a fist bump. "Have fun tonight, little guy! Miss Key, if you see Cav, ask him about our plan."

★★★

At Mistic Meadows, the excitement was as palpable as the barn scents. Regina and Jessie showed a determined Wain and a glowing Ell how to mount from the portable stairs, sit correctly in the saddle, use the reins, and keep their heels down. Bobcat exuded a monk-like patience, and Coco had several sparkly ribbons braided into her mane, courtesy of Ell. Horse magic. There was nothing like it.

"Ell's been helping Cav with some of the currying and whatnot," Lonny told Key. "She's got us all trained in the correct grooming procedures. Pretty sure I could curry a horse in my sleep."

"I think Ell does, her pillows have scratch marks," Gayle said, making them laugh. "She watches horse videos with GJ now on YouTube after school."

"So now my mama is an expert in equine husbandry," Lonny added dryly, using Dibsy's pink cowboy hat to fan away several persistent flies. "Let's hope it'll work out better than her human husbandry." Everyone laughed again. Lonny set Dibsy down. "Stay with your mama, baby. I'm gonna walk to the other side."

Within seconds, Gayle exclaimed, "Baby!" and ran to retrieve Dibsy, returning to the fence with her fussy daughter, who threw her cowboy hat on the ground.

Key picked it up. "I'll take her, Gayle."

"You're sure? Wain will be all right? I'd love to watch Ell a little longer. Seeing her like this … It makes my heart happy."

"Wain will be fine for ten minutes without me. In fact, I think it's good for him." She'd already taken several pictures, and aside from waving a couple times, Wain had been fiercely focused on following instructions.

"Thank you, Miss Key!"

Key was sure she'd admired every rock between the corral and the courtyard when Dibsy pointed and said delightedly, "Cav!" and began toddling as fast as she could toward her brother, who'd just emerged from the tack shed.

Cav swung her up. "Hey, y'all." He looked taller; Key couldn't tell if it was the cowboy hat, or the thick soles of his work boots. After a few minutes of small talk, he met her eyes. "Uh, Miss Key, Ell told me about Tally Mayweather. The flower power thing made a impact on her." He lowered his squirming sister to the ground. Dibsy took her hat from Key, plopped down in the grass, and began filling it with clover and rocks.

"Flower power. That's one way to put it." Feeling a massive rush of relief that Cav didn't think she was interfering, Key said, "I hope someday Ell feels comfortable telling your parents what's going on."

He kicked at a clump of dirt. "Um, the jail baby thing would be real tough on my daddy. Like, that part pissed me off so bad."

"Me too, Cav. I will never understand why some people deliberately inflict unkindness on to others. What ugly well are they tapping from? Why choose to be like that?"

"Mama says some people is just born mean." He met her eyes. "So, like, you know I helped at Tally Mayweather's birthday party that day y'all stopped by."

"Yes! Regina told me you were more popular than the horses."

Cav grinned. "Wasn't nothin' special. Just goofed around, did my same three dumb magic tricks that I practice on Ell, made jokes, all that. But it was hard to see them having such a good time without my own sister invited. Ell's a little nutty but such a good kid." He swallowed.

Key's eyes misted. "She is the best. Wain has *healed* because of her! And, Cav, you're a wonderful brother. Cissy said you two have a plan?"

"It's mostly Cissy's plan." He leaned down to admire a rock Dibsy was showing him. "She said maybe I should ride the bus with Ell, then hang out with her before school starts. Tomorrow Cissy's gonna come hang out, too, maybe with some other Lady Bullfrog basketball players."

*Cissy, you little genius.*

"Anyway," Cav went on, "that first day I showed up with Ell—hate to sound like I'm bragging—but them little girls was so shocked I was her brother. They was like, 'Cav, Cav, what are you doin' here?' And I was like, 'Hangin' with my sister.'"

Key clapped her hands, surprising Dibsy and Emmaline the border collie, who had materialized out of nowhere and was sniffing interestedly at the hatful of rocks and grass. "I would have given anything to see that!"

"Ell told me the girls are already being nicer to her. It seems crazy, but ..."

"And shallow," Key added shortly, then regretted it. "Sorry. I know they're just kids, Cav, but they know better."

"The funny thing is, Ell told me she ain't havin' such a hard time now 'cause she can talk to me and Cissy, and she gets to go home and see Coco."

Key gave him a quick, impulsive hug. "Cav, you've made my day! I feel like a weight is off my shoulders! And ... Cissy is awesome!"

He blushed. "Yeah, she's cool. Well, I better get back to work. Stay with Miss Key, baby."

Key dusted off the back of Dibsy's overalls. "Let's get you a drink, little girl. And before we go back to the corral, you can help me leave a new coffee maker beside the office door."

# Chapter 38

## REVELATIONS

"Wain is a wonderful asset to our class. His reading has improved immensely, and he gives full effort on all assignments. He still struggles with confidence, but he's considerate and friendly to everyone and has even helped one classmate overcome her fear of our classroom gerbil." Mrs. Goos beamed through her glasses at Key's phone, which was propped up where Guy could see both women.

Earlier, carrying Key's phone, Wain had proudly given his father and Key a tour of his classroom and was now lounging in a beanbag chair at the other end of the room, playing a math game on a tablet.

"Wain introduced me to Sheba," Guy replied, his humorous blue eyes focused on the camera lens. "She was working out. Getting some good gerbil cardio on that wheel. She's very *svelte*, Mrs. Goos." The teacher actually giggled.

Key blinked slowly and rolled her eyes at Guy, who laughed. Seven thousand five hundred miles away, his face on a four-inch screen, and even Mrs. Goos, the very personification of no-nonsense, wasn't immune to Guy's ridiculously disarming ways.

"I can see where Wain gets it," Mrs. Goos said in a low voice to Key as she walked them to the door. "You have a delightful family."

"I do, don't I?" *Her family.* Key was warmed to her core.

★★★

"How long before our party starts?" Wain asked for at least the fifth time on Saturday morning as they hurried the two blocks from their hotel to Imagine That. CartWheels Reveal Day had finally arrived.

Key pushed up her jacket sleeve to show him her watch. "Another minute has gone by. Nine to go."

"Whoa. Look at the line around the store!"

"And look at the cars waiting to get into the parking garage!" Key exclaimed, thankful she'd booked a hotel close enough to walk. "I'm afraid there are going to be some disappointed shoppers."

"I feel sorry for the kids who won't get one." Wain thought a moment, then added shamelessly, "But I don't want to give them mine."

Key gave him a side hug. "To that, Wain, I would say, count your blessings! Evie sent you a very special invitation! Turn here. We're supposed to use the back door."

In the alley, a jagged, squirming, colorful queue of mostly boys and men stood alongside a brick wall leading to a gray metal door with *IMAGINE THAT* stenciled in black. A sandwich sign, its attached helium balloons dangling lethargically in the cool air, read *CARTWHEELS VIP REVEAL PARTY!!!*

"Hey! That's my friend from the pool! Abby!" Wain waved enthusiastically at a girl near the front of the line, one of several young CartWheels fans he'd met the night before at the hotel.

*The pool.* Key grimaced. What, she wondered, did it reveal about herself that in defense of Wain, she had waded without a second thought not into the water but into a discomfiting confrontation, all because of a certain little car?

She'd been relaxing on a chaise lounge, keeping eagle eyes on Wain, who was swimming with several children. An older boy approached them and spoke directly to Wain; whatever he said was drowned out by the echoing noise, but Wain's eyes held a troubled expression that Key hadn't seen in months. She stood, ready to intervene, then watched as the older boy exited the pool and threw himself dramatically into a chair beside a bored-looking middle-aged couple.

Carrying Wain's towel to the edge of the pool, Key gestured him over. His eyes still contained that apprehensive flicker, and as she draped the towel over his shoulders, she asked softly, "Everything okay, buddy?"

"That boy keeps bugging me. He doesn't believe I have Black Diamond. He said I was a liar and said *prove it*. Can I go get my backpack and show him?"

Key thought a moment. "Let's talk to them." With Wain at her heels, she approached the parents and said pleasantly, "My grandson would like to show a picture to your son. If that's all right."

"Why?" the father asked, barely looking up from his phone.

Key had to hand it to him; he'd managed to wedge every facet of disdain into one three-letter word. She tapped her phone to wake it up, then gave it to Wain.

"Oh!" He nonchalantly held it out. "See? I'm not a liar. That's me holding Black Diamond. My *real* dad got it for me."

There was a short frosty silence. "Wow, lady," the father remarked loudly, yanking off his glasses and fixing flat gray eyes on Key. "If it's that important to you to brag to *strangers* how great your grandkid is, you've got a problem." Turning to his tight-lipped wife and sulky son, he snapped, "Let's go."

By now almost everyone was staring. Key knew her face was bright red. Feeling utterly humiliated and guilty, she tucked her wilting hair behind her ears. *Had* she been bragging? What was her motive in showing that boy the picture? What harm would there have been in simply letting the whole situation slide?

Wain watched the family slam out of the pool area. "Like the Ickies," he said knowingly.

"Which Ickies were those?" Key asked wearily.

"The ones that, like, called people names."

The knot in Key's stomach loosened as she began to laugh. Bending down to meet his eyes, she said, "Well, Wain, they *were* icky! I didn't think that boy should get away with calling you a liar."

He was beaming. "Me neither!"

Every day with Guy's son, it seemed, revealed another layer of protective strength she never realized she possessed.

Now, standing in line outside Imagine That, it was evident Key needed to muster a very different kind of strength: patience.

"How many minutes *now*?" Wain asked.

# Chapter 39

## A NUDE TO THE GENIES OF THE PASTE

The door opened, revealing a pink-haired girl in jeans and a white T-shirt featuring the CartWheels logo superimposed across a big blue question mark. "Good morning! We're gonna scan y'all in, do the reveal, and let you shop for a few." Cheers and applause.

"Hey there! I remember you, little man!" Evie exclaimed when they finally reached the door. "Still got the cool backpack, I see!"

The store was at capacity. Key slowly guided Wain to the front, where over the cash register a large banner hung from the ceiling, its wording concealed by a lightweight beach blanket resembling a vintage California beach map. A similar blanket was draped over the CartWheels display.

Evie's mother Charlie gave a short welcome speech. "And now, y'all, we are so thrilled to present the latest car in the CartWheels family .... Enginuity!" With a flourish, she swept the map-blanket downward as Evie simultaneously uncovered the display.

"It's a Woodie!" Key exclaimed, over cheers and applause.

"Like, a old-fashioned car." Wain studied the banner. "'A ... nude'? Nude! Ew!" He looked appalled.

"Nod," Key corrected, thankful she already had a wide smile on her face. "Like when you nod your head."

"Oh! 'A nod to the ... genies'?"

"Close! *Genius*."

"'A nod to the genius of the ... paste.'" Wain frowned. "What does that mean?"

"Past, not paste. Great reading, buddy." Key pointed to each word. "'*A nod to the genius of the past.*' It means they admire the people who designed and built these beautiful old cars."

Charlie let out an expert whistle. "Hey, y'all, internet's not working, so Evie's gonna read the announcement from John Cart, the inventor of CartWheels. Ya'll can look up the video later online."

Evie jumped up onto the counter. "'Way back when, a gas engine was attached to a wooden horse carriage, which eventually morphed into an ingenious combo of technology and nature known affectionately as the Woodie. Due to their boho vibe and roomy interiors, Woodies became synonymous with the California surfer world of the fifties and sixties. Enginuity is a replica of a 1946 Ford station wagon rocking teal paint, maple and mahogany panels, and a detachable yellow-and-red surfboard on the roof. CartWheels is proud to pay tribute to the inventors of this iconic car.'"

Wain tugged on Key's sleeve. "What's it called, again?"

"Enginuity." Key answered, enchanted with both the name, the car, and the little boy soon to assign it to its own mesh pocket. *A nude to the genies of the paste.* How did she get so lucky?

# Chapter 40

## URBAN LEGEND

*September 5, 1998*

I t was September-in-the-South hot and humid. Riggs hadn't considered how uncomfortable he'd be in blue jeans. Lonny in his shorts might not score as high on the fashion meter, but at least his legs could feel what little breeze there was.

Shasta Harrison and her entourage had joined them half an hour earlier, and at her insistence, they'd all immediately posed for a group shot, taken with Shasta's camera by an attractive girl passing by. As they'd been arranging themselves, Ayo had tried to engage the photographer with his off-putting, proprietary flirting, but the girl had ignored him, instead giving Riggs her red bandana, which he'd tied around his head.

"You look like a freaking idiot, *Riggsy*," Ayo had declared, wedging himself between Riggs and the girl to his left. "Find Bunny Eleanor," he added, smirking as he held two fingers up behind Riggs's head, but no one paid any attention, especially Riggs, who pointedly leaned away. As the girl snapped the picture, Lonny let out a derisive, snorting cough that sounded suspiciously like the word "jackass," which *did* cause Riggs and everyone else to crack up as the group disbanded. Ayo was humiliated and smoldering, but Riggs didn't care. Nothing, not even the thundercloud on Ayo's face, was going to ruin this once-in-a-lifetime experience.

On the drive to Richmond, Ayo had made it clear that it was *his* benevolence, *his* generosity that allowed Riggs and Lonny the privilege of seeing the Foo Fighters, but as was typical, he hadn't requested monetary repayment. His currency of choice was hero worship, and he fully expected their public acknowledgment of his superiority.

It wasn't working. When Riggs and Lonny refused to accompany him to the souvenir booths, Ayo furiously stalked off alone, his hands shoved deep into his shorts pockets. Judging by the queues, if they were lucky, he'd be gone for a while. Riggs helped himself to a beer. *Catch-22. If it wasn't for Ayo, I wouldn't be here, but even looking at the guy makes me want to puke.*

"Dude looks like he took a wrong turn in his pink golf cart somewhere off the back nine," the guy who'd brought the moonshine remarked, watching Ayo disappear into the crowd.

"After hitting a ten and recording a par," Lonny drawled. They'd witnessed it many times at the municipal golf course in Troy.

"He's a puke," Moonshine Guy said, echoing Riggs's thoughts. "I've told him twice now to stay the hell away from my girlfriend."

"Now *that's* par for the course," Riggs shot back. Everyone laughed.

Thirty minutes later, Riggs and Lonny were surrounded by even more partiers they didn't know, but it didn't matter; everyone was friends now. Ayo still hadn't returned.

Nodding his head to the music, his beer sloshing gently, Riggs immersed himself in the music. The day was *almost* perfect. The only thing missing was Carly. With all his heart, he wished she was one of the girls in their group. If only he could call her, share the total awesomeness of this concert dream come true. The only cell phone, though, as far as he knew, belonged to Ayo, and Riggs wasn't about to ask to use it.

"What's that word when, you know, life feels perfect? Starts with an *E*?" Riggs asked the thirty-something guy next to him. They'd been talking lyrics and music composition, and Riggs still didn't know his name.

"Elated? Enraptured?" the man guessed, slightly slurring the words. "No! *Exhilarated!*" He did a fist pump, then gave Riggs a questioning look. "Right? Right?"

"Ain't any of those. Thanks for trying, Dictionary Dude. Be right back." Riggs set his cup on the ground. "Hey, man," he said to Lonny, who'd taken off his shirt and secured it with a fat knot to the back of a lawn chair, "I'm going to the john."

Lonny gave him a distracted clap on the back, his familiar smile crinkling the corners of slightly glazed blue eyes. "Okay, bro." On stage the Foo Fighters began "February Stars."

"Hey, Riggs Plummer!" the man called.

Riggs turned.

"*Euphoria!*"

"*Yes!* Big props, dude!" Riggs flashed him a thumbs-up, laughing as the man did a comical little victory dance in his too-small Teva sandals.

Picking his way through the densely packed chairs and blankets and bodies, Riggs groaned. There had to be fifty people in line, waiting for six portable units.

In front of him was a couple sharing a pair of binoculars, swaying and singing along. *Binoculars!* In his excitement, Riggs had forgotten his in Ayo's van. He surveyed the area. The VIP parking was right there. He could easily exit the concert, take a leak on the far side of the van, grab his binoculars, and get more of his money from the glove box to buy souvenirs for Carly and DP. He didn't need a key; Riggs knew the perfect jiggle-and-yank that would unlock the van's damaged back door handle. Abandoning the line, he made his way toward the exit. He'd be back before the dancing couple even reached one of those smelly johns.

Out of nowhere came a taunting voice. "Ooh, it's Eleanor Riggsy Plummer! The world's minorest minor celebrity from the subbest of subpar bands! Where do you think you're going?"

*No.* Riggs gritted his teeth and forced himself to sound halfway civil. "Getting my binoculars from the van." *One more day. That's all. One more day, then Ayo's brushed out of my life like a spider off my shoulder.*

*A spider off my shoulder.* Riggs made a mental note—there were potential lyrics there. It was always in his mind, this search for lyrics, and lately, he and his father had been collaborating on a new set of songs for Orion. "Snake in the Grass" was their latest. Already it had become a huge hit. Obnoxious people made for good music.

Ayo slammed his shoulder into Riggs's, knocking him off balance. "You weren't going to ask permission? To access *my* vehicle?"

"I know how to jiggle the lock."

"Still my rig, *bro.* Am I allowed to call you that, or is that reserved for your boyfriend Loony?"

"Whatever." Riggs refused to engage, and anyway, they'd reached the exit. Seeing their wristbands, a middle-aged woman waved them through. When she saw where they were headed, however, she cheerfully called them back.

"Hey-hey! Y'all can't go in there. That's the VIP lot."

"Wanna bet?" Ayo replied churlishly, managing to make it sound as though she'd insulted his honor. "I have a pass."

"May I please see proof?" The woman pointed at their wrists. "'Cause y'all don't have the right wristbands for the VIP lot."

Ayo fished in his shorts pocket for the stub from the parking pass and held it close to her face, slowly shaking it back and forth. "Hey-hey, *y'all*! Satisfied?"

The woman gave Ayo a level stare. "Should have gotten these green wristbands. Gotta change 'em out."

"Not our fault *y'all* suck at your job," Ayo retorted, turning to stare at Riggs.

Experience had taught Riggs that in situations like this, he was expected to play wingman, laugh at his companion's witty, derisive comments, make sure Ayo's superior status had been appropriately noted. Instead, Riggs kept his eyes on the distant stage as the woman searched for a pair of scissors, then cut the gold bands off their wrists and replaced them with green ones. He could feel Ayo's irritation mounting, and he knew it was directed at him. He wasn't playing by the rules.

"*Come on.*" Ayo stormed toward the VIP lot.

Riggs hung back. "I apologize, ma'am."

The woman nodded, watching Ayo's retreating back. "Ain't nothing new under the sun, but thank you."

"Listen," Riggs said quietly, "is there any chance I could have my gold wristband? I know my little brother would love it."

Her face softened. "Sure thing. Take 'em both."

"Thank you, ma'am." Riggs stuffed both gold wristbands deep into his jeans pocket, then took off the bandana and pushed it in too.

The woman gave him a searching look. "It's zero of my business, son, but you need better friends."

"He's not my friend. But I take your point. Thanks again." Riggs caught up to Ayo, who was standing by the gate, glowering.

"You are such a freaking wuss." Ayo waved his wrist in Riggs's face. "See, numbskull? You wouldn't have gotten into the lot without me." When Riggs didn't reply, Ayo added, apropos of nothing, "And you owe me Shasta."

For the first time, Riggs looked straight at him. "What does that mean?"

"I have to draw a picture? You and Loony gave her permission to ride home with us. Never even *asked* me. Who do you think you are? She wants a ride home in my van, she shares it with me."

"She's not into you." *That's putting it mildly.* Riggs wasn't worried for Shasta. He and Lonny were more than a match for Ayo.

There was no one else in the parking lot. At the van, Riggs relieved himself on the passenger side while Ayo unlocked the back. "Get in, get the binoculars, get out," he commanded.

"Got one more thing to do." Riggs entered the van through the back, then clambered into the front passenger seat. He hated that his mother and little brother had witnessed his argument with Dawson, who truly adored his sons and had not deserved the impulsive, blistering words Riggs had hurled at him. *I am an idiot. Sorry, Daddy.* He sighed, then set his jaw. *Just absorb the here and now.* The issues with his father would all blow over once he apologized to his family. He opened the glove box.

"What are you *doing*?" Ayo followed Riggs into the van and picked up the binoculars, then leaned into the front seat, his breath hot on Riggs's neck.

Repulsed, Riggs forced himself to stay calm. "Get *back*, would you? I need to get some money. Gonna get T-shirts for me and Carly and my little brother."

Ayo snorted in his ear. "Better get one for *Mama and Daddy* while you're at it."

Used to Ayo's jealous, obsessive comments about his dedication to Carly and his close-knit family, Riggs ignored him, but Ayo refused to let up. "Bet Carly would love to hear how you're all over Shasta today. Not to mention flirting with your little bandana groupie back there. I should call Carly right now. Tell her you're a cheater."

"That's the stupidest thing you've said so far." He had never called Ayo "stupid" to his face before, but he simply didn't care anymore.

Ayo's voice turned to ice. "I'm not the ignorant one here. You think I don't know you and Loony are avoiding me? You think I don't know your frigid, dried-up mama is the reason I don't get invited to your place anymore? Or your stuck-up, suck-up father—"

"Shut up! *Just shut up!*" Whirling around, so furious he could hardly breathe, Riggs finally, comprehensively snapped. He shoved Ayo's face backward with all the force he could muster. "You know what? This is *it*." He held up his hands, punctuating his words with more shoves at the air. "Leave. Me. Alone. Stay away from my family! Stay away from my concerts. Stay away from my brother's baseball games. Stay away from Lonny and me. I want you gone, man. I want you out of my life! And it's not just me! Everyone is sick of you!"

Ayo recoiled like he'd been struck.

Riggs laughed. "Yes. That's right. You're a *laughingstock*. Everyone calls you *a-hole* behind your back. Oh, and *by the way*, I was wrong when I said Shasta's not that into you. She actually *despises* you. We're all done with you, you freaking repugnant Neanderthal. *Done*." He snatched the parking pass from the rearview mirror and hurled it into the back. "Lonny and Shasta and I will find our own ride home. Anywhere but in this low-life van with its VIP snake-in-the-grass driver." Shaking with fury, Riggs jerked his money envelope from the glove box, grimacing as he remembered the asinine reason he'd brought it along in the first place. What had he been thinking? Carly would have read him the riot act if he'd run off like that and showed up like a petulant baby whining at her door.

Pulling six twenties from the envelope, he slapped them down on the console. "That's for me and Lonny's tickets and gas. And give me my binoculars." He leaned forward to slip the money envelope into his back pocket, suddenly so eager to escape the van that he felt like his skin was on fire.

"You *actually* think you're better than me." The disbelief in Ayo's voice had devolved into a ferocious, white-hot hiss that sent chills down Riggs's spine.

Riggs turned. "I said, give me—"

His last words were lost in the explosion that followed as a muscular fist slammed viciously into his left temple, smashing him twice with devastating force against the window, the one-two blows stunning him so thoroughly that he never felt the unbreakable nylon binoculars strap snaking around his neck from behind.

Riggs barely resisted as he was dragged into the back of the van, his short twenty years falling away as noiselessly as the six bills that fluttered onto the floor where his now-still feet had been.

# Chapter 41

## SURPRISING?

"Hey, Ell! We have a surprise for you!" Wain yelled, launching himself from the Jeep. "You are gonna love it!" Key had finally shown him the fishing poles and metal detectors, and he was beside himself.

"What?" Ell bent to hug Faro.

"You'll see," Key answered quickly, before Wain could spill the beans. She did a quick, worried survey. Good. The chickens were inside the fenced coop. She still didn't trust Faro not to chase them.

Ell cupped her hands around her mouth and hollered at the top of her lungs toward Granny Jewel's front porch, where Cav now stood holding his baby sister, both waving as if they were setting sail. "CAV! I'M LEAVING! BYE, BABY!" To Key, she said, "Cav's watching Dibsy so Mama can help Granny Jewel take a bath. And he's gonna go play mini golf with Cissy. Ooooh! Kissy Cissy! He gets so mad when I say that!"

Yes, old Ell was back. In force. Already that morning, Ell told them after they'd all crowded into the overflowing Jeep, she and Cav had ridden their bikes to Mistic Meadows so she could curry Coco, which explained the faint horsey scent that accompanied her.

"What does your shirt say?" Wain asked. He attempted to read everything these days, but cursive was still a foreign language.

"'Crater of Diamonds State Park, Murfreesboro, Arkansas,'" Ell told him, pronouncing the state Ar-*kansas* and deliberately mangling the name of the town so badly that it came out sounding like a giant belch. "That's how Cav says it," she added, making Wain giggle until he fell sideways, like only Ell could. "It used to be my cousin's. Auntie Petra thought I would like it because, like, you know, I want to be a pirate and find treasure, and at this place, you can dig up diamonds and keep them! I want to go there!"

"That's our surprise!" Wain burst out, then clapped his hand over his mouth.

Ell stared at him. "We're gonna dig for diamonds?"

"*Kinda*. Something's in the back of the Jeep. But it's a surprise, so I can't tell you *any* more!"

"What's left to tell?" Key asked dryly as she parked at Pike House and waved at DP, who, in a red knit Carhartt cap and a thick plaid jacket, looked oddly unfamiliar as he stood at his truck's tailgate perusing a blueprint. "Wain, don't you have something *else* to show to Ell? Something tiny?" Wain was branching out in so many new ways that he wasn't nearly as consumed with his CartWheels as he'd been. The fact that he hadn't yet brought out Enginuity spoke volumes.

However, Enginuity *had* been the focus all weekend, lined up on the kitchen table with the rest of the CartWheels family, and when Guy called on Sunday afternoon, Wain had recounted every detail about their trip to Porterville, including their face-off with the "Picky Ickies." Guy, whom Key had never known to back down from any confrontation, was of course very supportive, but she still wasn't convinced she'd handled it exactly right. Well, it was over now. Nothing she could do about it. Live and learn.

She'd shown Wain the fishing rods, and he'd gone to bed clutching his backpack, full of seven-year-old philosophical observations. "It's like, I had a wish, oh, I want to ride a horse and *boom*! It came true. And I wish I had a fishing pole, and *boom*! It came true. *And* I got Enginuity! And I got to talk to my dad!"

She kissed his cheek. "Best weekend ever! It was very fun for me, too, buddy. And more fun tomorrow! Jukey and Mary are joining us!"

"Yay! Key, you're my grandma, right? Like, kinda anyway?"

How technical, really, did all this need to be? "Yes. I'm your grandma. Not even kinda. Forever."

"I thought so." He'd given a happy little sigh and immediately closed his eyes.

After Enginuity had been admired by both Ell and especially DP, who, as it turned out, had an affinity for old station wagons, Wain tucked it into its mesh pocket, and the children and Faro took off for the tire swing, their happy voices somehow reflected in the dappled sunshine festooning the changing leaves.

DP rolled up the blueprints. "My daddy's coming to help this week while Mama's in Alabama visiting her sister."

"Please thank him for me!" Key handed DP a small cooler. "Lunch for you guys. There's plenty for your dad too."

"Thank you, Miss Key!" DP began helping her unload. "You got enough activities for a week. Fishing poles, tackle … *metal detectors?* Y'all gonna uncover more rusty lures and old beer cans than you can carry."

"*Treasure,*" Key corrected him, laughing. "And fortunately, Jukey and Mary will be here in an hour with their ATV. They'll cart most of this to the pond."

"I was wondering! Need me to move my pickup?"

"No, they're parking down at the Morgans', where there's room for their trailer. They'll ride the ATV over here."

"Looks like y'all have a real fun day planned." DP removed his hat and ran his hands through his hair, lightly tapping his right forefinger on his earring.

Key hesitated a moment, then asked, "DP, um, is … is your earring unique?"

He tipped his head quizzically. "Unique? It ain't custom made or nothing like that."

"Do you know where Riggs got it? Is the diamond real?"

"No idea where he got it. The diamond is real. Why?"

"Well, I've been trying to think of ways Riggs could be identified, if ... if they ever find him." She wasn't ready to mention Vern Olson's matching earring. "Oh! I was also wondering. Have you ever put your DNA out there, to match to missing persons?"

DP's eyes grew cautious. "Uh, Daddy has," he replied carefully. "But for some reason Mama specifically asked that I didn't, and she hasn't either. We've never heard nothing anyway, though, like through missing persons networks or whatever."

*Interesting.* And surprising.

Or was it?

# Chapter 42

## TREASURE HUNT

When Wain showed Ell the metal detectors and the box they'd come in, her reaction was all Key could have hoped for, starting with a disbelieving, wide-eyed gape that morphed into an enormous grin, then a joyous leap into the air, which Key caught on camera. "A pirate-treasure hunter! I'm so geeked! Can I try it?"

"It's called a 'metal detector,'" Wain said as Ell launched herself dramatically at Key and threw her arms around her.

"They really work! Check it out, Ell." DP opened his fist to reveal four roofing nails. He had tested one of the detectors in the grass beside the driveway. "Flat tires prevented! But ain't it kinda bulky to tote real far?"

"Yes." Key had already told Wain and Ell that she could carry only one.

"Aw, Miss Key! I could totally carry mine the whole way!" Ell protested, hefting hers above her head. "See? And I'm getting stronger from helping with Coco." To Key's amusement, Ell managed to mention her horse in nearly every discussion.

"After a mile, Ell, you'd be singing a different tune." Key patted her shoulder. "Jukey and Mary will bring the other one."

"A fishing pole's not heavy," Wain suggested hopefully. "See? Easy peasy lemon squeezy! Greggo taught me that," he added, as Key and DP began to laugh.

"Let's wait until Jukey can show you what to do, honey," Key replied, beginning to feel as though she were sorting out the intricacies of base camp before scaling the Matterhorn.

DP held up crossed fingers. "Find lots of treasures; catch lots of fish."

"Oh! Speaking of treasure …." Key turned to the children. "Kids! Tell DP what we saw at Dogleg Pond last time." They stared blankly as Key prompted with a swirl of her hand, "White … swimming …"

"Swans!" they said in unison, and Ell added, "They swam really close to us."

"That's real awesome. High five." They slapped DP's upraised hand. "So something good's gonna happen 'cause you saw them, right? That's what my pawpaw always said."

"I'm gonna find a diamond!" Ell told him, and Key decided it wasn't the time to explain why, at least with a metal detector, she wouldn't.

Forty-five minutes later, Key relievedly leaned the metal detector (which now weighed at least a hundred pounds) against a tree, then slipped off her backpack and set her camera on top of it. She felt like a pack mule.

Ell, as it turned out, was a doggedly determined hunter. Dropping to her knees after getting a beep on the grassy swath that led from the path to the pond, she dug with the garden spade Key had brought and extracted a discolored 2004 quarter that she laid on a log. Wain's first find was a rusty bottle cap, which Ell said *of course* was part of their treasure collection. "We have to keep everything!" she told him.

"Stay where I can hear you. And fill in the holes you make!" Key called. She took the stick Faro had dropped at her feet and strolled down to the dry, cracked mud outlining the water, pausing to absorb the still dreaminess of a perfect autumn morning, the early nip in the air already nearly banished by the sun. Across the silvery expanse, early October reds, oranges, yellows, and greens created a forest fashion show, their vibrant reflections only slightly disturbed by the widening ripples where Faro's stick splashed down. She scanned branches, but except for a pair of orioles balancing delicately on bobbing reeds, the birds stayed hidden. No swans in evidence either. From the path she heard beeping, then Wain and Ell's joyful shouts. The pirates had again struck booty.

The unfamiliar, increasingly close growl of a motor cut through the sleepy silence, but only Mary stepped out of the rig. And no wonder—the ATV, which resembled a miniature pickup, was piled stem to stern with picnic supplies. There were even two lawn chairs strapped to the roof. Apparently, Key thought wryly, they were going to live here for a few months.

"I'm missing something!" Mary said teasingly, after they'd all helped unload.

"The fishing poles!" Wain exclaimed.

"Anything else?" Mary asked, laughing and ruffling his hair. "Or maybe I should say, *anyone* else?"

"Oooh. Jukey!" Wain's eyes widened. "Where is he?"

"Back at the house, talking to DP and Dawson. I won't tell him you thought *fishing pole* first! Would you kids like to ride with me to get him? If that's okay, Key?"

"Of course!"

"I want to go! I never rode in one of these! Come on, Ell!" Wain scrambled onto the front seat, but Ell wanted to keep hunting for treasure.

"I love this thing, Miss Key," she said after Mary and Wain had puttered away. "It's super fun! I can't wait to show Cav."

"You're a natural, Ell, obviously cut out of strong pirate stock." Encouraged when the little girl genuinely laughed, Key added, "I talked to Cav the other evening while you were riding Coco." They started south along the path, which, if followed for another mile or so, would end at the edge of Mistic Meadows' property.

"He told me," Ell said distractedly, sweeping the detector back and forth.

"Are things better for you at school these days? Now that Cav and Cissy have been hanging out with you?"

"Yeah. But Tally and them, they're only nice to me because of Cav." There was a beep, and Ell dropped to her knees.

"You're a bit of a detector yourself, Ell," Key said wryly. As much as she wished Ell's instincts weren't true, she was probably right. "If that's the case, you need to decide if they're the kind of true, real friends you can count on. Something similar happened to me the other day."

"It still happens when you're *old*?" Ell asked, her freckles bunched together as she squinted at Key.

Key laughed and sat down next to her, sifting through the dirt. "It does!" Keeping it simple, she recounted how Nina LaDane had inadvertently told her about her exclusion from the Sage Sleuths. "I would have enjoyed being in a detective club. Then I thought about what you and I talked about, you know, about giving your power away?"

Ell nodded and Key continued, "The best way to deal with it, I've discovered, is to concentrate on what you *can* do. Find new friends. Become an expert at your hobbies, like riding Coco and metal detecting. Talk about your feelings with people you trust. I'm so much happier now that I have real friends like you, your parents, Wain, his dad, Mary and Jukey, DP ..."

Ell held up a green-tinged coin. "It's a dime!" As she began brushing dirt back into the shallow depression, she added, "I made a friend in my class. His name is Javon, and he has a sister in third grade. Cissy knows them."

"I'm so glad!" Key exclaimed. "And you know you can always count on me too. Friends come in all ages." She patted Ell's back. "I do hope someday you're okay with telling your mom and dad."

Ell stood and brushed off her clothes. "Maybe someday. It's a lot better now because of Coco and Cav and Cissy."

"The three C's." Key stood too. "But Ell, remember, it's mostly better because of ..." She took a stick and drew a *U* in the freshly dug dirt, then patted Ell's shoulder. "It may not make your detector beep, but that, my dear, is pure treasure."

# Chapter 43

## PICKLES

Taro perked up his ears, whined, and raced toward the picnic site. Key and Ell arrived a few minutes later to find three more chairs set up, Mary already meandering through the pines, and Jukey and Wain baiting Wain's fishhook with a squirming, muddy night crawler.

Wain held up another worm just as Ell showed him her dime, and Key snapped a picture of the two of them comparing treasures. "Look, Key!" he called. "It's like the gummy worm my friend Ava gave me at school!"

"Mmmm! Looks delicious!" Key teased, noting the streak of mud on Wain's cheek where he'd scratched a fresh mosquito bite. *Insect repellent. Sunscreen.* She'd brought both, but they sat forgotten in the side pocket of her backpack. *Honestly,* she thought guiltily, as she retrieved the sprays, *how did we survive?* During her childhood, mosquito bites and sunburns had been insignificant rites of passage. *Grab the Solarcaine spray,* her mother would say complacently when Key showed her a reddened, coconut-scented shoulder. Not that she didn't see the point of taking protective measures, of course, but her to-do list seemed much longer than that of her mother's. Caring for Wain was a daily, multifaceted enterprise, and she was still an intern.

The subject of her concern, however, was completely unbothered by sun, mosquito bites, mud, worms, potential hook stabs, or anything else the great outdoors could throw at him. He just wanted to fish.

Key joined the trio. "Hi, Jukey!"

"Good morning, Key North! Ready to fish, Ell?" Jukey handed Wain his pole.

Ell crept a little closer. "I've fished before, with my daddy and Cav and my pappy in Florida."

Jukey nodded. "Want to grab a crawler, bait this hook?"

Ell locked her hands behind her back. "Uh-uh. Will you do the first one?"

Chuckling, Jukey attached a bobber to the line and began expertly tying on a hook. "Like I told your compatriot here, if you want to be a true fisherman ..." He stopped and looked expectantly at Wain.

Wain pointed at the worm. "You have to bait your own hook! I'm gonna do my next one by myself."

"I might not be a true fisherman," Ell gingerly accepted the pole, avoiding looking at the night crawler. "I'm, like, into treasure hunting."

"You ask me, two cuts of the same cloth. Hope and failure and success. Try both out," Jukey suggested, "then you can make an informed decision."

"Come over here, you two," Key said. Shaking a can, she sufficiently protected the children from UV rays and minute bloodthirsty predators.

"Been too long since Mary and I spent quality time with Mother Nature." Jukey snipped surplus line from a knot, then slung a folding chair over his shoulder and picked up an ancient once-green metal tackle box. Catching Key's smile, he held it out, saying, "It was my grandpa's," and she took a picture of the three of them, hoping the camera had sufficiently captured the stories in the tackle box's patina, Ell's ambiguous expression, and the anticipation practically pulsating from Wain's wiry body. "We're gonna work on casting over there on the south edge of the pond, where there's deeper water and not so many reeds. Grab the worms, son."

Wain gave a joyful skip. "Yahoo! I hope we see the swans again!"

"You all saw the swans?" Jukey exclaimed. "That's unusual. They normally hang out behind the jetty, away from the party scene."

"The party scene?" Key repeated.

"There used to be a path straight through the woods from Pike Road to here. Back in the day, teenage drivers dropped off their friends, then drove to a parking area where Mistic Meadows' property line now is. The unlucky driver had to hike back." Jukey pointed with his fishing pole. "I imagine those metal detectors would be buzzing like hornets at the drop-off spot. Can tabs and bottle caps, most likely. Ready, kids?" They headed toward the pond.

Key peered into the woods (where, as far as she could tell, there was absolutely no sign of a trail), then draped Faro's leash around her own neck, selected two seltzers from the cooler, and went to join Mary, who'd set up a pair of chairs near the water. "How'd Wain like the ATV?" she asked.

"Five minutes in, he told me he was pretty sure he could drive it himself because it was his size of car."

"Well, I certainly hope you let him! What could possibly go wrong?" They laughed, shading their eyes to watch the fishing trio traipse across the cracked mud, Wain in front, carefully toting the little Styrofoam bucket of worms, followed by Ell chattering to a nodding Jukey. Key whistled for Faro and snapped the leash on to his collar before he could take off after them.

"Oh, just look at the view! Why don't we schedule this kind of day like we do everything else?" Mary leaped aside as Faro shuddered off about a quart of water.

"Wain's going to remember this day forever, Mary." *Guy should be here, enjoying fishing and hiking and father-son activities.* The thought came out of nowhere. It would be two years before he would be home for good. It seemed like forever.

After about half an hour, Mary jumped up, shielding her eyes. "Ooh! Bite? It looks like Jukey might have one on the line!"

Key raised her camera and zoomed in, taking several shots as Jukey reeled in a smallish fish while Wain and Ell danced and cheered. They huddled around him as he removed the hook and gently slipped the fish back into the pond.

"Bass," Mary said when Key showed her the magnified picture. "They'll have fishing fever now that they know it can happen."

But by noon, after it had become so warm that Key and Mary had moved their chairs into the shade, Jukey's catch had been the only one, though Wain was sure he'd had several nibbles.

"Today's all about learning, and your time's coming, kids," Jukey assured them as they filled their plates. "But afternoons aren't the best for fishing this pond."

"We can treasure hunt," Ell said, looking relieved.

After the children had devoured everything (even, to Key's great surprise, her black bean salad), they headed for the path with metal detectors, spade, and cupcakes in hand.

Jukey called them back. "Dogleg's water level is low right now. In that dried mud around the edge of the pond, you got a chance to find lures, maybe even coins that might have fallen into the water back in the day. All manner of treasure courtesy of Dogleg's partiers and fishermen."

"Be careful of hooks!" Mary called as Wain and Ell raced off.

"What'd I tell you?" Jukey called with a touch of delighted smugness when both detectors went off almost immediately.

Ell and Wain easily unearthed two ancient lures, a Cheerwine bottle cap, a penny, and a single key. Each item was rinsed off and added to the treasure stash. It was obvious they'd be busy for a while.

"If I had a hammock, I'd take a nap." Jukey leaned back in his chair and put his hands behind his head. "Where'd you get the pickles, Key North? Put one of those on a sandwich and no caviar on a cracker is better."

"Honey, the closest you've ever come to caviar is if that bass you caught is female," Mary joked.

"The pickles are from Granny Jewel." Key recounted the pimpwich story, and when they'd all stopped laughing, she exclaimed, "Oh, I almost forgot!" She showed them the pictures from the concert. "These were in with Lonny's old things."

"Yep, that's the Ayo I remember." Jukey zoomed in for a better look. "I don't remember him being so muscular though."

Mary swiped back and forth between the two pictures. "Key, I think Ayo *could* be Vern. Don't you?"

Before Key could answer or point out Ayo's green wristband, their peaceful afternoon was shattered by Ell's scream.

# Chapter 44

## MUDDIED STRING

"Oh no!" Key bolted in a panic toward the pond, her frantic imagination conjuring up a fall into deep water, broken bones, a life-threatening injury, wild animals, or any horrifying combination of the four. To her overwhelming relief, however, the children were simply huddled with their heads together, gazing at whatever Ell was holding in her hand. Several yards away, Faro ambled casually through a grove of birch trees, his nose riffling a layer of sawtooth-edged golden leaves. Even the water was perfectly still.

"Kids! Are you all right?" Key exhaled the words in short, ragged bursts as she rubbed the stitch in her side.

Jukey and Mary showed up a few seconds later, panting. "What happened? Who's hurt?"

Ell held up what appeared to be a filthy string with a mud-coated medallion dangling from it. "Look what I found! Treasure! *Real* treasure!"

"Oh!" Mary leaned on her knees, laughing weakly. In one hand she held a small tin first aid kit. "So not a fishhook in a major artery, then."

"I'm gonna rinse it off!" Before anyone could stop her, Ell waded in, shoes and all. "Ooooh!" She danced a splashy little jig. "Diamonds! I *told* you I'd find diamonds! Cav is gonna be so super jealous!"

Jukey chuckled. "Some grandma is probably still wondering what happened to her necklace. Didn't realize she lost it skinny-dipping in 1978."

"Jukey *King*!" Mary shook her head as Key began laughing. "These children do not need to hear about skinny-dipping! Goodness!"

"Call of the wild," Jukey replied enigmatically, putting an arm around his wife. "Let's see what you've got there, Ell Morgan."

Ell squished back to the group, her leggings wet to mid-thigh, mud oozing through the eyelets of her sneakers. She laid the medallion on her palm. "One side has diamonds, and there's some scratches on the other side."

"Whoa," Wain reached out a tentative forefinger to gently sway what was not a string at all but a sturdy, untarnished chain with a broken clasp dangling from Ell's hand. "It *is* treasure!"

"*Real* treasure." Ell was basking in the glory. "I'm gonna keep it forever! So drippy!"

"Drippy?" Key asked, not necessarily expecting an answer. She took a closer look. "This might actually be genuine gold."

"'Drippy' means stylish, Key," Mary informed her, then said teasingly, "Try to keep up!"

"I'll add it to my vocabulary list, right under 'helicopter parents' and 'bougie.'"

"*Oh, no. No. Oh, no.*"

Key whirled around. Jukey had put on his glasses and was staring over Mary's shoulder at the medallion as if he'd seen an apparition. He extended a faintly trembling hand and said urgently, "Ell, I need to see that." All trace of his good humor had vanished.

"Why?" Ell closed both fists over the necklace and clutched it to her chest, retreating several feet from the group. "Jukey, finders keepers! That's what you *told* us!"

"Normally, yes." Jukey pulled a pristine white handkerchief from his jeans pocket and flicked it open, saying in that same strangled voice, "But please, Ell, give it to me. I need to look at it more closely."

"Please let Jukey see it, honey," Key said kindly after Ell again refused, though she couldn't make sense of any of this. "You know he wouldn't ask if it wasn't very important."

With a loud huff, Ell reluctantly dropped the necklace into Jukey's hand, then tightly crossed her arms. "No fair! I found it!"

Key gave Ell's stiff shoulders a comforting squeeze and glanced questioningly at Mary, who responded with a mystified shrug.

Jukey carefully placed the medallion on the handkerchief and began to rub it, flipping it over several times. Finally, he held it out on his palm. His disbelieving eyes met first Mary's, then Key's. He whispered, "Do you see it?"

"See what?" Mary asked. They all moved closer.

Jukey cleared his throat and began counting. "One, two, three, four, five diamonds. And here are three more, the stars on his belt. It's the constellation Orion."

It took a few seconds for his words to sink in. "*Jukey!*" Mary gasped, stumbling backward and pressing a hand over her mouth. She looked again. "Are you saying—Is that ..."

When Jukey turned the medallion over, it was Key's turn to gasp as he said somberly, "What Ell thought were scratches are engraved letters. *R-I-P.* Ah! I don't recall his middle name! Did it start with *I*?"

By now Key knew the name as well as her own. "Riggs Inman Plummer." Her voice sounded unfamiliar—hollow, distant. If Jukey was right, it was the very medallion Riggs had been clutching in the concert picture they'd been studying moments before.

Her next thought sent goose bumps tingling down her arms. *Lonny's dream!* He'd seen Riggs standing by a pond, clutching his neck and showing him an *L.* He hadn't meant *loser.* No, Riggs had shown Lonny who would find the necklace. *Ell.* And where the necklace was buried. *The pond!*

As if to certify her thoughts, the notes of a cardinal's cheery song fell like musical droplets into the solemn, uncanny silence, but Key and Mary were the only ones who tipped their heads, searching the upper branches of a nearby loblolly pine to discover the singer perched high above them, a slash of brilliant red juxtaposed against the shadowy green needles and shining patches of heavenly blue. *A visitor from beyond.* Key's grandmother had always believed cardinals were harbingers of love from those who had passed before.

"So fitting," Mary murmured, tears welling in her eyes, and Key knew she was thinking the same thing.

Wain finagled his way under Key's arm into the center, his nose almost touching Jukey's hand. "'*R-I-P.*'" He looked up at Key. "Hey! Like the tattoo on DP's arm!"

Curiosity trumped Ell's distress. "Who's *R-I-P?*"

"Riggs Plummer. DP's older brother." Key's eyes remained locked on the medallion. "He's been missing for twenty years, and most likely this necklace belonged to him."

"Ohhh!" Ell pieced it together. "My daddy's friend!"

"Yes." Jukey, still very shaken, flipped the medallion to the Orion side and rubbed more mud off the diamonds, then examined the broken clasp. Lifting his head, he studied the landscape. No one spoke. It was dizzying, hypnotizing—as though they'd been catapulted into the dark recesses of the past, then emerged into the sunny present with nothing gained but the necklace and the secrets it held.

"It looks like our mystery has moved from anywhere in the world to your backyard, Key North." Jukey reverently folded the necklace into the handkerchief, saying softly, "I'll drive back, get Dawson and DP. They need to identify it, see where Ell found it."

Ell touched the dirt-stained fabric. "But why was the necklace buried in the mud?"

"We'll do our best to find out, honey." Jukey's voice had returned to normal, but his alert, focused posture gave Key an indication of why he was such a successful tracker.

"We should mark this spot," she suggested, pointing at the shallow depression Ell had dug three feet from the water's edge. "Wain, please go find eight skinny sticks. We'll put them around the hole."

"Okay! Come on, Faro!" Full of importance, boy and dog dashed into the woods.

Jukey put his hand on Ell's shoulder. "Will you hold on to the treasure until I bring Dawson and DP back here? It's you who should show them what you found."

"Will I get to keep it after they see it?" Ell asked hopefully.

"If this is Riggs's necklace, it belongs to the Plummers," Jukey replied, and Ell's shoulders slumped once again. "It may even help find him! That would be the most priceless treasure ever, and Ell Morgan, you will always be a part of that gift. Does that make sense?"

"Yeah," Ell replied with a heavy sigh. She didn't sound at all convinced.

"Where did DP's brother *go*?" Wain asked as he and Key placed sticks in a crude frame around the hole.

Key explained Riggs's disappearance as simply as possible. "Now we need to figure out how the necklace ended up in the water."

Was Riggs in the pond? Buried beneath them right here in the mud? The thought gave her chills. She could clearly visualize the crossroads at which the Plummers now stood. In minutes, their world would be overturned once more, courtesy of the most bewildering yet hopeful news they'd had in two decades.

"But this isn't *water*," Wain argued. "Look! It's, like, cracked-up dirt!"

"When we have more rain and the pond is deeper, the water covers all this dried mud."

"How long has DP's brother been gone?" They started back to the picnic area, where a watchful Faro, who Key had leashed to Ell's chair once Wain had collected the sticks, began whimpering. He sensed the change in everyone's mood.

"Riggs has been missing for twenty years."

"Whoa. Is that as old as my dad?"

"Hmm." Key frowned. "If you're asking how old Riggs would be today, he would be forty. Your dad is thirty-three."

Wain halted in his tracks. "Wait. My dad is *that* old?"

Key smiled. "He is that old."

"Are *you* that old?"

She laughed outright. As usual, Wain's innocence added a refreshing luminosity to the most difficult conversations. "I'm way older than thirty-three. I'm almost fifty-eight!"

"*What?* Whoa! That is like ... I mean ... like grandma age!" Wain pretended to fall over, then staggered comically to the blanket and flopped down next to Faro and his backpack. *Ancient history*, Key thought, picking up the plates and cups they'd dropped in their mad dash to the pond. *And that's the way it should be.* Without new generations, pain would never grow distant.

Mary, sitting in a chair next to Ell, caught Key's last sentence. "Almost fifty-eight? You're just a year younger than me! When's your birthday, Key?"

"November fifth." Maybe, she thought, she should celebrate in light years because that's how far she felt from those days when Jeff handed her a card with his first name scribbled under some tepidly worded sentiment, accompanied by a professionally wrapped box containing a valuable piece of jewelry chosen by whatever assistant to whom he'd handed his credit card. (Jeff had never tried to hide that fact; in fact, he was proud of being successful enough to delegate the job.) She smiled. All of Jeff's gifts combined were no match for the value of a certain gold plastic star.

"Oh, we'll have to celebrate!" Mary exclaimed. "What's your favorite kind of cake?"

"I can never choose between carrot or German chocolate." Key knew Mary was purposely keeping the conversation mundane, but how strange it was to be discussing birthdays and cake when Ell was cradling such a monumental piece of the Plummers' life in her very grubby pirate hands.

"I've got a carrot cake recipe to die for saved on my phone." Mary rose and gave Key a knowing glance, and as they walked away, she said softly, "Vern's tattoo had those initials on the tombstone!"

"Yes. But again ... what does that prove? It's a typical tombstone sentiment!"

Mary made a face. "You're right. Are you going to tell the Plummers about Vern?"

"Not yet. We have zero proof. If this *is* Riggs's necklace, the Plummers need to focus on discovering what that means."

"Key, somehow this medallion traveled from a concert in Virginia to right here in Dogleg Pond! But *how*? And how long has it been there?"

"By the looks of it, a long, long time, I'd say. I'm as bewildered as you are."

Mary tapped her head. "Jukey has tracked birds and deer his whole life. That man has got something going on in that brain of his."

"I can't wait to hear what he's thinking. Who could have ever predicted our day would end like this?" Key glanced over at the children. Wain lay on his back on the blanket, using a sleeping Faro as a pillow, one foot crossed over a bent knee, examining Enginuity once again. He'd detached the tiny surfboard. Ell was softly humming "You Are My Sunshine" and rotating the medallion between her fingers.

It was heartbreaking to think of the years the necklace had languished under water and silt while its owner's loved ones grieved. The answers remained buried, but something otherworldly had occurred that day. Orion was on the hunt. Riggs was tugging that muddy string.

Correction—he was tugging a golden chain.

*Hallelujah!* the cardinal sang.

# Chapter 45

## FATHER AND BROTHER

" Key?" Wain sounded serious.

"What's up, buddy?" Key carried cookies and juice to the children, along with two dog treats. She might have trouble remembering sunscreen, but snacks? Never.

"Should I show Enginuity to DP again?" he asked as Ell silently looked on. "I found something else on it to show him. It might make him feel better."

So he wasn't as unaffected by the afternoon's events as she'd thought. Key smoothed his hair. "Maybe later. He'll want to see what Ell found." She checked her watch: almost three o'clock. She and Mary had agreed that after Ell gave the Plummers the necklace, the children would be driven back to Pike House.

Mary hurried over. "I hear a motor. Oh, my stomach is in knots!" She let out a little gasp as a minute later, four men stepped out of the ATV. "Lonny's with them!"

"Afternoon," Dawson said courteously.

Key had been around DP's father only twice, and both times she'd been impressed with Dawson's understated, elegant style, so it was strange to see him in construction gear, a pair of leather gloves reaching like empty hands from the back pocket of his pants. She now knew, too, that his was the face of a man who daily forced himself to operate in a realm beyond his own pain.

"Daddy!" Ell stood up, and Lonny hurried over to her. Both Plummers watched curiously as, still holding the wrapped necklace, she dropped her cookie (which Faro immediately ate), threw her arms around his waist, and burst into tears.

"Hey, hey," Lonny said soothingly, smoothing her hair. "You're gonna be okay, baby girl."

"Dawson, DP …" Jukey said, gesturing toward two chairs. "Ell found something today."

"What'd you find, darlin'?" Dawson asked casually as he and DP sat down. "Something that belongs to us?"

Ell's uncharacteristic lack of drama added an almost-unbearably simple intensity to the moment. "This," she said, her startling violet-blue eyes meeting first Dawson's, then DP's. Opening her fist, she displayed Jukey's now very wrinkled, muddy handkerchief, but the necklace wasn't showing. As she dropped it into Dawson's outstretched hand, the necklace slipped from the fabric and landed on his thigh, engraved side up. It was as though, Key and Mary later agreed, Riggs couldn't wait a single second longer.

Time and sound were suspended as Dawson and DP stared down at the medallion, clearly unable to process what they were seeing.

"See, DP?" Wain's eager voice broke the silence. "*R-I-P!* Like your tattoo! We were treasure hunting, and Ell found it!"

"What …?" DP leaned closer. "*What?*"

"*Riggs!*" Dawson choked out. It was a cry two decades in the making. Pressing the necklace to his chest, he tipped his head back and closed his eyes. DP simply leaned forward and rested his pale face in his palms. They said nothing more, asked no questions.

Key put her arm around Wain, and with the others, they quietly moved away.

"How did Jukey find you so fast?" Mary asked Lonny.

"I stopped by to show DP the pictures, was just gettin' out of my rig when Jukey drove up and told me what was goin' on." His face, too, was pale. "I can't believe it. That is for sure Riggs's necklace."

Jukey glanced over to where DP and Dawson were passing the necklace back and forth, rubbing the medallion as though it were an oracle. "Seeing some vestige of Riggs after all this time knocked the breath clean out of them."

"Have they seen the concert pictures?" Key asked Lonny.

"No, ma'am. Haven't had no chance to show or tell them nothing." He put his arm around a subdued Ell. "You did real good, baby girl. Jukey, sir, if I can use the ATV, I'll drive Ell and Wain and Faro to my mama's, then come back. Gayle's expecting them."

Key sagged with relief. She would gladly have taken the children, but she didn't want to leave Jukey and Mary to manage all the cleanup. Faro adamantly refused to climb into the ATV, though; and finally, Key gave up. "Leave him here with me," she told Lonny. "I'll walk him back."

"Wait!" DP called out. He and Dawson hurried toward them. "*Where* did you find this, Ell?"

"I found it down in the mud." Ell pointed toward the pond, then cried excitedly, "Look!"

From his seat in the ATV, Wain stood up to see. "The swans!"

# Chapter 46

## HELL OR LOW WATER

"This where my girl found the necklace?" Lonny queried, rejoining the group half an hour later.

"Right there." Jukey pointed to the hole in the mud.

Lonny frowned. "That don't make no sense whatsoever. One hundred percent Riggs was wearin' it the day he disappeared." He handed his phone to Dawson. "Sir. This was at the concert. That's why I was at Miss Key's house today when Jukey drove up. To show y'all some pictures Gayle found in my things."

Father and son took turns studying the picture, zooming in on the chain and the medallion just visible beneath Riggs's hand.

"Hey, bro," DP said wistfully. "It's real good to see him in a picture I never saw before."

Dawson, however, almost seemed to take offense. "Why am I only now seeing this?" he asked testily, thrusting Lonny's phone back at him. "We shoulda seen that way back in the day."

Lonny met his eyes. "I don't even remember getting them from Shasta Harrison, sir. In fact, her note says somethin' about Riggs bein' gone, real casual, like we was all still thinkin' he's gonna come back."

"The *note*?" Dawson's exasperation was evolving to anger. "Seems we're the last—"

DP lifted a hand. "Lonny said he was comin' to tell us, Daddy."

Lonny scrolled through his phone, frowning. "I thought I had a picture of the note in here."

"I have a picture of the note." Key passed Dawson her phone. "I was at Granny Jewel's the day Gayle found the pictures." The ensuing silence as Dawson read the note grew as thick as the mud on which they were standing.

"Seems we're the last to know anything," Dawson snapped. "How does a stranger come to get that information before I did?"

"Dawson …" Jukey said quietly, a strand of warning threaded through his voice. "We're all on the same page here. Searching for answers."

Dawson handed Key her phone, then lifted his cap and rubbed his bald head. Retreating several steps to a grassy spot, he sat heavily on the ground. "I hate to tell Olive *anything* till we get this figured out."

"Where is Olive?" Jukey asked.

"In Birmingham, visiting her sister."

"Just as well, Daddy," DP put in. "She'd have a real hard time with all of this."

"She would that." Dawson compressed his lips. "This fresh angle makes everything ten times more complicated. Now we gotta consider that Riggs came back, maybe went swimming and drowned, and we never knew?"

Key was startled. *Drowned?* She'd never envisioned a scenario where Riggs would have come back home and deliberately avoided his family. Judging from the guarded looks on everyone else's faces, neither had they.

"We'll get it figured out, my friend," Jukey said. He added quietly, "Swans are heading back west, toward the far side of the jetty." The magnificent birds glided effortlessly through incandescent ripples of water metamorphosed into silver and gold and diamonds by the late-afternoon sun.

"Don't go," Dawson whispered brokenly, and it seemed to Key that he hadn't meant to say the words aloud. "I'm so sorry, son." He began weeping—raw, soul-crushing sobs that sounded as though they'd been wrenched from a bottomless well of grief. Next to Key, Mary, too, was wiping tears from her face. It felt like a funeral.

DP crouched down and put a comforting arm around his father, whose tears obviously weren't new to him. *What a terrible burden for a surviving child to bear*, Key thought.

"Daddy," he said gently, "we're closer now than we've ever been. You know how I've told you I feel like Riggs is calling to me? We gotta believe this was meant to happen."

"I feel the same, DP," Lonny said, swiping a hand from his eyes to his chin.

The cardinal began singing again.

Jukey walked several steps toward the picnic area, made a measured full turn, and narrowed his eyes, contemplating the landscape. "Dawson, let's organize a search and start fresh tomorrow morning. Key North, could we meet at your place?"

"Of course!"

"Let's go." Dawson grasped the hand DP offered, scrambled to his feet, and started up the hill. The no-nonsense boss had suddenly emerged and was taking charge. "We'll be back tomorrow, and if Riggs is in this pond, I'm gonna find him. I'm gonna *find my son*."

With six people and all the equipment, they'd need to make multiple trips back and forth. After loading the ATV, Jukey left with Dawson and DP, and Lonny helped Key and Mary pack up the remaining supplies.

"Oh my goodness. Dawson was so torn up. I've never seen him like that." Mary still sounded shaken.

"No disrespect to Dawson, but he ain't thinkin' clearly right now. The hurt is coming out from the bruises on his soul." Lonny stacked the folded chairs, then leaned against a tree, crossing his arms and staring at the pond. "If Riggs *did* come back here, how did *no one* see him?" he asked. "There wan't a person in this county back then who didn't know Riggs Plummer. And to get here, he woulda gone right past Mama's house, where I was. Why wouldn't he stop there? Furthermore, Riggs could swim like a fish, so how would he *drown*?"

"I was surprised Dawson mentioned drowning," Key said as Mary nodded in agreement.

"I'm gonna say what we're all thinking," Lonny replied grimly. "Ayo murdered Riggs, then thrown his body in the pond."

"But ... how'd he do all that without you and Shasta seeing?" Key asked.

"We gotta figure that out." Lonny pressed a balled fist to his forehead. "Cause he *wasn't* in the van."

"Jukey's thinking it through," Mary assured them. "You'll see."

Key shouldered her backpack. "I'm going to walk with Faro. Easier than forcing him into the ATV. I'll see you back at my place." *

Patches of late-afternoon sun created shadowy stepping stones as she started down the path. Maybe, she thought hopefully, that same light would illuminate a medallion-shaped clue in the Plummers' dark mystery.

# Chapter 47

## PLANS

They made it back to Pike House in record time, her thoughts bouncing like loose marbles in every possible direction, all rolling to a stop facing one blazing question: How did Riggs's necklace end up *there*? As she joined the group gathered on her driveway near DP's pickup, she sensed the tension.

"For the first time since he went missing, we've got new information!" Dawson was saying forcefully to Jukey. "Riggs *could* have hitchhiked back here and camped at Dogleg! We got to start with draining the pond."

"I'm not saying you shouldn't drain the pond." Jukey appeared completely unruffled. "Just that maybe it makes sense to search the woods first—"

Dawson slammed his fist hard against the side of the pickup, making all of them jump except DP. "How would you feel, Jukey? If it was your son?"

"I would not leave a stone unturned, Dawson." Jukey laid his hand lightly on Dawson's shoulder. "We can start wherever you feel is best."

"Okay, then. We start with the pond." Dawson crossed his arms, breathing hard.

To Key, he suddenly seemed very fragile, as though the cracks and fissures he'd held at bay for two decades might at any moment crumble into a flood of irrevocable anguish. If the necklace didn't lead to finding Riggs (or at least provide answers), Dawson's grief might erupt one final time and harden, emptying him forever like the hollow lava tubes she'd once visited in Hawaii.

"What if we hired divers, Daddy?" DP suggested. "Be a lot faster than waiting for permission from the railroad to drain the pond."

"How deep is the pond?" asked Mary, who'd been quietly perusing her phone.

"Thirty feet at the most," Jukey replied. "You got an idea, honey?"

"Yes." Mary touched Dawson's forearm. "What if we started with cadaver dogs? They can smell human remains underwater. They'll search on land too."

"Best suggestion yet, honey," Jukey said.

It was the best suggestion yet, but Dawson wasn't convinced. "We're talking twenty years. Don't see how any dog can help after all that time."

"Dogs have found *bone fragments*, even after much longer," Mary replied. "If they alert to something in the pond, a diver can check it out."

"You know anyone with that kind of dog, Mary?" DP asked eagerly.

"No, but I know who would." Mary pointed at her sweatshirt logo. "This podcaster, Wolverine. He lives in Porterville. Riggs's case was the first one he covered." Mary showed Dawson the app. "Wolverine once hired dogs to search a lake in West Virginia for a missing teenager, and they found his body. It was so sad, but such a relief for his family."

"I think it's a great idea, Daddy," DP said. There was a silence.

Dawson tugged the necklace from his pants pocket and began flipping the medallion over and over between his thumb and forefinger. "Okay," he finally said grudgingly. "If pod man can get dogs in tomorrow, we'll start searching in the mud where this was found, then we move on to the water. How do we get ahold of him?"

"Key's met him," Mary said. All eyes swiveled to Key; Dawson's were unreadable.

Key pulled her phone from her pocket. "I'll call Wolverine right now." After a short, intense conversation, she returned to the group. "He's in," she told them to audible sighs of relief. "I'll let you all know when he finds someone. Can we set up a group text?"

After everyone exchanged numbers, Dawson announced, "Anyone who can, meet here at eight tomorrow morning. Bring shovels, gloves, water. DP, you talk to Molly's daddy about getting ahold of the railroad. If we do need to call in divers or drain the pond, I want all the ducks in a row."

"Use my outdoor patio as a base," Key suggested. "I'll bring lunch."

"Me and my brother are in," Lonny said. "Larry's gonna bring his four-wheeler."

"We'll leave our ATV here too," Jukey told Dawson. "And I'll be here."

"I've got to mind the store," Mary said regretfully. "Maybe I can find someone to fill in."

Key stowed Faro in the far back of the Jeep, then gave Mary and Jukey a ride back to the Morgans', where they'd parked their truck. "You know," she mused aloud as she drove, "in my mind, it all comes back to Ayo and the green wristband." The Kings both looked mystified. She tapped her wrist. "The one I told you about at lunch. When I showed you the concert pictures?"

Mary cocked her head. "Key, am I going crazy? I don't remember anything about a green wristband."

"Me neither," Jukey said.

"Oh, that's right!" Key smacked her forehead. "Everything went sideways after Ell screamed!" As they parked and unloaded supplies, she explained.

Jukey nodded. "Okay. Now we know for a fact that Ayo *did* exit the concert. That's got to be significant." He began unhitching the flatbed trailer from his pickup.

"Hey, Jukey!" Wain came bounding down the hill from Granny Jewel's and tossed his CartWheels backpack into the Jeep, then dug into his shorts pocket. "I gotta show you one more thing on my new car. It's so cool!"

"Yeah? What's the latest in CartWheels coolness?" Jukey put on his glasses, then sat down on the trailer, patting the spot next to him. He sounded weary and distracted, but as always, Key thought gratefully, he took the time to listen.

Up on Granny Jewel's porch, Gayle, Ell, and Dibsy appeared and began making their way at Dibsy-speed down the drive. Key unhooked Faro's leash from the Jeep bumper. She'd meet them halfway so she could properly thank Gayle.

"It does *what*?" she heard Jukey exclaim before she'd taken three steps. She spun around to see him examining Enginuity and Wain swinging his feet, looking pleased. "Has Key North seen this?" Jukey asked.

"Not yet. I just figured it out today! I kinda *thought* you'd like it." Wain sounded as proud as a new father.

"You thought right." Jukey pulled his phone from his pocket. "I gotta call Corny. Mary, honey, would you please text the group, ask DP and Dawson and Lonny to come over here right away? First the necklace, then the green wristband, now this. I'm telling you what, this has been the day to end all days."

# Chapter 48

## ABSENCE IS A PRESENCE

While they waited for the Plummers and Lonny, Jukey held an animated conversation with Corny, and Key and Mary caught an enthralled Gayle up on the day's events. Sprawled on the Morgans' front steps, Wain, Ell, and Dibsy devoured ice pops, and under the enormous magnolia tree, Gayle's free-range Rhode Island Reds pecked and clucked. Such normalcy on the surface, but an ultrasonic urgency hummed above them all.

Jukey finished his call and joined them, nodding with grim satisfaction. "Got news."

As they made their way up the hill to Granny Jewel's, Key's phone pinged. *Mack.*

I found a last-minute flight. Get in tomorrow 10 AM, leave Friday PM. I'll rent a car in Porterville. What do you think?

*Of all the days.*

-Oh, perfect timing! So much to tell you—I'll call in a bit

As the group trooped onto the porch, Granny Jewel greeted everyone from her wheelchair, her hugs for DP and Dawson especially poignant. With a sense of déjà vu, Key accepted a cup of sweet tea, grateful this time for the sugar boost. In the center of the ring of chairs, Dibsy played with her veterinarian set while inside Wain and Ell were curled up on the couch, enthralled by Dude Perfect videos.

Jukey, who was leaning against the porch railing, surprised everyone with his first question. "How much do you weigh, Lonny?"

Lonny shrugged. "We don't got a scale. Still wear the same size I did in high school, so maybe one-seventy?"

Jukey turned to Dawson. "Got a general idea of what Riggs weighed when he went missing?"

"One-sixty or so," Dawson replied. "Why?"

Jukey held up a finger. "DP, big strong guy like you, could you pick up Lonny, deadweight off the ground, and throw him over your shoulder?"

Judging by the puzzled faces, no one was following Jukey's train of thought, but DP, agreeable as always, simply answered the question. "I probably could."

"Could you carry him half a mile?"

DP looked doubtful. "It would be a struggle. Probably not without help or a hand truck or some such."

A grim picture materialized in Key's mind.

"Okay." Jukey sounded gratified at DP's answers. "For the purposes of this conversation, we're going to assume someone harmed Riggs at the concert and brought him back to this area. And let's say the name; it's Ayo Jones we're talking about."

"*How?*" Lonny asked, his puzzled face mirroring everyone else's.

"I'll get to that. So we all agree that even a strong man would struggle mightily to carry a one-hundred-sixty-pound body a half mile through the woods, then somehow conceal him well enough that for two decades, despite all the partiers and fishermen who hung out at Dogleg Pond, not a single molecule of this body or its possessions was found. Until the necklace today." Jukey shrugged. "In my mind, that is impossible."

"I agree, Jukey!" Granny Jewel boomed. "What's your thought, then? What happened?"

"I have a scenario that at least merits speculation. I've asked Wain to show us his new little car."

"I'll get him." Key opened the door. "Ready, buddy?"

"Wain, you want to show everyone what you showed Key and me earlier?" Jukey asked.

"It's my new CartWheel." Wain placed the car on his palm and made the rounds. "It's called Enginuity and it's, like, a old-time car called a Woodie that, um, they drived to the ocean to go surfing." He'd come up with that impromptu recap all on his own, and Key felt she would burst with pride.

"Where do you store Enginuity's surfboard?" Jukey asked.

"It snaps on to the roof, but—" Wain opened the little car's tailgate. "There's, like, a secret compartment where you can slide the surfboard into the back." Again, he made his rounds, displaying a compartment that extended for the length of the car under the seats.

"That's a real nice toy car, son," Dawson said in a tone that clearly conveyed, *Why are y'all wasting my time?* "But Jukey, I know where you're going with this, and it's a dead end."

"Hear me out, Dawson. Thank you, son." Jukey patted Wain's shoulder, and the children went back inside. "Corny says the regular vans used by Castle Phoenix had a raised floor. Under this floor, they stashed their longer tools on a piece of plywood with hinged legs. When they slid the plywood out the rear doors, the legs unfolded, providing a tabletop workspace. I asked Corny: Theoretically could a man—and I sincerely apologize that this is distressing, Dawson and DP—could a man's body fit in there, and Corny says no way. Not high enough."

"Jukey, I know all this!" Dawson burst out, exasperated. "I *went* to Castle Phoenix. *Talked* to Joe Castle. He *showed* me the vans. There's *no question* in my mind it was too small … a … a … space."

"Joe didn't show you one other van, a junker with no logo on it, busted back door. This one had a compartment that spanned the width of the vehicle, rear tire to rear tire, shallower over the axle, deeper toward the center of the van. A storage compartment for tarps and whatnot, accessed by a—a I guess it'd be something of a trapdoor. In this van, the rakes and shovels were attached to the inside walls."

Lonny's eyes widened. "There were tools attached to the inside walls of Ayo's van. And no logo."

Jukey nodded. "From what Corny described, I believe a body could have fit into the space I just described." Everyone froze.

"Oh, *no*." Lonny put a fist over his mouth, closed his eyes, and bowed his head.

"So you're telling me you think Riggs was in that compartment," Dawson said quietly, staring at the floor.

"Diabolical but genius," Jukey replied grimly. "And by suggesting that Riggs had gone to New Mexico, Ayo threw everyone off the scent for weeks—more than enough time to clean up any trace of evidence in that van, get out of town, disappear."

Dawson became more agitated. "I asked *repeatedly* about the vans! No one told me about the old junker!"

"I suspect Joe Castle didn't want you to know," Jukey answered slowly. "Corny has alluded to some issues the man had with the law. I thought tax evasion, that type of thing, but today Corny said it was common knowledge they were transporting something illicit."

"Drugs?" Mary asked.

"Corny thinks so," Jukey replied. "It's why he quit."

"Ayo lied like a rug all the time." For the first time Key heard in Lonny's voice a hard edge. "*I should have known*."

"Ayo made sure you didn't," Key said, somewhat tentatively, when no one answered.

Dawson, who was sitting on Key's left, turned and glared at her. "Mind if I ask, what's your interest in this? How you come to know so much?"

"Daddy, I told Miss Key all about Riggs," DP said hastily.

Lonny lifted his head. "She's tryin' to help, Dawson."

"Help? You a reporter or what?" Dawson snapped. "Maybe working with that guy you called today? Get a story?"

"No," Key answered calmly. She recognized deep pain masquerading as helpless anger, understood that she was looking into the eyes of a man venting his distress on the person in whom he was least invested. Even so, his words stung. "I hoped to—"

Three sharp claps, loud as backfire, startled them all and briefly woke Dibsy, who let out a little wail. "*Shiitake mushrooms,* Dawson!" Granny Jewel exclaimed, rubbing her hands. "*I'm* the one first told Key about Riggs! She ain't no dadgum *reporter*! Goodness glory, you wouldn't be holding that necklace if it wasn't for her! Take help where it's offered! Whyever would you not?" She sat back, glowering. There was a shocked silence.

"Shiitake mushrooms, Mama?" Lonny said wonderingly. "What the—"

"Larry's daddy used to say that when he was perturbed," Granny Jewel replied archly. "Because yes, I am perturbed that a woman who's been nothing but a good friend to all of us should be getting such treatment from someone I've known since Hector was a pup! And no, before y'all ask, I don't know no Hector. It's a *sayin'*. Goodness!"

Another dumbfounded silence, serenaded by distant wind chimes.

*Grandmas*, Key thought. Neither Dawson's intimidating personality nor his social stature meant anything to a woman who'd watched both him and his sons grow up. But this was becoming a massive distraction from the issues that mattered. Key clicked her pen to retract it and reached for her backpack

"No. Don't leave." Dawson seemed to have shrunk into his chair. "I sincerely apologize, Key. My years of frustration are getting the best of me. We owe you a debt of gratitude." He held out his hand.

Key shook it. It was hard and callused, exactly how she imagined he'd had to force his heart to become. "Dawson, I am so very sorry for all your family has been through. It's Ell, though, who deserves the credit. If she hadn't wanted to be a pirate, none of this would have happened. I sincerely hope the necklace leads to answers."

Dawson nodded, still looking ashamed. "Much obliged." He addressed the group. "Olive still don't know about this. I'll call her tonight. I can handle my own sorrows, but watching the ones you love struggle to cope ..." He cleared his throat.

"We all grieve with you and Olive and DP. We have these many years." Granny Jewel dabbed at her eyes with a wrinkled tissue.

"I know y'all have, Jewel, and I thank you. Hard to put into words what it would mean to find Riggs, put our boy to rest. But then all hope that he's alive goes out the window." Dawson rubbed his hands on the knees of his paint-covered pants, then pulled out the medallion once again. "You know what Olive told me, way back?"

He was again looking at Key, so she answered. "What?"

"His absence is a presence." His voice cracked. "*Absence is a presence. I've never forgot those words. She said we live with the unknown like it's a ghost in the house." Out of the corner of her eye, Key saw DP swipe at his cheeks.

Lonny was right. Though having committed no crime, the Plummers were serving a life sentence.

# Chapter 49

## PREPARATIONS

**K**ey called Mack on the drive back to Veronica View, telling him simply that their picnic had gone very unexpectedly sideways. "Meet me at Pike House tomorrow," she told him.

"You're going to leave me hanging?" he'd asked cheerfully, and when she replied, "I've got company," he immediately understood that Wain, who was nodding off and probably wouldn't have heard anyway, was with her in the Jeep.

Key had told no one, not even Mary, that Mack was coming, and now that she and Dawson had a precarious truce, she hoped he wouldn't be offended by a stranger's presence. Surely, though, Mack would be an asset in searching for Riggs, because she strongly suspected that he and Guy were somehow involved in locating people.

After a shower, Wain crawled into bed, gave her a hug, said drowsily, "Next time I'm gonna catch a fish," then instantly fell asleep.

Key had changed into sweats and was whipping up an omelet when her phone rang. *Gabriel.* He probably had news about the cadaver dogs. She rejected the call and sent a quick text.

I'll call you in 2 min

A thumbs-up emoji instantly appeared.

After checking on Wain, Key paused outside the front door. Within range of the doorbell camera, she said cheerfully, "Sylvia, I hope I don't lose you. I'm going to check the mail." Once at the mailbox, she pressed Gabriel's number, which still showed up as *Wolverine*.

*Because everyone should have a* Wolverine *in their contacts.*

"Hi there!" she said, hoping for a quick conversation. Her thin shirt was no match for the chilly breeze.

"Hi, Key! Good news. My contact, Paul Vicarman, will be bringing his Bluetick Coonhound, Gunnar Boy, tomorrow. You can't do better than these two."

"Oh, that's great news! A blue what?"

"Bluetick Coonhound. He's an incredible hunter. I'll be there too …. If you think that's all right?"

"Why wouldn't it be?"

"I don't want to intrude on the Plummers."

*I understand*, Key thought. How ironic that Gabriel's podcast fans were called "Insiders," because Dawson would surely view him, like Key, as an outsider. "You're a professional, Gabriel, with years of experience in dealing with families in these tough and sad situations. I'm sure you'll handle it with grace and understanding."

"Thanks, Key." Gabriel still sounded slightly dubious.

"Oh, and let's not mention my landlord to them." Shivering, Key tipped her head back, scanning the clear night sky. Orion was especially brilliant tonight. She hoped that was a good omen.

"I agree. Nothing provable. Text me the address, will you, please? We'll be there between nine and ten."

Key kept her phone to her ear as she stepped onto the porch. "Brr! It's chilly out! Have a good evening, Sylvia!" *Everyone should have a Sylvia in their contacts too*, she thought with a slight laugh. Now to line up dog- and childcare.

Yes, Bertie told her, she'd be happy to check on Faro the next day, and as Key devoured her omelet, she absorbed the latest gossip from the senior center. Indira Figg had broken her thumb when she'd tripped on a curb, and at lunch that day, Theodora Matthews, who had more money than the Queen of England, had them all laughing until they cried by describing a recent disastrous date with a man who was only after "a nurse and a purse." Key, too, was laughing when she hung up.

After arranging for Cissy to meet Wain after school and placing an online order for two dozen sandwiches from Troy Grocery, Key searched for *Bluetick Coonhound*. To her surprise, there was an article about Gunnar Boy, who had tracked a missing toddler to a barn where he'd fallen asleep behind a stack of hay bales. How overjoyed those frantic parents must have been—instead of drowning, they'd burst through the water's surface and embraced their child, able to breathe again.

# Chapter 50

## CONFAB AT THE FIREPLACE

onsidering the circumstances and the previous evening's caffeine, Key wasn't surprised when she woke very early the next morning, still gripped by a wacky dream where she and an unfamiliar dog had wandered through an enormous house searching for Wain. When she'd finally found him asleep behind a hay bale in a closet, the Wain who emerged was a teenager with braces on his teeth and a pink bandana tied around long, curly dark hair who kept saying, "I'm gonna catch a fish." That was all she retained before the dream faded like a drop of water on a hot sidewalk. She tiptoed into Wain's room. Still seven years old, thank goodness, and not a hay bale in sight.

Key let Faro out, made coffee, then checked the weather. Today and tomorrow would be mostly sunny and pleasant, but Thursday promised rain. Would they still be searching?

A text popped in.

At the airport. See you soon!

-Lots going on, can't wait to fill you in

Very mysterious! Want to talk now?

-I can't, but I promise it'll be a doozy of a discussion

OK...but not curious anymore =)

-Here's a link to a podcast. If you have time, give it a listen.

Will do. A chance to try my new ear buds... but still NOT curious.

She laughed aloud, then exhaled a small sigh. What would the next three days reveal? Yes, Mack was smart, engaging, and funny, but the truth was she barely *knew* the man. The first and only time they'd met in person, it had been at Pike House, and she'd been filthy, sweaty, and barefoot, but Mack had been as genteel as though they'd convened for a business meeting (which, in an oddball way, they had). Of one thing she was positive though: Guy never would have engineered an introduction if he didn't trust Mack implicitly.

Her thoughts racing, Key gave the guest bedroom a quick tidy-up. Maybe Mack was simply doing Guy a favor by checking in on her and Wain. Maybe he would be horrified to know she was viewing any horizon beyond their companionable friendship. Maybe he was seeing someone. Feeling annoyed that she'd even followed such a pointless train of thought, Key headed for her bedroom to put on the clothes she'd chosen. Considering she'd be outside all day, she spent more time on her cosmetic routine than was warranted, but she stubbornly refused to ask herself why.

★★★

To Key's surprise, at breakfast Wain enthusiastically discussed fishing but didn't mention the necklace. He vividly remembered Mack, though, when Key told him company was coming. "He's gonna be so excited to see Enginuity and Bobcat." He patted his heart. "You should wear the star."

"Great idea!" Ruffling his hair, she said, "You're the best, you know that, Wain?"

"You too," he replied with his mouth full.

After dropping Wain at school, Key picked up the sandwiches, then called Bertie to give her the door code. "Good morning, Bertie—"

"Key!" Bertie's voice was trembling. "Olive called me late last night! Oh, I can't believe the little Morgan girl found Riggs's necklace!" She sniffed. "I've been sworn to secrecy, but I pray we get answers. Olive is simply *torn up*, absolutely terrified to hope."

"Is she on her way home?"

"Tomorrow. I think she's half afraid to come back."

"Understandable." Key didn't feel it was her place to say more. "Thank you, Bertie, for your help with Faro!"

At Pike House, Benito explained in broken English that DP, Jukey, Dawson, and Lonny had taken the ATV into the woods. "Back here *diez*."

"Back by ten. Thank you, Benito!"

Key was pulling chairs out of the shed when Gabriel drove up. Behind him was a blue Jeep, older and more battered than Key's.

"Hi, Key!" Gabriel gave her a quick hug, then looked around. "Wow. Beautiful place. Peaceful."

"I bought it on a whim last March, and already it feels like Wain and I have lived here forever. We cannot wait to move back in! I'll be so glad to be out of Vern's house."

"The man who shall not be named," Gabriel replied dryly. "Things certainly escalated fast since our meeting!"

Key nodded. "It's surreal."

A wiry man with a long graying ponytail exited the blue Jeep, followed by a sleek, muscular hound with dappled fur and black-and-tan ears that snapped like sheets on a clothesline when he shook himself.

"Vicarman's a little offbeat, but the guy's a genius," Gabriel said as they watched the man extract a bag from the back seat, then fasten a green collar around his dog's neck. "Green collar for human remains, orange for a live search. I don't know how the dog knows the difference, but he does."

Key couldn't help wincing. *Human remains.* No matter the condition of his body, for this group of searchers, it was *Riggs* they hoped to find—a beloved young man with a name, a history, an adoring family, burgeoning talent, a sense of humor, a girlfriend, a loyal best friend, even a modicum of fame. A *life.* Key's thoughts went again to Olive, a mother fighting desperately not to expect any answers yet dreading what results they might find. *How, exactly, do you tamp down hope?*

After Gabriel made the introductions, Key explained how the previous day had unfolded.

"Almost sounds like divine intervention," Paul said. He had a drawl much like DP's. "No law enforcement here?"

"Not at this point," Key replied as several crows suddenly flapped raucously from the nearest giant oak. At the bottom of the hill, the ATV rumbled out of the woods.

"I brought doughnuts." Gabriel retrieved a large flat box from his truck. "Whew. I'm a little nervous."

Paul nodded understandingly. "Every time me and the pup do a search, I get butterflies."

*You see this dog, Riggs?* Key telegraphed to Orion, now concealed behind the brilliant sun. *His name is Gunnar Boy. Call him.*

# Chapter 51

## CHARCOAL BLUEPRINT

To Key's great relief, Dawson greeted her with a smile, cordially shook hands with Paul Vicarman and Gabriel, then immediately walked away from the group with his phone to his ear. As the rest of the introductions circulated along with the doughnuts, DP retrieved two five-gallon buckets for extra seating and Jukey, affable as ever, produced thermoses of coffee.

"Feel like I know you," DP said to Gabriel, who immediately stiffened, then visibly relaxed as DP went on. "I recognize your voice. My wife, Molly, listens to your podcast. She's real excited to meet you later today."

Jukey handed Gabriel a cup. "Mary's coming later too. She and Molly are gonna have to decide who's your biggest fan." Everyone was trying, Key thought, to keep conversation light, but a palpable tension threaded through the group. Even Gunnar Boy's alert body language spoke of the task ahead.

Dawson returned, informing DP, "Mama's doin' as okay as can be expected. She says to thank all y'all for your time and effort." He gazed apprehensively at the woods. "I gotta say, I'm dreading what we might find, or even worse, that we'll find nothin'. Every time we've allowed our hopes to rise, we hit harder on the landing. If we don't get answers this time ..."

"If your son's out there, Dawson, my dog'll find him." In a bright-orange knit hat and vest, Paul Vicarman stood out like a neon sign. There was a respectful silence as everyone contemplated the life-changing implications of a successful search. "This is the third time Wolverine and I have partnered up," Paul added.

"Wolverine?" Dawson looked confused. "Thought it was Gunnar."

"Gunnar Boy's the dog. Gabriel Mink, here, he's got a popular podcast called *Inside Outlines* where he's known as 'Wolverine.' Works with families of missing people."

"My hat, Dawson." Jukey touched the logo.

Dawson made the connection. "You're the reporter told Riggs's story."

"Yes, sir. I'm a podcaster. I'm truly sorry for your family's terrible loss."

Dawson nodded but didn't reply.

Lonny stubbed out his cigarette and tossed the butt into the fireplace, then held up a wet sneaker. "Jukey, you mind if I take the ATV back to my place real quick, to change into boots?"

"Welcome to it," Jukey replied. "And son, grab the jerrican out of the back of my truck while you're at it."

"Yessir, but ... *jerkin*? What am I lookin' for?"

"Gas can. Green. Military."

"Ah. Never heard it called that. Thought you meant beef jerky."

It was a relief to laugh.

"I'll hitch a ride with you up to the house," DP said. "Gotta check in with the guys."

Paul, Jukey, and Dawson began discussing strategy. "Gunnar Boy's life vest is in my backpack, if y'all want to start in the pond," Paul said. He hadn't explained the green collar. *Why would he need to*, Key thought ruefully.

Dawson cleared his throat. "Uh, Jukey's convinced me to start on land." He met Key's eyes. "Lonny told us about the green wristband. I now believe something happened to Riggs at the concert, and Ayo transported him back here in that ... van."

Gabriel, Key noticed, had snapped to attention at the mention of pictures and the wristband. *He doesn't know that piece yet.*

"Does anyone remember the year the real bad storm hit our area?" Jukey asked from his bucket perch. "Back in the nineties, had a couple mini tornadoes in it. Was it before Riggs disappeared?"

"Was it the year that Plummer Construction repaired Bertie Montgomery's house?" Key asked. "If so, Bertie told me it was 1997."

"That's right. We got more work than we could handle that year." Dawson helped himself to more coffee, then settled into the chair next to Key. "Riggs was on my crew. And that snake in the grass, Ayo, helped Mayweather's boys cut up the fallen tree at Bertie's place."

Key was stunned. "Ayo trimmed trees? I thought he worked for Castle Phoenix!"

"He worked for Mayweather now and then. The guy cuts up one tree and suddenly he starts referring to himself as an 'arborist.'" Dawson rolled his eyes. "What he really wanted was a job with my company. Not only no, but *hell* no. The guy's obsession with Riggs was pathological."

"Why *was* he so obsessed with Riggs?" Key asked, hoping she didn't sound too eager. In the chair across from her, Gabriel had stretched out his legs, one foot stacked on top of the other, appearing casual but alertly absorbing every word.

Dawson shrugged. "Hard to say. It's pretty much impossible for normal people to understand stalker mentality. He was a user. Possessive. Jealous. The most self-centered person I've ever met. Riggs gave him the benefit of the doubt for far too long, and Ayo took full advantage of that. Olive calls him a 'textbook narcissist.'" He jumped up and began pacing. "Man, I can't sit still. My nerves are on fire."

Lonny and DP returned and parked the ATV next to the patio. "Gayle wanted to help," Lonny explained, as Gabriel helped them unload an archaic military-style gas can, a platter of cookies, a dented pump carafe on which someone had written *COFFee*, a bucket-shaped orange cooler with a faucet spout, and a stack of Styrofoam cups.

"Thank her for us, Lonny," Dawson said with a nod.

Key noted how intently Gabriel studied DP, just as he had Dawson. Lonny, in turn, was staring hard at Gabriel. Key couldn't help but think of the word Gabriel had used that day at Java U: *tectonic.*

"We got a plan yet, y'all?" DP asked.

"Discussing it now," Dawson replied. "What's significant about the '97 storm, Jukey?"

"Riggs was still around when that storm hit, is what I'm getting at." Jukey sounded gratified, as though this piece of information had allowed his mind to track a certain path. He picked up a partially burned stick from the fireplace, using the charcoal tip to sketch a half circle. "Here's the pond, and this X is the spot where Ell found the necklace. Gunnar Boy will check here first."

*It looks exactly like a treasure map,* Key thought. Ell's desire to be a pirate had led them all into murky, uncharted waters fraught with mystifying undercurrents.

"If the dog doesn't alert, we'll spread out and search east from the shoreline into the woods, along the overgrown party path, toward Pike Road," Jukey continued, drawing a straight line from the X. "We're gonna be looking for fallen trees, big ones, root balls out of the ground. If you see a mound at the end of a fallen log, mark it, and our canine Sherlock will check it out." He gave Gunnar Boy a pat.

Dawson frowned. *"Fallen trees? Mounds?* What's the sig—"

Jukey held up a finger and began pacing. "Let's say I mortally attacked another man in my van in a parking lot outside a concert in Virginia. Then, because there was nowhere else to hide him— and I had people riding home with me—I stowed his body in a compartment under the floor in that van. On the way home, I insisted that the other guy drive, and I slept on top of the trap door. Got back here in the wee hours of the morning and dropped off my passengers, who live near a familiar wooded area. The sun's gonna come up soon, and I'm panicking. My victim is too heavy to carry very far." He paused, creating a mesmerized silence broken only by two Carolina wrens singing gaily back and forth. "Now. Though I have tools—a shovel, a rake—I can't dig two inches in these woods without hitting tree roots. But what leaves a big hole? A hole big enough to fit a body into. The roots of—"

"*A fallen tree*. The '97 storm!" Dawson leaped from his chair and grabbed Jukey by both arms. "Jukey King, sir, I know you are a tracking genius, but this is … This is masterful!"

Jukey put a cautionary hand on Dawson's shoulder. "It's a start, my friend."

"But the necklace, Jukey." DP sounded confused. "If Riggs isn't in the pond, how'd the necklace end up there?"

"Best Mary and I can figure, someone broke the clasp when he yanked it off Riggs's neck, took it as a trophy. Then he got real dirty digging a grave and needed to wash himself off and—"

"And lost it in the pond," DP whispered.

Another astonished silence. Chills ran down Key's spine. It all made so much sense.

"Let's head out," Dawson commanded, galvanizing the troops like a five-star general. "DP, Paul, and the dog come with Jukey and me. Lonny, are you okay waiting for your brother? Meet us at Dogleg?"

"Yessir!"

Jukey held up a bucket. "We got yellow plastic ribbons here—tie 'em high on trees next to any fallen logs that fit the criteria."

Paul snapped his fingers and pointed, and like an eager panther, Gunnar Boy vaulted onto the rear seat. "If my dog alerts, my recommendation is to do a cursory check, then best call law enforcement."

"We'll have to come back here to call, cell service is nonexistent out there." DP squeezed onto the back seat, and Paul climbed in on the other side and tugged the dog halfway onto his lap.

"I've got a friend, Mack Simons, coming to visit; he'll be here soon." Key nearly laughed at the subtly raised eyebrows. She took several ribbons from the bucket. "And I know of at least two fallen trees nearer to the house. Mack and Gabriel and I will check them."

Dawson looked skeptical. "Near *here*? That's further from the party path than the pond is."

Jukey glanced up at Key from where he was filling the ATV with gas. "Hmm. It's an area I hadn't considered, but ..." He capped the jerrican and climbed into the driver's seat. "We'll compare notes at lunch."

Gabriel was disappointed at being excluded, Key could tell, but she hoped he didn't take it personally. While they waited for Mack, she would bring him up to speed.

Dawson consulted his watch. "Meet back here in a couple hours."

"Y'all be safe," Lonny said. They watched the ATV disappear into the woods, the yellow ribbons in Key's hand fluttering like sunbeams blessing the voyage.

# Chapter 52

## GABRIEL

While they waited for Larry, Lonny focused his attention on Gabriel. "Mink. Never heard that last name before. That like a—a what they call a stage name?"

Gabriel laughed. "No. But it is a revised name. Way back in the late 1800s at Ellis Island, it got simplified from something much more difficult to pronounce."

"Ellis Island? That where you're from?"

Key felt instantly protective. *Do not embarrass him*, she mentally telegraphed to Gabriel, then felt ashamed of herself when he did no such thing.

"No, Ellis Island is where they processed immigrants. My parents' families settled in Virginia, but I was raised in California. I've moved a lot since then though." Gabriel slid on a pair of sunglasses. It was growing warmer but without the slushy humidity of summer. A perfect autumn day.

"Always wanted to see Cali. Check out the West." Lonny stood to check the driveway, then leaned against the fireplace, one hand shoved into his jacket pocket. "You got brothers and sisters? Wife? Kids?"

Gabriel shook his head. "Only me, separated from my wife, no kids. And in the last several years, both my parents passed. I miss them every day."

"Sorry to hear that. So ... no family around here?"

"Around here?" Gabriel repeated, shifting in his chair and crossing one ankle over a knee. After the tiniest hiccup of hesitation, he replied, "I've never been told there was."

*What kind of answer is that?*

"You remind me of someone is why I asked." Lonny, too, had put on his sunglasses.

"Really? Who?" Gabriel hadn't moved a muscle. Key held her breath.

"It's—" Lonny waved the cup he was holding. "Ah, it's nothin'. Forget it. This whole thing is makin' me crazy." To Key's relief, the conversation moved on to the previous day's events, and by the time a quad bike crested the hill and followed the parallel depressions in the grass, Gabriel and Lonny were talking like old friends.

Larry parked next to the pavers and tugged off a full-face helmet. In jeans, neckerchief, and a zipped-up black leather jacket straining at the seams, he looked every inch the quintessential, well-nourished urban biker dude of indeterminate age. (Key had met dozens of them; after all, she'd been married to one.)

"Lots of excitement at our place about all this," Larry commented after he shook hands with Gabriel. "Mama's with Gayle and Petra. They're monitoring social media for any mention of what's going on out here. Hopefully it stays on the down-low for as long as possible."

"We told Cav and Ell to keep it to themselves but ..." Lonny grimaced. "Eh. We'll see how it goes."

"Wain may say something. I didn't tell him not to." Key hadn't brought it up that morning; she suspected that forbidding him to talk about the necklace would have magnified the issue.

Tapping a helmet he'd clipped to the back seat, Larry said, "Put this on, little bro."

Lonny let out a guffaw. "Lar, guarantee you ain't gonna go more'n eight *M-P-H* on them rooty paths, so no, I ain't wearin' no *helmet*."

Larry shrugged, then buckled his own back on. "Suit yourself. Don't come cryin' to me when you bang your freakin' stubborn head on a low-lying branch. Or get ticks in your rock-star hair."

Lonny patted Larry's helmet. "Ain't that kinda overkill for tick protection?" After shoving a pair of leather gloves into his back pocket, he swung a long leg over the seat behind his brother. "See y'all later."

"Whew." Gabriel rubbed the back of his neck. "For a few minutes there, Lonny was grilling me like a salmon on hot coals." They started toward the house to retrieve the lunch coolers.

"He isn't usually so intense. I think they're all just very protective of one another; they like to know who they're dealing with." Key showed Gabriel the concert pictures and pointed out the green wristband. "Also, for the record, Lonny, Jukey, and Mary know why I think there's something to this Vern-is-Ayo theory, and they're—well, if not one hundred percent convinced, they think it's worth pursuing."

"So the visibly invisible landlord is still on the radar. Given that my team found zilch, I'm anxious to hear your reasons."

Back on the patio, Key handed Gabriel her notebook, open to a page titled *V.O.* "Here's everything I've discovered about Vern Olson that weirdly meshes with Ayo's possible involvement in Riggs's disappearance. It's all circumstantial, which is why I didn't share it with you at Java U."

Gabriel began reading aloud. "'Mentioned Lonny before podcast did?? Earring?! Beatles song,' with an arrow to—sheesh, I feel like I'm in one of those escape rooms—the lyrics to 'Eleanor Rigby,' and 'Father McKenzie' is underlined." He began to laugh. "Does—does this say 'Horse poop by P.H.?'"

Key waved her hand. "*P.H.* Pike House. I'll explain them all."

"Okay …. Maybe, madam, you are a Cold War spy. Because this is obviously written in code." He turned the page. "'No internet history found'—you and I discussed that—'Moved to Troy, why? Buys horse, rides in woods.' And here's a drawing of a gravestone with the letters *R-I-P* on it."

"It's a tattoo on Vern's arm."

"Riggs Inman Plummer," Gabriel said thoughtfully. "That's weird and creepy—but could have an innocent explanation."

"Exactly! That's been my problem all along, Gabriel! Everything weird and creepy about Vern Olson has an innocent explanation!"

"Last thing on the list. 'Tree trimmer gooseberry know it all.' And that's in red ink."

"I made that note this morning after Dawson said Ayo occasionally worked as a tree trimmer. Vern told Mary and me that he was an 'arborist.'" Key gave the last word air quotes.

One intense half hour later, Gabriel told her he was convinced that Vern warranted further investigation, but he was at a loss as to how to do it.

Key stood and stretched. "I'm glad you agree. Sometimes my list makes perfect sense, and other times, I feel like I'm manufacturing a villain out of whole cloth. She lifted the lid on the cooler. "Let's have a drink."

Gabriel shaded his eyes. "Looks like you've got company." They'd been so engrossed in their conversation, they hadn't heard a car drive up, and when Key turned to look, she felt her entire being break into smiles.

"Key." How did Mack make her name *sound* like that? As though she'd opened a window and in wafted the wistful, aromatic mystery of all outdoors. Sage. Pine. Rain. Sunshine. For some reason, Wain and his "easy peasy lemon squeezy" remark flitted into her mind, and without saying a word, she set down two dripping cans of seltzer and gave a man she'd met only once an impulsive and utterly authentic hug.

# Chapter 53

## THE UNSAID (SORT OF) SAID

"Mack Simons, this is Gabriel Mink." Key adjusted her cap (gone askew when a slightly disconcerted Mack returned her hug), then gave them each a seltzer, taking a moment while they engaged in small talk to perform a quick, surreptitious inspection. Yes, Mack looked as put together and handsome as she remembered, and he was dressed casually enough to traipse through the woods. Yes, she was extremely happy to see him. No, she still had no idea where this would all lead.

Gabriel held up his phone. "Key, I need to make a call. Back in a few."

Mack surveyed the scattered personal belongings, upside-down buckets, the gas can, the trampled grass, Lonny's abandoned helmet, the doughnut box lying crumpled in the cold fireplace, the coolers stashed in the shade of the arbor. "Wow. What's going on?"

"An impromptu search for Riggs Plummer. There are six guys and a cadaver dog in the woods right now." Key could hardly believe she was talking to Mack in person.

Mack's eyes widened. "I just listened to the podcast!"

"It's been a crazy turn of events, but I want to wait for Gabriel before I say more."

"Okay. It's truly good to see you, Key," Mack said easily, surveying the woods. "North Carolina in the autumn is spectacular. Another reason I regret having to cancel the fishing trip."

"It worked out for the best. You're here at the perfect time."

"Good to know." They chatted for several minutes about Lainey's broken arm and other generalities, then Mack said, "Gabriel seems like a nice guy."

"He's great. We met a week or so ago." Only a week? It seemed much longer.

"Like on a date?" he asked casually.

Key was momentarily speechless. "Oh, no! No. Gabriel is ... is ... a friend who has a part in all this." She explained.

"Ah! I thought I recognized the voice! This is getting curiouser and curiouser." He caught her off guard again with his next words. "You look great, Key."

"Compared to grubby overalls and bare feet and dirty fingernails?" she asked lightly, still seeking footing, but as soon as the words left her mouth, she cringed. She sounded ... fake, flirtatious—like she was compliment fishing, a trait she abhorred. What was the matter with her? *Get a grip, Key.*

Mack tilted his head, regarding her curiously. "You may not believe this, but that's not at all what I saw that day. For the record, I loved the overalls."

"It's great to see you too, Mack." Her words emerged stiff and perfunctory, as though they'd just shaken hands over the sale of a used Oldsmobile. Why was it so easy to talk to him on the phone and proving to be so awkward face-to-face?

"You know," Mack said, taking a deep breath and slowly rotating the can in his hands, "when Guy asked me to come to North Carolina to talk to you, he described you as his mother's cousin without going into one iota of detail. In fact, I suspect he deliberately used vague words that conjured up a sweetheart of a ... well, a kind of elderly relative in a housedress and those slip-on shoes." (Key immediately thought of Bertie.) "A more typical ... well, you know, not doddering on the *brink*, exactly, but uh, extra mature and ... *ohhhkay.*" He grimaced, rubbing his nose, then said ruefully, "I'm going to stop digging. I already can't see my way out of this hole."

Key laughed but didn't reply. Thousands of miles away and Guy had managed to create exactly the situation he'd intended.

"Whew." Mack took another deep breath. "Well, what Guy never said was that your huge heart is encased in this, um, attractive and very fascinating woman who also happens to have a great sense of humor." He dipped his chin decisively, as if to say, *There, I said it.*

"Thank you," Key managed to utter. It was as personal a conversation as they'd ever had. Of all the scenarios she had imagined when she finally saw Mack again, especially considering their current location and circumstances, this one had not even made the Z-list.

"I know why Guy put it that way though," Mack went on determinedly. "If he had so much as hinted that I might hit it off with you, I would have balked. He knows I'm rabidly single. No offense." He helped himself to a handful of trail mix, then leaned against the wall next to her, crunching a pretzel.

"None taken." Two-word replies seemed to be her limit.

"Do you date, Key? If you don't mind my asking."

"I don't mind." Standing side by side made the conversation easier. "And no, I don't date. I'm very happy as is, and my life lately has been all about adjustment, especially with Wain. And the house renovation."

"You and Wain have had one upheaval after the other."

She nodded. "It's been crazy from the get-go, but oddly enough, as new as it all is, it never feels overwhelming. Who knew I had a Wain-shaped space in my life at the perfect time?"

"Simple words that belie the difficulty of putting them into action. That's what I find so fascinating. You roll with the punches; make it look effortless when I know it's not."

She smiled. "You know what else? It's *fun*. I never know what each day will bring, and Wain's the best kid, wonderful company."

"Guy hit the jackpot by coming to you."

"It's mutual! I can't imagine my life—or Wain's—if he hadn't called." Key rested her elbows on the wall. "Do *you* date?" she asked. A kind, confident, honest man, with Mack's exceptional looks? It would be far more shocking if there *weren't* women of all ages buzzing possessively about. In the short silence that followed, Key spotted Miguel on the screened deck, then came the whine of a table saw. She couldn't see Gabriel.

"Do I date." Mack contemplated a moment, then said carefully, "Ah, yes and no. Mostly no." He stopped to check a text, then said resignedly, "Speak of the devil."

*The devil?* Key kept her face neutral. "We don't have to discuss this if you don't want to."

"No, it's a relief. I need advice." He tapped an answer to a text, then pocketed his phone and sighed. "Toni is a real estate agent who I met when I sold our house after my wife died. She's in her late forties, divorced. She texts me constantly, bakes stuff that I usually pass along to my neighbors, brings gifts for my grandkids, invites me to dinner. But the few dates I've agreed to have been ... uh, underwhelming. When I'm around her, I feel ... uncomfortably tethered. Like she wants to own me." He glanced at Key. "Does that make sense?" When she nodded, he added, "In contrast, Key, talking with you is uncomplicated and interesting; and invariably, I find myself wanting more." He held up his empty can. "What is this stuff? Truth serum?"

"Yes. I injected sodium pentothal into that very can before you got here." They laughed, but it was odd to hear Mack so unsure of himself. "Mack, I feel the same way about our conversations."

"But ...?" He turned to look her in the eyes.

"No *buts*. I already consider you a valued friend." She wasn't sure which of her words were the reason relief washed over his face.

"Key, I would hate to lose this friendship by ... you know, by being too ..."

"Ambitious?"

"I was going to say *aggressive*, but ambitious is better."

Key took a deep breath and laid her hand on his elbow, her words finally emerging honest and unforced. "No pressure from me, Mack. What I need most right now is your friendship. I would *hate* to lose that."

"Me too. On all counts. So we're good?"

"We're very good!" she said emphatically. The atmosphere suddenly grew much lighter, as though they'd come to an agreement that didn't need further definition—doors left open but neither feeling any need to rush through.

"And as for your friend Toni," Key continued, "maybe you should seek advice from my neighbor Bertie and the ladies at the senior center. They'd probably tell you that if you know it's going nowhere, you should be honest with her, rip off that Band-Aid." She recounted Bertie's "nurse and a purse" story, which was just the additional humor they needed.

"Poor lonely old guy. In one way, I can totally relate." Mack removed his jacket and tossed it over the back of a chair, then asked teasingly, "By any chance, are you a rich nurse, Key? Asking for a friend."

They were still laughing when Gabriel reappeared. "Any news, Key?"

"Nothing so far." To Mack she said, "But now we can get you caught up! It wasn't a conversation I could have over the phone." Her eyes met his. "Wain is always around …."

There was an instantaneous switch in Mack's demeanor. Gone was the bemused, handsome grandpa untangling a folksy dating issue, replaced by a man laser focused on the whole of his surroundings. "I'm all ears. But do you mind giving me a tour while we talk? I need to stretch my legs."

Thirty minutes later, from Pike House's covered deck, the three of them watched the searchers rumble into view. Even from a distance, their disheartened body language was perfectly legible. Key's heart sank. *But what were you expecting?* she asked herself. The forest floor was a tangled mess of vines and undergrowth, and most likely, the roots of trees fallen two decades prior had rotted and collapsed. Even for a cadaver dog, it would be extremely challenging terrain. Worst of all, there was no guarantee that Riggs was even in the woods! He could be anywhere on Earth. The enormity of it made her almost nauseous.

Out of nowhere, an almost supernatural comprehension of the Plummers' despair flooded over and through Key; she could feel their piercing pain as though it were her own, and the sorrowful beat of Olive's broken, not-daring-to-hope heart made such a clear imprint on hers that it nearly buckled her knees. She leaned on a sawhorse, saying shakily, "I don't think they've found anything."

"It doesn't look like it." Gabriel spoke far too loudly when a drill inside suddenly cut off. He lowered his voice. "These searches are brutal on the emotions, no matter how they end. It's early yet, Key. Don't give up hope."

Mack laid his hand lightly on her shoulder but didn't speak.

# Chapter 54

## FRAGILE AND TECTONIC

ey wasn't surprised that Mack instantly found common ground with everyone, even conversing in fluent Spanish with Benito and Miguel. When Larry asked him what he did for a living, he said he was an accountant of sorts, "too boring to elaborate."

After lunch, Jukey pulled Key, Gabriel, and Mack aside. "What you said earlier, Key North, got me thinking. Back in the day, your house's previous owner, Elvin Grimes, had a substantial garden." He pointed to where Key's property abutted the woods and Pike Road. "Behind that row of pines was a little pull-in spot where Elvin parked his truck, impossible to see from the house. Grown over now, like everything else. But when you all search this afternoon, check around there." He gestured with both hands as though drawing a map. "The '97 storm blew in from the southeast, so walk perpendicular to the road, west to east. Look for logs fallen toward the west." Key could tell Mack and Gabriel were impressed.

She nodded. "Exactly where I was thinking. Wain and I have done some exploring over that way."

"Could he have been buried *in* the garden?" Gabriel asked. "No tree roots there."

"Good thought, but it was early September," Jukey replied. "Still a lot to harvest at that point, pumpkins and whatnot, and old Elvin would've seen the mess."

*One location eliminated. Only a gazillion to go.*

After the searchers left once again for the woods, Mack went to his car to change his shoes and make a call.

"DP's a really nice guy. Smart and savvy," Gabriel said as he and Key quickly tidied up.

"He's the best." It was getting warm. With a quick twist, Key put her hair into a bun and tucked it under her cap.

Gabriel moved one of the upside-down buckets closer to the fireplace wall and sat. All those chairs available and the buckets remained the seating of choice. "Great news about their baby. DP told me the name: Riggs Dawson. I about teared up. I had this very odd thought while I was talking to him."

"What's that?" Up at the house, the drilling and hammering had begun again, but at least down here they didn't need to yell.

"Ah ... I hope you don't think it's macabre. While we were talking about their baby, DP mentioned how his wife's shape has changed." With one hand, Gabriel drew a bump over his own stomach. "And he used the word 'mound,' which is a little unusual. I couldn't help but think of Jukey's instructions. 'Look for mounds.'" He swallowed, nodding his head slightly as he spoke. "You know, one Riggs is yet to be, growing in a warm, safe mound, soon to meet the parents and grandparents who love him to pieces already, and the other one may very well be concealed in another kind of mound .... Done growing, never to be with his family again. Both invisible at the moment, both equally loved." Gabriel's voice dropped so low on the last two words that Key barely heard them. He cleared his throat. "If there's anything I've learned by working with the families of the missing, *unseen* doesn't matter when it comes to love. Lost, passed away, relinquished, unborn ... doesn't matter. Their families just naturally ... love. I can't help but feel that the two Riggses are working together to heal their family."

"That's beautiful." *Relinquished.* Key pressed her hands against her cheeks. "Gabriel ..."

His eyes were as cautious as if there were land mines on the path. "You have a pretty good idea, don't you?"

"About ...?"

"Key. Come on." He shot her a lopsided grin. "Our conversation at Java U veered in a direction I never expected, and I've been agonizing over it ever since."

Her heart was beating so hard that she was sure Wain's gold star pin had to be jumping up and down, but she managed to ask calmly, "Am I right?"

He didn't even hesitate. "Yes."

The cloudy pane of delicate glass she'd been gingerly holding, refusing to contemplate, was rinsed clean, bringing with it the answer to the main question but conjuring up many more. "Are you okay with that, Gabriel? With me knowing?"

"I kind of have to be, don't I? I pretty much just jumped off a cliff just now. No going back."

"You landed safely. It's not my story to tell, and I never would." *Another secret to carry.*

He sighed. "Thank you."

"Does anyone else know?"

"My ex knows general stuff but had absolutely no interest in upsetting our lives by going further, which is partially what led to our breakup. I couldn't let it go."

Key glanced toward the house. To her delight, Mack, now in hiking boots, was strolling down the hill, carrying a large tote bag, accompanied by Mary.

"What are you going to do?" she asked.

"I wait. Like I have for a long, long time." Gabriel stood. "Key, if ... if you ever see an opening, a possibility of ... would you let me know?"

She couldn't imagine what that opening would be, but she simply replied, "Okay." Another ambiguous conversation fraught with unsaid, life-altering words. *What a day.*

"Did we just have an entire discussion in code, Cold War compatriot?" Gabriel asked as if reading her mind. Key laughed (probably so she wouldn't cry) and mentally slotted his fragile, tectonic secret into place, shut the vault, and locked it.

# Chapter 55

## ORION IN THE SUNSHINE

"Mary!" Key gave her a hug. "You've met Mack—"

"We're friends already." Mary gave Key a wide-eyed, approving nod.

"Gabriel, this is Mary King, who deserves all the credit for your presence here."

"It's truly a pleasure." Gabriel warmly shook Mary's hand. "I've heard so much about you from Key." Key noted how differently he interacted with Mary, compared to his polite but more formal demeanor with Nina LaDane at Java U. Mary's genuine and sunny personality simply had that effect on everyone.

"I'd recognize your voice anywhere," Mary exclaimed. "It's such a treat to meet you! You have no idea how many pies and cinnamon rolls Wolverine has helped me make in my kitchen! I'll try not to call you Wolverine if you prefer Gabriel."

"You can call me whatever gets me a sample of the contents of that bag."

Mary laughed. "An assortment of pastries I had in the freezer. They'll be thawed by the time everyone is back." She looked around and sighed. "You know, y'all, ever since Ell found that necklace, I've sensed that something strong and good is happening here."

"Everybody ready?" Key asked. Though they didn't need to cover much distance, she was anxious to get going.

Mary handed them each a small packet. "Wipes. Use them if you think you touched poison ivy. It'll get most of the urushiol off your skin." Trust Mary to think of everything.

"They're great," Mack told Key as they paired off and started toward the woods. "Jukey is an outdoors wizard, and they obviously love you."

"They've been a godsend." She lowered her voice. "Mack, I only pursued this mystery because I thought you or Guy might be able to unearth new information. Especially about Vern Olson. I still feel the chills I got when Wain said Vern's earring was 'just like DP's.'"

He held a branch aside for her, saying so quietly that she barely heard him, "I'll do what I can."

At the edge of the woods, the four of them spread out and began wrestling their way through the underbrush, west to east. Key tied a ribbon on the first log they found, but it had been decaying for far longer than twenty years. The second and third were small and had toppled recently, their needles still green. After that, they found nothing, and as they grew closer to Pike Road, it felt like a dead end in more ways than one.

"Jukey may need to rethink his theory," Mary said regretfully.

"Look at this." Key pointed out a maple tree with deep grooves encircling its trunk. She'd shown it to Wain one remarkable, life-changing day, when this very section of trees had reached out and embraced the two of them, merging their paths, erasing the distance between their disparate ages and quietly planting deep the seeds of their friendship and mutual healing. Now here she was on another extraordinary day, again seeking answers from the trees.

"Scarred by a kudzu vine," Mary said knowingly. "It's a blight on the South."

Mack grimaced. "Texas has the same problem."

Key pulled another ribbon from her jeans pocket. "We're close now to one more big log, the spot where Wain first opened up and talked to me. We sat on it and played I Spy and he—" She stopped. "There. Where the sun is shining through the trees."

"Oh, yes, there's the line of pines, so the garden and Mr. Grimes's blueberries would be ..." Mary gasped and clutched Key's arm.

They all saw it at the same time. At the end of the tall tangle of roots attached to Key's fallen log was a settled but noticeable mound, covered with grass blades that danced like slender green ballerinas in the light breeze.

"*Oh my goodness.*" Mary's whisper hung suspended like the dust motes floating around them in the autumn light, disappearing and reappearing, tiny reflections of fragile hope mingling with robust disbelief.

On that memorable day five months prior, Key's entire focus had been the nearly catatonic little boy beside her; she had noticed neither the roots, the mound, or the single young beech with a mass of now-gold-and-orange leaves rustling above lovely gray camouflage bark, the perfect embodiment of a gallant blond soldier standing guard over a tomb.

With trembling fingers Key tied her ribbon around the beech tree's trunk, then sank onto the log and dropped her face into her hands. *No wonder DP and Lonny heard him calling.* Riggs was *here.* In the sunshine. She had no doubt that the Plummers' agonizing search had come to an end exactly where her journey with Wain began.

Instantly, Mary was by her side, wrapping warm arms around her. "We all feel it, Key."

Gabriel knelt and placed a hand on the mound, as though checking for a heartbeat, and what followed was a quiet so all-encompassing that they could hear the steady course of a jet miles overhead, its occupants unaware that they were momentarily privy to an enormous drama unfolding under the branches of the minuscule forest below.

"I'll go get the others," Mack said quietly, then hurried away.

Gabriel remained where he was, head bowed, and they waited, serenaded by birdsong and deferential, whispering leaves.

★★★

For the rest of her life, Key would look back in awe at the muted, savage beauty of what happened next. While Gabriel filmed at Dawson's request, the entire group held their collective breath as Gunnar Boy gave the area a thorough investigation. There were no outbursts, no exclamations of surprise when the Bluetick Coonhound, almost reverently, lay down and put his head on his paws, signaling that here, in an impeccable shaft of sunlight, with the leaves landing like lazy meteors onto a sacred green planet, the search for Orion's star had ended.

When Jukey and Dawson subsequently discovered disintegrating scraps of blue plastic tarp several inches under the soil, their deliberate, almost archaeological digging came to a halt.

At Pike House, Jukey phoned the sheriff and requested he come right away. "But Gordon, please keep it on the down-low," he said soberly. "Because there's gonna be more to this story."

"There's always more to the story," Mack remarked quietly to Key and Mary as the magnitude of the day began to soak in. "Always."

# Chapter 56

## THE OLIVE BRANCH

live's white Lexus was the only other vehicle in the parking area behind Troy Methodist Church. Key slid her keys, sunglasses, and lip gloss into her pocket, then picked up the bouquet on the seat next to her and exited the Jeep. Wain's gold star shone reassuringly from the lapel of her navy tweed blazer, and a pair of turquoise-and-gold earrings added a splash of color. Though she had no idea why Olive had asked to meet, Key had dressed up a little today. It felt like the proper way to pay her respects.

Riggs was here too. Once he'd been positively identified and the coroner had released his body, the Plummers had laid him to rest after a private funeral. *Cemeteries and fallen leaves share a wistful beauty all their own.* Following the asphalt path, Key thought back to her conversation with DP on the screened deck at Pike House several days before.

★★★

"Daddy's planning a public memorial service," DP had told her after describing Riggs's funeral. "It's gonna be at the high school gym. We want to share our gratitude."

Inside the house, where Benito and Miguel were painting, the bright shop lights and Mexican ranchera music added an incongruously upbeat backdrop to both the ominous gray sky and the sober conversation, brought on by Key's simple question, "How are *you* doing, DP?"

He'd waited so long before answering, rubbing his earring and gazing through the screen toward the woods, that she wondered if he'd heard her. Finally, he said, "I got to be honest. It's complicated. Don't get me wrong, Miss Key, thanks to you and Ell and Jukey, Riggs is home. We don't wake up wondering where he's at. There's light where there was darkness."

"Want to sit?" Key tugged the protective covers from two cushioned chairs.

DP sank into the closest one and leaned forward, his paint-speckled hands loosely laced together. "Before Riggs was found, I could visualize him anywhere, keep him alive." He held his thumb and forefinger a millimeter apart. "That tiny thread of hope. But now, every time I look over there, I see … mmmh." His next words poured out. "Those bones wrapped in that tarp was *Riggs*. My *brother*. He was *murdered*! Thrown away! It breaks my heart, knowing what he went through. So how am I doing?" He shrugged. "The answers just provided a new kind of sorrow." When Key didn't answer, he added, sounding almost embarrassed, "It's not that I'm not grateful; it ain't that at all. Like I said, complicated. It's just something I gotta work through, 'cause I can't change it. You know?"

"Yes." If there was anything Key North understood, it was complicated grief.

DP gestured toward the woods. "You got people coming onto your property, leaving stuff at the spot where Riggs was found. Have you seen all the flowers out there?"

"I have. No one stays long, and they're very respectful. If it becomes a problem, I'll address it."

"It's already become another piece of the urban legend."

Key smiled sympathetically. "But this time it's real, isn't it?"

"Sure is." DP rubbed a spot of paint on his thumbnail. "Miss Key, is living here gonna be hard for you?"

"*Hard* for me?" she asked, taken aback. "Why would you think that?"

DP shrugged. "Maybe it feels ... I don't know ... sad. Or creepy. You know people are gonna talk, like, say the place is haunted, what have you."

With all that the Plummers had endured, she would not allow them to add her perfectly fine mental well-being to the worry list. "DP, listen to me," Key said crisply, causing him to look up in surprise. Good. She had his attention. "Do you remember saying you felt your brother was calling to you?"

"Yes, ma'am."

"I've thought a lot about the incredible chain of events that have transpired since you told me that."

DP listened, rubbing his earring, as Key explained how she'd gone to Imagine That hoping to find fishing poles and discovering metal detectors instead. "For some reason, DP, I felt very strongly that I should buy them. My motive was simple: to create a fun, pirate-related experience for Ell and Wain. But given how it all played out, I've asked myself what other voice might have been speaking, what else might have been urging me to pick up those boxes."

"Like that butterfly effect," DP mused, "where one thing leads to another."

"Exactly." Key drew a circle in the air. "It all coalesces in such a beautiful way. Look at all the pieces that connected to help bring Riggs home." She ticked her fingers. "A dog. Trees. A little girl and a little boy. A toy car. A metal detector. Shasta's pictures. A podcaster. Jukey and Mary and Lonny and Gayle and so many others. Even your unborn baby boy had a part, because when you told me his name, it led to our first discussion about Riggs." DP simply sat silently, staring at the woods, so she went on, "You know, my grandmother used to say that cardinals were visitors from beyond. On the day—almost the moment—Ell found the medallion, a cardinal sat in a tree above us, singing its heart out. Why? Why right then?"

"So you're sayin' there's an unseen element." DP touched the corners of his eyes.

"Hmm." Key tilted her head. "Maybe unseen, or maybe ... *unnoticed.* I believe that there's a very real but invisible side to life. Some things just can't be explained in the usual way."

He nodded slowly. "It's pretty dang amazing when you look at it like that. Like my brother was in on it somehow."

Key pointed to the woods. "What I see out there is a miracle that I'm honored to share with you and your family. What was lost is found. What was dark is illuminated. I see Orion in the sunshine."

DP's eyes were bright with tears. "That's truly beautiful, Miss Key."

★★★

"Key." Just one word showcased Olive's cultured Alabama drawl as she stood up, elegant in black wide-leg slacks and a silky champagne-colored boatneck sweater. Her dark-blond hair was pulled back into a short ponytail, and Riggs's necklace, now repaired and polished to its original luster, hung on its shining gold chain around her neck. She leaned down and picked up two wine glasses from a tray at her feet. "Hello. I hope you like pinot noir, but please don't feel obligated."

"Hi, Olive. I do. Thank you." Key took the glass and handed Olive the bouquet. It had taken her days to decide what kind of flowers to bring. "These represent strength and courage, both qualities that your family has shown for two decades."

"Sunflowers! How beautiful! Flowers from Key, Riggsy." Olive pressed them against her cheek, then laid them lovingly on the brick-red rectangular mound next to the blanket, exposed like a livid scar in the impeccable cemetery lawn. "Thank you so much." She sounded nervous.

"Thanks for inviting me."

They settled on a quilt, Key with her legs stretched out in front of her, ankles crossed, and Olive with hers folded to the side, shoulders gracefully squared. She wore a pair of black leather ankle boots that probably cost more than all of Key's shoes combined.

With a manicured finger, Olive traced a line of stitching between alternating blue and gray squares. "Dawson's mother made this quilt for Riggs. It was in a box I finally found the courage to open." She met Key's eyes. "He was so much more than a young man who went missing."

"Yes."

"At last, thanks to you and so many others, I'm able to say, *This is where my son is!* It gives me a peace I'd forgotten existed." Olive set her glass carefully on the tray. "To finally know that Riggs didn't *choose* to leave ... means more than I can ever express. And yet ..." She was openly weeping now, pressing her palms on high cheekbones. "Finding him has also created the deepest grief. The kind with no shred of hope."

*Myriad, perpetual ripples from the same deadly stone.* "I'm so sorry, Olive." Key lifted the wine bottle and handed her the floral paper napkin it had been sitting on.

"I think I've wept twenty years' worth of tears since Riggs was found. I feel like a block of ice melting." Olive lightly blew her nose. "I imagine you're wondering why I asked you to meet me here."

"I was surprised," Key admitted. "But I'm glad you did."

Olive tucked the napkin into her pocket and picked up her glass. "I feel like I know you much better than I do. DP speaks so highly of you and Wain."

"You have a wonderful son. DP has been a godsend to Wain and me for so many reasons."

"He is wonderful, isn't he? Dawson and I are so proud of him. Somehow, he's managed to overcome living nearly two-thirds of his life with parents who've been barely available. Knowing that DP still needed me saved my sanity, but I wasn't the mother he deserved to have. The guilt I've felt because of that, on top of everything else ..." She compressed her lips and fixed her gaze on the pristine sky. "Riggs's shadow was everywhere. No matter how hard Dawson and I tried to keep it from happening, every celebration, every holiday, every vacation, every milestone DP experienced, simply amplified the fact that Riggs wasn't there. We could never escape."

*Twenty years (and more) of living inside the outlines of guilt, unrelenting sorrow, and answerless questions.* Key laid a tentative hand on Olive's arm.

"It's small consolation, but DP was the first man Wain learned to trust. He paved the way for Wain to trust his own father."

Olive nodded. "He's told us how much he respects your decision to take Wain in."

Key smiled. "I don't even remember what thoughts occupied that portion of my mind that Wain now fills."

"Yes. It's ... pervasive. Once our children join our lives, they're front and center forever." Olive shifted her position. After a moment, she asked, "Are you Catholic, Key?"

"Catholic?" *What a strange question.* "No."

"Neither are we. Sometimes, though, I think, *If only I had a confessional booth, where I could tell some anonymous priest my secrets, it might ease the burden.*" When Key didn't answer, Olive added, to Key's astonishment, "You have secrets too."

"I do?" She did, but how would Olive know any of them?

"Please don't take offense, but I looked you up online. The young woman who died in the motorcycle wreck with your late husband ... am I right that there's more to the story?"

"Ohhh." Key had journeyed so far from the bitterness and hurt Jeff had caused that it may as well have happened to someone else, in an era long past. Hoping she'd successfully hidden her relief, she replied, "Yes. Jeff was seeing her. I only found out after he died."

"That must have been devastating! But I sense no anger in you." Olive took a sip and fixed questioning blue eyes on Key. *Eyes I've seen before.*

"Well, I was angry," Key replied honestly. "But in my experience, perpetual bitterness and guilt condemn many undeserving humans to the worst kind of life sentence." Above them, a cardinal began to sing. "And I think sometimes we extend to others far more grace than we are willing to give ourselves." *Come on Riggs, help me.*

Olive twirled a maple leaf she'd picked up, blurring the reds and yellows into orange. "Why is that, Key? Why are we so reluctant to extend grace to ourselves?"

"Human nature?" Key asked with a friendly little shrug, watching an intrepid ant navigate the gigantic fabric desert on which they sat.

"All I know is that when you extend grace to yourself, you can't help but begin charting a new course."

"You're speaking from experience."

Key nodded. "It started after my husband died. I *desired* to live differently, but having the courage to actually *make* the changes was, well …" She smiled, recalling Gabriel's words. "Quite honestly, it was like choosing to walk off a cliff, not knowing where or how I'd land. But it was the best decision I've ever made. Life has gone from sepia to color." The ant dropped off onto a blade of grass and disappeared into his jungle.

Olive seemed to be listening—to what, Key had no idea—then laid the leaf on the red dirt, patted the grave, and said decisively, "Okay." Sitting up a little straighter and grasping Riggs's medallion, she asked, "Key, do you have time to hear a story?"

"Yes! How about a walk while we talk?"

# Chapter 57

## IN THE DARKEST DARK

Olive had a drawl that added syllables to words, but she was a brisk walker. "This *must* stay between us," she said as they made their way to the path that twisted and turned like a life metaphor through a sedate community of headstones, tiny flags, and floral tributes.

"Of course." *Secret keeper*—it seemed to be Key's lot in life since she'd moved to Troy.

Olive described how she'd grown up in a socially prominent family in Tidewater, Alabama, under strict parental rules. "My sister and brother and I were constantly warned that our family's reputation rested on our behavior."

"That's a tough burden to put on children," Key said sympathetically.

"Yes," Olive answered thoughtfully. "And even as an adult, I never got over wondering what my parents truly thought of me."

"Why?" Key asked, though she suspected she knew exactly why.

Olive didn't answer directly. "You know, I've read studies that say the brain, especially the frontal lobe, the decision-making part, is nowhere near fully developed during the intense teen years."

Key nodded. This conversation needed to meander wherever Olive chose. "Ironic that it's deficient at an age when, arguably, we most need it to be fully functional."

"Isn't that the truth!" Olive gave a little laugh and crossed her arms, as though unconsciously protecting her heart. "It's that profound fact that allows me to give myself at least some grace, as you put it. Because at age sixteen, my life went off my parents' preplanned map when I met a Swedish exchange student named Vidar Axelsson. He ticked all the boxes—handsome, nice as could be, an accent to die for—and every girl in my class fell hard for him. And for some reason, he chose me."

"*Some reason?* Olive, you're beautiful!"

Olive smiled. "Thank you, Key. But I was a late bloomer, the awkward, smart girl who loved reading and psychology and preferred staying home to social events. In my less practical moments, though, of course I dreamed of the fairy-tale romance, the perfect prince."

"As we all did!" Key felt strangely protective of the woman beside her.

"Then my braces came off, and I got contacts, and ..." Olive gestured somewhat ruefully at her still-very-attractive figure. "The girls suddenly saw me as a competitor, and the boys who up until then had completely ignored me were ..."

"Way to confuse them, Olive. How *dare* you."

Olive gave Key a startled glance, then let loose a genuine, loud belly laugh, revealing a hint of the less polished girl she'd just described. "I was every bit as confused as the boys were!" She sat down on a cast iron bench and patted the space next to her. "Anyway, long story short, I fell head over heels for Vidar as only a naive sixteen-year-old girl with an unformed frontal lobe can." She paused. "He loved me too, in his way."

"In his way? What does that mean?" Key was riveted.

"Well, of course he planned to return to Sweden and his life there, and I couldn't imagine leaving my beloved Alabama. It was all very *Romeo and Juliet.* So we made the most of the time we had. In every way. More unformed and *uninformed* frontal lobe decisions, if you get my drift."

"I do."

Olive stood and, from her pocket, extracted a small square photograph with rounded corners and faded colors. "I wasn't sure where my conversation with you today would go, but just in case, I brought this. Vidar and me. Prom 1972." She handed it to Key as they began walking again.

Key let out an involuntary gasp, then quickly added, "You're such a beautiful couple!" Fortunately, Olive didn't seem to notice anything odd in her reaction. "Where is Vidar now?"

Olive made a sad little noise. "He died not long after that picture was taken."

"What? *Oh, no.*" How many incarnations of grief did this woman have to suffer? For nearly her entire life, Olive Plummer had been forced to negotiate sympathetic words in lieu of the casual, upbeat everyday conversations that added lightness and joy to life. Conversations Key took for granted. It was so unfair.

"He and a friend were on their way to the beach to meet my friend and me, and a drunk driver crossed the center line. Neither boy survived, but of course, the intoxicated woman did." Olive shook her head. "Why is that so often the case? Vidar's family was absolutely devastated …. And very angry."

"Oh, I'm so sorry." Key handed the picture back.

Olive's voice took on an entirely different, quieter tone. "It wasn't long after the accident that I realized I was pregnant."

"Oh, Olive." Impulsively, Key reached out and clasped her hand.

Olive shook her head. "I avoid thinking back to the absolute horror of telling my parents, and those awful, ugly days that followed. I was allowed to stay home until I started showing, then I was shipped off, ostensibly to 'assuage my grief' over Vidar's death at a distant relative's home in Florida, a story that to this day most people still believe. In reality, I was sent here."

"Bertie." *Oh, beautiful Voile, you of the anagrammed name and the peachy, bruised roses. You, the darling girl who Bertie loves most.*

Olive nodded. "I owe Bertie Montgomery my life, and I mean that literally. I was very close to wanting to end my misery, both before and after my little boy was born. I thought I was sad about Vidar. It was nothing compared to the pain of giving up my son. Our son."

*Two sons lost.* It was inconceivable. "How old would your first son be?"

"Forty-five," Olive replied with no hesitation. *A mother's answer.*

"Does Dawson know?"

"Oh, yes. We met at Bertie's while I was pregnant, stayed in touch, and eventually got married. Dawson has always kept my secret, always been my rock." She sighed. "Sometimes he's *too* cautious when it comes to protecting me."

*Interesting,* Key thought. *Helicopter parents, helicopter husbands.*

"Then the boys were born," Olive went on, "and although not a day went by without missing my first son, who I had always thought of as my angel baby, I was very, very happy with my life. Riggs and DP were simply wonderful to raise, until ..."

*Until Ayo came along, shredding their lives into tatters,* Key thought angrily. "Does DP know about your first son?"

"No. Neither did Riggs." Olive stared straight ahead. "Rightly or wrongly, Dawson and I felt there was no reason to tell them they had a half brother who they'd never meet."

"Do you know where your son is?" Key asked.

Olive's voice turned inexplicably frigid. "I don't have the faintest idea."

"Would you want to meet him if you could?" Key held her breath.

"I would never want a relationship with him!" Olive replied emphatically, crossing her arms, her steps quickening, and Key's heart sank. "Because Key, I live with the deepest, darkest terror that Vidar's son is ... that he's Ayo Jones."

# Chapter 58
## OFF THE CLIFF

"Ayo!" Key stopped in her tracks. "*Ayo?* But *why* do you think that, Olive? *Why?*" No wonder Olive had kept DP from submitting his DNA to any database!

"When he and Riggs first became friends, Ayo told me he was adopted but that he didn't know his real birthday. He was in the correct age range."

"Did Ayo have any idea that you ...?"

"That I'd given up a child?" Olive was wringing her hands. "I don't know! He never said so, but his smug, secretive ways and the way he'd call me *Mama* so mockingly ..." She shuddered. "His possessiveness of Riggs, as time went on, became so intense that I did wonder if there was some sort of unseen, um, brotherly kind of connection. I finally asked Riggs not to invite Ayo over anymore. It tortured me to think I could be so repulsed by my own child."

"Why do you think Riggs chose to stay friends with Ayo?" Key asked as they settled back on the quilt.

Olive sighed. "I could write a book, but in a nutshell, Riggs was much younger, exceptionally kind, and somewhat naive. Ayo was a narcissistic master manipulator. I would put *nothing* past him."

Her shoulders drooped. "Key, I've never told a soul about my fears. Until now."

It sounded every bit the hellish purgatory Mack had described. Key placed her hand on Olive's back. "How can I help?"

Olive took a deep breath and rubbed her forehead. "Well, Bertie Montgomery told me after Riggs's funeral that she's been keeping a secret from me." Olive, staring at the clouds, didn't seem inclined to say more.

Key waited for a full minute. Finally, she ventured, "What was Bertie's secret?"

Another silence. "Bertie told me that eighteen years ago, a man called, asking if she could help him find his mother. He didn't give his name, but he gave his birth date, which, of course, matched my baby's. She sternly told him she couldn't help him and never to call again. Then she got an unlisted number."

"Does it bother you that Bertie decided to withhold that information?" Key asked.

Olive wearily shook her head. "She says that with all we were dealing with, she felt I couldn't handle the extra trauma. I would have had to explain it all to DP. It would have been more gossip fodder …." Olive crushed a clump of dirt between her thumb and forefinger, letting the red powder drift onto the quilt. "She was right."

"And you think the caller was Ayo?"

"Yes." More dirt fell on the blanket.

Key frowned. "Wait. Didn't Ayo tell you he didn't know his actual birth date?"

"He could have found out. Oh, Key, I just want the *truth*!" Olive declared angrily. "No matter where it leads or how ugly it gets. No matter who Ayo is to me or what secrets come to light." Her jaw tightened. "Ayo Jones, whoever he is, murdered my son. I want him brought to justice."

"The police *are* looking for him."

Olive scoffed. "It's been twenty years, so I'm not holding my breath." She laid a hand on Key's forearm. "I realize I may be asking for the impossible, Key, but you were instrumental in finding Riggs and … I wondered if you could possibly … help me uncover the truth in all this." Gone was the anger. The pain in Olive's eyes before she turned away to once again rearrange the flowers on her dead son's grave nearly broke Key's heart.

As if joyfully giving permission, the cardinal began to sing. This was the opening Key had promised to walk through. Time for darkness and fear to be cast aside. Time for Olive to join the living. Key sat up a little straighter, then laced her hands together and drew them toward her chest. "Olive … it's … it's not Ayo who called Bertie all those years ago."

"It's not …." Olive studied her face uncomprehendingly. "How do you know? What do you mean? Key, *what do you mean?*"

*How utterly perfect that her two missing sons led one another home.*

*How utterly* tectonic.

Clasping both Olive's hands in hers, Key stepped with Gabriel's mother over the cliff and into the light.

# Chapter 59

## BLINDSIDED

"Twas a cowboy! And I got all this!" From his chair at the kitchen table, Wain held up a candy-filled plastic bag toward the tablet Key had placed on top of an upside-down mixing bowl. Both Halloween and Key's birthday had come and gone, and Wain was catching Guy up on all the news.

Guy raised his eyebrows. "Nice loot! Let's just say you didn't inherit *my* Halloween genes. I plowed through my trick or treat candy in two days."

"Me too!" Key called from across the kitchen, where she was grating a huge zucchini Bertie had snagged from the senior center. "But I never got half that much!"

She'd have to wait to share with Guy the story Wain had told her about his previous Halloween. "My mom and Cal made me throw my candy away," he'd told her matter-of-factly, "because I forgot to say 'thank you' at the last house. I wasn't polite."

*Venomous.* As usual, Lyric had gone out of her way to inflict guilt and punishment, creating yet another joyless, haunting memory. Key was encouraged, though, at how easily Wain had recounted the story. The hurt was fading.

After Wain had shown Guy the card he'd made for Key (a picture of a giant cupcake with a horse and a boy on top), Guy wished her a happy belated birthday, promised they'd celebrate at Christmas, and rang off.

At Mistic Meadows the next day, Key distributed zucchini muffins, accepted the chorus of good wishes after Wain announced her birthday, then said, "I need to run back to Pike House for a minute. DP just texted me that he's not sure if he turned off a space heater."

"I'll go with you, Key," Petra offered. She and Larry had brought Granny Jewel to watch Ell ride. "If you don't mind. I'd love to see your place. Heard so much about it."

DP had been right. The heater was indeed still on. Key turned it off, then gave an admiring Petra the tour, ending on the screened deck.

"Oh, you'll *live* out here in the summers!" Petra exclaimed, then moved closer to the screen and peered into the woods, frowning. "Hey. What's that light?"

"Where?" Key joined her. "I don't see a light."

"There! See?"

Sure enough, out in the woods, an occasional flash beckoned like a lightning bug, then disappeared, as though someone was moving carefully through the trees.

"People have been stopping by to leave flowers at the spot where Riggs was found." Key hadn't been around after dark to see whether there were nighttime visitors, but she wouldn't be surprised. "It hasn't been a problem though. The sheriff told DP they were keeping an eye on the site."

Petra nodded. "Good. It's unreal that Riggs was there all that time." They chatted for a few more minutes, watching the light, which had stopped moving. "If they were only leaving flowers, they should be gone," Petra said suspiciously.

Key sighed. "Hopefully not teenage partiers."

Petra put her hands on her hips. "They shouldn't be partying at that … that sacred spot or trespassing on your property. Larry has a friend who installs fences. Remind me to give you his number." She strode purposefully toward the screen door. "Let's go check it out. Surprise the little turds."

Though it was almost fully dark, they could see well enough as they made their way toward the pine trees lining the old garden area. Insects were singing, and above them, the sky was still starless. It wasn't terribly chilly, but Key was glad for her *Inside Outlines* sweatshirt. A few steps later, they heard grunting noises, the slap of a shovel against soil, the faint plop as the dirt landed.

"What the *heck*?" Petra whispered, clutching Key's elbow. "Someone is digging! Hey!" she hollered at the back of a bent-over figure. "What are you doing? You're trespassing!"

"*Petra!*" Key whispered urgently through clenched teeth, horror and adrenaline flooding her body. Yanking desperately at the other woman's shirt, she gasped, "Back up, back *up*!"

But it was too late. The digger, who was dressed all in black, straightened and turned around, recognized her wide, terrified eyes, then raised his shovel above his head like a club and charged full force straight at them.

Petra let out an exclamation, and with incredible strength shoved Key backward, causing her to lose her balance and slam shoulder-first into a tree. As she slid painfully down the rough trunk to the ground, she raised her forearms to shield her face, bracing for the blow to come.

# Chapter 60
## A BIT OF A SITUATION

There was a loud *pop*, an almost simultaneous metallic *ping*, then a faint thud and an otherworldly howl. Key uncovered her eyes just in time to see her attacker drop his shovel like it was molten hot and bend over, moaning and clutching his fingers. From somewhere above her, an icily calm, authoritative voice was issuing commands.

"Stand *up*, sir, and put your hands up, or I promise you I will shoot those fancy boots right off your feet."

The man straightened but continued whimpering and rubbing his fingers, glaring at Petra, who, to Key's disbelief, was calmly grasping a compact pink-camouflage revolver in two hands, her extended arms as steady as the tree branches surrounding them. "UP! Put your hands up!" His face twisted in fury, the man reluctantly raised his hands. "You just attacked us!" Petra exclaimed. "Why?" Silence. She tried again. "What's your name?"

Positive her pounding heart was echoing all the way to Mistic Meadows, Key scrambled to her feet, pine needles and dirt and pebbles cascading from her backside. Rubbing her stinging shoulder, she said coldly, "That's my landlord, Petra. His name is Vern Olson." *Where* had Petra's gun come from? The woman was wearing skintight yoga pants, for heaven's sake!

Vern's eyes darted back and forth from the shovel to a bag resting against a tree trunk. Petra read his mind. "Don't even think about moving, mister," she snapped, then in a completely normal tone of voice, said, "Key, call 911. Gordon Ellicot is the sheriff. Have them send him out here."

"My phone's in the house on the kitchen counter." Key hadn't even thought about it when they'd impulsively walked out the deck door.

"Mine's in my pocketbook at the corral." Petra thought a moment, her eyes never leaving Vern. "Okay, Key, grab a stick and pick up that bag. Don't touch it. Get the lantern, too, but leave the shovel. The police can sort this out."

Key unhooked the lantern from a tree branch and found a sturdy stick, which she slid under the handles of the same briefcase Vern had brought with him the day he'd fixed the modem.

"Walk ahead of me toward the house with your hands up," Petra told Vern, who had not uttered a word.

They were almost to Key's front yard when headlights appeared, a car door slammed, and Larry hurried toward them.

"I was just comin' to find you …." Larry stopped, his jaw dropping as Vern stumbled forward, gloved hands in the air, Petra's gun pressing into his back. Key followed, carrying the electric lantern and balancing Vern's bag on a stick over her shoulder like Huckleberry Finn with a kerchief full of johnnycakes. If it hadn't been so deadly serious, she would have laughed. "What in the … Petra, honey, what are you *doin'*?"

"Well, as you can see, Lar, we got a bit of a situation. Call Gordon." Petra gestured with her gun. "Go through the gate, then sit," she commanded Vern. Pale and breathing hard, he lowered himself heavily onto the dew-soaked grass.

"Who is this?" Larry asked, tugging his phone from his jeans pocket.

Key carefully set Vern's bag and lantern on the porch and ran to the kitchen to retrieve her own phone.

"… and he attacked us with a shovel, so … I pulled my gun on him," Petra was saying calmly as Key rejoined them. "Sheriff's on the way," she told Key.

Larry raised his eyebrows. "Wrong soldier you messed with," he remarked casually to Vern. "Sergeant Oakes here ain't never not packin' heat."

★★★

After a disheveled and still-mute Vern was handcuffed and driven away, Larry left (Key would have loved to be a fly on the wall as he explained to the group at Mistic Meadows why she and Petra were delayed), and she, Petra, and Sheriff Endicott moved inside, away from the strobing red and blue emergency lights. In the woods, two deputies wrapped yellow tape around trees.

"Oh! Be sure to check for an earring," Key pinched the helix of her ear. The sheriff made a note. "Earring. Okay. What's the significance?"

"I strongly suspect Vern's earring will match one that Riggs's brother DP wears. In fact, I have a notebook full of information that has convinced me that Vern Olson is Ayo Jones."

Petra gave a startled exclamation, but the sheriff didn't look at all surprised. "I'd like to see your notebook, ma'am."

"I'll bring it to your office tomorrow."

"What was he digging for?" Petra asked.

"Can't divulge that at the moment," Sheriff Endicott replied slowly, "but I *can* tell you that in our press conferences, we deliberately withheld information about the evidence we found, hoping it would entice Riggs's killer to come looking for what we didn't mention. We been monitoring the site, but nothing come of it, and today of all days, we cut back on our surveillance." He shook his head. "Y'all did real good."

"Petra gets all the credit," Key said. "He came at us with that shovel, and she instantly had the gun on him. She was fearless."

The sheriff looked pleased. "Exactly what concealed carry's supposed to do—diffuse a situation that coulda ended tragically." He shook their hands. "Thank you, ladies. Ain't every day we get the assistance of such competent crime fighters. See y'all tomorrow."

As they walked to the Jeep, Petra turned to Key. "You gonna be okay, honey?"

"Maybe a little shook up." Key gave her a hug. "Thank you! You saved my life, Petra!"

"What'd I tell you, way back when?" Petra sounded the tiniest bit smug.

"Um …" Key drew a blank. "What?"

Petra scratched furiously at the air. "Mama. Frickin'. Wildcat."

# Chapter 61

## TWO SIDES OF THE SAME COIN

"Hi!" Mary and Olive, coffees in hand, slid into the booth across from Key. It had been several days since she'd talked to either of them, and she suspected they were as eager as she was to catch up.

Olive wasted no time. "Key, we told Mary and Jukey about Gabriel."

"Yes!" Mary put an arm around Olive. "Jukey and I cried. It was almost more than we could take in. We're so very happy for you all. To think I've been listening to your son all these years! No wonder I loved him!"

"DP and Molly have been so welcoming," Olive said. "And Gabriel absolutely adores them."

"What about Dawson?" Key asked.

"You know Dawson. When it comes to family, he's very protective," Olive replied, sounding, Key thought, somewhat noncommittal. "He's … relieved, but coming on the heels of finding Riggs, it's been … well, intense."

Mary nodded. "Such lows to such highs. It's got to be complicated."

"Yes and no," Olive said decisively. "Gabriel will never replace Riggs, and no one with an ounce of sense would ever think he would! But Gabriel alone has owned a very specific part of my heart since I was sixteen. He will never *not* be my son. Meeting him was the most natural thing in the world. Dawson will come around."

"Where did you and Gabriel meet?" Key asked. She'd been dying to hear this part of the story.

"In Porterville, in the lobby of the Andover Hotel."

"Oh, Olive, I can't even imagine how nervous you must have been!" Mary was as enthralled as Key. "Were you alone?"

"Dawson and DP and Molly were there, but Gabriel and I met alone first." Olive pressed her hand on her heart. "I was a wreck! But as soon as he walked into the room, I had exactly the same thought as the day he was born: *Of course it's you!* And we both just broke down and gave each other the biggest hug!"

"When you showed me that prom picture, I couldn't believe it," Key said. "Gabriel looks so much like Vidar. But I see your boys in him too. You want to know what got me wondering? The way Gabriel and DP both stack one foot on the other when they stretch their legs out."

Olive laughed delightedly. "We've all said that! Did you know that Lonny noticed it right off too? He told DP that he thought he was going crazy!"

So Lonny and Gayle knew too. It made Key very happy.

Olive showed them pictures on her phone. "Since then, all five of us—Dawson and DP and Molly and Gabriel and I—have talked for hours. Gabriel wants to know everything, and though there is such sadness that Riggs isn't with us, it's a joy to share stories with his older *brother!* Gabriel was searching and grieving *with* us all those years. He sincerely loved Riggs without ever meeting him."

Key described how Gabriel had knelt and placed his hand on the grassy mound the day they found Riggs. "It was something a brother would do."

Olive nodded. "He told us. We all just cried. And Bertie ... Well, she's in heaven. Gabriel is the only one of her girls' babies she's met. She's shown him my rosebush, which she says is partly his." Her voice, Key thought, reflected a new lightness. Olive had broken free.

"Voile." Key nodded, smiling.

Olive chuckled. "Bertie anagrammed my name in case anyone made the connection. You suspected, though, didn't you, Key?"

"Yes," Key admitted. "From the day I saw it. But it wasn't my business, so I just locked it away. Who could ever have predicted that this is where your story would end up!"

"It's the start of a new chapter, Olive," Mary said. "And I can't think of anyone more deserving than you. You must feel set free."

"I do. No living in terror that my secrets will get out." Olive paused. "And yet, there are so many years ahead without ... I mean, Riggs would have wholeheartedly embraced his big brother. That piece of his life was stolen from him along with everything else. Stolen from all of us." Tears rolled down her cheeks. "Oh, I'm so sorry. I go from laughing to crying without warning these days. Two sides of the same coin." She reached for a napkin. Before she could pick it up, Key laid her hand on Olive's, then Mary put hers on top of Key's, and without warning, Olive leaned forward and set her forehead on the back of Mary's hand. Oblivious to the sympathetic stares from the tables around them, they sat that way for a moment, no words necessary, allowing a freshly minted friendship to absorb just a sliver of Olive's pain.

# Chapter 62

## CLARITY

*Early December*

"I'd hate to pass my cold on to anyone"—Bertie sniffled to Key over the phone—"so I'll hear all about the open house later from you and Olive. But if you don't mind, would you pick up the container of cookies on my porch? DP loves my toffee pots, so I suspect Gabriel will too!"

Key dropped Wain off at Greggo's for a playdate, then spent a blissful three hours at the Kings' annual holiday open house, where she finally got to meet Corny and his wife.

After helping Jukey and Mary clean up, several people were still gathered around the kitchen island.

"How long till Wain's daddy gets here, Miss Key?" Gayle asked. Her freshly colored hair was swept up in a jeweled clip, showcasing a pair of dangly Christmas-tree ball earrings Ell had proudly purchased for her at the school holiday fair.

"Twelve days," Key replied. "Thirty years in Wain time." Everyone laughed.

"And how long till you're back in your place at Pike Road?" Jukey asked.

Key looked at DP. "What do you think?"

"A week, ten days." He grinned. "Twelve years in Miss Key time."

"I admit to being the world's most impatient client," Key admitted amid more laughter. Her suspicions about cameras inside the Veronica View house, as it turned out, were unfounded, but she still could hardly wait to leave. She had every box packed and ready, which was just as well because a blindsided Deirdre, who'd already filed for divorce, was putting the Veronica View house on the market. "I can't leave Troy fast enough," she'd told Key in an emotional phone call. "I should have left long ago."

Jukey turned to Dawson. "What's going on with Ayo's case these days?"

"They're fighting for bail, which we've been assured will never happen," Dawson replied to a suddenly quiet room. "He's a flight risk." Ayo had been caught by a classic sting, Dawson told them. After Riggs's body was found, the sheriff had publicly announced that they'd found only a red bandana buried with him. In truth, they'd unearthed his binoculars under several inches of dirt, below the blue tarp. In Lonny's second concert picture, Ayo wore those binoculars around his neck.

The police also found two gold wristbands (their numbers sandwiching Lonny's) lying near Riggs's disintegrated Levis, as well as a green band still poignantly looped around his wrist bones, proving that he'd left the concert to access the VIP lot. Shasta would testify that she'd removed Ayo's green wristband shown in the same picture as the binoculars.

It all amounted to significantly damning circumstantial evidence, but it was what detectives found in Vern's briefcase that sealed his fate: a folder full of stories about Riggs, pictures of the burial site, and a homemade map showing spots where he'd obsessively searched for the necklace in the woods during his horseback rides. Added to that was the earring matching DP's. He'd also been charged with the attack on Key and Petra. Vern Olson would never be a free man again.

"Is it true he was adopted, then put back into the foster system?" Granny Jewel asked from the living room. "I have no truck with his ugly crimes, but that is a harsh sentence for any little boy."

Dawson shook his head in disgust. "He wasn't adopted. He's just a pathological liar." There were a few gasps.

"I *knew* it!" Lonny exclaimed. "He always knew the right words to get him the wrong things."

"A bad seed." Granny Jewel nodded knowingly, fiddling with the multiple necklaces draped around her neck. "There's no explaining bad seeds."

*All those years,* Key thought. *All those years Olive tortured herself, wondering, because Ayo Jones decided to lie.*

"He's got family somewhere in Pennsylvania who ran a very successful carpet-cleaning business," Dawson went on. "Sheriff tells me his parents did kick him out *as an adult,* after a series of escalating incidences. Stealing, fraud, dealing dope, that type of thing. He changed his name to Ayo Jones somewhere along the line. When he left Troy, he took back his real name ...." He paused, frowning.

"Alvern Overton," Gabriel said. "That's why he was impossible for my team to find."

"Right." Dawson nodded. "Thanks, Gabe. At some point, he changed his last name yet again, this time to Olson. Got married. Not a whiff of illegal activity since then."

"But why Troy?" Mary asked. "What was here for him? How'd he end up working for Castle?"

Dawson shrugged. "Just one of those things. Castle was using that junky van to transport drugs, and that was Ayo's particular job. I wonder sometimes if Riggs found out and ..." He sighed. "Unless Ayo confesses—and it doesn't look like he will—we'll never know what caused him to snap." He nodded at Lonny. "Those pictures, especially the one with the binoculars, are gonna be key evidence. We sent a portion of the reward money to Shasta, knowing how much her testimony will help the case."

(The Morgans had received nearly two-thirds of the reward. "It's life-changing for us," Gayle had told Key one evening at the corral.

"Ell's gonna buy Coco, and Lon can pay off his debt." Gayle and Lonny would never know that Key had asked the Plummers to add her portion of the reward to theirs. )

"Why'd he come back here, then? Buy old Gerald and Georgia's house?" Lonny asked.

"Now that's an interesting bit of information," Dawson replied. "We suspect Ayo obsessively tracked Riggs's case, but nothing new happened until 2014, when Gabriel's podcast put a spotlight on the case, and on Troy. Deirdre could never understand why he insisted on moving here so suddenly. He bought a horse because the land he needed to search had become inaccessible. The police also expect Vern's computer to be a treasure trove of information."

"And here you was looking for your own brother!" Granny Jewel exclaimed to Gabriel. "Did you know he was your brother when you cast the pod?"

Everyone laughed.

"I did."

Mary raised her cup. "Now, Gabriel, you just tell me to mind my own business if I'm getting too personal. Olive has told us her piece, but I'd love to hear your side of this amazing story."

"Starting from about age nine or ten, I felt something was missing." Gabriel hesitated. "Crazy as it sounds, and much as I loved my adoptive parents, I could never shake the feeling that my birth family needed me. I told myself I didn't need to be involved in their lives. I just wanted to know they were okay."

"Did you tell your adoptive parents you were searching?" Gayle asked.

"Not until I was an adult and had hit dead end after dead end. It was a slog, trying to find information. Back then, DNA databases for personal reasons were nonexistent."

"Why any sane person would willingly hand over their bloodlines to strangers is something I'll never fathom!" Granny Jewel shook her head.

"You're not wrong," Gabriel acknowledged with a polite nod. "But DNA also exonerates innocent people."

Granny Jewel looked unconvinced. "Sorry to interrupt. G'wan. Your story is real interesting."

"I finally told my parents about my search, and they gave me Bertie's name. When she shut me down, I almost gave up. Not long after that, though, I was trying out this new thing called Google—"

Amid the laughter, DP's wife Molly looked mystified. "Don't know how y'all existed without Google." She patted her very large belly. "This Riggs is gonna grow up in a real different world."

"My nephew," Gabriel said proudly. "Anyway, I searched for Troy, North Carolina, and first thing, up popped an old story about Riggs's disappearance. I can't explain why it resonated so deeply with me, but it did. I stared at those grainy online pictures, looked up every article I could find. I felt like I knew him."

"Y'all have the same eyes," Granny Jewel said. "Lonny noticed it right off."

Gabriel nodded. "Maybe that was it. By 2013, both my parents had passed away, and DNA had progressed to the point where I could submit mine. It led me to my biological father's family, who, to my great surprise, all lived in Sweden. And they had absolutely no idea I existed. That has been a less ... serendipitous outcome," he added ruefully. "My father's siblings wanted nothing to do with the complications I'd bring, but they did provide the only thing I wanted: Olive's name."

"It's a gift from Vidar," Olive said with a smile.

"You must have been shocked to realize Riggs was your brother!" Mary exclaimed.

Gabriel nodded. "Shocked and yet ... not. A connection I couldn't explain suddenly made sense. And Bertie's words became clear. Olive and Dawson and DP were going through too much for me to show up and add another layer of trauma. I decided not to contact them, but it was the most painful decision I've ever made. So instead, I made it a mission to find my brother."

"So you started your podcast," Gayle marveled. "And it worked. You found Riggs."

Gabriel waved a hand around the room. "*We* found Riggs."

"And Riggs brought you back to Mama and us," DP said. "Brothers and hunters."

Granny Jewel dabbed at her eyes. "Riggs, I know you can hear me. We miss you to this day. Always will, honey." She raised her water glass. "To Riggs."

"To Riggs," everyone chorused as Olive leaned over and kissed Granny Jewel on the cheek.

*Life. A series of good and tough jars. A path of thorns and roses.*

# Chapter 63

## A GATHERING

"Hold still, buddy." Key fastened a lime-green clip-on tie to the collar of Wain's white dress shirt. "There. Turn around." She put her hands on his shoulders. "What do you think?"

"It's good." Wain stared seriously at their unfamiliar, formal reflections: he in his new suit and Key in a charcoal-gray belted dress and knee-high black boots, her pearl earrings and star pin her only jewelry. He touched the tie. "I look like a grown-up. I look like my dad."

"You do. But you look like you, too, Wain!" They were headed first to a service at the high school, then a private reception at Dawson and Olive's residence on the outskirts of Troy. As close as she and Olive had become in the past few weeks, Key had never visited their home, and she was looking forward to it.

Key pressed a tape roller to her dress to remove a fringe of black dog hair, then tucked extra tissues into her purse. "Wain, please grab the bouquet on the table and check Faro's water."

Her phone pinged. Mack.

Hey Key! Please hug the Plummers for me. Wish I could be there!

-Me, too! We're just about to head out

BTW, finally broke it off w/ Toni. Didn't go well. Lesson learned

Key was happy to hear it, as much for Toni's sake as for Mack's.

-Can't wait to catch up!

I'll call you later. I made a chart with stickers for how many days til I get back to NC. =)

Wain reappeared with the sunflowers. "Who are these for?"

"For DP's family. It's a way to say we're sorry for the sadness they've experienced."

"Because, *R–I–P.*" Wain always referred to Riggs that way.

"Yes. Riggs."

"Is the bad guy still in jail?" Wain asked as Key backed down the driveway.

"Yes, he is." Key knew Wain wasn't worried; he just liked discussing the night Vern Olson was arrested. Another urban legend in the making, no doubt.

"My dad says he's *never* gonna get out."

"That's true." Key grinned. Every other sentence these days started with *My dad says.*

"How'd the necklace get into the pond?" Wain asked. "Like, *everyone* asks me that."

"No one is really sure, honey," Key replied. No way would she put the images of Jukey's theory into Wain's mind.

Thankfully, he'd moved on. "What's gonna happen to the bad guy's horse?"

"He's staying at Mistic Meadows." Key had spent a couple hours with Jessie and Regina doing paperwork because at Christmas Wain would be told that Guy had purchased McKenzie from Deirdre, changed the horse's name to Hunter, and hired Cav to ride and care for him.

At the door of the packed gymnasium, latecomers were directed to the school cafeteria, where a video feed had been hastily set up. "We lost count at two thousand," an usher informed Key as he showed them to their seats. "Maybe they ain't never met Riggs, but they love the Plummers and Orion. And a good amount is just curious, just *gotta* see what's goin' on." In the last category was the media; Key had noted a Porterville news van in the parking lot. Though the discovery of

Riggs's body had made only a slight ripple in the river of national news, it was a huge story locally.

On the stage, three large pictures of Riggs—age five at the beach, teenager posing proudly next to a motorcycle, handsome young man sitting on a stump holding his guitar—rested on easels positioned between four pots overflowing with December greenery. After greeting the Plummers and Gabriel, Key and Wain placed their flowers alongside the tributes lining the stage. Among the notes, photographs, and stuffed animals was a toy guitar with *MISS YOU MAN* written on the front, a bobblehead doll bearing an astonishing resemblance to Riggs, and a Troy High School yearbook open to his senior picture with a dollar bill inexplicably taped to the page with a note, *never laughed so hard, still got the dollar!!* Everyone, it seemed, had felt a connection with Riggs Plummer.

As touchingly emotional as it all was, the sheer scope of the event provided even more insight into the reasons Dawson and (especially) Olive had retreated so far from the limelight. "Even the good side of fame will consume you if you let it," Key once heard a popular actress say; it had to be exponentially harder when trauma and grief were partly the reason for that fame.

Directly across the aisle from Key were Jukey and Mary with their three handsome sons and daughters-in-law, easily creating the best-looking row in the entire gym. Behind them, Granny Jewel was seated in what she'd told Key was her "go-to-meeting wheelchair," accompanied by Larry and Petra. Next to Molly's family in front of Key, already blotting under her glasses with a tissue, was Bertie, her shiny white hair freshly styled.

"Hey!" From her seat with her family at the end of the row, Ell skipped over, adorable in a gauzy floral skirt and long-sleeved shirt featuring a sequined red rose. On her feet were brand-new Converse high-tops, and in her smooth brown hair she wore a sparkling tiara-type headband.

Key hugged her. "Ell! You are gorgeous. Love the tiara."

"I got all this at Mayweather's." Ell kicked up a foot. "Except the shoes. Granny Jewel got me these."

"Really? You got this outfit at Tally's mom's store?"

"Yeah. Someone sent me a gift certificate in the mail. But we don't know who."

"You have a secret admirer!" Key had weighed the pros and cons of going to Mayweather's boutique, then decided it was worth a try, if only to get a closer look at Ursula the Honker. Maybe she'd misjudged the woman. Ursula had been retail-polite, but she had shown no sense of recognition when Key told her who the certificate was for, until Key had said, "The little girl who found the necklace."

Ursula shuddered. "Ugh, horrible! Do you know, we drove right past those haunted woods to the horse barn where *my Tally* had a party!" Key sensibly decided to take it no further. It wouldn't have ended well. At least Ell was happy in her new clothes.

"Ell, how are things going with Tally?" Key asked.

"Eh." Ell shrugged.

"She's being nicer?"

"Kinda. But I have other friends now. *Everybody* wants to hear about the necklace!"

Key laughed. Now *there* was a string she hadn't expected Riggs to tug, but who was she to question? "I'm so glad to hear that."

"Miss Key, I got some people I want you to meet." Lonny introduced Shasta (attractive, blonder, and more matronly than in the concert pictures) and Carly, (beautiful, fashionable, and demure). Key found it slightly disconcerting to meet them as forty-something adults. Time had simply folded in on itself.

Dawson stepped forward and waited for the anticipatory hum to still. "I want to share a miracle." Starting with the day Ell found the necklace, he narrated Riggs's story to a spellbound audience. "Finding Riggs was a collaborative effort, involving many people. We would like to honor them now." To applause and curious stares, he introduced Key, Wain, Ell, Lonny, Jukey, Mary, Shasta Harrison, Petra, and Gabriel. Gunnar Boy, emerging with Paul Vicarman from behind the curtain, caused a minor sensation. "Without these wonderful folks, we would not be here today." Cheers and applause exploded from the crowd.

Back at their chairs, Wain laid a hand on her arm. "Key, is it sad yet?" he whispered. "Because I don't feel like crying!"

She smiled. His confusion was understandable. So far, this service bore no resemblance to the sober church funeral she'd described to Wain the day they'd gone shopping for his suit. Instead, today was an extraordinary mix of somber and celebratory, and Key suspected Riggs approved. She squeezed Wain's shoulder. "Dawson's going to talk. Let's listen."

# Chapter 64
## CONTRITION

"Our family is honored to be here with y'all, remembering with love our son and brother and friend, Riggs Inman Plummer."

With the band behind him and the mic in his hand, Dawson strolled between the pictures on the stage, sharing memories of Riggs. "And all y'all Orion fans from way back know Riggs was also one of those musicians whose personality and talent would have taken him as far as he wanted to go."

He paused by the picture of Riggs as a small boy. "Any parent who's lost a child, no matter what stage in life, understands that searing ache that lodges deep in your bones and hardens into the marrow. For the families of the missing, though, the unknown steals the very breath from your lungs. I've heard it described as a 'hellish purgatory,' and I find that to be the perfect description."

From where she sat, Key could see Carly's lovely profile, tears rolling down her cheeks, a mother now who no doubt related to Olive and Dawson's anguish as much as she did herself as the teenage girl who'd lost her first love. *This open sorrow, this is what finding Riggs has allowed.*

"Life goes on though, don't it? For twenty years, hope was our tenuous and fickle lifeline," Dawson continued. "I tried to make myself believe Riggs had chosen to leave—because painful as that thought was, it allowed hope we'd someday hear him say, *Hey, Daddy. Hey, Mama. Hey, little bro. Ah.* Bear with me. This next part's the hardest." He took two deep breaths and momentarily closed his eyes. There was a rustle as everyone sat up a little straighter in their chairs. This was no gossipy rumor, no urban legend. Here, in this gymnasium, was truth.

"Y'all know the Bible verse that warns us not to let the sun go down on our wrath." Soft *amens* rolled like whispering tide around the gym as Dawson placed a hand on the picture of Riggs with the guitar. "On the day Riggs disappeared, he and I had the first and only strong disagreement we'd ever had. No fisticuffs or nothin' like that, and what it was about don't matter. What *does* matter is that Riggs left the house red-hot fuming, and I stayed in the house equally angry, and—"

He swallowed hard, nodding. "—and we never saw our son alive again. The last words Riggs heard from me were hurtful words I could never take back."

Another prolonged silence, broken only by sniffles and muted nose blowing, ensued while Dawson composed himself. Wain scooted out from under Key's arm to the front of his chair.

"One year to the day after Riggs disappeared, I wrote a song for him—a song borne of corrosive sorrow and ... and soul-crushing regret. Then I buried it deep in a desk drawer, vowing that no one would ever hear it unless Riggs found his way home.

"Olive, DP, and I had no crystal ball to tell us that song would languish for another *nineteen* years, until—thanks to a genuine miracle, caring people who didn't give up, and the incredible dog y'all just met—we *did* find Riggs." This time, there was no holding back the applause that swelled to a roar; people simply couldn't help themselves.

Wain leaned toward Key. "He's talking about Ell! And us!"

Dawson fitted his guitar strap over his shoulder. "Thank y'all for coming to listen to Orion over the years. And while we truly appreciate the applause, we respectfully ask that after this song, y'all offer us the pure gift of silence. *Remember* the thousands of families still dwelling in that same hellish purgatory from which we've finally been set free. And y'all—consider the heavy toll of unnecessary or unresolved anger. Practice grace and forgiveness."

The band began to play.

"This song is called 'Contrition.' A song to my beloved son, Riggs Inman Plummer."

My heart is
Parched and dry,
Its chambers
Echo with
Your absent voice.
I pray
My burning eyes
Are dreaming and
I'll wake up
To the usual noise.
The words I hurled
Have boomeranged,
I beg to change
That time, this place.
I should have said
I love you son,
I could have
Offered you my grace.
The bleakest night,
The brightest day,
Indifferent parts
Of the broken whole,
Are suspended in
This bruising haze,
Mirroring my soul.
If sorrow is a river,
I've drowned
A million times.
If breath is for the living,
Come back,

I'll give you mine.
Now your absence
Is a presence,
No reflection in the mirror.
I would have
If I could have
Gifted you my life, my years.

The simple chords and Dawson's rich, soulful baritone circulated the healing words deep into the veins of past, present, and future, fortifying still-beating hearts and miraculously incorporating another invisible, forgiving voice along the way, as though the lyrics were being sung back to the singer. In the magnificent stillness that followed, two thousand people telegraphed as one their healing sympathy to a father and a family finally emerging from exile.

# Chapter 65

## THE CARDINAL'S SONGS

"And now," Dawson said quietly after a full two minutes of heartfelt silence, "my son DP would like to share a few words."

"Thank y'all for celebrating with us the life of my brother Riggs. I miss him more, not less, as time goes on." DP unfolded a piece of paper and began to read. "Recently I had a conversation with a good friend." He put his hand over his heart and inclined his head toward Key, who beamed back at him. "We talked about how one simple action might propel us to an unexpected place, and from there another, and so on. We in our limited and puny human scope cannot fathom or explain why the path opens up this way, but I believe that our family recently saw the hand of God at work through the people, animals, and nature placed around us." He smiled over at Olive, Molly, and Gabriel. "Without these connections, we wouldn't have found *either of my brothers*." Though he emphasized the last four words, he didn't elaborate.

*Oh, this will set tongues wagging,* Key thought, as the murmurs and neck craning began, *but the ladies in the senior center will certainly set it straight.* Because there was Bertie, beaming like a heroic lighthouse keeper who'd safely guided a boatful of lost souls to the white pebbled shores of her rose garden.

DP ignored the stir. "To all y'all struggling—don't give up hope. You never know what mountains the butterfly wings are gonna move." The band began to play. "This song is called 'Orion in the Sunshine.'" His voice, no longer a backup to his father's, emerged clear and strong, introducing a rapt audience to the most beautiful lyrics Key had ever heard.

Your meteor fell, burning deep,
A flash, a flame we could not keep.
Where did you go? I wait for night
To beg your star to share its light.
I pray the sun will rise for me,
Chase the darkness, bring me peace.
Orion in the sunshine
You've been there all along,
Orion singing to me
The hidden hunter's song.

I cast my eyes across the skies,
Somewhere out there, the answer lies.
Someday a butterfly will land
On a tree leaf or an outstretched hand.
A breath of hope will move its wings,
Start the song the hidden hunter sings.
Orion in the sunshine
You've been there all along,
Orion singing to me
The hidden hunter's song.

I throw my net upon the waves
Of sorrow, deep as ocean caves.
Someday a swan will glide just so
Across the bay, into the cove,
A ripple grown into ten more

Guides our hunter to his final shore.
Orion in the sunshine
You've been there all along,
Orion singing to me
The hidden hunter's song.

Our heartbreak's drawn a map of lines,
A journey of seek but never find.
One day a sunbeam shining clear
Will part the clouds on the pathway here.
The warmth will spread into our bones,
Our star, Orion, has come home.
Orion in the sunshine
You've been there all along,
Orion singing to me
The hidden hunter's song.

The last notes faded into another reverent stillness. On the stage, Dawson embraced DP.

Wain swiped at his eyes, then patted Key's leg. "That's a good song," he whispered. "DP's brother likes it, I think. *R-I-P.*"

*The cardinal*, Key thought through her tears, as she handed Wain a tissue and hugged him tightly. *These are the cardinal's songs.*

# Acknowledgments

The inspiration for *Orion in the Sunshine* flowed from the well dug by my first novel, *The Alphabet Woods*, where my readers were introduced to Key North, Wain, and the characters who comprise their fictional North Carolina world. As a sequel, *Orion* was easy to write but extremely difficult to edit! Thank you to everyone who helped me carve this story out of so many superfluous words and kept me tracking and encouraged.

Thank you to my beta readers: my daughters, Lindsay Meekin, Danica Markus, and Courtney Tiencken; my husband, Ken; and my two sisters, Raye Pride and Patti Clark. It takes time and effort to navigate a huge, unwieldy first draft, not to mention answering my long list of questions. ("Does this character need fleshing out?" "Should I include these poems?" "Did you pick up on this subtle clue?" etc.) Thank you so much for your willingness to critique and analyze! I appreciate every bit of your honesty and humor and insight!

Thank you to every one of my readers, who have overwhelmingly and enthusiastically embraced the idea of a sequel. Thanks to my friends who consistently check in to ask how it's going and gift me their words of encouragement.

Thank you once again to everyone at Warren Publishing: Erika Nein, my developmental editor who rearranged, deleted, suggested, encouraged, and ultimately said, "It's great." Thank you to Amy Ashby, Melissa Long, Mindy Kuhn, Lacey Cope, copy editor Danielle Lange, and others who added their unique touch to this book. They are a great team, and I'm honored to collaborate with them.

Thank you to the memory of Maxwell, our beloved dog, who died in 2023 just before *The Alphabet Woods* was launched. How we miss our beautiful best friend. I'm so happy he lives on in Wain's dog, Faro.

Thank you to all of our children, children-in-law, and grandchildren and our extended family (which is huge). I especially want to recognize my mom, Wini Pierson, who has lived nearly her entire adult life with absence as a presence; and my mother-in-law, Helen Poelman, one of my staunchest supporters! I'm so happy the book is finally in your hands!

Thank you most of all to Ken, for his unwavering support and love. I am blessed.

www.ingramcontent.com/pod-product-compliance
Lightning Source LLC
Chambersburg PA
CBHW020535020726
47494CB00006B/1775